Clare Connelly [...] among a family [...] of her childhood [...] hand. Clare is m[...] and they live in [...] two children. She is frequently found staring into space—a sure-fire sign that she's in the world of her characters. She has a penchant for French food and ice-cold champagne, and Mills & Boon novels continue to be her favourite ever books. Writing for Modern is a long-held dream. Clare can be contacted via clareconnelly.com or at her Facebook page.

USA TODAY bestselling author **Natalie Anderson** writes emotional contemporary romance full of sparkling banter, sizzling heat and uplifting endings—perfect for readers who love to escape with empowered heroines and arrogant alphas who are too sexy for their own good. When not writing you'll find her wrangling her four children, three cats, two goldfish and one dog…and snuggled in a heap on the sofa with her husband at the end of the day. Follow her at www.natalie-anderson.com.

THE GREEK'S BILLION-DOLLAR BABY

CLARE CONNELLY

THE INNOCENT'S EMERGENCY WEDDING

NATALIE ANDERSON

MILLS & BOON

First Published in Great Britain 2019
by Mills & Boon, an imprint of HarperCollins*Publishers*
1 London Bridge Street, London, SE1 9GF

The Greek's Billion-Dollar Baby © 2019 by Clare Connelly

The Innocent's Emergency Wedding © 2019 by Natalie Anderson

ISBN: 978-0-263-27360-1

THE GREEK'S
BILLION-DOLLAR
BABY

CLARE CONNELLY

For Emma Darcy,
who wrote the first Mills & Boon I ever read
and thus gave me one of the greatest gifts of my life:
an enduring love of passionate escapist romance.
There is a piece of Emma Darcy in every book I write.

PROLOGUE

BEING EQUAL NUMBER TWO on the international rich list might have made Leonidas Stathakis the envy of the world, but Leonidas knew from personal experience that money was a poor substitute for having what you really wanted in life.

Billions in the bank didn't take away the empty throb of loss that dogged your steps when you'd had to bury your loved ones.

Being rich didn't take away the grief, nor the guilt, nor the pain and the sense of impotence at knowing you had put someone in harm's way—that you had failed to protect them.

This was his fourth New Year's Eve without his family. The fourth year he'd seen draw to a close with only memories of his wife, Amy, and their two-year-old son, Brax.

It felt like a lifetime.

When he closed his eyes, he saw her as clearly as if she were standing in front of him. He'd never forget the way she smiled, as though she'd struck a match inside and happiness was exploding out of her.

How could someone so full of life and vitality simply cease to exist? For all her strength, she'd been so weak at the end, so fragile. Ploughed into while walking Brax to the playground. What chance did either of their bodies stand against that hunk of metal, commanded by a madman?

Hair that had been a vibrant russet with eyes that were

the same shade as the ocean beyond this hotel; he saw her as she'd been in life, and then, as she'd been in death.

He would never forget Amy Stathakis, nor the violent fate that had awaited her, murdered because of his father's criminal activities.

Dion Stathakis had destroyed their family, and, with Amy and Brax's death, had destroyed Leonidas's life.

Anger surged inside him and he curved his fingers more tightly about his Scotch glass, wondering how many of these he'd had. Not so many as to dull the pain yet, though in his experience it took more than a few quick drinks in a bar to get anywhere near the obliteration he sought. Especially at times like this, when his memories were at their clearest.

Happiness surrounded him. Loud, exuberant noises of celebration. People seemed to love marking the close of a year, celebrating the arrival of a new one, and he could understand that. At one time, he'd felt just the same—he had celebrated life with Amy.

Now, every day was something to be got through. Every year was simply something he survived—without them. His very existence was a betrayal. How many times had he thought he would give his life to return theirs? He was the son of the criminal bastard—he, Leonidas, should have paid for his father's crimes. Not his innocent wife and their beautiful son.

Bitterness threatened to scorch him alive.

He threw his Scotch back and, without his signalling for another, a hostess arrived at his table, replacing it with a substitute, just as he'd requested. There were some perks to being the owner of the place, and this was one of them.

He lifted his head towards her in acknowledgement, noting dispassionately how attractive she was. Blonde hair, brown eyes, a caramel tan and pale pink lips that were quick to turn into a smile. A nice figure, too. She had the kind of looks he had once found irresistible.

But not any more.

Yes, he could have opened himself to the hint of desire that stirred inside him. That started in his gut and, as his eyes dropped to her breasts, to the hint of lace he could see beneath the cotton shirt she wore, spread like flame, threatening to make him hard right there in the skyline view bar of his six-star hotel on Chrysá Vráchia.

But he refused the impulse. He turned his attention to his Scotch, taking pleasure in denying his body any hint of satisfaction on that score. It had been four years. Four years without Amy, four years without knowing the pleasure of a woman. It was a habit he had no intention of breaking…

CHAPTER ONE

HANNAH HADN'T COME to Chrysá Vráchia to lose her virginity.

She hadn't come to this stunning Greek island for any reason other than she'd been in shock and needed to escape Australia. Her controlling aunt, uncle, and the cousin she'd thought of as a sister—who'd been sleeping with Hannah's fiancé.

She'd discovered them in bed together and been at the airport two hours later, booking the first available flight—which just happened to bring her here.

This stunning paradise she'd heard of all her life and wanted to visit. Golden cliffs, white sand beaches, turquoise waters, lush green forests—it was paradise on earth and the perfect place to chew through her honeymoon savings and rebuild her heart.

So apparently even the darkest storm clouds had silver linings.

No, Hannah hadn't come to Greece to lose her virginity but as her eyes kept straying to the man across the hotel bar, she felt the pull of desire deep in her chest, and something more.

Vengeance? Anger? No. It was less barbaric than that, less calculated.

Fascination.

She looked at the man across from her, cradling his Scotch with a brooding intensity that tied her tummy in knots, and she felt a surge of white-hot desire that was as unfamiliar as it was intriguing.

Waiting until they were married had been Angus's idea, but she'd gone along with it. She loved Angus, she liked the way he made her feel, the way he kissed her and held her tight. But she'd never really longed for him. She'd never trembled at his touch nor fallen asleep imagining his kisses.

And the idea of carelessly giving something away to a stranger, sleeping with a man she didn't know, felt like the perfect way to respond to her fiancé cheating on her with her cousin.

Hannah's chest tightened as flashbacks of that moment sliced through her. It was too raw. Too fresh.

Still…he looked like a man who wanted to be left alone. As she watched, a blonde waitress approached and said something *sotto voce*. He didn't even meet her eyes when he responded, instead looking towards the view beyond them, the dark night sky inky for now—though it would soon be illuminated with the fireworks that marked the conclusion of one year and the start of another.

Midnight ticked closer and Hannah sipped her champagne thoughtfully.

She'd never approached a man before. She had no idea what to say. And it was a stupid idea. Hannah was twenty-three years old; there was a reason she was so woefully inexperienced with the opposite sex.

She was completely clueless.

No way could she click her fingers and change her personality, even if she wanted to.

Suppressing a sigh, she stood and moved towards the bar. If she wasn't going to do something *really* out of character and have a random one-night stand with a stranger, then she could do something *slightly* out of character and get a little bit tipsy.

She stood and looked about for a waiter, moving to the other side of her table, and deciding to go direct to the bar when she couldn't find one. But as she spun to the bar she connected with something impossibly hard and broad.

Something strong and firm, like concrete. Something that almost sent her flying across the room for the latent strength contained within its frame.

A hand snaked out to steady her and Hannah lifted her gaze, right into the obsidian eyes of the man she'd been unable to look away from for the past hour. He was rubbing his shoulder distractedly and a little pain radiated from her own, so she presumed they'd bumped into each other—hard.

'It's you,' she exhaled on a tremulous breath, trying to swallow even when her mouth was bone dry.

'It's me,' he agreed, his expression unchanging.

'You're like a brick wall,' she said before she could stop herself. The man's brows furrowed, and, if anything, he looked even hotter when he was all handsome and forbidding.

'Are you hurt?'

My pride is hurt. My heart is hurt. But this was not what he was asking. 'No, I'm fine.' And something like courage lashed at her spine, so she heard herself say, 'But I should at least buy you a drink. For getting in your way.'

A stern expression crossed his face and she felt the beginnings of embarrassment, certain he was going to say 'no', that she'd just made a complete fool of herself.

She bit down on her lower lip, wishing she could recall the words to her mouth. He stared at her for a long time, saying nothing, and with every second that passed her heart rate accelerated; she was drowning.

'That is not necessary,' he said, but made no effort to

move. That alone was buoying. At least, Hannah hoped it was.

Her fingertips shook a little as she lifted them to her hair, straightening the auburn mane behind her ear. His eyes followed the gesture, a contemplative frown on his face.

'I wasn't watching where I was going,' she said.

'Nor was I. In which case, I should buy you a drink.'

Hannah's heart turned over in her chest, desire like a wave that had picked her up and was dragging her with it.

'How about I buy this round and you can get the next?' she said with a lift of one brow.

It was by the far the most forward she'd ever been in her life but seeing Angus in bed with Michelle had robbed Hannah of the ability to feel embarrassment.

His frown deepened. Then, he nodded a little, just a shift of his head. 'You have a deal, Miss...'

'Hannah,' she said, her own name emerging a little husky. She darted her tongue out and licked the outline of her lower lip, her eyes holding his so she saw the way the black shifted, morphing to inky and coal.

'Hannah,' he repeated, his European accent doing funny things to the simple two syllables, so her gut lurched.

'And you are?'

Surprise briefly flashed on his features. 'Leonidas.'

His name was just what she'd expect. Masculine, spicy and sexy, it suited him to a T.

'You have a table?' she asked, shifting her eyes to where he was sitting. A couple had already claimed it. She spun around and saw the same fate had befallen her own seat.

'I was just on my way to my room.' He said the words slowly, the frown not leaving his face, the statement almost spoken against his will.

But the question in the words didn't fail to reach Hannah's ears, nor her awakening libido. Desire throbbed low down in her abdomen, so heat flamed through her.

'Were you?'

Plan for seduction or not, Hannah knew she was moving dramatically out of her realm of experience.

'It has a view back towards Athens. Perhaps we could have our drink on my balcony?'

Hannah had no idea if he was seriously offering to show her the view, or if this invitation was for so much more—she hoped the latter, and had every intention of finding out.

It was stupid. So stupid, so completely out of character, but she wasn't acting from a rational place. Hannah had had her heart and trust broken and, wounded, she needed something. She needed to know she was desirable. She wanted to know what sex was all about. She had to push Angus way out of her mind.

And this man with his darkly quizzical gaze and mysterious, brooding face was everything she wanted—for one night only.

'I...' This was it. Her moment of truth. Could she do this?

The bar was busy and a woman passed behind Hannah, knocking her forward so Hannah's body was once again pushed against Leonidas's. This time, his hand reached out to steady her but it lingered, curving around her back and holding her there. Her eyes lifted to his, and doubts filled her. They were mirrored back to her, a look of confusion in his eyes, uncertainty on his face.

'I want you to come upstairs with me.' He said the words almost as though they were a revelation, as though he was completely surprised by the pull of this desire.

Hannah's pulse was like a torrent of lava, hot and demanding in her bloodstream. She wanted that too, more than anything.

'I just got out of a relationship,' she heard herself saying, her expression unknowingly shifting so her green eyes were laced with sadness. 'I was engaged, actually, until recently. I'm not looking for anything. You know, anything more than...' She looked away, shyness unwelcome, yet impossible to disguise.

'I don't do relationships,' the man said quietly. 'I don't generally do one-night stands, either.'

Generally.

The word was like an axe, preparing to fall. Hannah's eyes slid back to his and the hand that was at her back, holding her pressed to him, began to move up a little, running over her spine with a possessive inquiry that warmed her from the inside out.

'Nor do I.'

'Theos...' He said the word under his breath. 'I didn't come here for this.'

There was an undercurrent of emotion to his words, a sense of powerlessness that pulled at Hannah's heartstrings. And if she weren't completely drowning in this torrent of desire, she might have asked him about it. She might have insisted they find somewhere to talk. But desire was taking over Hannah's body, and she reached her hand around behind her back so her fingers could lace with his.

'Nor did I.'

His eyes glittered as they saw right through her, boring into her soul. 'A night out of time,' he said, pulling her with him, away from the bar, weaving with skill and ease towards the glass doors that led to the hotel foyer.

People seemed to move for him—he had a silent strength that conveyed itself with every step he took.

And with every inch they covered, Hannah's mind was yelling at her that this was stupid, that she was going to regret this, even as her heart and sex drive were applauding her impetuosity.

The hotel had been more than Hannah had expected, despite its billing as one of the world's finest. It was true six-star luxury, from the white marble floor to the gold columns that extended to the triple-height ceilings, the glossy grand piano in one corner being expertly played by a renowned pianist, the enormous crystal chandeliers that hung overhead.

As they approached the lifts, a suited bellhop dipped his head in deferential welcome. 'Good evening, sir,' he murmured. 'Madam.'

His gloved hand pressed the button to call the lift and Hannah stood beside Leonidas, waiting in complete silence. The lift arrived seconds later and Leonidas stood back, allowing Hannah to enter before him.

She stepped into the plush interior, her breath held, her senses rioting with the madness of what she was about to do.

But the moment she felt regret or doubt, she closed her eyes and conjured the image of Angus's pale face brightened by his sensual exertions with Michelle and determination kicked inside her.

Not that she needed it—desire alone was propelling her through this, but anger was a good backup.

'You are no longer engaged?'

The lift pulled upwards, but that wasn't why her stomach swooped.

'No,' she said. 'I've left him—everyone—far behind.'

'You are angry?'

'No.' She was. And she wasn't. She was…hurt. Reeling. Confused. And if she *was* angry, it was mostly with herself, for having been so stupid as to believe him, to care for him, to get so hooked on the idea of the picture-perfect future that she'd stopped paying attention to the present, to whether or not Angus even made her happy.

The lift doors eased open silently, directly into a large living room. It took only a moment to realise they were on the top floor of the hotel and that this magnificent space must surely be the penthouse.

'Wow.' For a second, everything but admiration left her—this place was amazing. Every bit as decadent as the foyer but even more so because it was designed with a single occupant in mind. Everything was pale—cream, Scandinavian wood furniture, glass, mirrors, except for the artwork that was bold—a Picasso hung on one wall. There were plants, too, large fiddle-leaf figs that added a bold hint of architectural interest.

Sliding glass doors led to a balcony that showed a stunning view of Athens in the distance—glowing golden warm, an ancient city, so full of stories and interest.

'This is beautiful.'

He dipped his head in silent concession, moving towards the kitchen and pulling a bottle of champagne from the fridge. She recognised the label for its distinctive golden colour.

She watched as he unfurled the foil and popped the cork effortlessly, grabbing two flutes and half filling them.

'What brings you to Chrysá Vráchia, Hannah?'

There it was again, her name in his mouth, being kissed by his accent. Her knees felt shaky; she wasn't sure she trusted them to carry her across the room.

'A change,' she said cryptically. 'And you?'

His lips twisted and she felt something sharpen within him, something that sparked a thousand little questions inside her. 'It's routine. I come here every year.'

'What for?'

He didn't answer. Instead, he strode across the room,

champagne flute in hand, passing Hannah's to her as though he were fighting himself, as though he were fighting this.

And she couldn't understand that.

If it weren't for the gale-force strength of her own needs, she might have paused to ask him why he was looking at her with such intensity, why he stared at her in a way that seemed to strip her soul bare.

But the incessant thrumming of her own desire was all Hannah was conscious of.

'Habit,' he said simply, swallowing so his Adam's apple bobbed in his throat.

She bit down on her lip, and his eyes dropped to her mouth, so her desire became louder, more urgent, desperation rolling through her. This was crazy. Madness. Necessary.

Outside, a spark of colour exploded through the sky— bright red, vibrant, its beauty an imperative they both resisted.

'Happy new year,' she said quietly, unable to take her eyes off his face.

Happy new year? He stared at the woman he'd brought up to his penthouse, completely at a loss for what the hell had come over him. For four years he'd come here to pay his respects to Amy, he'd undertaken this pilgrimage, he'd come here to remember her.

For four years he'd resisted any woman he found desirable, he'd ignored his body's hungers, he'd resisted anything except the debt he felt he owed Amy.

Then again, no other woman had ever slammed into his body. She had literally hit him out of nowhere, and the second his hand had curled around her arm, simply to steady her, his body had tightened with a whole raft of needs he no longer wanted to ignore.

He'd sworn he'd spend the rest of his life single, celibate. Amy's.

But right here, with the starlit sky exploding beyond the glass wall of his penthouse apartment, something within him shifted. It was as though an ancient, unseen force was propelling him to act, was reminding him that grief could coexist with virility, that he could have sex with a woman without it being a betrayal to his wife.

He had loved Amy, even when their marriage had been fraught and neither of them particularly happy. She was his wife, he'd made a promise to her, and he had sworn he'd love only her for the rest of his life. So wasn't it loving another woman that was the true betrayal?

What did sex have to do with it?

No, denying his libido wasn't about what he owed Amy. It was punishment.

Punishment for being the son of a criminal mastermind. Punishment for being careless, for thinking he could turn his back on Dion Stathakis and live his life without the long, gnarled fingers of that man's sins reaching in and shredding what he, Leonidas, possessed.

He had been punishing himself because he deserved to feel that desperate pain of denial, that constant throbbing of need.

And he still should.

But there was something about Hannah that weakened his resolve to the point of breaking. He didn't believe in angels and ghosts, he didn't believe in fairy tales and myths, and yet, in that moment, it almost felt as if she'd been sent to him, a fragment of his soul, a promise that he could weaken, for one night, and go back to hating himself again tomorrow.

In the light of day, with the breaking of another year over this earth, he could resume his uneasy life.

But for tonight, or what was left of it, he could forget. With determination in his gaze, he put their champagne flutes down, knowing there was no turning back from this, no changing the immediate future.

'Happy new year.' And he dropped his head, surprising her completely if her husky little gasp was anything to go by, parting her lips so he could drive his tongue deep inside her and feel every reverberation of her body, he could taste her desire and welcome it with his own.

Just for this night, he would be a slave to this—and then, everything could go back to normal...

CHAPTER TWO

PERHAPS SHE'D EXPECTED him to kiss her gently, to explore her slowly, but there was nothing gentle about this, nothing slow. It was a kiss of urgency and it detonated around them.

She made a groaning noise into his mouth, her desire roaring through her body, taking control of her.

This was not a warm, comfortable kiss. It was a kiss that redefined everything in her life, pushing new boundaries into place. She clung to his shirt for dear life and he kissed her deeper, his mouth moving over hers, demanding more of her, his tongue duelling with her own, his body cleaved to hers so not a breath of space remained between them.

It was a kiss of complete domination and she succumbed to it utterly.

'Just this one night.' He pushed the words into her mouth as he spun her body, tightening his arms around her waist and lifting her in his arms. He sat down on the sofa, pulling her onto his lap, pushing at her dress and making a guttural sound of frustration when he found the cotton of her underpants.

It was everything she wanted—the impermanence, the perfect treatment. She wanted to lose her virginity—it seemed ridiculous to be twenty-three and not know what sex was all about, yet the idea of a relationship made something inside her shrivel up and die.

She'd never trust another man, she'd never want love,

or believe in love. She'd never be foolish enough to believe *she* was lovable.

But sex?

This?

This was a balm to her soul.

She tilted her head back as he pushed her dress higher, over her arms and then from her body altogether, so she wore only her underwear, flimsy cotton, with no care whatsoever that this man she'd met less than an hour ago was seeing her like this.

If anything, she found her total abandon to this—to him—liberating.

There was no room for any such rational consideration, though, when he unhooked the bra and discarded it carelessly, then began to trace one of her nipples with his tongue, circling the peach areola lightly at first, so she was trembling on top of him, straddling his lap.

He moved his mouth closer to the tip of her nipple and, finally, surrounded it completely, sucking on her flesh in a way that burst starlight behind her eyes.

She swore, uncharacteristically, and he echoed it in his native tongue, reaching between her legs and pushing at the trousers of his designer suit, unzipping them, unbuttoning them so that the arousal she could feel through the material was hard and naked.

He transferred his mouth to her other breast and the first, so sensitive from his ministrations, felt the sting of the cool, air-conditioned air and she arched her back in response.

It was completely overwhelming.

Or, she thought it was. But then, he moved his hand between her legs and through the waistband of her underwear, sliding a finger into her moist core, and she cried his name.

He stilled for a moment then moved his finger deeper, finding her sensitive cluster of nerves and tormenting it until she was panting, desperate, so desperate, before pulling his finger out, fixing her with a look of wonderment.

'You are so wet.'

She was, and shaking all over, desire like an electrical current and it was frying her completely.

'I know,' she groaned as his hands moved to the top of her underpants and began to push at them. She shifted her body, lifting herself up so he could undress her completely, needing to be naked, needing him.

She had no experience but she had instincts and they were driving her wild, needing her to act, to feel, to do. She groaned as she stood shakily, naked before him, wanting to experience everything. There was a type of madness overtaking her, building within her.

She reached a hand out for his and he stood, wrapping his arms around her, crushing her to his frame.

'Who are you?' he groaned into her mouth, the words making no sense.

'Hannah,' she said unevenly and he laughed, a husky sound.

'Yes. But what kind of mermaid or angel or fairy are you to come here and do this to me?'

She swallowed his words, kissing him right back, her tongue duelling with his, passion making their breath harsh and loud in the still night air.

'Leonidas,' she groaned his name and his hands curved around her naked rear, lifting her up, wrapping her legs around her body as he strode through the penthouse towards what turned out to be a bedroom. It was huge with the same view towards Athens. He eased her down without bothering to turn on the lights so every sparkle of fireworks was like a jolt into the room.

Her hands tugged at his shirt with such desperation a button popped off and flew through the room.

She cursed softly under her breath, her eyes apologetic when they latched to his.

He shook his head. 'Don't worry.'

She nodded, but he finished the job, stripping the shirt from his body to reveal a broadly muscled chest that had her pulse ratcheting up yet another gear so she was almost trembling with the force of her own body's demands.

'Wow.' She stared at the ridges of his torso, transfixed by the obvious strength there, and lifted her hands to trace his abdominals almost without realising it. 'Work out much?'

She didn't see the way his lips flickered into a smile, nor could she have any idea how rare that smile was. Her hands ran down his chest, finding the waist of his pants and pushing at them, her eyes lifting to his as she sucked her lower lip between her teeth.

She was completely inexperienced and yet Hannah felt no anxiety, no nervousness, nothing except desire bursting through her, jolting her body as though she'd picked up a bundle of live wires.

'I want you,' she said, in awe of how true that was. It went beyond needing revenge on Angus, it went beyond anything to do with Angus. There was nothing and no one in Hannah's mind as she lifted onto the tips of her toes so she could claim Leonidas's mouth with her own, her kiss curious, questioning and then desperate.

He kissed her back, their bodies moulded together, desire a flame that was growing bigger than either could control. 'I want to take this slow,' he groaned, his hands tangling in her russet hair, curling it up and holding it against her head. He took a step forward, pushing her backwards until Hannah collapsed onto the bed, his body following, the weight and strength of him an impossible pleasure.

'I want this,' she said again, more to herself than him. 'Don't take it slow.'

He lifted himself up to stare at her, his eyes showing emotions she couldn't comprehend, or perhaps her ability to comprehend was blunted by the sheer force of her own feelings, which were overwhelming her, robbing her of sense and logic and reason.

'You don't know...'

His words were engulfed by her kiss. Hannah was sick of being patient; she was sick of waiting. She'd never known desire like this but that didn't mean she wasn't prepared to answer its call. 'Please,' she groaned. 'Make love to me.'

The words were breathed into his being, sparkling like the light show beyond the window. Explosions of light, intense, glowing, hot. He separated her legs, nudging the tip of his arousal against her womanhood, and Hannah held her breath, she held everything.

For a split second, she contemplated telling him she was innocent, that she'd never done this before, but there was no time. He thrust into her and with her gasp he stilled, pushing up to stare down at her, his features harsh in the darkened room.

'*Theos*, Hannah, was that...were you?'

'Don't stop,' she said, shaking her head, but Leonidas was already pulling away from her, his body rock hard, his eyes pinning her with intensity. 'Please don't stop.' Her heart crumbled. She hadn't realised until that moment how desperately she wanted to know herself to be desirable. To know that someone wanted her enough to be unable to control their desire.

He swore under his breath and moved to the night stand, sliding open the drawer and pulling out a foil square. 'Not once have I forgotten protection,' he said thickly, the words coated in his own desires, which began to put Hannah's heart back together again.

She watched as he unfurled a condom over his length

then came back to the bed, his body weight returning to hers, bliss fogging into her mind.

'You should have told me.' The words lacked recrimination. They were simple. Soft. Gentle. Enquiring. As if he was asking her to assure him she was okay.

'I didn't know how.'

'I'm a virgin?'

She laughed, despite the desire that was pulling at her gut. 'I was a virgin.'

'You are sure this is what you want?'

She nodded, lifting her hands up to cup his face. 'Please.'

But he didn't respond. Something tightened in his expression, his jaw moving as though he were grinding his teeth. 'I meant what I said, Hannah. One night. Nothing more.'

'I know that.' She nodded, thinking of the situation she'd left behind, the mess her private life was in. The last thing she wanted was the complication of more than one night.

And it was the freedom he needed, the reassurance he obviously craved, because he pushed back into her. Gently this time, slowly, giving her time to adjust and adapt, allowing her inexperienced body a chance to get used to this invasion, to feel his presence and relish in it before taking more of her, more of her, until finally she was crying his name over and over, the foreign syllables tripping off her tongue as rushed breaths filled her lungs.

His mouth moved from hers to her cheek then lower to the sensitive flesh at the base of her neck, his tongue flicking her pulse point while his hands roamed her body, feeling every inch of her, pausing where she responded loudest to his inquisition, teasing the sensitive flesh of her breasts, tormenting her nipples with the skill of his hands.

It was heaven.

Pleasure built inside Hannah like a coil winding tighter

and tighter and she dug her nails into his back, moaning softly as the spring prepared to burst. She arched her back and rolled her head to the side, the fireworks gaining momentum as her own pleasure began to detonate. She lifted her hips in a silent, knowing invitation and he held her, his hands keeping her close to him, reassuring her as she lost herself utterly to the compelling, indescribable pleasure of a sexual orgasm.

It was intense and it was fast and it robbed her of breath and control. Her eyelids filled with light, her mouth tasted like steel. She pushed up on her elbows, staring into Leonidas's eyes, feeling quite mad and delirious with what she'd just experienced.

But it was nowhere near over.

He braced himself above her on his palms, watching the play of sensation on her features, and then he began to move again, his body stirring hers to new heights, his dominance something that made her want to weep.

She knew though, instinctively, that giving into the salty tang of tears would be a bad idea. Even while she was part mad with pleasure, she didn't want to show how completely he'd shifted something inside her, nor how much this meant to her.

Because Hannah felt a surge of feminine power and it was instantaneous and went beyond words. She didn't need to tell him how much this meant to her; she felt it and that was enough.

Angus had made her feel precious and valued, he'd made her feel like an *objet d'art* and that had been nice. It had been better than knowing herself to be an unwanted nuisance, which was how she'd spent a huge portion of her childhood since the loss of her parents. But he'd never looked at her as though he would die if he didn't kiss her.

He'd never looked at her as though the push and pull of their chemistry was robbing him of sense.

Leonidas was, though.

He moved his body and he stared into her eyes and she felt a cascade of emotions from him to her and none of them would be worth analysing, because this was just one night. A temporary, fleeting, brief night—a slice out of time.

Sitting on the edge of the bed, Leonidas cradled his head in his hands, staring at the floor between his feet. Early dawn light was peeking through the window. Hannah's rhythmic breathing filled the room, soft and somehow sweet. Sweet? How could breath be sweet? He turned to face her on autopilot, his expression grim.

He didn't know how, but it was.

She was sweet.

She'd been innocent.

He cursed silently, standing and pulling his pants on, watching her through a veil of disbelief. What the hell had come over him? Four years of celibacy and then he'd spontaneously combusted the second the beautiful redhead had literally bumped into him?

And it wasn't the red hair, nor the passing resemblance to Amy. If anything, that would have been a reason to keep his distance. No, this was something else. A kind of sexual starvation that he supposed was only natural, given he'd denied himself this pleasure and release for such a long time. But, *Theos*, a virgin?

He hadn't wanted that! He had wanted meaningless, empty sex. A quick roll in the hay to satisfy this part of him, to obliterate his grief, to remind him that he was a man, a breathing, living man with blood in his veins.

And instead, he'd taken a young woman's innocence. He'd been her first.

A sense of disbelief filled him as he watched her sleeping, her gentle inhalations, her lips that were tilted into a smile even in her sleep.

He'd always be her first. No matter what happened, no matter who she slept with, he was that to her.

It wasn't meaningless; it never could be. Thank God he'd remembered protection. He'd have put money on the fact she wasn't on birth control—why would she be? He could think of nothing worse than that kind of consequence from a night of unplanned pleasure.

And it had been a night of pleasure, he thought with a strong lurch of desire in his gut. Despite her inexperience, she had matched him perfectly, her body answering every call of his, her inquisitiveness driving him wild, the way she'd kissed and licked her way over his frame, tasting all of him, experimenting with what pleased him, asking him to tell her what he needed.

He groaned, a quiet noise but she stirred, shifting a little, so the sheet fell down and revealed her pert, rounded breasts to his gaze.

His erection throbbed against his pants. He took a step back from the bed.

One night, and dawn was breathing its way through the room, reminding him that this was not his life.

Hannah was an aberration. A mistake.

He had to leave. He had to forget this ever happened. He just hoped she would, too.

Hannah woke slowly, her body delightfully sore, muscles she hadn't felt before stretching inside her as she shifted, rolling onto her side.

A Cavalcanti masterpiece was on the wall opposite, the morning light bathing its modernist palette in gold, a gold she knew would be matched by the sheer cliffs of this spectacular island.

But none of these things were what she wanted to see most.

She flipped over, her eyes scanning the bed, looking for Leonidas. He wasn't there.

She reached out, feeling the sheets. They were cold. Her stomach grumbled and she pushed to sitting, smothering a yawn with the back of her hand. When had they finally fallen asleep? She couldn't remember.

A smile played about her lips as she stood, grabbing the sheet and wrapping it toga style around her, padding through the penthouse.

'Leonidas?' She frowned, looking around. The glass doors to the balcony were open. She moved towards it, the view spectacular, momentarily robbing her of breath for a wholly new reason.

He wasn't out there.

She frowned, turning on her heel and heading back inside. It was then that she saw it.

A note.

And there was so much to comprehend in that one instant that she struggled to make sense of any of it.

First of all the letterhead. It was no standard issue hotel notepad. It bore the insignia of the hotel, but the embossed lettering at the bottom spelled 'Leonidas Stathakis.'

Leonidas Stathakis? Her heart began to race faster as she comprehended this. She didn't know much about the Stathakis brothers—she wasn't really *au fait* with people of their *milieu*, but no one could fail to have at least *heard* of the Stathakis brothers. To know that they were two of the richest men in the world. There were other facts, too, swirling just beneath the surface. Snatches she'd heard or read but not paid attention to because it had all seemed so far away. Crimes? The mob? Murder? Was that them? Or someone else?

She swallowed, running her finger over the embossing, closing her eyes and picturing Leonidas as he'd been the night before. As he'd stood so close to her and their eyes had seemed to pierce one another's souls.

Her pulse gushed and she blinked her green eyes open, scanning the paper more thoroughly this time, expecting to see a few lines explaining that he'd gone to get breakfast, or for a workout—those muscles didn't just grow themselves—or something along those lines.

What she wasn't expecting was the formality and finality of what she read.

Hannah
It shouldn't have happened. Please forget it did.
The penthouse is yours for as long as you'd like it.
Leonidas

She read it and reread it at least a dozen times, her fingers shaking as she reached for the coffee machine and jabbed the button. Outrage warred with anger.

It shouldn't have happened.

Because she hadn't been what he'd expected? Because she hadn't been any good?

Oh, God.

Was it possible that the desire she'd felt had been one-sided? Angus had been engaged to her and been able to easily abstain from sex, yet he'd been fooling around behind her back.

Had she been a let-down?

Hurt flooded inside her, disbelief echoing in her heart. She'd wanted to come to Chrysá Vráchia almost her whole life, but suddenly, she couldn't wait to leave.

CHAPTER THREE

A WEEK AFTER leaving the island, Leonidas awoke in a cold sweat. He stared around the hotel room, his heart hammering in his chest.

Hannah.

He'd been dreaming of Hannah, the woman he'd met on Chrysá Vráchia. He'd been dreaming of her, of making love to her. His body was rock hard and he groaned, falling back onto the pillows, closing his eyes and forcing himself to breathe slowly, to calm down. To remember his wife.

And nausea skidded through him, because he knew he would never forget Amy. But for those few moments, when he'd lost himself inside Hannah, when he'd pierced her innocence, and possessed her so completely, he had felt...

He had felt like himself.

For the first time in many years he had felt like a man who was free of this curse, this guilt, this permanent ache.

He had lost himself in Hannah and, just for a moment, he had lost his grief.

He swore under his breath, and pushed the sheet back, his heart unable to be calmed. Leonidas walked to the plush kitchen of his Hong Kong penthouse, pressing a button on the coffee machine.

He watched it brew, an answering presentiment of disaster growing inside him.

* * *

'Do you need me to talk to him?'

Leonidas focussed on sounding normal. But in the month since leaving Chrysá Vráchia, he'd had a growing tension, balling in his gut, and nothing he did seemed to relieve it. It was guilt, he knew. Guilt at having betrayed his vows to Amy. At having broken the vow he made himself, that Amy would be the last woman he was intimate with.

The limousine slid through Rome, lights on either side.

'Yeah, sure, that's even better,' Thanos responded with sarcasm. Leonidas's younger brother shook his head. 'Kosta Carinedes will take one look at you and see Dad. Sorry.'

Leonidas winced—the physical similarities between himself and Dion were not news to him. 'So how are you going to convince him to sell?'

'He wants to sell,' Thanos murmured, tilting his head as the car slowed at a corner and paused near a group of beautiful women wearing skimpy shorts and singlet tops. 'He just doesn't want to sell to us.'

'Because of Dion?'

'Because of our name,' Thanos conceded with a nod. 'And because I am, quote, "a sex-mad bachelor".'

At this, Leonidas laughed, despite the bad mood that had been following him for weeks. 'He's got you bang to rights there.'

Thanos grinned. 'Hey, I don't think there's anything wrong with being sex-mad. We can't all live the life of a saint like you.'

Leonidas's expression shifted as though he'd been punched in the gut. He was far more sinner than saint, but he had no intention of sharing his slip-up with his brother.

'Offer him more money,' Leonidas suggested, cutting to the crux of the matter.

'It's not about money. This is his grandparents' legacy.

They built the company out of "love",' he said the word with sardonic derision, 'and he won't sell it to someone who's constantly in the headlines for all the wrong reasons.'

Leonidas shrugged. 'Then let it go.'

'You're kidding, right? I told you what this means to me? And who else is interested in buying it?'

Leonidas regarded his brother thoughtfully. 'Yes. Luca Monato. And I know you two hate each other. But this is just a company. Let him have it, buy its competition and drive him into the ground. Far more satisfying.'

'It might come to that. But I'm not done yet.'

'What else can you do? I hate to point out the obvious, but Kosta's right. You're a man whore, Thanos.'

Thanos laughed. 'And proud. You could take a couple of pages out of my book. In fact, why don't you? I've got a heap of women you'd like. Why don't you call one of them? Take her for dinner and then back to your place...'

Leonidas turned away from his brother, looking out of the window of the limousine as Rome passed in a beautiful, dusk-filled blur. He thought of Hannah, his body tightening, his chest feeling as if it were filling with acid. 'No.'

'You cannot live the rest of your life like this,' Thanos insisted quietly, his tone serious now, their banter forgotten. There weren't many people on earth who could speak plainly to the great Leonidas Stathakis, but Thanos was one of them, and always had been. Side by side they'd dealt with their father's failings, his criminality, his convictions, the ruin he'd brought on their fortune and the Stathakis name.

Side by side, they'd rebuilt it all, better than before, returning their family's once-great wealth—many times over. They were half-brothers, only three months apart in age, and they'd been raised more as twins since Thanos was abandoned on their doorstep by his mother at the age of eight. Their insight into one another was unique.

Leonidas understood Thanos as nobody else did, and vice versa. Leonidas knew what it had done to Thanos, his mother abandoning him, choosing to desert him rather than find a way to manage his dominant character traits.

'What would you do?' Leonidas drawled, but there was tension in the question. Tension and despair.

Thanos expelled a sigh; the car stopped. Thousands of screaming fans were outside on the red carpet, here to catch a glimpse of the A-list Hollywood stars who'd featured in the film of the premiere they were attending.

'I can't say. I get it—you miss Amy. What happened to her and Brax—do you think I don't feel that? You think I don't want to reach into that prison cell and strangle our father with my bare hands for what he exposed you to? But, Leonidas, you cannot serve her by living half a life. Do you think Amy would have wanted this for you?'

Leonidas swept his dark eyes shut, the panic in his gut churning, the sense of self-disgust almost impossible to manage. 'Don't.' He shook his head. 'Do not speak to me of Amy's wishes.'

But Thanos wasn't to be deterred. 'She loved you. She would want you to live the rest of your life as you did before. Be happy. Be fulfilled.'

'You think I deserve that?'

'It was our father's crimes that killed her, not yours.'

'But if she hadn't met me…' Leonidas insisted, not finishing the statement—not needing to. Thanos knew; he understood.

'It's been four years,' Thanos repeated softly. 'You have mourned and grieved and honoured them both. It's time to move forward.'

But Leonidas shook his head, his time on Chrysá Vráchia teaching him one thing and one thing only: it would never be time. He had failed Amy during their marriage, in many ways; he wouldn't fail her now.

'Tuna salad, please,' Hannah said over the counter, scanning the lunch selections with a strange sense of distaste, despite the artful arrangements. In the four months since arriving in London and taking up a maternity-leave contract as legal secretary to a renowned litigator, Hannah had grabbed lunch from this same store almost every day.

Her boss liked the chicken sandwiches and she the tuna. She waited in the queue then grabbed their lunches and made her way back to the office as quickly as she could.

There was a wait for the lift and she stifled a yawn, sipping her coffee. Her stomach flipped. She frowned. The milk tasted funny.

'Great,' she said with a sigh, dropping it into a waste bin. Just what she needed—spoiled milk.

But when she got to her desk and unpeeled her sandwich, she had the strangest sense that she might vomit. She took one bite of the sandwich and then stood up, rushing to the facilities. She just made it.

It was as she hovered over the porcelain bowl, trying to work out whether she was sick or suffering from food poisoning, that dates began to hover in her mind. Months of dates, in fact, without her regular cycle.

Her skin was damp with perspiration as she straightened, staring at the tiled wall with a look of absolute shock.

No way.

No way could she be pregnant. Her hand curved over her stomach—it was still flat. Except her jeans had felt tight on the weekend, and she'd put it down to the sedentary job.

But what if it wasn't just a little weight gain? What if she was growing thick around the midsection because she was carrying Leonidas Stathakis's baby?

She gasped audibly, pushing out of the cubicle, and ran the taps, staring at herself in the mirror as the ice water ran over her fingertips.

Surely it wasn't true? It was just a heap of coincidences. She had a tummy bug and her weight gain *was* attributable to the fact she was chained to a desk for twelve-hour days. That could also account for her recent exhaustion.

That was all.

Nonetheless, when she left the office much later that day, still feeling unwell, Hannah ducked into a pharmacy around the corner from the Earl's Court flat she'd rented a room in.

She'd do a pregnancy test. There was no harm in that—it was a simple precaution.

In the privacy of her the bathroom, she unsealed the box, read the instructions, and did precisely what they said. She set an alarm on her phone, to tell her when two minutes was up.

She didn't need it, though.

It took fewer than twenty seconds for a second line to appear.

A strong, vibrant pink, showing that she was, indeed, pregnant.

With Leonidas Stathakis's baby.

'Oh, jeez.' She sat down on the toilet lid, and stared at the back of the door. Her hand curved over her stomach and she closed her eyes. His face appeared in her mind, unbidden, unwanted, and unflinchingly and just as he had been for months in her dreams, she saw him naked, his strong body and handsome face so close to her that she could breathe him in, except he was just a phantom, a ghost.

But not for long.

It shouldn't have happened. Despite the fact she'd torn his note into a thousand pieces and left it scattered over the marble bench-top of the luxurious penthouse kitchen, his words were indelibly imprinted into her mind.

Well, regardless of his regret, and the fact he hadn't respected her enough to say that to her face, she'd have to see him again.

There was nothing for it—she had to face this reality, to tell him the truth.

And she would—when she was ready.

Hannah checked the name against the piece of paper she clutched in her hand, looking around the marina with a frown on her face.

There was some event on, Capri Sailing Week or some such, and the whole marina was bursting with life. Enormous boats—or 'superyachts', as she'd been told they were called—lined up like swans, so graceful and imposing in the evening sun.

She knew from the search she'd done on the Internet that Stathakis Corp owned a boat that took part in the event. She also knew that Leonidas and his brother came to the event annually on their own 'superyacht'. Photos had shown her a suntanned Leonidas relaxing on the deck, casting his eye over the race.

She'd closed out of the images as quickly as she could.

She didn't need to see him again. Not like that.

This was going to be quick, like ripping off a plaster. She'd tell him she was pregnant—not that she'd really need words. At more than five months along, she was quite visibly carrying a baby.

She'd been so tempted just to call him. To deliver the news over the phone and leave it at that, just as he'd written her a note instead of having the courage to face her the next morning.

But it was cowardly and she wasn't that. They were

having a baby together—she couldn't ignore the ramifications of their night together and nor could he. At least she knew that, no matter what happened next, he'd regretted that night.

He'd regretted it, he wished that it hadn't happened, and he'd treated her with complete disdain and disrespect, skulking out in the middle of the night, leaving a note! It wasn't as if she'd have begged him for more—they'd both agreed to it being one night only. It was the salt in the wound of him vanishing, not even bothering to say goodbye.

That was the man she was having a child with.

She grabbed hold of that thought; she needed to remember that.

The Stathakis yacht was the biggest in the marina, and it was pumping with life and noise. Her eyes skimmed the yacht, running over the partygoers moving around with effortless grace, all scantily clad, from what she could see. Music with a heavy beat sounded loud and somehow seductive, so something began to beat low in her abdomen. There were staff, too, their crisp white shirts discernible even at a distance, the trays they carried overflowing with champagne flutes.

She narrowed her eyes, lifting a hand and wiping it over her forehead. She was warm—the sun was beating down, even now in the early evening, and she'd been travelling since that morning.

She was tired, too, the exhaustion of the first trimester not giving way in the second.

She moved closer to the yacht, mindful on her approach that security guards stood casually at the bridge that led to the deck.

As she approached, one of the men spoke to her in Italian. At her blank expression, he switched to Greek and then, finally, English. 'Can I help you, miss?'

'I need to see Leonidas Stathakis. It's important.'

The security guard flicked his gaze over Hannah, his expression unchanging. 'It's a private party.'

She had expected this resistance. 'If you tell him my name, I'm certain he'll want to see me.'

The guard's scepticism was obvious. 'And that is?'

'Hannah. Hannah May.' Her voice was soft, her Australian accent prominent.

The guard spoke into his walkie-talkie, the background noise of the party coming through louder when he clicked the button at its side. She discerned only her own name in the rapid delivery of information. Then, he clicked the walkie-talkie back to his hip.

'He says you can go up.'

'Thank you.'

Nerves were jangling inside her, doubts firing in her gut. Maybe she should turn around. Go back to London, or even Australia, far away. Call him with this information. Or not. She had no idea. She just knew suddenly the thought of coming face-to-face with Leonidas filled her with ice.

She was going to be sick.

'Miss? Are you okay?'

But she'd come all this way. She'd grappled with this for weeks now, she'd faced the reality of being pregnant with Leonidas's baby, trying to work out the best way to tell him. She had to tell him—there was nothing for it.

'I will be.'

Yes, she would be. She needed simply to get this over with. The faster the better. 'This way?' she prompted, gesturing towards the boat.

'And to the left.'

Hannah's smile was tight as she surveyed the crowd, not

particularly relishing the idea of weaving her way through so many people. 'Thank you.'

She stepped onto a platform and then went up a set of polished timber and white stairs. At the top, another guard opened a section of the boat's balustrade, forming a gate. The noise was deafening up here. She braced herself for a moment, frozen to the spot as she recognised at least a dozen Hollywood celebrities walking around in a state of undress. Men, women, all in their bathers, suntanned, impossibly slender and toned with very white teeth and enormous eyes.

Hannah stared at them self-consciously, this world so foreign to her, so foreign to anything and anyone she knew. These people were his friends?

There was a loud noise, a laugh, and then the splashing of water. She turned, chasing the interruption, to see a handsome man standing above the pool, a grin on his chiselled face. It wasn't Leonidas, but she recognised him nonetheless from the few photos she'd pulled up while trying to find out how to contact Leonidas.

Thanos Stathakis, the playboy prince of Europe, all golden and carefree, and surrounded by a dozen women who were quite clearly vying for a place in his bed. She pulled a face, straightened her spine and began to cut through the party.

She didn't belong here. She didn't want to be here. She just needed to tell him and get out.

'Miss May?' A woman wearing a crew uniform approached Hannah, a professional smile on her pretty face. 'This way, please.'

Hannah nodded stiffly, falling into step beside the woman, almost losing her footing when she saw a Grammy award–winning singer breeze past, laughing, arm in arm with the undisputed queen of talk-show television.

Hannah stared after them, her heart pounding. She felt like a fish way, way out of water. The crew member pushed a door open and Hannah followed, grateful for the privacy and quiet the room afforded.

'Would you like anything to drink, miss?'

Hannah shook her head. 'No, thank you.'

She waited until she was alone and then scanned the room, her eyes taking in the obvious signs of wealth that were littered without care. The yacht was unlike anything she'd ever seen, the last word in luxury and money. Designer furniture filled out this room, a television the size of her bed on one wall, and through the glass partition a huge bedroom with a spa against the windows.

Leonidas's bedroom?

Her pulse picked up a notch and on autopilot she wandered towards it, her heart hammering against her chest as she pushed the door open.

Yes. She couldn't say how she knew, only there was something in the air, his masculine, alpine fragrance that instantly jolted her senses.

She backed out quickly, as though the very fires of hell were lining the floor in there.

She had to do this. She would tell him, and then leave, giving him a chance to digest it, and to consider her wishes. This would be over in minutes.

Minutes.

She waited, and with each moment that passed her nerves stretched tighter, thinner, finer and more tremulous, so, five minutes later, she honestly thought she might pass out.

She was on the brink of leaving the room and going in search of Leonidas herself when the door burst inwards and he strode into the room, wearing only a pair of swimming shorts, and a look that—in the seconds before surprise contorted his expression—showed his impatience with her arrival.

He was partying.

He was probably the centre of attention, being just as fawned over and celebrated as his brother. Jealousy tore through her, but Hannah told herself it was outrage. Outrage that she'd been agonising over the baby they were going to have while he'd slipped out of bed and gone back to his normal life as though it had never happened.

If she'd held even a single shred of hope that he might be glad to see her, it disappeared immediately.

'Hannah.' His eyes roamed her face and then dropped lower, until he was staring at her stomach, and she felt the force of his shock, the reverberation of his confusion. It slammed into the room, slammed against her, and if she weren't so consumed with her own feelings she might almost have felt sympathy for him.

'Yes.' She answered the unspoken question, her voice slightly shaky. 'I'm pregnant. And you're the father.'

CHAPTER FOUR

HIS EYES SWEPT SHUT, almost as if he could wipe this meeting from reality, as if he would open his gaze and she'd be gone. It wasn't until that moment Hannah realised that she'd been partly hoping he would react well to this news. While neither of them had planned this, nor wanted it particularly, a baby was still cause for celebration, wasn't it?

Apparently not.

When he opened his eyes and his gaze pierced her soul, it was with a look of rejection, and panic.

'No.' He glared at her. 'This cannot be happening.'

Hannah curved a hand around her stomach, trying to be generous, to remember he was shocked, that she'd had time to adjust to this news and he was being presented with it all now.

'Really?' She arched a brow, her obvious pregnant state contradicting that.

He swore in his native tongue and moved towards a bar in the corner, pulling out two bottles of mineral water. He stalked towards her and held one out and she took it without thinking, her fingers curving over the top.

But, oh, she was so close to him now, and the last five months disappeared, everything disappeared, except this wave of intense recognition and need, that same spark of hunger that had incinerated her on New Year's Eve.

Her breath escaped her on a hiss; she stood frozen to the spot, her eyes glued to his, her face tilted upwards, her body on alert for his nearness. It was an instant, visceral, physical reaction and it shook her to the core.

But even before her eyes, Leonidas's surprise was giving way to comprehension. His jaw tightened and he nodded slowly, releasing the water bottle into her grip and stepping away from her, turning to stare at the ocean.

'How do you feel?'

She was surprised by the question—she hadn't expected it, this rapid assimilation of information, acceptance and then a hint of civility.

'I'm mostly okay.' She nodded, opening the bottle and taking a sip gratefully. 'I'm quite tired but otherwise fine.'

He didn't react. 'Do you know what gender it is?'

Hannah nodded again, but he wasn't looking. 'Yes.' She reached into her handbag, her fingers fumbling a little as she lifted out an ultrasound picture. 'Here.'

At that word, he turned slowly, his expression grim, his gaze lowering to the flimsy black and white photograph. He made no effort to take it.

'It's a girl,' she said quietly.

He still didn't reach for the picture, but his eyes swept shut as though he were steeling himself against this, as though it wasn't what he wanted. Hurt scored her being. But before she could fire that accusation at him, he was shooting another question at her.

'When did you find out?'

She swallowed in an attempt to bring moisture back to her dry throat. 'A while ago,' she admitted.

'When?'

A hint of guilt flared in her gut but she reminded herself she'd done nothing wrong.

'I've known for a few weeks.'

He stared at her, long and hard, for several moments. 'You didn't think I deserved to know when you did?'

She shook her head once, from one side to the other. 'You didn't think I deserved more than to wake up to a crummy note?'

He froze, completely still, and the sound of the glamorous party outside the room thumped and crashed. Hannah didn't move. She glared at him, waiting for his answer.

It came swiftly, his brow furrowing. 'So this was payback? Retaliation of some kind?'

She shook her head. 'What? No. It was nothing like that.' She sucked in a breath, not wanting to be dragged off topic. 'I just wanted a chance to get used to this before I had to deal with you.'

'And you are now used to it?' he demanded, heat in the question.

She let out a small laugh, but it was a sound completely without humour. 'I'm not sure I'll ever adjust.'

'I don't want anything from you, Leonidas,' she said firmly, not registering the way something like admiration sparked in his eyes. 'I had no idea who you were that night, nor that you're worth a squillion dollars. I have no interest in asking you for any kind of support payment or whatever.' She shuddered in rejection of the very idea.

'I mean it. This isn't my way of asking you to support me in any way. I don't want that.'

He spoke then, his voice low and husky. 'So what do you want?'

She bit down on her lip then immediately stopped when he took a step closer, his eyes on the gesture, his body seemingly pulled towards hers.

'I want…to know you'll be a part of her life,' she said quietly, her own childhood a black hole in her mind, swallowing her up. She would do whatever she could to make sure her own daughter never had to live with the grief she'd felt.

He was quiet, watching her, and nervousness fired in Hannah's gut. 'Don't misunderstand me,' she said thickly. 'I would happily never see you again. But our daughter deserves to know both her parents.' She lifted a hand, toying with the necklace she wore, running her finger over the chain distractedly. Hannah needed the security of knowing their child would have two people who loved her, two people in case something happened to one of them.

'I appreciate this news is probably an even bigger inconvenience to you than it was to me,' she said simply. 'I understand you didn't want this. You were very clear about that.' She cleared her throat, sidestepping him and moving towards the windows that framed a sensational view of the waters off the coast of Capri. 'But we are having a child together, and I don't want her to grow up thinking she's not wanted.' Hannah's voice cracked and she closed her eyes, sucking in breath, needing strength.

'You want me to be a part of our daughter's life?'

'Yes.' The word rushed out of her. She spun around, surprised to find Leonidas had come to stand right behind her, his eyes on hers, his expression impossible to comprehend.

'And what kind of part?'

She furrowed her brow, not understanding.

'Tell me, do you expect me to see her once a year? At Christmas, perhaps? Or for her birthdays, as well? Do you envisage I will spend time with my daughter according to a stopwatch?'

Hannah's eyes rounded in her face. 'I don't understand…'

'No,' he said succinctly and now she understood what was holding his face so completely still. He was angry!

'I will not be a figment of my child's life—the kind of father who exists like a tiny part of her.'

Hannah didn't get a chance to reassure him.

'My child will be raised by me.' His eyes were like flints of coal as he spoke. 'She will be raised with my name, and will have everything I can provide her with. She will be *mine*.'

At the completely possessive tone to his voice Hannah shuddered, because it was exactly how she felt, and they couldn't both raise their daughter.

'Don't make me regret coming here,' Hannah said quietly.

At this, his features grew taut, his jaw locked and his eyes showed a swirling comprehension that filled her with ice. 'Are you saying you contemplated not doing so?'

She paled, tilting her chin with a hint of rebellion. 'I've contemplated a great many things since I found out about her.'

'And was not telling me that I fathered a child one of those things you considered?'

Her cheeks glowed pink, revealing the truth of that statement. 'Briefly,' she conceded. 'Yes, of course. Wouldn't it be easier that way?'

Fury contorted his features and she rolled her eyes.

'I contemplated it for about three seconds before realising I could never do that. Obviously you deserve to know you're going to be a father. She's your child. I'm not saying you don't have a claim on her. But she's an innocent in this, she doesn't deserve to be pulled between us just because of that night.'

'I do not intend for her to be pulled between us.' He seized on this and, for a moment, she felt relief. Perhaps he was going to be reasonable after all, and not make this so difficult.

'You can be *very* involved,' she promised. 'I'm a reasonable person, Leonidas, and what I want most in this world is for our daughter to grow up secure in the love of her parents. But I want full custody. Full rights.' He didn't speak and she took strength from that. 'It's better this way, don't you see that?'

'Better for you,' he drawled, and then shook his head angrily. 'At least, you seem to think it is, but you do not have all the facts, Hannah.'

'No? What am I missing?'

He ground his teeth together. 'Does it not occur to you that there are risks to you, to her, in being connected to someone like me?'

She blinked, and something tapped the back of her mind, something she'd seen on an Internet search. Only she'd tried not to look too deeply at his life, his past—she'd felt dirty enough having to look him up on the internet to find the name of this boat.

'No one needs to know.'

His laugh was a mocking snort. 'That's simplistic and naïve. The tabloid press probably already has paparazzi on your trail. That's before you show up to this—one of the most hotly photographed events of the year—heavily pregnant and asking to see me.'

'I am not heavily pregnant,' she said, and then clamped her mouth shut in frustration and the sheer irrelevancy of that. 'And so what? Who cares? Lots of people have illegitimate children. There'll be a rumour. We'll say nothing, and then it will die down.'

'You are missing my point,' he insisted darkly. 'From the minute this news hits the public domain, you will become a part of my world, and so will she, whether you want to be or not. Thinking you can just hide away from that is unrealistic.'

'So?' she said, though she hadn't considered this, and didn't particularly like the way it made her feel. 'I'll cope.'

'As a bare minimum, you will find yourself and your

every move open to speculation in the gossip papers, and our daughter will be photographed and written about even when doing the most mundane things. You will want my protection from this, Hannah, and she will certainly deserve it.'

'I'd rather find my own way to protect her,' Hannah said crisply. 'I can handle a few photographers, and as for the stories, I just won't read them.'

His smile was a grim flicker of his lips. 'Sure, give that a go.' It was pure sarcasm.

'In any event, it is not,' he continued, 'the photographers that I am concerned with.'

She waited, holding a hand protectively over her stomach without realising it.

'I was married once,' he said, finally, the words like steel.

She remembered. Oh, it had been buried deep inside her mind, but as soon as he said it she recalled reading that, somewhere, at some time.

'And my wife was murdered.'

Hannah sucked in a gasp, sympathy pushing every other emotion from her mind.

'As was my two-year-old son.'

Hannah was hot and cold, sorrow and pain shooting through her. She almost felt as though she might faint.

'They were murdered as a vendetta against my father.' The words were strained and urgent. 'They lost their lives to hurt him and punish him. They were killed because of who they were to Dion Stathakis, and to me. I will not let that happen again. I will not let that happen to our daughter.'

Hannah's chest hurt. She'd known she was pregnant for a few weeks and already she knew she would give her life for this baby. She couldn't imagine the desperate agony of losing a toddler, of knowing a toddler to have met such a violent end.

'I'm so sorry.' The words were thick with tears. 'That must have been unbearable.' She swallowed, but the tears she was so adept at fighting filled her eyes.

He didn't respond—what could he say?

'But isn't that even more reason for me to hide away? To let me move far away from you and your world?'

'You cannot hide her. Not from men like him.'

A shiver ran down Hannah's spine.

'Only I can protect you both.'

Fear made Hannah tactless. 'I beg to differ, given the past...'

His expression cracked with pain and she winced.

'I'm so sorry. That was an awful thing to say. It's just...'

'No, you're right.' He held up a hand to stall her. 'I did not appreciate the danger to Amy and Brax. I failed them.' His voice was deep and her heart ached. 'I had no idea they were being watched, nor that a madman would use them to seek revenge on my father. His conviction did much damage to our business, and my brother and I worked tirelessly to make amends there, to return Stathakis Corp to its position of global prominence. That was my focus.

'I failed them, my wife and child, and I will never forget that, nor forgive myself.'

He straightened, his expression like iron. 'I will not make that mistake with her.'

He moved closer to Hannah, and she held her breath.

His hands curved over her stomach and she felt so much in that moment. It was as though a piece of string were wrapping from him to her, binding them, tying them together. If this had been a wedding ceremony it would have felt like a lesser commitment.

He focussed all his attention on Hannah. 'I will put everything I am into protecting you both, into ensuring men like that cannot get you. I cannot let you get on with your life as though this is simply an aberration when there may very well be a target over her head. Or yours, just because you happened to make the regrettable decision of sleeping with me one night.'

'You were the one who regretted it,' she pointed out and then shook her head, because that didn't matter any more. Panic was surging inside her; she felt as though she were falling back into a well only there was no light at the top of it.

She sucked in a breath but it burned through her lungs. 'Leonidas,' she groaned. 'I don't want anything to happen to her.'

'I won't let it,' he promised, lifting his hands to her face, holding her steady for his inspection. 'I promise you that.'

'How can you stop it?'

His eyes roamed her face intently. 'I will protect you and our daughter with my dying breath, that is how.'

She shook her head, the madness of this incongruous with the sounds of revelry beyond the room. Fear had her forgetting everything they were to one another, the brevity of their affair, his quickness to leave her, the fact he'd intended for them never to see one another again—and she'd agreed to that. In that moment, he was her lifeline, and she lifted a hand to his chest to take hold of it.

'Do you really think we're in danger?'

His eyes held hers and she felt the battle raging within him—a desire to reassure and placate her and a need to be honest.

'I will make sure you are not. But you must do what I say, and trust me to know what is right for you, for her, for our family.'

Family.

The word seemed to tear through both of them in different ways, each reacting to the emotion of that word, the harsh implications of such a term.

He looked stricken and Hannah felt completely shocked. She hadn't had a family in a long time. And even though this had been foisted on both of them, the word felt warm and loaded with promise. She swallowed past a lump in her throat and shook her head, nothing making sense.

'How? What? Tell me, Leonidas. I need to know she'll be okay.'

'Marry me,' he said simply, the words like rocks dropping into the boat.

'What?'

'Marry me, as soon as is legally possible.'

She sucked in a breath, his words doing strange things to her. In a thousand years, she hadn't expected this, and she had no way of processing how she felt. Marriage? To Leonidas Stathakis?

'How the heck is that going to help?'

'You'll be my wife, under my protection, living in my home. We will be raising our child together.'

The picture he painted was so seductive. Hannah took a fortifying breath, trying to disentangle the irrational desire to make sure her daughter didn't suffer the same miserable upbringing as she had from what was actually the *right* decision. It was impossible to think clearly.

Hannah shook her head slowly. 'It would never work between us.'

'What is there to "work"?' he asked simply. 'You love our child, do you not?'

Hannah's eyes sparked with his. 'With all my heart.'

'And you want to do what is best for her?'

Hannah's chin tilted in silent agreement.

'So trust me. Trust me to protect you both, to ensure her safety. I will never let anything happen to either of you.'

She nodded, listening to his words, hearing the intent in them.

'I cannot have my daughter raised anywhere but in my home,' he murmured, clearing his throat. She jerked her gaze to his and the depth of feeling in his eyes almost tore her in two. 'I need to *know* she is safe. That you are safe.' He turned away from her, stalking towards the table. He placed his palms on it, staring straight ahead, out into the water. The party raged outside their doors, but inside this room, it was deathly silent.

'We don't really even know each other,' she said quietly, even as her heart was shifting, and her mind was moving three steps ahead to her inevitable acceptance.

Two main points were working on her to accept. Whatever threat he perceived, there was enough of a basis in fact for Hannah to be seriously concerned. His wife and child had been murdered. His father was in the mob. These threats did not simply disappear—she was in danger, and so was their daughter.

And even if it weren't for that, there were other considerations. Hannah's parents had died unexpectedly and her whole world had imploded. She'd been moved to her aunt and uncle's—who she'd barely known—and been left to their dubious care. She'd been miserable and alone.

There were no guarantees in life, but weren't two parents better than one wherever possible? Wasn't it more of an insurance policy for their daughter to know both her mother and father? What if Hannah insisted on raising her alone, with Leonidas as a 'bit player' in their lives, and then something happened to Hannah? And what if by then he'd married someone else, and their child was an outsider?

As Hannah had been.

She expelled a soft breath, the reality of that like a punch in the gut. Because marrying Leonidas would mean she'd always be on the edge, that she'd never find that one thing she knew she really wanted, deep down: a true family of her own. A family to which she belonged. People who adored and wanted her.

But this wasn't about her; it wasn't about her wants and desires. All that mattered was their baby.

With resignation in her turbulent green eyes, she lifted her head a little, partway to nodding.

He saw it, and his eyes narrowed then he straightened, relief in his features. 'We will fly to the island today. My lawyer will take care of the paperwork.'

But it was all so rushed. Hannah spun away from him, lifting her water bottle from the table's edge and sipping it.

'I have a job, Leonidas.'

'Quit.'

There were only two weeks left of her maternity contract. It wasn't the worst thing to do, though she hated the idea of leaving her boss in the lurch. She dropped her hand to her stomach and thought of their baby and nothing else seemed to matter.

For her? She'd do anything.

'You will be safe on the island,' he insisted, as though he could read her thoughts and knew exactly which buttons to press to get her to agree.

'On Chrysá Vráchia?' she asked distractedly.

'No.' His expression took on a contemplative look. 'My island.'

'You have your own island?' Disbelief filled the tone of her words.

'Yes. Not far from Chrysá.' He moved closer, his eyes scanning her face. 'It is beautiful. You'll like it.'

She was sure she would, but it was all happening so fast.

Even knowing she would agree—that she had agreed—she heard herself say softly, 'This is crazy.'

And perhaps he thought she was going to change her mind, because he crossed the room and caught her arms, holding her close to him, his gaze locked to hers.

'You have to see that I cannot let our child be raised away from me. And, following that logic, that it is best for us to be married, to at least try to present our child with a sense of family, even when we know it to be a lie.'

Her heart squeezed tight, her lungs expelled air in a rush. Because it was exactly what she wanted, exactly what she'd just been thinking. Still, cynicism was quick to follow relief. 'You really think we can fool our child into believing we're a normal couple?'

His lips were a grim slash and she had the strongest impression that he couldn't have been less impressed if she'd suggested he set fire to this beautiful, enormous yacht.

'I think we owe it to our child to try.'

CHAPTER FIVE

HIS STATE-OF-THE-ART HELICOPTER flew them from the yacht to the airport, where his private jet was waiting.

It was the kind of plane Hannah had flown to Italy aboard, the kind that commercial airlines used, only it bore the name 'Leonidas Stathakis' in gold down the side. When she stepped on board it was exactly like walking into a plush hotel.

As with the yacht, everything was white or beige, and incredibly comfortable. Enormous seats, like armchairs, chandeliers made of crystal, and, deeper into the plane, a boardroom, a cinema and four bedrooms.

'Have a seat.' Leonidas indicated a bank of chairs, and as she did she couldn't shake the feeling that it was more like a job interview than anything else.

For the hundredth time since leaving his yacht, since lifting up into the sky and hovering over the picture-perfect Capri marina, Hannah questioned the wisdom of what she was doing.

But every time doubt reared its head and begged her to reconsider, she heard his words anew. *'My wife was murdered. As was my two-year-old son.'* And a frisson of terror sprinted down her spine and she knew she would do anything to avoid that same fate befalling their daughter.

Every primal, maternal instinct she possessed roared to life. She wouldn't allow their child to be harmed.

And nor would he.

She'd felt that promise from him and trusted him, had known he would lay down his own life if necessary to protect hers, to protect their child's.

And suddenly, the world seemed frightening and huge, and Hannah knew that if she walked away from Leonidas now, she would be alone, with unknown dangers lurking, with threats to their child she couldn't possibly appreciate, let alone avoid.

'The usual month-long notification period for weddings will be waived,' he explained, sitting opposite her, his long legs encroaching on her space so that if she wasn't very careful, they would be touching and the little fires still buzzing beneath her skin would arc into full-blown wildfires once more.

It took her a moment to collect her mind from the fears that were circulating and bring herself back to the present. 'Why?'

'What do you mean?'

Her sea-green eyes showed confusion. 'Well, isn't that the law? Why would that be changed for us?'

He lifted a brow and comprehension dawned.

'Because you asked for it to be, and you're Leonidas Stathakis.'

He shrugged. 'Yes.'

'And you get whatever you want?'

His eyes were like coal once more. 'No.'

Her heart twisted because of course he didn't. He'd just told her he'd lost his family—clearly his life wasn't that of a charmed man.

'Why rush, though, Leonidas?'

All of his attention was on her and she trembled for a different reason now, as the heat of his gaze touched something deep in her soul, stirring the remnants of their passion and desire anew. She swallowed, her throat dry, her cheeks blushing pink.

'Because there is no point in delay. Because I want you to be protected from this day, this moment. I will take no risks with our daughter's life,' he said firmly. 'Nor with yours. You should not have been brought into this.'

She opened her mouth to confront him, but he continued. 'Having sex with you was a moment of weakness, a stupid, selfish decision that I regretted instantly. Believe me, Hannah, if I could take that back, if I could have never met you...' He shook his head, looking away, as the plane began to move on the runway.

'I am sorry to have drawn you into my world. I am sorry that we must marry, sorry that we are having a child together. It is my fault, all of it. I cannot change that night, what happened between us, but I can do my damned best to ensure no further harm befalls you.'

'Harm?' she repeated, the word just a croak. 'You think of this pregnancy as harm?'

'I think it is a mistake,' he muttered. 'But one we must live with.'

Her temper spiked, disbelief at his callous words making her chest hurt. 'How can you talk about our baby like that?' she found herself whispering, even though that 'baby' was still very much inside her.

'You said as much yourself,' he pointed out logically. 'You didn't want this.'

'I didn't *plan* on it happening,' she corrected caustically. 'I'm twenty-three years old; I thought children would be way off in the future.'

He dipped his head in silent concession.

'But, Leonidas, almost as soon as I learned of this pregnancy, I have loved this baby, and I have wanted our daughter, and I have known I would put this child first. For ever and always.'

He digested her words, his expression giving little away, and then he nodded, as the plane hurtled faster down the runway before lifting into the sky.

'And in marrying me, I understand you are doing just that—putting our baby first. You do not wish for this marriage, and nor do I.' He ground his teeth together. 'And yet, for this child, here we are.' He reached into his pocket and pulled out his phone, not seeing the way her face paled at his harshly delivered words. 'I have some questions for you. My lawyer emailed them across.'

'Questions?' It was a rapid change of subject, one that made her head spin. 'What for?'

'The marriage licence. The prenuptial agreement. Setting up your bank accounts and the family trust.'

'Woah.' She was still reeling from his repeated insistence of how little he wanted this marriage, and, even though he was surely echoing her own thoughts, hearing them voiced made her head spin a little. It was all too much, too soon.

'Can't we just…take it one day at a time?'

'Let me make this clear,' he said, leaning forward, his expression that of a hard-nosed tycoon.

She swallowed, but refused to be cowed by his closeness, by his look of steel. 'Yes?'

'One week from today we will be married. You will be my wife: Mrs Hannah Stathakis. You will be marrying someone who is worth over a hundred billion American dollars. Your life, as you know it, is about to cease completely. There is no "taking it one day at a time". In what? Three months? Four? We will have a child. That is the deadline hanging over our heads. Within four months, we need to be able to find a way to relate, to exist as parents. We cannot delay. Surely you see that?'

It was all so shocking, so impossible to comprehend and also so reasonable. She heard his words and closed her eyes, because the final sentence was what really got through to her.

His net worth was awe-inspiring, his suggestion that she too might be worth a fortune, even his reminder that their daughter would inherit such a sum, were all details that caused her heart to pound, and not necessarily in a good way. But what he'd said that had really spoken to Hannah had been right at the end.

They had a deadline. A tiny little time bomb ticking away inside her belly.

They needed to find a way to make this work and he was showing himself to be cognisant of that.

'Your full name is Hannah May?'

'Hannah Grace May.' She nodded, tightening her seat belt and looking out of the window on autopilot. Capri was tiny beneath them, just a beautiful picture-book piece of land, looming from the sea, all verdant green against the deep blue of the Med, the superyachts tiny white shapes now, clean and crisp.

Was it really only that morning she'd flown in over Italy, and stared down at this exact same view? How certain she'd been then of being able to tell Leonidas she was pregnant and then depart, confident he'd accept her suggestion of being a small but vital part of their daughter's life.

'Birth date?'

She responded, thinking back to her last birthday, right before Christmas. Angus had thrown her a surprise dinner party and she'd pretended to be thrilled, but Hannah hated surprises, and she'd wondered how he couldn't know that about her. She'd wondered how he could think she'd like being the centre of attention like that, with everyone in the restaurant staring at her, waiting for her to smile and make a little speech thanking them for coming.

Hannah didn't like surprises but she'd chalked the party up to something they'd laugh about in ten years' time. Besides, he'd gone to a huge amount of effort, she wasn't about to be ungrateful in the face of that.

She'd had no idea, though, that a way bigger surprise had been in store for her, nor that his 'effort' in arranging such an elaborate party was undoubtedly his way of compensating for the fact he was sleeping with Hannah's cousin behind her back.

Her jaw tightened, and unconsciously she gripped her hands tightly in her lap, the past rushing towards her, wrapping around her, forcing her to look at it, to be in it even when it was strangling her. To remember the sight of her cousin and her fiancé, their limbs entwined, the dark black sheets of Angus's bed in stark contrast to their flesh, Michelle's white-blonde hair glistening in the evening light.

It was a betrayal on two fronts. That her fiancé would cheat on her was bad enough, but with someone she'd been raised to think of as a sister?

Indignation and hurt made her breath burn a little.

Capri swam beneath her, ancient and striking, and it offered a hint of perspective. How many millions of people had walked those shores, swum in these seas, each of them with their own problems and concerns, none of those concerns mattering, really, in the huge scheme of life and this earth? One day, she'd forget the sting of this betrayal, the second loss of family she'd had to endure.

'Parents' names?'

She swept her eyes shut, thinking of her biological parents, seeing her mother's smile as she tucked Hannah into bed, stroking her hair, singing their goodnight song.

'Ellie—Eleanor—and Brad.'

There were more questions and she answered them matter-of-factly—it was easier to simply provide the information than to launch into explanations with each point.

'Why did your engagement end?'

That question had her swivelling her head to him, and she was grateful that a flight attendant chose that exact moment to enter the cabin, offering drinks.

'Just water,' Hannah murmured.

'Coffee.' He focussed on Hannah. 'Are you hungry?'

She was. 'A little.'

'And some dinner.'

'Yes, sir.'

The attendant left, and Hannah thought—for a moment—Leonidas might have forgotten the question he'd posed. But of course he hadn't. This man probably never forgot a thing. 'Your fiancé?'

'Right.' She was surprised at how well she'd kept her voice neutral.

'He cheated on me.' She shrugged as though it didn't matter. 'It kind of killed my interest in marrying him.'

'I can imagine it would.' He was watching her as though she were a puzzle he could put back together if only he had enough time. 'You hadn't slept with him. His idea, or yours?'

'His.'

His expression showed surprise. 'Why?'

The flight attendant reappeared with drinks, placing them down on the armrest table each had in their seat and leaving again.

'Romance.'

Leonidas lifted a brow. 'You think sex isn't romantic?'

Heat exploded through her body and she clamped her knees close together to stop them from shaking. Sex with Leonidas had gone beyond romance. It had been passion and fire, everything she could imagine wanting from a lover.

'I wouldn't know.' She dipped her eyes lower, studying the carpet on the floor of the aeroplane as though it were a fascinating work of art.

'So how come you were a virgin?' he pushed.

Hannah lifted her gaze, forcing herself to meet his curious eyes. 'We decided we'd wait.'

'There was no one before him?'

She bit down on her lip, shaking her head from side to side. 'Is that so unusual?'

His expression showed cynicism and disbelief. 'In my experience, yes.'

She laughed then, shaking her head a little. 'Stop looking at me like that.'

'Like what?'

'As though I'm some kind of… I don't know. As though I'm an alien.'

'Your inexperience is rare, that's all,' he corrected. 'Particularly given the fact you were engaged.'

'Angus and I…' She swallowed, the bitterness impossible to completely suppress. 'We were friends for a long time. The dating thing came out of nowhere and I guess our relationship didn't completely transition. Sex wasn't a drawcard for me. I guess it wasn't for him, either.'

'You did not desire him?'

Ridiculously, Hannah felt a buzz of disloyalty at admitting as much. 'Not really. We weren't about that.'

'What were you "about"?'

'I loved him,' she responded, simply, 'and I thought he loved me. That was enough.'

Leonidas nodded thoughtfully. 'So that was also a pragmatic marriage.'

Hannah's eyes widened at his description. 'What do you mean?'

'You agreed to marry a man simply because it made sense, because you thought you loved each other, without having any idea if you were physically compatible. So this marriage—ours—already has more going for it.'

Hearing him refer to their marriage caused her heart to trip a little, banging against her sternum. 'How do you figure? Angus was one of my closest friends...'

'Which means very little given that he betrayed your trust and slept around behind your back.'

'Woah. Don't go easy on me, will you?'

'I don't think you want anyone to go easy on you, Hannah May.'

She startled a little at his unexpected perceptiveness. 'It was less than six months ago. It's still kind of raw.'

His expression barely shifted yet she had the feeling he was saving that little revelation, storing it away. 'He cheated on you. He doesn't deserve a second thought.'

She nodded, having said as much to herself.

'Is he still with her?'

Hannah reached for her water, sipping it, trying to tamp down on that little bundle of pain. 'No. Not according to my aunt.'

Leonidas nodded sharply, as if filing away that information. 'There is no love between you and me, Hannah, but there is desire enough to burn us alive if we are not careful. And there is a baby—which we both want to protect and cherish.'

'Yes. I do.'

'Neither of us wanted this, but we can make our marriage a success.' He said it with such fierce determination she almost laughed, as though she were simply a property he wanted to acquire, a piece of real estate he needed to buy.

Her own questions zipped through her. She sipped her water, balling her courage. 'Your wife and son…when did they…?'

His eyes were coal-like in his autocratic face. 'Almost five years ago.'

'I'm so sorry.' She spoke gently, softly. 'You said they were murdered?'

His eyes narrowed and his skin paled almost imperceptibly. 'Yes.'

'By whom?'

He held a hand up, silencing her with the gesture. 'I have no intention of discussing it, Hannah. My first marriage is off limits.'

The words smarted and she couldn't resist pointing out his hypocrisy. 'But you were just asking me about my fiancé.'

'You were happy to talk about it.'

Hannah's brow furrowed. 'No, I wasn't. I answered your questions because we're getting married.' How strange those words felt in her mouth. 'And if you're going to be my husband, it seems like the kind of thing you have a right to know about.'

He tilted his head in concession but his gaze was steady. 'I will not discuss Amy and Brax.'

Hannah expelled an angry rush of breath. 'Well, that seems kind of dumb.'

He clearly hadn't been expecting that response. 'Oh, really?' There was danger in the silky drawl.

'Yeah, really.' The flight attendant returned, brandishing a platter loaded with Italian delicacies. Cheeses, ham, fruit, vegetable sticks and dips, breads, olive oil and vinegar. The aroma hit her in the gut and she realised she was actually starving.

But other feelings still took precedence. When they were

alone again, she continued, 'You were married and had a son, and you lost them. You lost your family.'

Her voice caught because she knew more than enough about how that felt—to be safe in the bosom and security of your loved ones one day, then to be adrift at sea, cast out, alone, bereft, with none of the usual place markers to help you find your bearings.

'Thank you for the neat recitation of this fact.'

Her nostrils flared. 'I only mean that's a huge part of you. Don't you think our child will want to learn about her half-brother one day? That's a part of *her* life.'

Despite the fact his expression remained the same, his breath grew louder, and she would have sworn she saw panic cross his eyes.

'No.' He said the word like a curse, harsh and compelling.

Hannah sat perfectly still.

'She will never know about Brax. *Never.*'

Hannah's heart thumped hard in her chest.

'I will not speak of them. Not to you, not to her, not to anyone.'

She truly didn't think he meant it as an insult—he was caught on the back foot and the sheer strength of his emotions made him speak without thinking. But the vitriol in the statement sliced through her, filling her organs with acid.

'You're seeing this marriage, and our daughter, as an abstract concept,' she said gently, even when her heart was hurting. 'You're thinking of her as a baby only. What about when she's ten? Fifteen? Twenty? When you and she are friends as well as family, when she's sitting here where I am, on a plane, opposite you, and she's asking her father about his life. Do you really think you can keep such a huge part of yourself shielded from her? And me, for that matter?'

He drank his coffee, before piercing her with his jet-black eyes. 'Yes.'

'You're being incredibly obtuse and naïve.' But the words lacked zing. They were said with sympathy. No one knew more about the toll grief took when it was kept locked deep inside a person.

'I am sorry you think so.' He pushed his untouched plate aside and pulled a newspaper from the armrest. He flicked it up, pointedly blanking her.

It was galling, and only the fact that his stance was obviously driven by a deep, painful sadness kept her silent.

He didn't want to talk about his family. Yet.

They barely knew each other, despite this bizarre agreement they'd entered into. They would marry—in a week—and the very idea stirred her pulse to life. But despite the marriage, they'd spent only a few hours in one another's company. They were virtually strangers. Of course he didn't want to crack his heart open and lay everything out before her.

He was guarding his privacy, as befitted the newness of all this. Over time, as they grew to know one another, he was bound to change, to open up to her more.

She lifted a strawberry, popping it in her mouth, tasting the sweetness, relishing its freshness. She wanted him to trust her, and she had to show him how. To keep opening up to him, even when it felt counterintuitive, even when the past had shown her to be more guarded with herself, to protect her feelings.

'I felt undesirable,' Hannah murmured, reaching for another strawberry.

Leonidas pushed the top of the paper down, so his eyes could meet hers. There was a trace of coldness there, from their earlier conversation. She pushed on regardless.

'With Angus. I didn't really feel anything for him, physically, and he suggested we wait until we were married, so I agreed. I heard about couples not being able to keep their hands off each other and, honestly, I thought there was something wrong with me.'

She bit down on her lower lip thoughtfully. 'I presumed I just wasn't really sexual. I thought he wasn't, either. Then I saw him in bed with someone else, and I found out they'd been sleeping together for over a month, and the penny dropped. He was sexual. He liked sex. He just didn't want me.'

Leonidas placed the paper on his knees, his steady gaze trained on her face.

'I never felt like I wanted to rip a guy's clothes off. It was as though hormones left me completely behind.' She shrugged and then homed her own gaze in, focussing on his lips. Lips that were strong in his face, powerful and compelling. Lips that had kissed her and tipped her world upside down.

'But you...'

He arched a brow, silently prompting her to continue.

'You left me breathless,' she admitted, even when a part of her wondered if she should say as much, if it didn't leave her exposed and vulnerable, weakened in some way. 'I can't explain it. I felt desire for the first time in my life and I...'

'Go on,' he prompted, the words a little throaty, and she was so glad: glad that maybe he was affected by her confession in some way.

'I felt desirable for the first time in my life, too. I liked it. I liked the way you looked at me.' She turned away now, clearing her throat, looking towards the window.

Leonidas leaned forward, surprising her by placing his hand on hers. Sparks shot from her wrist and through her whole body. 'Your fiancé was an idiot for giving you a moment's doubt on this score.'

Her laugh was dismissive, but he leaned further forward, so their knees brushed. 'You are very, very sexy,' he said, simply, and heat began to burn in her veins.

'I don't mean that,' she said, shaking her head. 'You don't need to... I just meant to explain...'

'I know what you meant.' He sat back in his seat, regarding her once more. 'And I am telling you that you are a very sensual woman. You have no idea how I have been tormented by memories of that night, Hannah Grace May.'

CHAPTER SIX

THE MEDITERRANEAN GLISTENED just beyond the window of his study. On the second floor of his mansion, and jutting out a little from the rest of the building, this workspace boasted panoramic views of the ocean. Leonidas braced his arms on the windowsill, staring out at it, his breath burning in his lungs, his head spinning as comprehension sledged into him from both sides.

In Capri, he'd acted purely on instinct.

His wife and child had died, but here was another woman, another child, and they weren't Amy and Brax—they'd never be to him what Amy and Brax were—but they were still his responsibility.

The fact he would never have chosen to become a father again was a moot point.

She was pregnant.

They were having a child—a daughter.

His chest clutched and he slammed his eyes closed, the taste of adrenalin filling his mouth. A thousand and one memories tormented him from the inside out, like acid rushing through his veins.

Amy, finding out she was pregnant. Amy, swelling with his child. Amy, uncomfortable. Amy, in labour. Amy, nursing their infant. Amy, watching Brax learn to walk. Amy, patiently reading to Brax, loving him, laughing at him.

Amy.

His eyes opened, bleakness in the depths of their obsidian centres.

If sleeping with another woman was a betrayal of Amy, what then was this? Creating a whole new family, and bringing them to this island?

He grunted, shaking his head, knowing that wasn't fair. Amy would never have expected him to close himself off from life, from another relationship, another family.

But Leonidas had sworn he would do exactly that.

The idea of Hannah ever becoming anything to him besides this was anathema. Theirs was a marriage born of necessity, a marriage born of a need to protect his child, and the woman he'd made pregnant. It was a marriage of duty, that was all.

Flint formed in his eyes, his resolution hardening.

They would marry—there was no other option. Even if it weren't for the possible threat to Hannah's life, Leonidas acknowledged his ancient sense of honour would have forced him to propose, to insist upon marriage. Growing up in the shipwreck of his father's marriages hadn't undone the lessons his grandfather had taught him, nor the unity he'd seen in his grandparents' marriage.

Their child, their daughter, deserved to grow up with that same example. Hannah deserved to have support and assistance.

And what else?

His body tightened as he flashed back to the way he'd responded to her that night, the way desire had engulfed him like a tidal wave, drowning him in his need for her. The way he'd kissed her, his mouth taking possession of hers, his whole body firing with a desperate need to possess her, even when he'd spent the past five months telling himself their night together had been a mistake.

It *had* been a mistake. It should never have happened, but it had, and, looking back, he didn't think he could have stopped it. Not for all the money in all the world. There had been a force pulling him to her; the moment their bodies had collided he'd felt as though he'd been jolted back to life. He'd looked at her and felt a surge of need that had gone beyond logic and sense. It had been an ancient, incessant beating of a drum and ignoring it had not been an option.

Perhaps it still wasn't…

Glass. Steel. Designer furniture. Servants. More glass. Famous art. Views of the ocean that just wouldn't quit. Hannah stared around Leonidas's mansion, the luxury of it almost impossible to grapple with, and wondered if she'd stepped into another dimension.

Did people really live like this?

He had his own airfield, for goodness' sake! His private jet had touched down on the island, a glistening ocean surrounding them as the sun dipped towards the horizon. She'd expected a limousine but there'd been several golf carts parked near the airstrip and he'd led her to one of them, opening the door for her in a way that made her impossibly aware of his breadth, strength and that musky, hypermasculine fragrance of his.

When he'd sat beside her, their knees had brushed and she'd remembered what he'd said to her in the plane. *'You have no idea how I have been tormented by memories of that night.'*

Her belly stirred with anticipation and heat slicked between her legs.

At first, she hadn't seen the house. Mansion. She'd been too distracted by the beauty of this island. Rocky, primal in some way, just like Leonidas, with fruit groves to one side, grapevines running down towards the ocean and then, finally, a more formal, landscaped garden with huge olive and hibiscus trees providing large, dark patches of shade in the lead up to the house.

Leonidas had given her a brief tour, introducing Hannah

to the housekeeper, Mrs Chrisohoidis, before excusing himself. 'I want to get some things organised.' He'd frowned, and she'd felt, for the first time, a hint of awkwardness at being here, in the house of a man she barely knew, whom she was destined to marry and raise a child with.

'Okay.' She'd smiled, to cover it, thinking that she had her own 'things' to organise. Like the room she was renting in Earl's Court and the job she was expected back at in a few days, and an aunt and uncle who deserved to know not only that she was pregnant but also that she was getting married.

None of these were obligations Hannah relished meeting and so she decided, instead, to explore. There was plenty of house to lose herself in, and with the approach of dusk, and only the occasional staff member to interrupt, she went from room to room, trying to get her bearings.

The property itself was spectacular. The initial impression that it was a virtual palace only grew as she saw more and more of it. But what she did realise, after almost an hour of wandering, was that there was a distinct lack of anything personal. Beyond the art, which must surely reflect something of Leonidas's taste, there was a complete lack of personal paraphernalia.

No pictures, no *stuff*. Nothing to show who lived here, nor the family he'd had and lost.

The sun finally kissed the sea and orange exploded across the sky, highlighted by dashes of pink. Hannah abandoned her tour, moving instead to the enormous terrace she'd seen when she'd first arrived. No sooner had she stepped onto it than the housekeeper appeared.

'Miss May, would you like anything to eat or drink?'

Hannah thought longingly of an ice-cold glass of wine and grimaced. 'A fruit juice?' she suggested.

'Very good. And a little snack?' The housekeeper was lined, her tanned skin marked with the lines of a life well-lived and filled with laughter. Her hair, once dark, had turned almost completely silver, except at her temples, where some inky colour stubbornly clung.

'I'm not very hungry.' Hannah wasn't sure why she said the words apologetically, only it felt a little as if the house-keeper was excited at the prospect of having someone else to feed.

'Ah, but you are eating for two, no?' And her eyes twin-kled, crinkling at the corners with the force of her smile, and Hannah's chest squeezed because, for the first time since discovering her pregnancy, someone seemed com-pletely overjoyed with the news.

Her flatmates had been shocked, her boss had been dev-astated at the possibility of losing someone he'd come to rely on so completely, and Leonidas had been…what? How had he felt? Hannah couldn't say with certainty, only it wasn't happiness. Shock. Fear. Worry. Guilt.

'My appetite hasn't really been affected,' she said.

'Ah, that will come,' the housekeeper murmured know-ingly. 'May I?' She gestured to Hannah's stomach.

Mrs Chrisohoidis lifted her aged hands, with long, slen-der fingers and short nails, and pressed them to Hannah's belly and for a moment, out of nowhere, Hannah was hit with a sharp pang of regret—sadness that her own mother wouldn't get to enjoy this pregnancy with her.

'It's a girl?'

Hannah's expression showed surprise. 'Yes. How did you know?'

At this, Mrs Chrisohoidis laughed. 'A guess. I have a fifty per cent chance, no?'

Hannah laughed, too. 'Yes. Well, you guessed right.'

'A girl is good. Good for him.' She looked as though she wanted to say something more, but then shrugged. 'I bring you some bread.'

Hannah suppressed a smile and turned her attention back to the view, thinking once more of the beautiful coastline of Chrysá Vráchia, of how beautiful that island had been, how perfect everything about that night had seemed.

She'd longed to visit the island from the first time she'd seen footage of it in a movie and had been captivated by the cliffs that were cast of a stone that shimmered gold at sunrise and sunset. The fact she'd been able to book her flights so easily, the fact Leonidas had been there in the bar and she'd looked at him and felt an instant pull of attraction...the fact he'd reciprocated. It had all seemed pre-ordained, right down to the conception of a child despite the fact they'd used protection.

When she heard the glass doors behind her slide open once more, she turned around with an easy smile on her face, expecting to see the housekeeper returning. Only it wasn't Mrs Chrisohoidis who emerged, carrying a champagne flute filled with orange juice.

'Leonidas.' Her smile faltered. Not because she wasn't happy to see him but because a simmering heat overtook any other thoughts and considerations.

'I am sorry I left you so long.'

'It's fine.' The last thing she wanted was for him to see her as an inconvenience—a house guest he had to care for. She knew the feeling well. Being foisted upon an unwilling aunt and uncle taught one to recognise those signs with ease. She ignored the prickle of disappointment and panic at finding herself in this situation, yet again.

This wasn't the same. She was an adult now, making her own decisions, choosing what was best for her child. 'You don't need to feel like you have to babysit me,' she said, a hint of defensiveness creeping into her statement.

His nod showed agreement with her words and, she thought, a little gratitude.

He didn't want to be saddled with a clinging housemate any more than she intended to be one.

'I will show you around, after dinner.'

'I've already had a look around,' she murmured, but her mind was zeroed in on his use of the word 'dinner'. It had all happened so fast she hadn't stopped to think about what their marriage would look like. Would it be this? Dinner together? Two people living in this huge house, pretending to be here by choice?

Or polite strangers, trapped in an elevator with one another, having to stay that way until the moment of escape? Except there was no escape here, no one coming to jimmy the doors open and cajole the lift into motion.

This was her life—his life.

'And I mean what I said. Please don't feel you have to keep me company, or have dinner with me or anything. I know what this is.'

'*Ne?*' he prompted curiously.

Mrs Chrisohoidis appeared then, carrying not only some bread, but a whole platter, similar to the one they'd shared on the flight, but larger and more elaborate, furnished with many dips, vegetables, fish, cheeses and breads.

'I make your favourite for dinner.' She smiled at Leonidas as she placed the platter on a table towards the edge of the terrace.

'Thank you, Marina.'

They both watched her retreat and then Leonidas gestured towards the table.

'She's worked for you a while?' Hannah eyed the delicious platter as she sat down and found that, to her surprise, she was in fact hungry after all. She reached for an olive, lifting it to her lips, delighting in its fleshy orb and salty flavour.

'Marina?' He nodded. 'For as long as I can remember.'

That intrigued her. 'Since you were young?'

He nodded.

'So she worked for your parents?'

'Yes.'

A closed door. Just like his wife and son.

Hannah leaned against the balcony, her back to the view, her eyes intent on the man she was going to marry. 'Did you grow up here?'

He regarded her thoughtfully. 'No.'

'Where, then?'

'Everywhere.' A laconic shrug.

'I see. So this is also "off limits"?'

Her directness clearly surprised him. He smiled, a tight gesture, and shook his head. 'No. I simply do not talk about my parents often. Perhaps I've forgotten how.'

She could relate to that. Aunt Cathy had hated Hannah talking about her own mother and her father. *He was my brother! How do you think it makes me feel to hear you going on about them? Heartbroken, that's how.* And nine-year-old Hannah had learned to keep her parents alive in her own mind, her own head, rather than by sharing her memories with anyone else who could mirror them back to her.

Angus had asked about them, but by then she'd been so used to cosseting her memories that it hadn't come easily to explain what they'd been like.

'They divorced when I was young.'

'That was hard on you?'

'Yes.'

Mrs Chrisohoidis appeared once more, this time with a little bowl of chocolates. 'For the baby,' she said, and winked as she placed them down on the table.

'But there was a silver lining, too, because part of the divorce was a new brother.'

'How does that work?'

'My father had an affair. Thanos was the by-product. It caused my parents' divorce, but they'd been catastrophically miserable, anyway. I was glad they were separating; glad there would at last be some peace. And Thanos arrived, only three months my junior.'

'That must have been strange. How old were you?'

'Eight.'

'And he lived here?'

At this, Leonidas's expression was thoughtful, darkly so. 'His mother gave my father full custody.'

'That must have been hard for her.'

Leonidas shook his head. 'Hardest of all for Thanos, I'm sure.'

'How so?'

'His mother gave him up quite willingly,' Leonidas said softly, his expression shifting to one of compassion so Hannah's heart turned over in her chest. 'Thanos was—and remains—an incredibly strong-willed, stubborn character. She could not cope with him.'

Hannah's jaw dropped open. 'But he was just a boy! Surely there were ways of making him listen to her?'

'Who knows? But one day, when he was eight, she showed up and left him with my father. She said she couldn't do it any more.'

Sympathy scored deep in Hannah's veins. 'That must have been so hard for him. And your mother!'

'My mother hated him,' Leonidas said grimly. 'She treated him like a street dog.'

Hannah felt as though she could cry! Having experienced exactly this treatment herself, she felt an odd link to Leonidas's brother, a desire to look at him and comfort him, to tell him he was worthy, just as she'd always wished someone would say to her.

'But your father took him in,' Hannah said quietly, hoping there was a happy ending for the little boy Thanos had been.

'My father was bullish about custody. He had money, resources, staff. He ensured he had the raising of us. We were *his*, you see. Not boys so much as heirs. Proof of his virility. As I got older, I came to realise that he enjoyed the story of Thanos and my closeness in age. Far from finding it awkward, he relished the proof of his desirability. He boasted about it.'

Hannah ground her teeth together.

'You're not close to him?'

Leonidas took a sip of his wine; Hannah's gaze didn't falter. 'No.'

She had the feeling she was moving closer to ground he wished to remain private, topics he'd prefer not to discuss. Rather than approach it directly, she circled around it this time. 'Would you have preferred to stay with your mother?'

He frowned, thoughtfully. 'My mother was American. She moved to Las Vegas when they split. I didn't want to go.'

'It must have been hard for her. Leaving you, I mean.'

Leonidas's smile showed disagreement, but his response was a banal, 'Perhaps.'

'Do you see her much now?'

'Once a year, for an obligatory birthday visit.'

'Yours, or hers?'

'Hers.' He sipped his wine again, then turned to face Hannah. 'And you, Hannah?'

'What about me?'

His eyes swept over her face and then zeroed in on her lips, staying there for so long that they parted on a rushed breath and began to tingle; she was remembering his kiss and aching for it anew.

'What about your own parents?'

It was like being dragged into a well that was completely dark. She felt the blackness surround her and her expression closed off, her skin paling. She jerked her head, turning away from him and looking towards the horizon. The sun was gone but the sky remained tinged with colour.

Her breathing felt forced and unnatural and she struggled to find words.

'Hannah?'

She nodded. He had every right to ask—this street went both ways. She wanted to know about him, she had a strange, consuming curiosity to understand him. It made sense he would expect the same courtesy.

'My parents are dead.' How was it possible that those words still stung? It had been a long time; the reality of being orphaned was one she'd lived with for many years.

'I'm sorry.' She felt his proximity rather than saw him move closer. His body was behind hers, warm and strong, and instantly reassuring.

'It was years ago. I was only a child.'

He didn't say anything, but he was right there. If she spun around, they'd be touching.

'My mum used to love that movie—*The Secret Princess*. I watched it a little while after she'd died, and I wanted to go to Chrysá Vráchia ever since.'

He made a noise of comprehension and now she did turn, and, just as she'd expected, it brought their bodies together, his so strong and broad that she felt as if she could weather almost any storm if he was there.

'And then?' he prompted, shifting a little, so his legs were wider than her body, and he pressed his hands to the balcony balustrading behind her, so she was effectively trapped by him.

'Then?' Her voice was husky.

'You came to the island for New Year's Eve, to see the fireworks. What were you going to do then?'

'I hadn't really thought about it. But I guess in the back of my mind I always thought I'd end up in England. My mum was English so I have a passport and I've wanted to travel through Europe for ever.' Her expression was wistful. 'My honeymoon was going to be to Paris. I used to have a picture of the Eiffel Tower on my bedside table, and when you tapped a button on it the lights twinkled.' She shook her head wistfully. 'My parents gave it to me after a ballet recital and I've never been able to part with it.'

'You did ballet?'

'Only as a child,' she said, thinking of how her aunt had donated all Hannah's tutus and leotards to a community charity shop when Hannah had moved in. She pushed the memory aside, focussing on the present, on the circumstances that had brought her here. 'After I found Angus and Michelle in bed together, I just wanted to run away.'

'Naturally.'

'It seemed as good a time as any to pack up and see the world.' Her smile was wry. 'I left before I could change my mind.'

Leonidas nodded thoughtfully. 'Have you spoken to him since you left?'

'No. There's nothing more to say there.'

'You were friends before you became engaged?'

'Yes.'

'You don't miss his friendship?'

Hannah thought of Michelle and Angus and her life in Australia and dropped her gaze. 'I miss a lot of things. It's hard, having the rug pulled out from under you.' She lifted her eyes to his, sympathy softening her features as she remembered his own harrowing past. 'As you would know.'

A warning light glinted in his eyes. *Don't go there.*

'Who was the other woman?' His voice was gruff.

Hannah's heart constricted with now familiar pain. 'That was the really hard part.'

'Harder than your fiancé cheating on you?'

'Yeah.' She angled her face, so Leonidas had a perfect view of her profile, delicate and ethereal.

'Who was she?' he repeated, and Hannah sucked in a soft breath.

'My cousin, Michelle. More like a sister, really. After Mum and Dad died, I went to live with my aunt and uncle, and Michelle.'

He let out a soft whistle. *'Christós.'*

'Yeah.' Her laugh was a low rumble. 'You could say that, and I did—worse, in fact. I was devastated.'

Admitting that felt good. Saying the word aloud, Hannah recognised that she hadn't spoken to another soul about the affair.

'I lost everything that afternoon.'

'What did your aunt and uncle say?'

Hannah lifted her gaze to his, and a ridiculous sense of shame made it difficult to maintain eye contact. Hannah shook her head, that awful afternoon burned into her brain like a cattle brand. 'Do you mind if we don't go down this particular memory lane?'

She flicked her gaze back to his face, catching surprise crossing his features. But it was banked down within a moment, and he stepped back, almost as though he hadn't realised how close they were, how he was touching her.

'Of course.' His smile didn't reach his eyes. 'Have a seat.' He gestured towards the table. 'There is much we have to discuss.'

CHAPTER SEVEN

'WHAT WORK WERE you doing in London?'

Hannah sipped her fruit juice, a pang of guilt scrunching her chest when she thought of her boss, Fergus, and how she planned to leave him completely in the lurch.

'I'm a legal secretary.'

'Have you done this for long?'

She nodded thoughtfully. 'Since I left high school. My aunt and uncle lived in a small town. There weren't a lot of options for work. I would have loved to go away to university but it just wasn't practical.'

'For what reason?'

'Money, mainly.'

'I thought universities in Australia were subsidised?'

'They are,' she agreed, lifting a piece of fish from the platter. 'But I'd have had to move to the city, found a place to rent. Even with governmental assistance, I wouldn't have been able to afford to live out of home, to cover textbooks and rent.'

'Your parents left you nothing when they died?'

She felt censure in his voice and her back straightened, defensiveness stirring inside her. 'They left a little. My aunt and uncle took a stipend each year, and what's left I can't claim until I'm twenty-five.'

At this, Leonidas was completely still. 'Your aunt and uncle took money from you?'

'It wasn't like that,' she said quietly. 'They took money to cover the cost of raising me.'

His face showed pure contempt.

'You think that was wrong?'

A muscle jerked in his jaw and she felt he was weighing his words, choosing what to say with care. She didn't know him well and yet she felt for herself how uncharacteristic that care was.

'I do,' he said finally. 'Were they struggling financially?'

Hannah shifted her shoulders and repeated the line she'd frequently been given. 'An extra person is an extra expense.'

He studied her thoughtfully for several seconds, but he evidently decided not to pursue this line of questioning, and she was glad.

Glad because she didn't like to talk about it, much less think about it.

As a teenager, she'd been able to ignore her niggling doubts, but as she'd grown older, and met more people, she had come to see more and more at fault with the way her aunt and uncle had treated her. A desire to defend them didn't change reality, and the reality felt an awful lot as if they simply resented her presence in their lives.

She felt it in her heart, but to confess that to Leonidas was too difficult.

'What would you have studied?'

She relaxed visibly. 'That's easy.'

He waited, his eyes not shifting from her face, so that even when their conversation was smoother to navigate, her pulse was still racing.

He had beautiful eyes, but she doubted many women told him that. There were too many other things about him that required mention. His body, his lips, his clever, clever hands. But his eyes were breathtaking. Dark, rimmed with thick black lashes, and when the full force of their focus was given to one's face, concentration was almost impossible.

'Am I to guess?' he prompted, after several seconds.

Heat flooded her cheeks. 'I wanted to be a lawyer,' she said, curling her fingers around the stem of her orange juice–filled champagne flute, feeling its fine crystal. 'Law degrees take years and cost a bomb. The textbooks alone would have bankrupted my aunt and uncle.' She said it with a smile, as though it were a joke. 'Becoming a legal secretary was the next best thing. There was a conveyancing firm in another town, just a half-hour drive away. Angus worked there.' She cleared her throat, sipping her drink. 'That's how we met.'

'I see.' If it were possible, his expression darkened even further.

'I loved working at the firm, and I'm good at what I do.' Pride touched her voice. 'So maybe everything worked out for the best.'

'I can't say I agree with that,' he drawled, after several long moments. His eyes roamed her face. 'However, you no longer have any kind of financial impediment to you undertaking a law degree. You will obviously be based here, on the island, but there are many universities that offer degrees via distance. You could enrol in one to start next semester.'

Hannah's eyes were huge, and she was struck dumb, for many reasons.

'This island is beautiful,' she said thoughtfully, trying to imagine her future. 'But very remote.'

His expression glittered. 'Yes. By design.'

She nodded, the loss of his family naturally having made him security conscious. Nonetheless, the idea of being stuck here sat strangely in her chest. She liked a tropical paradise as much as the next person, but not without an easy escape route.

Not necessarily for ever. She shelved her thoughts,

though. They'd only just arrived. There was time to find her groove as they adjusted to this new life.

'I love the idea of studying law as much as ever,' she said sincerely. 'But I'm kind of going to have my hands full for the next little while...'

'A baby is not an excuse to turn your back on your dreams,' he said simply. 'You will want for nothing, and help will be available whenever you need it. I will be available,' he added. 'This is *our* daughter, not your burden alone.'

Her heart turned over in her chest and his completely unexpected show of support and confidence had her opening a little of herself up to him.

'I'm nervous, Leonidas.' She lifted the fish to her mouth, chewing on it while she pulled her thoughts into order. 'The idea of becoming a mum scares me half to death.'

'Why?'

'How can it not? I have no idea what to do, or if I'll be any good at it. I mean, it's a *baby*. I've never even had a pet.'

His laugh was just a dry, throaty husk of a sound. 'A baby is not really anything like a pet, so I wouldn't let that bother you too much.'

'You know what I mean. I've never had the responsibility of keeping something alive, something totally dependent on me.'

She heard the words a second too late, before she could catch them, but as soon as they landed in the atmosphere she wished she could gobble them right back up. 'I'm sorry.' She leaned across the table and put a hand on his, sympathy softening her expression while his own features tightened to the point of breaking.

'Don't be. I know what you meant.'

She nodded, but the easy air of conversation had dissipated.

'Being nervous is normal. You just have to trust that you will know what to do when our baby is born.'

'And you have experience,' she said, watching him carefully.

'Yes.' He nodded, curtly, placing his napkin on his side plate and sipping his wine. Then, he stood, fixing her with a level stare. 'Marina will show you to your room when you are finished. In the morning, a stylist will arrive to take your clothes order, and then a jeweller will come to offer you some rings to choose from.'

She blinked up at him, his abrupt change of temperament giving her whiplash. He was obviously hesitant to discuss his first wife and son, but jeez!

'Leonidas...' Hannah frowned, not sure what she wanted to say, knowing only that she didn't want him to walk away from her like this. 'I can't ignore the fact you had a family before this. I get that you don't like talking about it, but I can't tiptoe around it for ever. You had a son, and I'm pregnant with your daughter. Don't you think it's natural that we'll talk about him, from time to time?'

'No.' He thrust his hands into his pockets and looked out to sea, the expression on his face so completely heartbroken that something inside Hannah iced over, because it was clear to her, in that moment, how hung up he still was on the family he'd lost.

And why wouldn't he be? They'd been wrenched from him by a cruel twist of fate, by the acts of a madman. Nothing about this—his situation—was by his choice.

Nor was it Hannah's, she reminded herself. She knew more than her fair share about cruel twists of fate.

The sky was darkening with every second, but pinpricks of light danced obstinately through, sparkling like diamonds against black sand. She followed his gaze, her own appetite disappearing.

'I don't want to force you,' she said gently, standing to move right in front of him. 'It's your grief, and your life. But I will say, as someone who's spent a very long time bottling things up, that it's not healthy.' She lifted a hand, touching the side of his cheek. He flinched, his eyes jerking to hers, showing animosity and frustration.

Showing the depths of his brokenness.

It called to Hannah; she understood it.

'You are an expert in grief, then?' he pushed, anger in the words.

'Sadly, yes,' she agreed quietly.

'Do not compare what we have experienced,' he said. 'To lose your parents is unbearable, I understand that, and I am sorry for you, what you went through. You were a child, robbed of the ability to be a child. But I caused my wife and son's death. As sure as if I had murdered them myself, I am the reason they died. Do not presume to have any idea what that knowledge feels like.'

That Hannah slept fitfully was hardly surprising. Leonidas's parting shot ran around and around her mind, the torment of his admission ripping her heart into pieces. To live with that guilt would have driven a lesser man crazy.

But it wasn't only sadness for the man she'd hastily agreed to marry.

It was worry.

Fear.

Panic.

Stress.

And something far, far more perplexing, something that made her nipples pucker against the shirt he'd given her to sleep in, that made her arch her back in her dreams, and meant she felt warm and wet between her legs when she finally gave up on trying to sleep, before dawn, and stood, pacing to the window that overlooked the ocean.

Memories.

Memories of their one night together and fantasies of future nights were all weaving through Hannah's being, bursting upon her soul and demanding attention.

The sun had just started to spread warmth over the beach. Darkness was reluctantly giving way to light, and the morning was fresh.

It was Hannah's favourite time of day, when the air itself seemed to be full of magic and promise.

She had only the clothes she'd worn the day before, and the shirt she'd slept in, which was ridiculously big even when accommodating her pregnant belly. Still, it was comfortable and covered her body. Besides, it was a private island. Who was going to see her?

Pausing only to take a quick drink of water in the kitchen, Hannah unlocked the front door of the mansion and stepped out, breathing in the tangy salt air.

Excitement and a sense of anticipation rushed her out of nowhere, like when she was a small girl, around six or seven, and her parents had taken her away on their first family vacation. They'd gone to the glitzy beachside resort of Noosa, in tropical Queensland, and Hannah had woken early and looked out on the rolling waves crashing onto the beach, the moon still shimmering in the sky, and her stomach had rolled, just like this.

There's something elemental and enlivening about the sea, and this island was surrounded by a particularly pristine shoreline and ocean.

Without having any real intention of going to the beach, she found herself moving that way quickly, her bare feet grateful when they connected with cool, fine sand, clumps of long grass spiking up between it every now and again.

Dunes gave way to the flatness of the shore. She walked all the way to the water's edge, standing flat-footed and staring out to the sea, her back to Leonidas's mansion, her eyes on the horizon.

This was not the tropical water off the coast of Queensland. Here, there were no waves, only the gentle sighing of the sea as the tide receded. With each little pause, each undulation back towards the shore, the water danced over Hannah's toes; the cool was delicious given the promise of the day's heat.

She could have stood there, staring out at the mesmerising water, all day, were it not for the sudden and loud thumping from directly to her left. She turned just in time to see Leonidas, earphones in and head down, eyes trained on the shore, galumphing towards her. There was barely enough time to sidestep out of his way.

He startled as he ran past, jerking his head up at the intrusion he'd sensed, then swore, pulling his earphones out and letting them dangle loose around his neck.

She wished he hadn't.

The simple act drew her eyes from his face to his body. There was nothing scandalous about what he was wearing. Shorts and a T-shirt—only the T-shirt was wet with perspiration and the firmness of his pecs was clearly visible.

She took a step backwards without realising it, not to put physical space between them but because she wanted to see him better. Her aunt would have told her to stop staring, but Hannah couldn't. As much as the tide couldn't cease its rhythmic motion, Hannah found it impossible to tear her eyes away.

She remembered everything about him and yet...seeing him again sparked a whole new range of wants and needs.

Thick, strong legs covered in dark, wiry hair looked capable of running marathons but she couldn't look at him without imagining him straddling her, pushing her to the sand and bringing his body over hers, his hard arousal insistent between her legs. Without remembering the feeling of his weight on her body, his strength, power and skill in driving her to orgasm again and again.

Her throat was dry and the humming of the ocean was nothing to the furious pounding of her own blood in her ears.

She dragged her eyes up his body, over dark shorts that showed nothing of his manhood, even when she was suddenly desperate to see it—to see all of him again, in real life, not her very vivid dreams.

She prepared to meet his gaze, knowing he must surely be regarding her with mocking cynicism, only he wasn't.

He wasn't looking at her face, wasn't looking at her eyes to see the way she'd been eating him alive. No, he was performing his own slow, sensual inspection and it was enough to make her blood burn.

His eyes were on her legs, desire burning in the depths of his gaze as he lifted his attention to the curve of her breasts and, finally, to her lips. They parted under his inspection as she silently willed him to kiss them. To pull her into his arms and remember how well that worked between them.

And when he didn't, she took a step forward herself, knowing it didn't matter who moved first, knowing it was imperative only that they touch once more.

It broke the spell. His gaze slammed into hers, surprise there, confusion and, yes, desire. So much desire that it almost drowned her. He made a deep, husky sound and stood completely still, his body hard like steel.

Hannah moved closer, her eyes holding a silent challenge. *Stop me if you dare.*

He didn't.

One more step and their bodies connected, just like that first night in the bar, when fate had thrown them together and passion had held them there.

The air around them cracked and sizzled as though a localised electrical storm had touched down. He was so much bigger than she was. Hannah stood on the tips of her toes, which brought her body flush to his, her womanhood so close to the strength of his arousal that she echoed his own guttural moan with a soft whimper.

'Hannah.' Her name on his lips wasn't a request, nor was it a surrender. He spoke her name as though he simply couldn't resist and she lifted higher onto her toes and kissed him, hungrily.

He was still. Completely still, so her mouth moved over his, her tongue tracing the outline of his lower lip, her breath warm against him, and then, after the briefest moment, he lifted his hands to the back of her head, holding her where she was, keeping her so close to him, and he opened his mouth, kissing her back. But not in the way she had kissed him.

This was a kiss driven as much by a need to possess as his kiss had been the first night they'd met. There was madness in his kiss, his desperation for her completely overwhelming.

The water rushed around them, chasing their ankles, its fervent pursuit matched by the coursing of blood in their veins.

Hannah couldn't have said if he pulled her to the sand or if she pulled him, but she was lying down then, her back against the cold ground, her legs bent, Leonidas's body on hers, just as she'd fantasised about, his weight sheer bliss.

His kiss didn't relent, even as his hands pushed her shirt up, revealing the scrap of her underwear.

He disposed of them and then his own shorts, lifting

himself up to look at her, his eyes piercing her, confusion and something else moving through him.

'I told myself we wouldn't do this,' he groaned, his voice tormented.

She bit down on her lower lip, her own heart tripping in her chest as his arousal nudged at her sex.

'Why not?'

His answer was to nudge his arousal inside her, and she moaned low in her throat as she felt the power of his possession. It had been five months but her body welcomed him back as though he were her saviour. She arched her back instinctively, needing more, and he drove himself deeper, pushed up on his elbows so he could see her, watch her, as well as feel her reactions.

Her insides squeezed him tight, muscles convulsing around him as he stretched her body to accommodate his length.

'What are you doing to me?' he groaned, and then said something in his native tongue, the words, spiced and warm, flickering inside her blood.

'I don't know but you're doing it right back,' she whispered, digging her nails into his shoulders before running them lower, finding the edge of his shirt and lifting it, trailing her fingertips over his back, feeling his smooth, warm skin beneath her and revelling in the contact.

Higher the shirt went, until he pushed up off one arm, ripping it from his body and casting it aside, so that he was naked on top of her. She wanted to stare at him, but she was incapable of forming the words to demand that when he was moving inside her, his body calling to hers, demanding her response, invoking ancient, soul-deep rhythms and needs.

'Christós...' The word was dark, a curse and a plea. His expression was taut as he looked down at her, unable to fathom her, this, them. 'Who are you?'

There was no answer she could give; the question made little sense.

He didn't require an answer, in any event. He moved faster then, his hands cupping her breasts, his mouth possessing hers as he kissed her until she saw stars and his hard arousal thrust deep inside her and everything she was in the past and would be in the future seemed to be coalescing in that one single, fragile moment.

She dug her nails into the curve of his buttock as pleasure pounded against her, like one of those waves from her faraway childhood, incessant, demanding, ancient. She cried his name and he stilled, his body heavy on hers, but as she exploded with pleasure her muscles squeezed him tight and Leonidas dropped his arms to his side, holding himself steady above her, staring down at her, watching every last second of delirium take over her body.

He stared at her so that when she blinked her eyes open, her own disorientation at what had just happened filling her with uncertainty, he saw it and he dropped his head, kissing her again, as though he knew how much she needed it.

It was a brief reprieve, nothing more. She'd been drowned by their passion and then emerged for air, and now Leonidas was taking her back under with him, tangling her in his limbs, his hands roaming all of her body now, until he curved them behind her bottom and lifted her a little off the sand, so his arousal reached even deeper and she found insanity was once more in pursuit.

His name tripped off her tongue, pushing into his mouth. With every thrust of his arousal, his body tightened, his buttocks squeezing, his muscles firm. She felt him beneath her palms, all of him, and then he moved faster, deeper and she was lifting into the heavens again, her body weightless and powerless to resist.

He moved inside her and she called his name as she burst apart at the seams, *Leonidas*, over and over. She called to him—willing him to answer—and he did. He tangled his fingers through hers, lifting Hannah's arms up above her head, his eyes on hers intense as his own explosion wracked his body, his release simultaneous with hers.

Their breath was frantic, louder than the ocean and the flapping of birds overhead, their exhalations thick and raspy, drenched in urgency. Pleasure had made her lungs expire. He lay on top of her and she ran her fingers down his back, still mesmerised by the feeling of his skin, and this: the closeness, the weight, the intimacy.

It lasted only seconds, and then Leonidas was rolling off, beside Hannah, onto his back on the sand beside her, staring at the dawn sky.

'*Christós...*' He said the word low and thick. 'What are you?'

Again, a question that was almost impossible to answer. He turned his head to stare at her and there was confusion in his eyes, and a look of resignation.

'What do you mean?'

He reached out as though he couldn't help himself, his fingers catching a thick section of her hair and running through it, his eyes on the brassy tones.

'Are you real?'

The question made no sense.

She raised an eyebrow, propping up on one elbow, a smile tugging at her lips. 'I'm pretty sure I am.'

He didn't smile. 'I swore we wouldn't do this.'

Hannah expelled a sigh. 'You said that. I heard you. It doesn't make sense, though.'

His frown deepened. 'For four years I have been able to resist any woman in the world. For four years I have been single, and then you...'

Hannah was quiet as his words ran through her mind and their meaning became clear. 'You mean you hadn't been with anyone since Amy died?'

His expression was shuttered. He shook his head, his lips a grim line in his face. 'No.'

Hannah's chest hurt, as if it had been sliced in half and cut wide open. 'Why not?'

His nostrils flared. 'Many reasons.' His hand lifted to her hair again, toying with the ends. 'I enjoyed resisting temptation, choosing to be celibate, to be alone. And then I saw you and it was just like this. As though you are some kind of angel—or devil—sent to tempt me even when I know how wrong this is. I spent four years flexing my power here and you take it away from me completely.'

Hannah's voice was thick; she didn't know if she was flattered or insulted. She suspected a bit of both. 'Why is it wrong?'

He pushed up to standing then, just as he had the night before when she'd touched on areas he preferred not to discuss.

But she wasn't going to let him get away with it twice. 'I'm serious, Leonidas. *Why* is this wrong?'

CHAPTER EIGHT

SHE WAITED AND WAITED and after a moment, she wondered if he wasn't going to answer her. He simply stood there, naked as the day he was born, staring out to sea, and she moved towards him, coming around in front of him so she could look up into his stubborn face.

'I don't know much about sex,' she said slowly, when he remained silent. 'But I do know that I want to feel more of this.' She gestured from him to her. 'I do know this is amazing and hot and incredibly addictive.'

He ground his teeth together, the action making his jaw tight, his expression grim. 'That night shouldn't have happened.'

Hannah shook her head, rejecting both the words and the sentiment. 'Neither of us planned that it would, just like we didn't plan for this to happen, but that doesn't mean it was wrong.'

He looked at her then, his expression impossible to interpret. 'You are so young.'

He said it as though it were a criticism.

'I'm twenty-three.'

'Yes, but you've been very sheltered.' He cupped her face then. 'You deserve better than this.'

'Than marriage to you?'

'Better than a lifetime with me.' His lips were grim. 'I'm not the man you want me to be.'

'And what do I want you to be?'

He expelled a soft breath then stepped back a little, just enough to put some distance between them. 'A clean slate.'

The words were strange. Discordant. At first, she couldn't make sense of them. But as he turned and pulled his shorts on, she saw the weight on his shoulders, the ghosts that chased him, and comprehension shifted through her.

'You're wrong.' She dropped the words like little, tiny bombs. He didn't turn around, but he froze completely still, so she knew he was listening. 'I know you have a past, just like I do. But I'm not going to marry you if you're telling me I'm going to be living with a brick wall. I'm not getting married if I think there's no hope of having a living, breathing, red-blooded man as my husband.'

He turned around then, his expression bleak at first, and then filling with frustration. 'And sex ticks that box for you?'

Hannah frowned. That hadn't been what she'd meant, but at the same time she knew it was a start. What they shared, physically, was a true form of intimacy. She didn't need to have loads of experience to recognise that. She could see it in his eyes when he held her. She could feel the uniqueness of what they shared. He was trying to fight it, and she knew why.

Intimacy like this must surely lead to more.

With Angus, she'd operated on the reverse assumption. She'd hoped their friendship would bridge the way to a satisfying physical relationship. And it might have, but it would never have been like this.

Nothing like it.

This kind of connection couldn't be learned.

It was raw and organic, primal, between two people.

She glared at him, challenging him from the depths of her soul. 'Yes,' she agreed. 'I'm not going to live here like a prisoner in a gilded cage, Leonidas.' Her voice cracked as she firmed up on that resolution. 'This island is stunning but it's no place to live if you're going to freeze me out.'

'Does it look like I am freezing you out?'

'But you want to,' she insisted. 'You want to fight this, not build on it.'

His features tensed, his lips just a gash in his face, and she knew she was right.

'And I won't stay here if that's the case.' She tilted her chin bravely, when outside this island was a world she wasn't sure she trusted any more. The reality of his wife and son's murder was still exploding inside her, and she didn't doubt there could be a risk to her.

But there was risk here, too. Risk in living with a man who was determined to ice her out. What if he acted the same with their daughter? What if she were born and Leonidas made no effort to get to know her?

His eyes narrowed. 'How? You forget my island is practically inaccessible to anyone but me...'

Hannah was breathless again, her pulse racing but for a wholly different reason. 'Are you seriously threatening to kidnap me?'

Frustration zipped through his body. 'No.' He raked a hand through his hair. '*Christós*, Hannah. You can't leave the island.'

'Ever?' she demanded, crossing her arms over her chest to still the frantic hammering of her heart.

'Not on your own,' he amended. 'I was careless once before, I cannot risk it again. I won't have more on my conscience.'

And her rapidly thumping heart softened, aching, breaking for Leonidas.

'I'm so sorry you lost them,' she said quietly. 'But I'm not going to be a prisoner to your fears.'

'They should be your fears, too.'

'I want to keep our daughter safe.' Her voice was level, careful. 'Somewhere between me living out there on my own and the luxurious prison you're proposing is a middle ground we need to find.'

His eyes held hers for several beats. 'I cannot agree to that.' The words were wrenched from him, gravelled and thick with emotion.

'Why not?' she demanded, her hands shifting to her hips.

'You cannot imagine what it was like,' he said, grimly. 'To get that call, to see their bodies.' He shook his head from side to side and stopped speaking, but his face was lined with grief.

Tears bit at the back of Hannah's throat; sympathy rushed through her. 'I can't even imagine that, you're right.' She lifted a hand to his chest, running it over his muscled flesh.

'I made a choice after they died. I planned to stay single for the rest of my life.'

Hannah's stomach clenched.

'I didn't want this. I have done everything I could to avoid it.' His words were heavy with despair. She felt it and wished she could take it away, but how? 'I knew we shouldn't have slept together. It was so selfish of me but I was careful, Hannah. I did everything I could to make sure this wouldn't happen. I didn't want this.'

She wasn't sure when she'd let herself care enough about him that his words would hold such a latent power to wound, but they cut her deep.

'You shouldn't have to live in this—what did you call it? Gilded prison? Because of me.'

She couldn't speak.

'But you do.' The words were grim. 'Surely you can see that? I can't risk anything happening to you, to her.' He lifted a hand to Hannah's stomach, curving it over the bump there. His eyes met Hannah's with a burning intensity.

'Let me protect you both. Please.'

'I am,' she said, quietly, stroking his chest, her eyes determined. 'But this is my life we're talking about.'

He gazed at her, his expression strangely uncertain. 'I know that.'

'I want to marry you.' The words felt right, completely perfect. 'I know it's the sensible decision.' And strength surged inside her. 'When my mum and dad died, I lost everything. Our home, my community, my school, my friends. I went to live somewhere new and different and I was miserable,' she said, frankly, so captivated by her past that she didn't see the way his expression changed with the force of his concentration.

'I don't want our daughter to ever know that kind of uncertainty. You're her dad, and by doing this together, she'll have two people who can love her and look after her. And as she grows older, we'll surround her with other people who'll love her and know her, so that if anything *ever* happened to us and she were left alone, she would eventually be okay. Don't you see that, Leonidas? I need her to be okay, just like you do, but, for me, one of the worst things we can do is isolate her. Keep her locked up from this world, so we're the only people she ever really knows. She deserves to live a full and normal life.'

'How come you were sent to live with your aunt and uncle?'

Hannah frowned. 'There wasn't anyone else.'

'And you didn't know them well?'

'No.' She shook her head. 'I'd only met them a few times. They weren't close to my parents.'

He frowned, lifting his hands to her face and cupping her cheeks. He stared down at her, his eyes ravaging her face. 'You were deeply unhappy there?'

Hannah didn't want to think of her life in those terms;

she hated feeling like a victim. And yet, what could she say? She'd been miserable. Only now that she was on the other side of the world and free from her aunt's catty remarks did she realise what an oppressive weight they'd been on her shoulders.

'I wasn't happy.' She softened the sentiment a little. 'I'm not sure my aunt ever really liked me, let alone loved me.'

He scanned her face but said nothing.

'I spent more than a decade living with people who cared for me out of a sense of obligation. People who resented my presence, who undoubtedly wished I wasn't in their life. I won't do it again.' Her eyes showed determination. 'We didn't plan this, we didn't intend for it to happen, but that doesn't mean we can't make this marriage work.'

Still, he was silent.

'Less than six months ago, I was engaged to another man. I had my whole life planned out, and it looked nothing like this. I'm not an idiot, Leonidas. If I ever believed in fairy tales, I've learned my lesson many times over. This isn't a perfect situation, but there's enough here to work with. Our marriage can be more than a business arrangement, a deal for shared custody. We can make something of this—we just have to be brave enough to try.'

His jaw was square as he turned to the water, looking at it, his face giving little away. 'I want you to be safe and, yes, I want you to be happy, Hannah. I want our daughter to have the best life she can. But beyond that, stop expecting things of me. You say you no longer believe in fairy tales? Then do not turn me into any kind of Prince Charming in your mind. We are a one-night stand we can't escape, that's all.'

CHAPTER NINE

HANNAH STARED AT the black velvet box with a sense of disbelief. The jeweller was watching her, a smile on his face, and Hannah imagined how this must look from the outside. A tailor had arrived on the island earlier that day, armed with suitcases of couture, beautiful dresses, jeans, shirts, bathers, lingerie—everything the wife of Leonidas Stathakis might be expected to wear.

The dressmaker had stayed for hours, taking Hannah's measurements, and photographs of her for 'colour matching'—whatever that was—and to discuss wedding dress options, before disappearing again. All the while some servant or other had taken the suitcases and carefully unpacked them into the room Hannah was using.

'Her room,' though she had no idea when she'd ever think of it like that.

There had also been a doctor, who'd come to check her over and implement a new vitamin regimen, and promised fortnightly check-ups. Then there'd been a more detailed conference with Mrs Chrisohoidis regarding Hannah's favourite foods, flowers and any other thoughts she might have as regards the running of the house.

Hannah had changed into one of the simple white shift dresses—for comfort on a hot day—and pulled her red hair into a bun on top of her head. As she looked at the dozen engagement rings the jeweller presented, all set against signature turquoise velvet, she knew it must appear to be some kind of Cinderella fairy tale. Leonidas looked on, not exactly playing the part of Prince Charming, though what he lacked in warmth he more than made up for in physical appeal.

He was casually dressed, in shorts and a white shirt, but that did nothing to diminish his charisma and the sense of raw power that emanated from his pores. It burst into the room, making it almost impossible for Hannah to keep her mind focussed on this task.

'Just something simple,' she said with a shake of her head, thinking that each and every ring was way too sparkly and way, way too big. 'Maybe this one?' She chose the smallest in the box.

'Ah!' The jeweller nodded. 'It is very beautiful.' He lifted it out, holding it towards Hannah. 'Try it on.'

This was all wrong! She didn't want to choose her own engagement ring, and no matter how many pretty, sparkly, *enormous* diamonds twinkled at her, it didn't feel right. She closed her eyes for a moment and imagined Leonidas going down on one knee, proposing as though this were a real wedding, and a bolt of panic surged inside her. But this wasn't a fairy tale and he wasn't Prince Charming, just as he'd said.

We are a one-night stand we can't escape.

Her heart began to churn. With a sense of unease, as though she were about to commit massive tax fraud, she slid the ring onto her finger. It was a perfect fit. She stared down at it and, ridiculously, tears filled her eyes. Now! Here! After becoming so adept at blocking them, she felt their salty promise and quickly sought to disguise them in what should have been a happy moment.

'It's beautiful.'

Leonidas came to stand beside her, his presence a force, a magnetic energy, pulling her eyes upwards.

'Don't you think?' she asked him.

His eyes met hers and they were back on the beach, just the two of them, his body inside hers, his strength on top of her.

'It is.' He nodded, hesitation in his tone. 'But you do not have to decide now.'

'Of course not,' the jeweller agreed. 'I can leave the tray, if you would like to try each for a time?'

Hannah's head spun. Each ring had to feature a diamond of at least ten carats. What must the whole tray be worth?

She didn't want to spend a week prevaricating over which enormous diamond she'd drag around. She just wanted the jeweller to go. She wanted Leonidas to go. Her head was spinning; it was all too much.

We are a one-night stand we can't escape.

He was right, and yet she rejected that description, she recoiled from it with everything she was.

'That's fine.' She shook her head, the beginnings of a throb in her temples. 'This one will be fine.'

She wanted to be alone and perhaps it showed in her voice, because Leonidas was nodding his slow agreement. 'Very well. Thank you for coming, Mr Carter.'

The jeweller left and Hannah watched the helicopter lift off from the cool of the sitting room, taking him from the island and to the mainland of Greece, the sun setting in the background, casting the beautiful machinery in a golden glow.

The day had lived up to the morning's promise. Heat had sizzled and Hannah, having spent so much time preparing for what lay ahead, wanted to simply relax. She'd spied a pool in her explorations the day before and she thought of it longingly now.

'Greg Hassan is scheduled to sit with you today,' Leonidas said as he entered the room.

Hannah's temples throbbed harder. 'Who?' She failed to conceal her weariness.

'Head of security at Stathakis.'

Hannah's throat shifted as she swallowed. 'What do I need to see him for?'

'There are protocols you will need to learn.' He was tense, as if braced for an argument.

'I thought you said this island is far from the mainland, inaccessible to just about anyone...'

He tilted his head in agreement. 'This island is secure, *sigoura*. But there are still protocols to follow and there are always risks.'

His fear was chilling. But it was also very, very sad. She saw the tension in his body, and she wished there were some way she could take it away for him, that she could tell him everything was going to be okay.

She didn't know that it was, but she knew you couldn't live looking over your shoulder.

'Can't you just go through the security stuff with me?'

'You will need to have a relationship with Greg,' he said firmly, his eyes roaming Hannah's face. 'He'll coordinate your movements, and our daughter's, arrange her security detail as she gets older.'

Panic flared inside Hannah. It was all too real and too much. To say she was overwhelmed was an understatement. 'Do you mind if we don't talk about that right now?'

His expression shifted. 'Your safety is important.'

She nodded. 'I know. I'm just—well, I'm worn out, to be honest.'

Concern flashed in his expression. 'Of course. You must be, the day was full and in your condition...'

'It's just a lot to take in.' Her smile was more of a grimace. 'I thought I'd go for a swim and just let it all percolate in my mind.'

'Fine.' He nodded. 'I'll ask Marina to prepare a simple dinner for you, for afterwards.'

Hannah nodded, unable to express why her stomach was swooping. 'Thank you.'

She didn't see Leonidas again that evening. She swam, gently pulling herself through the water, enjoying the lapping of cool against her sun-warmed skin, and then she ate the dinner Mrs Chrisohoidis had prepared—a small pasta dish with some fruit and ice water.

She contemplated going in search of Leonidas afterwards, but the revelations of their conversation from that morning were still sharp inside her.

She slept heavily, which surprised her. When Hannah woke, the sun was up, the sky was bright, and everything felt calmer. Better. Just as her mother had always said it would.

She had a feeling she could handle anything.

She showered, luxuriating in the sensation of the water on her body, lathering herself in the luxury coconut-fragranced products before towelling dry and slipping on a pair of shorts and a loose shirt.

Her stomach rumbled and she put a hand on it unconsciously, smiling as she felt their baby inside her. She looked down, her eyes catching the glinting of her engagement ring and her heart twisted, because she'd worn another man's ring, once upon a time, and she'd become used to seeing that on her finger. Then she'd become used to her hand being empty and bare—she'd been grateful. Grateful she'd found out what Angus was really like before she'd married him.

And now, she was to marry Leonidas. It was a gamble, and she wasn't sure she had the nerves to gamble any more, but here she was, closing her eyes and hoping for the best— all for their daughter's sake. This was all for her.

She had a coffee and some pastries for breakfast and was contemplating a walk on the beach when Leonidas appeared, wearing a similar outfit to the day before.

He wasn't alone.

'Hannah.' He nodded and she wondered if the man behind Leonidas thought the stiff formality of Leonidas's greeting unusual.

'This is Greg Hassan.'

The man in question didn't look anything like what Hannah had imagined. For some reason, 'head of security' conjured images of some kind of black belt muscleman in her mind, someone more like Leonidas, who looked as if they could snap someone with their little finger.

Greg Hassan was on the short side, and slim, with fair skin and bright blue eyes. Hair that had at one time been blond was now balding on top. Hannah was lost in her own thoughts so didn't notice the way he startled a little at the sight of Hannah. But then, he smiled, moving towards her with one hand extended. She met it, belatedly forcing a smile to her own face.

'Miss May, this won't take long.'

In fact, it took hours.

Greg Hassan left some time after noon, and Hannah's head was back to feeling as if it had been through a washing machine.

The island itself had state-of-the-art monitoring, there were panic buttons in each room, and alarms that were activated by unexpected air activity, including drones—the paparazzi had occasionally tried to send drones into the airspace to capture images but the new detection methods effectively made that impossible.

'As for when you travel,' Greg had continued, 'you'll have a team of four bodyguards. One of them will be with you at all times, and another with your child.' He'd smiled reassuringly, as if this were *good* news, but Hannah had felt as if she were having her head held under water.

She was drowning and it hurt.

'As much as possible, we'll coordinate your movements in advance. If you wish to travel to Australia, for example, to see family, we'll send a team out ahead to set up and prepare for your arrival. When your daughter starts school, I presume you'll move to the mainland—' At which point Leonidas had interrupted and said that had not yet been decided. Greg had continued that in the event of their daughter attending a school in Athens, or a major city, the campus would be vetted, and their daughter would wear a watch with an inbuilt panic alarm.

Questions mushroomed inside Hannah's brain, but she hadn't wanted to ask them in front of the security chief.

Leonidas had escorted Greg Hassan from the building and then disappeared to work, leaving Hannah with a million uncertainties scrambling around her brain.

She kept busy, calling her boss, Fergus, and informing him of her decision, and sending a polite, carefully worded email to her aunt, advising her, as a courtesy, that she was pregnant and getting married. She didn't even want to think what the reaction would be. Hannah was careful to leave out any other details—particularly who the groom was.

She texted her flatmates and let them know she wouldn't be coming back, but saying she'd pay rent until they found someone else and she could get back to pack up her room.

It all felt so official, and officially terrifying, but also bizarrely right.

She didn't see Leonidas again until that evening. Hannah stood on the terrace, watching the sun set, her heart lifting as the golden orb dropped, already feeling some kind of soul-deep connection to this land.

She heard his approach, and then she felt his proximity, even though he didn't touch her. It was as simple as the air around her growing thick, sparking with an electrical charge that fired her blood.

She turned slowly to find him there, his eyes locked to her as though he couldn't help himself. But the minute Hannah looked at him, he blinked and looked away, turning his attention to the ocean.

They stood there in silence for a moment, Hannah trying not to react to the throb of awareness low in her abdomen, trying not to act on an impulse to throw herself at him.

As the stars began to shimmer, she found herself remembering the meeting of earlier that day, recalling all the questions that had flooded her. 'You don't travel with a bodyguard.'

'I always have security,' he contradicted.

'Not on New Year's Eve. I didn't see anyone else...'

'My hotel is a fortress when I am there.' He tilted his head towards her, his eyes scanning her face. In the evening light, his sharp features were all harsh angles and planes. 'Additional guards would have been superfluous.'

'Was it like this before the accident?'

'It was no accident,' he responded, whip-sharp.

'Before you lost them,' Hannah corrected.

'Euphemisms? Perhaps if we call it what it is—murder—you will accept the security measures more readily.'

Hannah wasn't sure she agreed.

'And no. Before they were killed, I was stupid and lax with their safety. I was arrogant and thought myself, and everyone around me, invincible, despite my father's connections.'

Hannah moved towards Leonidas, her heart sore for him.

'Isn't that better than living with fear?'

'Living with fear might have kept them alive,' he said, darkly.

'You don't know that.'

'I know they should never have been out wandering the streets.' He ground his teeth. 'And that you and our daughter will never be exposed to that kind of risk…'

Hannah tried not to feel as if she were drowning again. She tried to breathe slowly, to feel the freedom of this island, to understand why he felt as he did.

And she did. She could imagine what pain he must be suffering, and the added layer of guilt. But the picture he was painting was grim. Hannah couldn't imagine not being free to simply wake up and decide to go to the shops, or to visit a friend without having bodyguards do a preparatory security sweep.

'So she'll wear a panic button?' The idea turned Hannah's blood to ice, but then, so did the idea of anything happening to her.

His voice held a warning note. 'At least you'll both be safe.'

His feelings were completely understandable, but Hannah railed against them instinctively. She'd felt loss, she knew its pain well. Losing her parents, then losing her engagement to Angus, she understood what it was like to have everything shift on you.

And yet, being fearless in the face of that was a choice.

'How come there are no pictures of them?'

Leonidas shifted to face Hannah, complex emotions marring his handsome face. 'What?' The word was sucked from him.

'You were married, what, three years? How come there are no wedding photos? No baby pictures of Brax? If I didn't know about them, I would never have guessed they even existed.'

Leonidas shut his eyes, but not before she saw his grief, his heartache.

'It is not your concern.'

Hannah's insides flexed with acid. Another reminder. His wife and child were off limits. They weren't her concern. His life before her was not up for discussion.

More boundaries. Rules. Distance. It slammed against her and she ground her teeth, the limitations of this like nails under her feet.

'I understand it hurts.' She spoke quietly, lifting a hand to his chest. His heart was pounding. 'But not talking about it doesn't make sense.'

'Please, stop.' She felt his frustration like a whip at the base of her spine.

'Why?'

'Because it is my choice. Because she was my wife and he was my son.' His voice cracked with awful emotion and she swept her eyes shut for a moment, sucking in a breath.

'I know that. And they're a huge part of you, just like our daughter will be.' She carefully kept herself out of that summation.

'But I do not want to discuss them.'

'Why not? Don't you want to remember your son? Don't you want to talk to me—to someone—about his laugh, his smile, his first steps, his night terrors—all the things that made him the little boy he was?'

Leonidas's skin was paler than paper. 'I will never forget my son.'

'I know that,' she said quietly. 'But you can't honour someone by burying their memories.'

Her words hung between them, sharp like an insult, bony and knotty and troublesome and almost too much. She partially rejected the truths of that observation, but she knew from experience what this felt like—she'd been made to stay silent for years, to hold her grief inside, and she'd lost so much of her parents as a result. So many memories she should have been free to relish, to smile about, were gone for ever because of forced disuse.

'He was the light of my life!' he said suddenly. The words were torn from him, animalistic for their pain. He held his ground, staring at her as though she were covering him in acid. 'He was the light of my damned life! Amy and I... I loved her but, God, she drove me crazy and we weren't...in many ways, we weren't well-suited.' He dragged a hand through his hair, his eyes pinpointing Hannah with his grief. 'We'd argued the week before they died. She'd gone to Athens and I was glad.' He groaned, his displeasure at reliving that time in his life evident in every line of his body. 'I was glad because I was sick of fighting with her, sick of disagreeing over unimportant matters. But Brax was my reason for living, my reason for breathing, the reason I would *never* have left Amy.'

Hannah's grief was like dynamite in her chest.

She waited, letting him speak, letting him finish. 'I loved her but Brax was my everything and then he was dead. Because of me.' He dug his fingers into his chest and her eyes dropped to the gesture, to the solid wall of tanned flesh that hid a thundering heart.

'You think I am at risk of forgetting a single thing about him? You think I need to speak to you about my son to remember the way balloons made him laugh riotously, or the way clowns terrified him, or the way he loved to swim and chase butterflies?' His expression softened with grief and love and Hannah held her breath, all of her catching fire with the beauty of that look—of the expression on Leonidas's face.

'Do you think I will ever forget how much he loved strawberries? Cheese? The way he called me Bampás, except he couldn't say it properly so he said Bappmas instead?

These things are burned inside my brain, Hannah, whether I speak of them or not.'

It was too real, too raw. She needed to say something, but words failed her. She opened her mouth, searching, seeking, but Leonidas shook his head and then kissed her.

It was a kiss to silence Hannah, a kiss to suck away whatever she'd been going to say and swallow it up, because he'd made it obvious he didn't want her grief, her sympathy, her conversation.

He kissed her, and she resisted for a moment because he was finally opening up to her and she wanted to talk to him, to help him, to hear him. She stiffened in his arms, wanting to push at his chest, to tell him not to run away from this conversation but then he groaned, a guttural sound of such utter, devastating need, and any fight wavered, leaving only surrender.

Surrender and such deep, deep sympathy.

She *understood* the complexity of his emotions.

And the way he kissed her now, she understood what he needed. He wished he didn't want her like this; he'd said as much on the beach, but this flame was burning out of control no matter how they tried to manage it.

'Damn it,' he groaned, swooping down and lifting her up. Regardless of the fact she was five months pregnant, he carried her effortlessly, moving through the mansion with a determined gait.

He shouldered the door to his room open—Hannah hadn't been in here. She looked around, seeing the dark wood, the masculine touches, gathering a brief impression of a space that was huge and elegant before he laid her on the bed, his body coming over hers, his mouth seeking hers as his hands pushed at the waistband of her shorts, lowering them, his hands running over her body.

A gentle breeze rustled in off the Mediterranean, bringing with it salt and warmth. Hannah lifted herself up, kissing him as her hands pushed at his shirt, guiding it over his chest, up to his head. He broke the kiss so she could remove it and then she lay back, breathless, her eyes running over his chest.

The room was dark, but she could see enough. She drank in the sight of him as quickly as she could because he kissed her again, his tongue flicking hers, his hands worshipping her body.

He brought his mouth lower, pushing at her shirt, lifting it to her throat so he could take one of her breasts into his mouth, his tongue swirling over a nipple until she bucked beneath him, stars flashing in her eyelids.

'God,' she moaned, digging her heels into the bed, arching her back, begging him to take her, to thrust inside her.

His mouth moved to her other breast and his fingers took over, his palm feeling the weight of her breast, his thumb and forefinger teasing her nipple until she was a puddle of whimpering nerves.

'Please,' she husked, running her nails down his back.

His arousal was hard between her legs; his knee nudged her thighs further apart and then he thrust into her, the ache unmistakable, the same urge overrunning them both. She felt his need and mirrored the depth of it.

She lifted herself onto her elbows, finding his mouth, pulling his lower lip between her teeth and biting down on it, so he let out a sharp sound of shock and then a groan as he pushed her head back to the mattress, his kiss a complete domination and sublime pleasure.

Only she wanted more, she wanted to be in control of this. She kissed him back, just as hard, needing him to understand her—this. Needing to reassure him in some way.

She moved herself over his arousal, her breath pinched, her body screaming in relief.

Hannah's heart hammered against her ribs and pleasure burst, touching every single part of her, until she was all fire and flame, no room for thoughts and feelings, doubts and uncertainties.

Concerns of security, the future, their relationship, his grief, her loss, they all disappeared. What room was there for anything when there was this pleasure in life?

Her breathing was rhythmic and he couldn't take his eyes off her.

Her vibrant red hair spread over his crisp white pillows, glowing like copper, and his gut throbbed painfully.

Leonidas Stathakis had tormented himself for the four years after his wife's death, staying celibate even when his body had begged him to relent, even when he'd wanted to lose himself in a willing woman's arms.

He hadn't.

He hadn't given in, until he'd seen Hannah and something inside him had begun to beat, a drum he could no longer ignore.

And it was still beating, but harder and faster now. With Hannah under his roof, it was impossible to ignore this; just as she'd said.

Theirs wasn't a normal marriage, but they did have this, and suddenly, Leonidas didn't want to fight it any more.

He watched her sleep, her beautiful, pregnant body naked to his hungry gaze, and he gave up fighting altogether. Perhaps in the morning he'd feel differently, but, for now, Leonidas allowed himself to curve his body behind hers, to place an arm possessively over her stomach and to fall asleep for the first time in a long time with a woman in his bed.

CHAPTER TEN

HANNAH WOKE, STRETCHING until her back connected with something hard and warm behind her. Her heart was racing, the meeting with Greg Hassan the day before having left a lingering sense of anxiety in her so that alarm was her first emotion, followed swiftly by something much warmer, much more tempting, when she corkscrewed in the bed and realised where she was, and who she was with.

Leonidas.

And he was awake.

Staring at her.

His naked body was not a mystery to her, and yet this was the first time she'd woken up beside him, or any man, and a hint of self-consciousness made her cheeks blush.

'I fell asleep,' she said quietly, her eyes dropping to his chest. 'I'm sorry.'

She didn't see the way his brows curved reflexively into a frown.

'Why are you apologising?'

Hannah lifted her gaze to his. 'I don't know. I guess I would have thought you'd want your space. Or to not have me here.'

His frown deepened and there was silence for several beats. 'I would have thought so, too.'

More silence.

'You were right, on the beach, Hannah. There is something between us. This chemistry.' His eyes were hollow when they met hers. 'I don't want to fight it any more.'

Her blood hammered inside her, hope was rolling inside her but she stayed completely still, watching him, listening.

'I have been single a long time. Single by choice. I have no idea how to do this. And I don't want to hurt you.' His expression showed his doubts on that score.

'Why do you think you're going to?'

His face bore a mask of wariness.

'I don't want you to think that great sex is more meaningful than that.'

Hannah swallowed, her brain turning his words over, making sense of them. He was afraid—afraid to risk falling in love, afraid to risk getting close to anyone. She understood that. He'd loved and lost. He was gun-shy now. But opening himself up to their intimacy was one thing—it was a definite step, and for now that was enough.

Hannah smiled slowly, her eyes sparkling in a way that made Leonidas draw in an audible breath.

'Don't worry, Leonidas Stathakis,' she said, pushing at his shoulder so he fell back on the mattress and straddling him at the same time, surprising him so his eyes flared. 'I'm very happy to just use you for sex for now.'

His laugh was throaty, his expression shifting into one of complete fascination.

'Is that right?' She took his erection in her hands, feeling his strength, running her fingertips over his length, her smile pure sensual heat.

'Oh, yes.' She pushed up on her haunches, then brought herself over his arousal, taking him deep inside her but so slowly that he dug his fingertips into her hips and pulled her the rest of the way, his eyes holding hers.

She bit down on her lip and arched her back and he pulled up then, sitting, wrapping his arms around her, sucking one of her nipples in his mouth, flicking it with his tongue. Her breasts were so sensitive that his touch was like an arrow firing right into her central nervous system. She cried out, his name heavy on her lips, her nails on his shoulders, and he held her tighter, thrusting into her. With her on top, he reached different places, and she felt a different kind of explosion building, more intense somehow, taking over her body.

'Leonidas.' She ran her fingers through his hair and then cupped his face, pulling him away from her chest so she could kiss his mouth, and he kissed her back, hard, their tongues duelling, even as he shifted their body weight, spinning her, rolling her onto her back so he could take even more of her, thrusting into her hungrily, deep, hard and fast, and Hannah pushed her hands up, wrapping her fingers around the bedhead and holding on for dear life, and pleasure threatened to explode her out of this world.

He leaned forward, catching her hands, peeling them off the bedhead, lacing his fingers through hers and, as on the beach, he pinned them above her head, so his hair-roughened torso was hard against hers and every single cell in her body reacted to this tactile contact, to his nearness.

Her orgasm splintered her apart and it was Leonidas who put her back together, each gentle murmur, his voice speaking in Greek, his kiss gentle now, soft, reassuring as she flew straight into the abyss.

'You don't think this is overkill?' Hannah murmured, surveying the island from the vantage point he'd driven her to. From here, she could see so much more than the house, including a full golf course, a helipad as well as the airstrip, and in the distance what looked to be a whole little village. There was a jetty, too, and another yacht was tied to it— not as large as the one in Capri, but still what Hannah had to imagine would be classed as a 'superyacht', beautiful and shimmering white.

'What is?'

'This island.' She couldn't help the smile that teased her lips. She'd woken that morning, in his bed, and something had felt easier between them. She knew there were demons driving him, controlling him, but they weren't the sum total of Leonidas Stathakis.

He shrugged nonchalantly. 'You don't like it?'

'Oh, I like it very much,' she contradicted, rolling her eyes a little. 'But who wouldn't? I just don't think I'll ever get used to living like this.'

'It's just a bigger home than you're used to.'

Hannah laughed at that, lifting the takeaway coffee cup she'd brought with her, sipping on it, wondering if she'd ever con herself into enjoying decaf. 'By about three thousand times. And then there's the expansive private beach.'

He looked at her, a smile pulling at his lips, and her heart turned over because he was really, exceptionally handsome, and when he smiled, it was as if someone had turned the music up full volume.

Her eyes dropped to his lips and her pulse gushed through her body, stirring heat in her veins and anticipation low down in her abdomen.

'I haven't thought about it in a long time,' he said simply. 'It's just the island, to me.'

'Naturally.' She was still smiling as she turned her eyes back to the view. 'Did you grow up here?'

'No.'

'Where, then?'

'Athens, mainly—Kifissia. My father's offices were in the city.' The words were flat, carefully blanked of any emotion.

But Hannah felt it. She felt it rolling off him in waves, crashing against her, just like the ocean to the shore. She swallowed, butterflies in her tummy making her hesitate a little.

'What happened with him?'

'You don't know?'

She shrugged, awkwardly. 'I had to look you up on the Internet, to work out how to contact you.'

His eyes roamed hers, probing thoughtfully.

'I mean, I saw a headline, but I didn't click into it.'

'Why not?' His expression showed genuine surprise.

'Because it kind of gives me the creeps. Doesn't it you?'

He arched a brow, clearly not comprehending.

'Well, it's not really any of my business. It seemed private to you and your family.' She wrinkled her nose, lost in thought. 'I guess there's a lot about you out there, and your brother, and your dad. But what kind of stalker would I be to read it?'

'Your stalkerishness is someone else's due diligence,' he said with a quirk of his lips. 'What if I'm some kind of pathological cheat?'

'Are you?' She turned her face to his, her eyes scanning his features.

'No.' The word was sombre.

Silence arced between them, electric and sharp. He seemed to be peeling her away, looking deep inside her, even though the question had been Hannah's.

'And see? I believe you.' Her own voice was a little husky.

'Why?'

Hannah replaced her coffee cup in the golf cart they'd been touring the island in, then spun around to face him, so their bodies were almost touching. 'Because you've never lied to me, Leonidas.'

His expression tightened imperceptibly, his jaw square.

'You told me on New Year's Eve that we'd only ever be

one night. You didn't make big promises to get me into bed. You were honest. You were honest with me this morning. I don't think you know how to lie.'

Leonidas looked beyond her, to the horizon. 'Honesty is generally the best policy, is it not?'

'Yes.' Her smile was uneven.

'I would have thought, having learned of your fiancé's infidelity, you would be slow to trust anyone.'

'So would I.' Her voice was a little shaky. 'But you're nothing like Angus. You're nothing like anyone I've ever met.'

At this, Leonidas's expression tightened, and she understood that he was closing himself off, that she'd moved them into territory he couldn't yet traverse.

'What did he do, anyway?'

'Who?'

'Your father.'

'Ah.' He expelled a slow breath, as though fortifying himself for what would come next.

'I gather he's in prison?'

'Serving a twenty-year sentence.'

'I'm so sorry.'

'What for? Prison is where criminals should be.'

'Yes, but he's your dad…'

'Not any more.'

Hannah frowned. 'You hate him?'

'Yes.'

She nodded thoughtfully. 'Why?'

'My father turned his back on the Stathakis Corporation. He almost destroyed what my grandfather, great-grandfather, and his father had spent their lifetimes building. Ancient, proud shipping lines that funded investments in foreign hotels and then hedge funds—our operations were crippled because of him.'

'How? Surely your company's too big for any one man to destroy?'

'He began to fund the mob, Hannah.' His eyes were haunted now, furious too, zipping with tightly coiled emotions. 'My father—who was richer than Croesus—didn't just want money and the lifestyle it afforded. He wanted power. No, not power; he wanted people to be afraid of him. He wanted notoriety and reach.'

'I can't even imagine what drives a man to think like that,' she said with a gentle shake of her head. 'How could he have even met that element?'

'It's everywhere. Casinos, bars, commercial investments.' Leonidas expelled a harsh breath. 'He was always enamoured of that lifestyle. I'm only surprised it took so long for him to be arrested.'

'That must have been so hard for you.'

'I think of myself as a strong person but I have no idea how I would have coped without Thanos.' The confession surprised her, and softened her, all at once. 'Investigators from every country in which we do business went over our records with a fine-tooth comb. We lost anything that had been used to fund crime. Despite the fact Thanos and I had been groomed from a young age, at our grandfather's knee, to love our company like a member of this family, to work hard to better it, we had to watch it being pulled apart, piece by piece, to see it crumble and fail.'

Sadness clouded Hannah's eyes; the image he was painting was one that was loaded with grief.

'What did you do?'

His expression was laced with determination and she thought of a phoenix, rising from the ashes. 'We cut the failing businesses, sold them off piece by piece, got what we could for them and recouped by aggressively buying into emerging markets. It was a high-risk strategy, but what did we have to lose?'

Hannah felt the conversational ground shift a little beneath them. She knew there was danger ahead, but, again, something had changed, there was more clarity, as if a valve had given way and now there was a clear flow of comprehension, an understanding.

'You said Amy was murdered in a vendetta against your father?'

His features tightened, and his jet-black eyes glittered with hatred—not for her, but for the men responsible. 'Yes.'

It was like pulling fingernails, she knew. He didn't want to do this, and yet, he wasn't hiding from her, even when it was causing him pain.

'He cut a deal with a prosecutor. Multiple life sentences were reduced to a twenty-year term, all because he handed over the names of his associates.' Leonidas's contempt was apparent, his lips little more than a snarl. 'He didn't, for one second, think of how that would affect us—those of us out here, living in this world.'

'Perhaps he was just trying to do the right thing?'

Leonidas surprised Hannah then, because he smiled—a smile that was tinged with grief. 'You see the world through the veneer of your goodness,' he said after a moment. 'You think because your motivations are pure and good, everyone else's must always be?'

'No.' She frowned; it wasn't that at all.

'Yes,' he insisted. 'How else could you have become engaged to a man who was cheating on you? You trust and you forgive.'

'Is that a bad thing?'

He was quiet, staring at her for several beats. 'I hope not.'

Hannah expelled a soft breath. 'Maybe I do give people more than their fair chance. But I also see the truth—I know what people are capable of, Leonidas. I've seen it. I've felt it.'

She looked away from him then, her eyes gravitating to the yacht as it bobbed on the surface of the Mediterranean. Everything was clear and pristine, and so very beautiful, like stepping into a postcard.

Leonidas's fingers curled around her chin, gently pulling her back to face him.

'He hurt you?'

Hannah's eyes widened, and it took her a moment to think who he was referring to.

'He was my fiancé, and he had an affair... Of course that hurt. But it wasn't him alone; it was her, too. It was the fact that two of the people who were supposed to love me most in the world had been happy to betray me with one another.' She shuddered, the shock of that moment one she wasn't sure she'd ever get over. 'It wasn't losing Angus. It was the whole situation.'

His eyes devoured Hannah's face, tasting her expression, digesting its meaning. 'Have you spoken to her?'

Hannah shook her head. 'I couldn't. I can't. I don't know what I'd say. Growing up, our relationship wasn't always... easy.'

'Why not?' he pushed, and she had a glimpse of his formidable analytical skills. She felt his determination to comprehend her words, to seek out what was at the root of them.

'She was competitive, and frankly insecure. Her mother—Aunt Cathy—spurred her on, making comments about how we looked, or about grades.' Hannah sighed. 'I never bought into it. I mean, we're all our own person, right? Run your own race. That's what my mum used to say.' Her smile was nostalgic, and then, it slipped from her lips like the sun being consumed by a storm cloud. 'But my aunt…'

He waited, patiently, for her to continue. Hannah searched for the words.

'She measured us against each other non-stop.'

'And your cousin didn't measure up?'

Hannah's eyes shot to Leonidas's. 'I didn't say that.'

'No, you are being deliberately tactful on that score.'

There was enough praise in that observation to bring heat to Hannah's cheeks, but she denied it.

'I'm not being coy. I just don't think like that. Michelle struggled at school; I didn't. I suspect she has some kind of undiagnosed dyslexia—no matter how much time we spent going over things, she found the comprehension impossible. I think she wasn't able to read clearly, and covered it by acting uninterested.'

'You mentioned this to your aunt?'

Hannah nodded. 'Once. She was furious.' Hannah's expression was unconsciously pained, her features pinched tight as her gaze travelled back towards the ocean.

'And you, in comparison, excelled at your studies?'

Hannah nodded slowly. 'Some people respond well to the school system, others don't. I'm lucky in that I'm one of the former.'

'And a lifetime of feeling compared to has made you downplay your natural abilities even now, here, to me.'

She startled at that insight. 'It's the truth.'

'It is also the truth to say you are intelligent, and I would bet my fortune on the fact you worked hard at school, too.' He softened his tone a little, but didn't quit his line of questioning. 'Isn't it possible that your aunt resented how well you did, compared to Michelle? That she couldn't get help for her daughter because it would be admitting she was, in some way, inferior?'

'If I'm right and Michelle had a learning difficulty of sorts then she could have been helped, and achieved far better results than she did.'

He dipped his head in a silent concession. 'But your aunt didn't want to pursue that. And so, instead, she took away your dreams, condemning you to a life of mediocrity so her own daughter would look better in comparison?'

Hannah sucked in a sharp breath, his words like acid rain against her flesh. 'I don't think you could call my life mediocre...'

'You should have been studying law, poised to move into the career you really wanted. And your aunt should have been supporting you. This is what you meant, when you said you have felt what people are capable of?'

She opened her mouth to deny it, but he was too insightful. Too right. She shrugged instead, lifting her shoulders and turning away from him.

'Where was your uncle in all of this?'

'Gary?'

'You speak of your aunt and your cousin, but I have not heard you say his name once.'

'He worked a lot. We weren't close.'

'And yet he must have known how his wife was behaving. He did nothing?'

'It's not like that. Aunt Cathy isn't a monster. It's complicated.'

'How?'

Hannah shook her head thoughtfully. 'It was so long ago, and I don't really know anything for certain. It's more just things I've picked up from throwaway comments. I think she was very close to my dad—her brother. And when Mum entered the scene, Aunt Cathy was jealous. Hurt. My mum was...' Hannah's smile was melancholy and she closed her eyes, seeing Eleanor May as she'd been in life—so vital, so beautiful. 'She was a pretty amazing woman. A diplomat for the United Nations, well travelled, passionate, funny, and so stunning.'

'So this is where you get it from,' he murmured, the compliment wrapping around her, filling her with gold dust.

Hannah smiled slowly, memories of her past pulling at her. 'I used to love watching her get ready for parties. She had this long, dark brown hair, like chocolate, that fell to her waist. She would coil it up into a bun, high on the top of her head, so that whatever dangly earrings she chose to wear would take your breath away.' Hannah felt him come closer, his body heat and proximity firing something in her blood.

'And she and Dad were so happy together. They used to laugh, all the time. I was just a kid when they died, but I'll never forget them, I'll never forget how lucky I was to have them as my example in life.'

He was quiet, but it didn't matter. Some part of Leonidas had slipped into Hannah, forming a part of her, so she understood—she understood his silence equated to disapproval of Aunt Cathy, and her inability to let Hannah properly grieve.

And long-held needs to defend Aunt Cathy were difficult to ignore. 'Cathy and Gary weren't like my parents. They married young, because she was pregnant. She lost the baby but they stayed together and it always felt a bit like they resented each other.'

She turned to face him then, her chest heavy with the myriad sadnesses of the past. 'I don't want our marriage to be like that, Leonidas.'

Her eyes raked his face and she chewed her lower lip thoughtfully as he stared at her, his eyes unshifting from hers, his expression impossible to interpret.

'I was wrong about you.' Leonidas's words came out hoarse, thickened by regret.

'When?'

'I presumed you did not know enough of grief to counsel me, to offer me any thoughts on my own experiences. That was incredibly arrogant.' He lifted a hand, running it over her hair, his attention shifting higher, as if mesmerised by the auburn shades there, flecked with gold. 'I downplayed what you have been through because I couldn't believe anyone could feel loss like mine.'

'It's not like yours,' she said softly, gently, her heart breaking. 'No grief is the same. I can't imagine what it's like to lose your partner, nor your child.' She shook her head sadly from side to side. 'I'm five months pregnant and the idea of anything ever happening to our daughter fills me with a kind of rage I can't put into words.' Her lips twisted in a humourless smile. 'You must be a mix of anger and fury and pain and disbelief all the time.' She swallowed, rallying her thoughts. 'You don't need to apologise to me. I understood what you meant.'

'But I didn't understand you,' he insisted. 'I didn't realise that beyond the somewhat sanitised phrase of "orphan" are all the memories of parents you loved, parents who made you happy and secure, parents who were replaced by an inferior substitute—an insecure and competitive woman who spent her life trying to diminish you.'

Hannah's lips pulled downwards, as she tried to reconcile his vision of Aunt Cathy.

'You should have studied law,' he said, simply. 'And anyone who loved you would have pushed you to do that, supporting you, encouraging you, making it easier—not harder—to pursue your dreams.'

Hannah's heart turned over in her chest, because he was right. Even Angus hadn't said as much to her.

'Your parents left you money. That could have been used to fund your studies.'

'I couldn't access it yet, not for another two years.'

'But a bank would have loaned against that expectation, if your aunt and uncle couldn't cover your expenses in the interim. There were ways for you to live your dreams but she held you back because she didn't want you to succeed.'

Something sparked in Hannah's chest because he was right, and she'd made excuses for Cathy and Gary all her life and she didn't want to do it any more.

'I miss my mum and dad every day,' she said, simply, focussing on the only kernel of good she could grasp at. 'Especially now.' She ran a hand over her stomach, thinking of the daughter growing inside her, and love burst in her soul.

The air between them resonated with understanding, with compassion, and then Hannah blinked away, moving her focus to the vista before them.

Their conversation was serious, and yet she felt a shifting lightness in her heart, a sense of newness. Perhaps it was simply the beauty of the day, or looking down over the horizon and seeing so much that fascinated her, so much to explore, but she found herself smiling.

'What's down there?' She nodded towards the village she could see in the distance. 'I thought this was a private island.'

'It is. That's the staff quarters.'

'Staff quarters?'

His smile was teasing. 'Where did you think all the people in the house went to at night?'

'I didn't think about it,' she said, and he smiled then, a smile that was natural and easy and that made her pulse feel as if it had hitched a ride on a roller coaster and were zipping and whooshing through her body.

'There are about fifteen gardeners, Mrs Chrisohoidis,

her husband Andreo, who oversees the island, the domestic staff, chefs, and I have two personal assistants based out of the island for when I need to work.'

Hannah's eyes flew wide. 'Seriously?'

'And their families,' he said, still smiling, the words lightly mocking.

She shook her head from side to side, wondering at how anyone could have this kind of money.

'It takes a team to manage all this.' He gestured with his palm to the island.

She nodded. 'And then the yacht crew, too?'

He nodded. 'They stay on board, though there are dorms for when the boat is here over winter.'

'You must spend a fortune in salaries.'

'I suppose I do.' He wasn't smiling now, but he was looking at her with a heat that simmered her blood. He lifted a hand to her hair once more, tucking it behind her ear slowly, watchfully.

'There's the security team, as well,' he said, and she felt his past pulling him deep into a raging ocean.

'Greg Hassan lives here?'

'Greg lives in Athens. He oversees Stathakis Corp, including my brother Thanos's security arrangements, and our company procedures. He has a manager on the island, and there are thirteen guards permanently placed here.'

'Thirteen?' She exhaled. 'Security guards?'

'It used to be only four,' he said nonchalantly.

'But because of me it's thirteen?'

'Because of you, and because of her.' He dropped a hand to Hannah's stomach, and right at that moment one of the little popping sensations Hannah had become used to reared to life, and Leonidas's eyes widened in wonder.

'Did she just kick me?'

Hannah laughed, but there was a sting of happy tears

against her eyelids. 'She's telling you we don't need anything like that kind of security.'

'I think she's giving me a high five of agreement.'

Hannah laughed and Leonidas did, too. She had no way of knowing how long it had been since he'd felt genuine amusement, or the occurrence might have taken her breath away even more than the sound did on its own.

Hannah lay with her head on Leonidas's chest, in the small hours of the next day, listening to his heart. It beat slow and steady in sleep. She lay there, her naked body close to his, their limbs tangled with the crisp white sheets, their bodies spent, her body round with the baby they'd made, and she smiled.

Because there was such randomness in this, and yet such perfection, too.

How could she have known that one night of unplanned sensual heat would lead to this? She lay with her head on his chest, listening to the solid beating of his heart, and admitted to herself there was nowhere on earth she'd rather be.

CHAPTER ELEVEN

'YOU'RE GETTING MARRIED?'

Thanos's voice came to Leonidas from a long way away.

'Where are you?' Leonidas stretched his long legs out in front of himself, crossing them at the ankles.

'Somewhere over the Atlantic.'

'You're going to New York?'

'It's model week.' Leonidas could hear his brother's grin, and experience told him that in approximately twenty-four hours there'd be tabloid headlines about Thanos's latest stunning conquest. 'Did you say you're getting married?'

Leonidas's eyes drifted to the window of his study, and beyond it, to where Hannah was lying beside the pool. The bathing costume was really just a couple of scraps of Lycra, and his fingers itched to remove it.

'Yes.'

'*You're* getting married?'

Leonidas grimaced. 'On Friday.'

'As in three days away *Friday*?'

'Yes.'

'*Christós.* I didn't realise you were seeing anyone.'

'I'm not. I wasn't.' He swept his eyes shut, his stomach clenching painfully. 'It's not like that.'

'So what is it like?'

Leonidas's chest felt as if it were being scooped out, replaced with acid. 'She's pregnant.'

Silence.

It stretched for so long that Leonidas thought they might

have lost reception. The phones on their state-of-the-art jets were good, but not one hundred per cent reliable.

'Thanos?'

'I'm sorry, I'm just surprised. I thought you'd sworn off women for life.'

'So did I.'

'And yet?'

'And yet,' Leonidas agreed, his eyes roaming her body with a hunger that was not a part of him. He'd given up on fighting this, on fighting Hannah. She was breathing herself into his soul, and taking over small parts of him, forming his building blocks back into shape. Except for his heart, which would always be locked away, reserved for Amy and Brax.

The rest of him, he could share. Especially if it made her smile the way she had been.

'When? I mean to say, when will you have this baby?'

'She's due in four months.'

Thanos let out a low whistle. 'So you're marrying her for custody?'

The description turned Leonidas's stomach. 'I'm marrying her for security.'

A moment of silence and then, gently, 'Leonidas, the man who killed them is locked up for life. He'll never get out. There's no reason to think he wasn't acting alone.'

'It's organised crime. Do you really think he'd have operated without instruction?'

'Yes,' Thanos spoke swiftly. 'I think he was a lunatic, angry that our father had turned on his brother and so he took that out on you—an eye for an eye. There is no risk now.'

'Would you bet someone's life on that, Thanos? Would you bet the life of an innocent woman you were too weak to resist and that of her unborn child?'

More silence, and eventually, 'No.'

Leonidas didn't realise until that moment how badly he'd needed to hear that. 'Here with me, on the island, she is safe. Our child will be safe.'

'What's she like?'

'She's…' Leonidas tried to put into words a hint of Hannah, but it proved hard for some reason. 'She's nice. You'll like her.'

Thanos's disapproval came across in his silence. 'Nice?'

'Yes, nice. What's wrong with "nice"?'

Thanos was quiet. 'Does she know about Amy?'

Leonidas stiffened. 'Yes.'

'Leo.' Thanos rarely used the diminutive version of Leonidas's name. It slipped out, the boyhood moniker coming naturally to him now. 'You don't think it's a bit of an extreme way to keep someone safe? You couldn't just give her a security detail?'

Leonidas was surprised to realise he hadn't even considered that. Not for a moment. But he understood his reasoning. Having lost Amy and Brax, he couldn't risk anything else happening to the mother of his child, and the only way to be sure of that was to have her within eyesight. He and Amy had fought—often. They'd begun spending more and more time apart. He'd missed Brax like anything but he'd relished his space from Amy, even when he'd known he loved her—or that he had loved her once and needed to honour that love, for the sake of their child.

But he'd been careless, letting her go without taking an interest in how she was spending her time. He hadn't seen the danger and they'd paid the ultimate price.

No. Hannah would be by his side, 'til death do them part. And if they were separated and he couldn't protect her, then he'd make sure she had an army at her disposal.

'A detail wouldn't have been enough. It's my job to keep them safe.'

'I see.' It was clear Thanos didn't agree, though. 'And is this what she wants?'

Leonidas stood, moving to the window, and his legs felt a little like jelly when he thought about what Hannah might want. Perhaps she caught a hint of his movement in her peripheral vision, or perhaps she felt the tug of him in that strange way she had, but she lifted her gaze to the window of his study, lifting her sunglasses from her head so she could pierce him, through the glass, with the intensity of her emerald eyes.

His pulse slammed inside him.

'She agrees it's for the best.'

Thanos was quiet for a moment. 'It all sounds very sensible and safe, then.'

Leonidas nodded, but his insides were clenching in a way that wasn't even remotely sensible.

'Maybe you could take over negotiations with Kosta Carinedes now that you're about to be married with a kid. That's the kind of respectability he's looking for.'

Leonidas stiffened—the reality of that still difficult to contemplate. And though Thanos had obviously been joking, he was quick to retort, 'There is no way on earth I'm telling anyone who doesn't need to know about Hannah and our daughter. I plan on keeping this secret as long as I can.'

There was safety in secrecy.

Hannah smiled up at him, and lifted her hand, motioning for him to come to her, then pointing to the water.

He shook his head on autopilot, the last vestiges of restraint reminding him that there needed to be some boundaries, some restrictions.

She shrugged, standing up slowly, unfurling her petite

frame and turning her back on him. She reached behind her as he watched, pulling on the string of her bikini top and lifting it over her head. Her hair, shimmering like a flame in the afternoon sunshine, ignited down her back.

He held his breath as she turned once more and blew him a kiss, her smile contagious, spreading over his lips, exploding out of her like diamond dust. And then she eased herself into the pool, her beautiful, pale breasts only half covered by the water.

He disconnected the call to Thanos, threw his phone on his desk and was already stripping his clothes as he made his way to the deck.

It was just a swim on a very hot day, nothing more.

Leonidas told himself he was simply doing what Hannah deserved. That it was easy for him to deliver on her dreams and that someone should do that for her, after everything she'd lost.

She was marrying one of the richest men in the world—she could have anything she wanted in life and Leonidas was going to make sure she knew that.

He couldn't give her his heart, he couldn't give her the version of happily ever after she wanted, but he could spoil her with every material possession so that she never noticed there was a gaping void inside her chest.

He told himself a thousand and one things but as he observed Hannah with undisguised interest, watched the way her face glowed with happiness and wonderment, he knew there was something more base in his reasons for bringing her here, to Paris.

The idea had come to him while they were swimming, earlier that day. They were marrying for somewhat pragmatic reasons, but that didn't mean he couldn't make some of her dreams come true. And she had always wanted to see Paris, had grown up staring at a tourist souvenir of the Eiffel Tower, and he could give her the real thing. He'd wanted her to have it.

Why?

Because it had mattered to him.

Because he could.

Because someone should spoil Hannah May.

'Leonidas.' She turned to face him, tears in her eyes. 'It's so much more beautiful than I'd imagined.'

Their penthouse hotel room looked over the glowing construction of the city's heart, the Eiffel Tower. He handed her a glass of non-alcoholic champagne, moving closer to her, still unable to tear his gaze from her face.

'Many locals would beg to differ.'

But even his cynicism couldn't dampen her mood. 'Then they're crazy.' She grinned. 'I've never seen anything more beautiful.'

'Haven't you?' His voice was thick and guilt rolled through him. He banked it down. This wasn't about him and Amy and Brax and the mess that was his life. This was about Hannah—she deserved to be happy, she deserved to feel joy, she deserved this. And he wasn't going to ruin it by brooding and regretting.

She lifted her eyes to his and heat seared him, as it had the first night they met, as it always did.

'I guess you come here all the time. You're probably used to it.'

He skipped his gaze to the Eiffel Tower thoughtfully. 'Often enough.'

'I can't imagine seeing it as just another landmark. It's extraordinary.'

As she looked at it the hour struck and the tower went from glowing gold to glistening with silver and starlight. Hannah drew in a sharp breath and moved closer, through the billowing curtains and onto the small Juliet balcony with an unrivalled view of the tourist favourite.

'Tomorrow I want to go right to the top,' she said with a broad grin, turning back to face him.

'Why wait until tomorrow?' he prompted, holding a hand out to her.

'Because it's eight o'clock. Surely it's not open to visitors?'

'It's open until midnight,' he said with a smile.

'Then what are we waiting for?' she asked breathlessly, yet he didn't move. He stared at her, drinking in the sight of her like this, and something shifted in his gut—hope, lightness, release.

He ignored it, taking her hand and squeezing it tight in his own. 'Not a thing. Let's go, *agape mou*.'

Hannah slept with a smile on her face and woke with it still drifting over her lips. Her sleeping mind had been full of all the dreams that Leonidas had made a reality. The surprise trip to Paris—touching down in his private jet at Charles de Gaulle and being whisked through the ancient city in his sleek black limousine.

She hadn't been able to speak, she'd been too thrilled, too fascinated, intent on catching every detail she possibly could. She'd craned forward in her seat, staring at the city as it passed and her heart had begun to throb and twist and race for how much the city lived up to her every dream.

And for how close she felt to her mother here. It had been Eleanor's favourite city—she'd spent a lot of time in Paris for the UN and had come home speaking about it, bringing the city to life in a young Hannah's imagination.

The Stathakis Hotel was in the heart of this thriving metropolis, poised on the edge of the Seine, showcasing views in one direction of the Eiffel Tower and in the other of the

Arc de Triomphe, and in between all the winding streets and tiny little houses that made this city so singularly unique.

The penthouse was exquisite, just like the one on Chrysá Vráchia, only it was different—there was more of a flavour of France in its styling. The artwork was done by the hand of famous Impressionists, the furniture a little more elaborate and baroque; everything about it was sumptuous and romantic.

And it had been waiting for them when they arrived.

It had all been so perfect and Hannah had almost been able to ignore the presence of the security officers who'd accompanied them on the flight and through the streets of Paris. Constantly walking a discreet distance behind but always there, always watching and waiting.

And despite the joy of this city, a frisson of alarm travelled down her spine, a hint of worry at what had befallen Amy and Brax and the threats Leonidas seemed to imagine were still out there.

She turned over in bed, lifting a finger to his shoulder and tracing an invisible circle distractedly across his tanned flesh.

His eyes lifted and he turned to face her, a look on his face she couldn't interpret before he smiled.

Her heart turned over in her chest.

'Bonjour.'

His smile widened. *'Bonjour, mademoiselle.'*

'I like it here,' she said simply, dropping her head to his chest but keeping her gaze trained squarely on the picture-perfect Eiffel Tower beyond the window. It was a perfect day—a bright blue sky called to her and Hannah was already excited to explore this ancient city.

'I thought you might.'

And so he'd arranged this. Something pulled inside her

chest—pleasure—and she smiled softly. 'Is it possible, Leonidas, that you are a romantic at heart?'

His chest slowed, his body completely still. 'No.' The word was like thunder in the midst of a sunny day. She pushed up to look at him, not cowed by the stern expression on his face. A week ago, she would have bitten her tongue, but something had shifted between them; she was different now. He'd made her different.

Hannah liked to think she wasn't the same girl who'd agreed to marry Angus, who'd taken her aunt's decrees as gospel. She bit down on her lower lip, watching him, thinking, and then said, 'How did you meet her?'

His eyes dropped to hers, his expression unreadable. She wondered if he was going to plead 'off limits', as he had at the start, but he didn't.

Though it clearly gave him no pleasure and considerable pain, he spoke slowly, quietly, the words dredged from deep within him. 'Through my brother.'

Silence. She didn't fill it.

'Thanos has a broad social circle.' Scepticism filled the words. 'Amy had just started modelling. She got pulled along to a party by some friends. I happened to be there.'

'She was a model?'

Leonidas nodded. 'She was beautiful and I was smitten.' His smile was dismissive but jealousy surged inside Hannah. She knew how petty that was. The poor woman had died and it was not for Hannah to envy her anything.

'Did you date for long before marrying?'

'No,' he laughed softly. 'I am not a patient man. When I see something I want I go after it.' His frown was another storm cloud on the horizon. 'We married quickly, privately, and before we really knew much about one another.'

Hannah tilted her head to the side, watching him. 'You say that as though it's a bad thing.'

'It can be,' he said thoughtfully.

Curiosity got the better of Hannah. 'Was she different from what you imagined?'

Leonidas flicked his gaze to Hannah's, his eyes showing torment. 'I loved her.' The words were defensive. 'But we weren't capable of making each other happy.'

Sympathy scored deep into Hannah's heart.

'I thought a baby might be the answer to that. I convinced her to fall pregnant, and by then she was so afraid of losing me I think she would have borne me a football team if I'd asked it of her.' He shook his head from side to side, anger in the tight lines of his lips.

'Why weren't you happy?' she asked curiously.

He expelled a soft sigh. 'Neither of us was happy.' He moved his gaze to the window, looking through it without seeing. 'Amy loved a certain lifestyle.'

'Money?'

He grimaced. 'Money was not the issue. Partying was. She loved to go out, to be seen, to be adored. She fell into my brother's crowd for a reason.'

Sympathy shifted inside Hannah's chest. 'And you're not like that?'

'I never have been. Thanos is the "playboy prince of Europe" and that suits him. He lives his life in the fast lane—life can never be loud enough, fast enough, drunk enough.' His smile showed affection. 'He's a tornado. And he attracts tornados.'

'Like Amy.'

'Yes. Like Amy. She was much more at home with his friends. I couldn't make her happy.'

'But you loved her.'

A heavy beat of silence throbbed between them. 'Yes.' He turned to face her. 'And I refused to let our marriage fail.'

Hannah expelled a soft sigh. 'You can't beat yourself up

for things not having been perfect. I sometimes think life is a knot full of different threads. Some of them happy, some of them profoundly sad, but they all form a part of you.' She pressed a finger to his chest.

Leonidas lay back and gave his fiancée the full force of his attention. 'And you think you would have been happy with him?'

Hannah considered that for a moment. 'I think I would have been free with Angus. Free of my aunt and uncle and their low expectations, free of Michelle's jealousy. At least, I thought I would have been—clearly those jealousies were going to chase me into my marriage.'

'Do you still love him?'

'Angus?' She wrinkled her nose. 'The more time that passes, the more I think I didn't ever really love him. Not as anything more than a friend. But he was the first person in a long time to tell me he loved me.' Her lips twisted painfully. 'He was the first person who made me feel wanted— needed. And I loved that feeling.'

'I have something for you.'

Hannah stifled a yawn, the whirlwind, one-night trip to Paris having been both spectacular and exhausting. She placed her book down on her lap, lifting her gaze to Leonidas's face and feeling that now familiar rolling in her stomach as her nerves exploded. Desire lurched inside her, but it was more than just a physical need.

She longed for him in every way.

'Oh, yeah?'

'Yes.' He crossed the floor of the private jet, propping his hip against the broad armchair opposite her. 'Here.' He reached into the pocket of his shirt and pulled out a small black velvet pouch.

'What is it?' She took it without looking away from his face.

'Open it.'

She did just that, sliding the tip of her finger into the pouch's opening and reaching for the contents. It was tiny and sharp. She tipped it into her palm and smiled. Because there in her hand was the most delicate and beautiful replica of the Eiffel Tower she'd ever seen. A closer inspection showed it was made of diamonds and it was attached to a delicate chain.

'It's truly beautiful,' she said, her voice cracking with emotion.

'I thought you should always have something that brings you so much happiness right by your heart.'

Her heart! Oh, how it flipped and flopped at his thoughtful, kind words.

She felt as though she were soaring high into the heavens, right alongside the clouds outside the porthole windows of this designer jet.

She looked up at him, a smile on her face, holding the necklace out. 'Would you mind?'

He took it from her, arranging it around her neck and clipping it into place. It was a mid-length chain so the stunning charm dangled perfectly between her breasts.

'I love it,' she said sincerely, looking up at him. 'Thank you.'

His smile was the most beautiful thing she'd ever seen. Her pulse fired inside her, but then, his smile flattened and his face assumed a serious, distracted expression. 'You were right on the beach.'

She frowned, searching her memory.

'You said we could make something of this marriage and you were right.'

Her stomach clenched and her heart trembled.

'When Amy and Brax died, my heart died with them,

and it's gone—for good. I cannot offer you what I think you deserve, but I can give you enough, I think, for you to want this. For you to be happy.' He crouched down at her feet, clutching her hands, staring into her eyes. 'Look at the life you can lead by my side. Look at how we can raise our child.' He lifted one of his hands to cup her cheek. 'There is enough here to build on, just like you said. We just have to be brave enough to try.'

She felt the once foreign but now familiar sting of tears in the back of her throat. He was speaking softly, as though he were offering a great gift, but all his words did was open up a hole in her heart and make her feel as though she were falling into it completely.

There was something so final and so *limiting* about what he was saying, and the timing of it filled her with despair. Their trip to Paris had been so full of magic and she'd felt so wanted and cosseted, but it had all been a sales pitch, him showing her what he could *give* her to make this marriage appealing. Because he wanted her to be safe, he didn't want the guilt of any harm befalling her, and because he wanted their child close. She'd seen the way he talked about Brax, the genuine love that had filled him—he'd be a great father to their daughter.

This trip hadn't really been about her—he hadn't brought her to Paris because he'd wanted her to see it, he'd done it because he'd wanted her to know what she could expect, being married to him. He'd thought showing her the enormous silver lining of being Mrs Leonidas Stathakis would compensate for the fact his heart 'had died' with his first wife and son.

She bit down on her lip, turning her face away from him without responding, not able to find any words that would express the enormous doubts that were harpooning her soul.

CHAPTER TWELVE

HANNAH HAD BUTTERFLIES in her tummy and they wouldn't quit. She looked at the dress the couturier had brought earlier that day—it was the perfect wedding dress for this perfectly fake wedding.

'Keep it simple,' she had instructed, feeling as if the wedding was enough of a farce without a frou-frou white cupcake dress. And simple it was. A silk slip with spaghetti straps and cut on the bias so it emphasised the curves of her breasts, hips and the roundedness of her stomach. It was not a dress one would wear to a public wedding, in front of hundreds of people.

It was a dress to be worn for a lover. Beautiful, but so incredibly sensual. She ran her fingers over the silky fabric, and then dropped her gaze to the floor, where a pair of rose-gold sandals had been teamed with it. They were casual and comfortable and the perfect bit of whimsy to offset such a stunning piece.

She heard a noise and startled, quickly putting the simple gown back in the wardrobe and slamming the door, spinning around almost guiltily as Leonidas entered their bedroom. When had she started to think of it as theirs, rather than just his? It had been just under a week since she'd arrived on the island and she barely recognised the woman she'd been then.

'Marina has set dinner up on the terrace,' he said. He looked at her as he had on the plane, with a smile that was at ease, as though he'd made his peace with how this would work—he'd slotted her into a space in his mind and he was content with that.

She wasn't his wife by choice, but they could still 'make this work'.

Hadn't she said something along those lines to him, right at the beginning of all this? She'd been happy to take a pragmatic approach then. But something had changed and now the limitations of that sat strangely in her chest.

'Okay.' Hannah returned his smile, but it didn't light up her face as usual.

They walked in silence to the terrace, and when they reached it, Leonidas held a chair out for her.

Mrs Chrisohoidis had gone to a lot of trouble.

Candles flickered everywhere, and fresh flowers had been picked from around the island, filling the terrace with an even more delightful, heady fragrance than usual.

She breathed it in and told herself to relax.

She told herself nothing had changed. They were two people who were forging a relationship, who were getting married the very next day, and all the reasons for agreeing to this marriage were still there. Aside from the possible danger to her and their daughter, Hannah's desire to provide their child with a father was as strong as ever. To know that if anything ever happened to her, Leonidas would be there—that she would know and love him.

She was doing the right thing—these doubts would lessen once they were married and she could get on with building their marriage.

They would have a lifetime together. A lifetime to make sense of this madness.

But as Leonidas took the seat opposite Hannah, she realised with a terrifying bolt of comprehension that she didn't need a lifetime to make sense of this. He took the seat opposite her and she breathed out, relaxing.

Because he was there; he was near her.

She clutched the stem of her wine glass—filled with ice-cold apple juice—and stared at her groom, as a thousand memories exploded inside her.

Perhaps it was the starlit sky overhead, just like the night they met, but suddenly, Hannah seemed to be looking through binoculars, seeing everything larger and bigger and more true to life.

Why had she slept with him that night?

She'd never done anything like that, and yet one look from Leonidas had made her want to throw herself at his feet. That couldn't be anything other than desire, could it?

So why had she thought of him every day since? Why had he tormented her thoughts and dreams and filled her chest with a strange palpitation?

What was the underlying reason that had made accepting his proposal easy? Beyond the very sensible reasons of security and support, what had really made her agree to this?

Because marriage meant this.

Time with him. Sitting opposite him. Lying with him. Kissing him. Making love to him.

No, not making love.

It was sex. Just sex.

Except it wasn't.

She swept her eyes shut, remembering every kiss, every touch, the way he laced his fingers through hers and stared into her eyes when she exploded with pleasure.

'Hannah?' He leaned forward, curving a hand over hers, and she startled, piercing him with her ocean-green eyes. 'Are you okay? Is it the baby?'

She shook her head, and tried to smile, but her pulse was frantic and her stomach was lurching.

There was no way on earth she'd done something as stupid as fall in love with the man she'd agreed to marry.

Every step of the way he'd told her he didn't want that. Their marriage wasn't about love. It was convenient. Sensible. And yet a rising tide of panic made breathing difficult because they were due to say their vows in the morning, and Hannah knew hers wouldn't be a lie.

In one week…no. Not one week. This thread had begun to stitch its way into her heart that very first night, on Chrysá Vráchia.

She hadn't understood it then—how could she?

It was only now that she comprehended what she hadn't been able to with Angus. Love wasn't a choice, it wasn't a sensible, practical formula one could apply to the 'right' candidate to ensure a lifetime of happiness.

It didn't work like that.

Love was as organic as breathing and laughing. Love was magic and, somehow, it had placed Hannah and Leonidas on the same island at the same time and the chemistry of their bodies had demanded something of them. It hadn't been about chemistry alone, though, she saw that now. He'd offered a one-night stand—and instead, she'd seen his heart and buried a piece of it in her own.

She gasped again, standing jerkily, moving to the balustrade and staring out at the inky black ocean. If it weren't for the sound of the waves, it would have been impossible to know what was beyond the balcony.

'Hannah? *Christós!* What is it?'

She shook her head, unable to speak, definitely unable to put any of this into words. She had to make sense of it herself first. 'I… It's nothing. I just wanted to look at the view.'

She felt his disbelief. 'There is no view. It's pitch black.'

She turned around to face him, surprised to find Leonidas standing right behind her. 'There are stars,' she said softly. 'Lights in the dark. See?'

Her huge green eyes shifted heavenwards, but Leonidas

didn't look upwards. He stared at Hannah, worry communicating itself in every line of his body.

'There is also dinner, on the table,' he teased, the words only slightly strained. 'And I am hungry.'

Hannah nodded, even though she wasn't sure she could stomach any food.

'In a moment.' She gnawed on her lip, the realisation of a moment ago doing funny things to her, making her look at him in a wholly new way.

Was it possible to fall in love with someone so quickly? Was love at first sight something she even believed in? Could she be so impractical after everything she'd been through?

It didn't matter how she queried herself.

Her eyes only had to glance to Leonidas and she felt the pull from his heart to hers. She felt a soaring of something inside her that was new and different and refused to be grounded.

She was suffocating, this knowledge desperate to burst from her, but she held it back, keeping her mouth closed even when the words pressed against her lips.

They would marry the next day, and she would say her vows, knowing they were true and honest, and then she would gently show him how she felt. She would give him time to adjust. To feel his way into this.

She exhaled, the sensible approach filling her with relief.

Calmed, she moved back to the table, taking her seat and eating as much as she could—the butterflies in her tummy left little room for food, though.

'Where are you going?' he asked at the door to his room.

Hannah's smile was soft, and inside, she carried the knowledge that was continuing to unfurl inside her. She loved him. She loved him in an everlasting, for-the-rest-of-her-life kind of way. And tomorrow, they'd marry.

'It's the night before our wedding, Leonidas. Don't you know it's bad luck to spend it together?'

His brows arched heavenwards. 'A superstition?'

'Yep.' She nodded. 'And one I intend on obeying. Go to sleep. I'll see you in the morning.'

He groaned, pulling her closer, his eyes locked onto hers. 'I don't want you to go back there.'

He nodded down the corridor, and her heart turned over in her chest. 'Why not?'

She held her breath.

'Because.'

She laughed. 'That's not an answer.'

A frown pulled between his brows but before he could answer, she disentangled herself from his arms. 'It's one night, and then a lifetime.' Her smile almost reached her eyes. Leonidas stared at her, completely silent.

And Hannah stared back, unable to look away, three words whispering through her, begging to be spoken—a question to be asked.

'Goodnight,' she said instead, simply. And she turned away, walking towards the bedroom she'd slept in when she'd first arrived, opening the door and moving into it for what she believed to be the last time.

Of course it did rain in the Mediterranean on occasion. Summer storms weren't unheard of. But the rain that lashed the side of the mansion woke Hannah before dawn, the unfamiliar ruckus causing her to frown at first. She pushed her sheet back, moving towards the window and staring out of it, so fascinated by the sight of everything that had become familiar looking so foreign and unrecognisable now. It took her a moment to realise what day it was. The significance of the morning.

And then, to remember.

To remember who she was marrying and what he meant to her.

She gripped the wall behind her for support, turning and pressing her back to it as fear tightened inside her.

'When Amy and Brax died, my heart died with them.'

His words had been hammering away at her chest from the inside out since they'd come back from Paris.

She'd decided, the night before, that she would marry him and let things play out. She'd had a sense of confidence, a sureness, that one day he would feel the same as she did.

But what if he didn't? What if he was right, and his heart was gone for ever, any kind of love no longer in his power to give?

The rain fell harder and she turned to face it, pressing her forehead against the glass. The rain lashed the other side.

What if he didn't love her, and never would? What if he was no longer capable of love? What if she was about to tie herself to another man who was incapable of giving her what she needed?

Panic flared.

When Angus had proposed, she'd been grateful. She'd been grateful that someone loved her and *wanted* her. That someone was choosing her to be their wife and partner. Since her parents had died, she hadn't felt that, and so she'd agreed to marry him out of gratitude rather than love.

She'd known that, and it hadn't mattered. She'd valued feeling wanted above anything else.

But he hadn't really wanted her. Not enough. He'd betrayed her before they'd even said their vows—he hadn't deserved the trust she'd placed in him.

And Leonidas?

Hannah stepped away from the window, padding back to the bed, sitting down on the end of it and looking at her feet. She'd painted her toenails pale pink the day before, thinking how nice they'd look through the strappy sandals she planned to wear for her wedding.

Leonidas didn't want her. If she hadn't been pregnant, they'd never have seen each other again. The thought made her gasp into the bedroom and she held a hand over her stomach, because that very idea seemed impossible to contemplate.

Hannah could no longer disentangle her life from Leonidas's.

They were like roots from neighbouring trees, intertwined and interconnected, dependent on staying where they were for life.

But what if he didn't—wouldn't—couldn't love her?

She'd decided the night before that she would simply wait. Wait for him to realise what they were, what they shared. But could she really do that?

Hannah pushed up from the bed, knowing in her heart what she'd known even over dinner on the terrace.

She couldn't.

She couldn't do this if he didn't know how she felt. She had to be honest with him. She had to...she had to tell him.

And words she'd bit back the night before refused to be silenced now, so she closed the distance between their rooms quickly and pushed the door inwards without knocking, too distracted to wonder how she might find him, her thoughts churning through her.

He was standing with his back to her when she entered, wearing only a pair of grey boxer shorts, his body momentarily robbing her of the ability to think straight. He held a square piece of plastic paper in his hands and, at the intrusion, moved quickly to place it down on the window-sill behind him.

'Hannah.' He was surprised; then worried as he saw the pinched expression on her features. 'Are you okay?'

'No. Yes.' She shut the door behind her, moving deeper into his room, looking at this man and feeling as though everything and nothing made any kind of sense.

'What is it?' He stood perfectly still, staring at her as though he barely recognised her.

'I...need to talk to you.'

His expression didn't shift. 'Okay.'

She nodded, wringing her hands in front of her body, knowing what she needed to say but not exactly sure how to express it.

'I've done something stupid,' she said, shaking her head.

'What is it?' He was quiet, patient, but there was something lurking just beneath his exterior. A darkness that she felt but couldn't navigate.

She expelled an uneven breath and padded across the carpet of his room until she was right in front of him. He stiffened a little.

'Leonidas, the night we met...' She tapered off into nothing, looking at him with eyes that were huge and awash with emotions.

'Yes?'

'It came out of nowhere. I've never done anything like that in my life but I know that there's no way that wouldn't have happened between us. From the moment we literally bumped into each other, I felt this...magnetic pull to you. I know that sounds...ridiculous. But I looked at you and felt like I couldn't *not* go to your room with you. And, once I was with you, like I couldn't not be with you. I feel like, from the moment we met, there's been something bigger pushing us together.'

He was quiet, but she didn't let that discourage her. She'd expected this. She'd known he wouldn't necessarily welcome this confession.

'And then you disappeared and you were angry and I told myself it was for the best. That I was messed up after Angus and so none of this was making sense and I'd made a mistake with you.'

He didn't say it was a mistake, and she was so glad for that, because it would unstitch a part of her soul in a way she'd never recover from to hear those words now.

'But it wasn't a mistake. I never really believed that.' She shook her head slowly, an unconscious smile on her lips. 'I went to London but a part of me stayed on Chrysá Vráchia with you. A part of me stayed with you from that night, and I took some of you with me. I didn't stop thinking about you, Leonidas.'

He stiffened in front of her and there was wariness in his features, a look of panic that was the antithesis of what she wanted, but she pushed on, knowing she needed to do this.

She couldn't marry him and hope for the best—that was what she'd been planning to do with Angus and it had been stupid. Stupid, and a recipe for disaster.

'I don't know if I would have had the nerve to contact you if I hadn't been pregnant. But I do know I never would have forgotten you. I do know I never would have met anyone who made me feel like you did. I always laughed at the idea of love at first sight, but in one hour, you reached inside me and changed who I was. In one hour, you transformed me and I can't marry you today without telling you that I…that this…isn't just about our baby or security or anything so pragmatic and rational as that. This is me offering all of myself to you, for all our lives.' She reached down and laced her fingers through his, as he'd done so often with her.

He didn't speak, though. Her words filled the room, developing a beat of their own, throbbing with the strength of what she had offered him, and every moment that passed with utter silence was like a tendril wrapping around her throat, constricting her airways, making breathing almost impossible. She stood there, her breath raspy, and she waited.

'Why are you telling me this now?'

It wasn't exactly the answer she'd expected, but it didn't matter. Having said what she'd been thinking, she felt as if a weight had been lifted.

'Because I can't not,' she said simply, and his brow furrowed, his expression dark.

'Hannah.' It was a sigh and a plea. 'Don't do this.'

Hannah stood very still, regulating her breathing, trying to stay calm. Because this was important. This mattered. 'I got engaged to Angus for all the wrong reasons. I thought I loved him, I thought he made sense. But nothing about what I felt for him was love. Love isn't a tepid, calm, considered choice. Love isn't a choice at all. Love is a lightning bolt—'

'*Desire* is a lightning bolt,' he interrupted, shaking his head, his expression tense. He took a step backwards, raking a hand through his hair, staring at her with obvious frustration. His body was a taut line of impatience. 'Desire is what you felt for me that night, and it's what you feel for me still. It's clouding your judgment, and you have no experience to discern the difference between that and love.'

'I'm not an idiot,' she murmured. 'I get that there's desire here, too. I know I feel lust as well as love.' She swallowed, trying to order her thoughts. 'One of those things makes my mouth dry when you walk into the room, and the other makes me feel as though my feet are two inches off the ground when you smile at me.'

He wasn't smiling now.

'I was going to marry Angus, you know, even when I wasn't in with love him. I was going to marry him and hope that everything would just work out. I nearly made that mistake once and I can't do it again.'

Now Leonidas was completely still, his face like thunder. 'What are you saying?'

Hannah didn't know, but the words tripped out of her mouth before she could consider them. 'If you don't love me, Leonidas—not even a little bit—if that lightning bolt struck me and me alone, then we can't do this.' Her eyes filled with tears and she found herself powerless to halt their progress. 'If I didn't love you, maybe it would be different, but feeling like I do and marrying you…it would be hell. Every day would be a torment.'

His nostrils flared as he expelled an angry breath. 'We have discussed this. There is so much in our marriage that would be good, so much you would enjoy.' He forced a smile to his face but his eyes remained intent, disconnected. 'You will see the world, travel to places you cannot imagine, and all in five-star luxury…'

'With an army at my back?' she challenged.

'No matter what happens, the army is something you will have to adjust to.'

She shook her head, pushing that aside for the moment. 'That's not enough.'

'It has to be!' He spoke loudly, the words thick with impatience. 'I have told you all along what I am offering. When you came to me in Capri I was clear, and I have been clear all along.'

'Are you saying you still feel that way? That nothing's changed for you since then?'

He regarded her through half-shuttered eyes, lifting his arms and crossing them over his broad, naked chest for good measure. 'Things have changed,' he conceded, finally.

Hannah relaxed, just a little.

'But I don't love you. I'm not free to love you, Hannah. I made a promise to someone and even though she's dead, it doesn't change that. I have told you this as well, and I cannot fathom why you can't just accept it.'

Misery exploded inside her. Hannah drew in a breath, her eyes firing to his, hurt unmistakable in their green depths. He looked away, his jaw rigid as he unfolded his arms and reached for the piece of plastic paper that was on the windowsill. It was a photo, she saw now, and he'd been looking at it right before she'd entered the room.

He handed it to her, his eyes holding a challenge when they met Hannah's.

She turned her attention to the picture slowly, scanning it and frowning as similarities leaped out at her. For the briefest second, she thought the photo was of her, but it wasn't. Close, though.

The woman in the picture was smiling, her lips painted a similar red to the colour Hannah favoured. Her eyes were wide-set and almond-shaped, like Hannah's, and an almost identical shade of green. Her skin was pale, like Hannah's, though Hannah had tiny freckles on her nose and it didn't look as if this woman had any.

Her hair was loose around her face, falling to beneath her shoulders, and it was the exact same auburn red of Hannah's own hair.

Hannah looked at the picture without comprehending, at first.

'Is this Amy?' she whispered, something in the region of her heart bursting, shattering his internal organs with the force.

'Yes. My wife.'

It was just three words, three tiny words, but they were wielded like a machete. Hannah lifted her face to Leonidas's, her skin completely blanked of colour, so that even in the midst of this conversation, he felt a blade of concern.

'Please sit down.' He gestured to the bed, putting a hand on her elbow, but she wrenched out of it, moving away from him, dropping her gaze to the picture. Her fingertips shook and her eyes were filled with tears, making it difficult to focus properly. But she'd seen enough.

Clarity—a different kind of clarity from what she'd experienced last night—settled about her.

'This is what you saw in me that night on Chrysá Vráchia, isn't it?'

Leonidas was quiet.

'If I didn't look like this—' Hannah lifted the photo in the air a little, at the same time she reached for her hair '—you wouldn't even have noticed me, would you?'

Still, he was silent. What could he say? How could he defend this? The evidence was staring back at her.

'Did you think of her when you slept with me?' Her eyes pierced him, the hurt and accusation in them like a physical weapon.

'No.' The word came out gravelled, and it was as if he were being roused from a long way away. 'You are similar, at first glance, but believe me, Hannah, I saw only you.'

She wanted to believe him, but pain was slashing her from all angles.

'But she was in my mind that night. She was a heaviness inside me.' He expelled a long, slow breath. 'That island is where I met her. On New Year's Eve, and it's where I proposed to her. I go there every New Year because I'm a sadist and it's my particular brand of torture. And this year, you walked in and for a moment, I felt like I'd slipped back in time…'

A sob filled Hannah's chest. She was such an idiot! She'd been falling in love with this man, and he'd been living with a ghost.

She groaned, spinning away from him blindly.

He moved after her, gripping her arm, holding her gently, turning her around to face him. 'But that's not why I slept with you.'

His eyes held hers. Even when she wanted to blink away, she couldn't. She was transfixed. Talk about sadism.

'No?' The word was just a whisper. She cleared her throat. 'So why did you?'

'I wanted *you*, Hannah. I've wanted you since that night. I've been tormented by how much I wanted you. And I've hated myself for that. When Amy was killed, I was furious. I swore I would never forget her, never move on with my life. I resisted any woman, any connection with anyone, until you. Even wanting you physically is a betrayal of what I promised myself, of what I owe Amy.'

His words were dragged from him.

'I had a family, Hannah, and they were murdered because of me. Do you think I have any right to close that book and pick up a new one? To simply move on because you're here and pregnant with my child?'

Hannah's heart broke a little more, but for Leonidas this time. He was trapped by his grief, and she couldn't fight that for him. He alone could forgive himself, could work out how to love Hannah and their daughter while still holding Amy and Brax in his heart.

Hannah looked down at the photograph of Amy, and felt a sense of kindredness with this woman, this poor woman. They had both loved the same man, and it bonded them in some way. Hannah handed the photo to Leonidas with an expression that was pure sympathy.

'What would she want?'

He shook his head slowly. 'Amy would want me to be happy.'

Hannah's heart chirruped a little. She stepped forward, so their legs brushed, and she lifted her hands to his chest. 'Then be happy, Leonidas. You'll never stop loving Amy and Brax, and I don't want you to. They're a part of you, and I want them to be a part of our lives. I want to hear more about the little boy who made you laugh, I want to hear about him, I want you to keep him alive within me and one day his sister. You can't live in stasis for ever. I'm here, and I love you, and I'm asking you to open yourself up to this. To look inside your heart and see that I'm there, too.'

She dropped her hands to his, finding his wrists and lifting his palms to her belly. 'I'm asking you to marry me today because you love me, not because you're worried I'll be hurt, not because I'm pregnant. Marry me because you don't want to live your life without me in it.'

He stared at her as though he were drowning, but she was too far away to help him.

He stared at her as though nothing and no one could ever help him. As though he didn't want to be saved.

'I didn't suggest this because I wanted it,' he said, finally, his voice hoarse. 'I can't bear to be the reason someone else is in danger. I shouldn't have slept with you and I shouldn't have got you pregnant, but now that I have and you are, the least I can do is make sure you're safe and looked after.'

His words, so reasonable, so decent, were the polar opposite of what she wanted to hear.

Hannah stared at him for several moments, as the small seed of hope she'd let grow in her chest began to wilt.

'I don't want to be safe and looked after,' she said quietly. 'At least, that's not a reason to marry someone.'

His eyes narrowed. 'You don't think?'

'No.' She tilted her chin defiantly, even when she'd begun to shake. 'I can take care of myself, and our baby.'

'You have no idea what's out there.'

'And nor do you,' she interrupted forcefully. 'Neither of us has a crystal ball, but I know this: if I stay here and marry you, I'm going to regret it. I'm going to be miserable, and our child's going to be miserable. After my parents died, I went to live with my aunt and uncle and saw for myself how damaging this kind of relationship can be. I won't put our child through that.'

'Damn it, Hannah. You agreed to this…'

'Yeah,' she choked out the agreement. 'But that might as well have been a lifetime ago.'

'Not for me.'

She grimaced. 'No, not for you. And that's the problem. You can do this—you can marry me and sleep with me and hold me through the night and not feel a damned thing.' Tears burned her lashes but she dashed them away angrily. 'I'm not like that. This is real to me.'

'So stay for that. Stay because you love me. I'm not going to hurt you. Stay because you love me and I'll spend the rest of my life taking care of you, making sure you are happy in every way. Stay here, marry me. I promise you, Hannah, you will have everything you could ever want in life.'

'I'll have *nothing* I want,' she contradicted, but it was sad now, not angry. She blinked, as if she were waking up from a nightmare. 'I can't do this.'

His eyes didn't waver from hers. He stared at her, and she felt a pull within him, a tug between two separate parts of him, and then he straightened, his expression shifting to one of calm control.

'You must.' He hesitated; she felt that pull once more, as if he were at war with himself. 'I cannot allow you to walk away.'

'Are you going to keep me here as your prisoner?'

He stared at her for several seconds. 'No.' His hesitation wasn't convincing. 'But I will fight you for our child. I need to know she's safe, Hannah, and only here, under my protection, will I believe that to be the case. I will sue for custody if I have to. I will do everything within my power to bring her to this island—I would prefer it if you were a part of that. For our daughter's sake.'

She drew in a breath, her eyes lifting to his as those words sliced through her. Words that made her body feel completely weak. The idea of someone as wealthy and powerful as Leonidas Stathakis suing her filled Hannah with a repugnant ache.

But then, she was shaking her head, and her heart thudded back to life.

'No, you won't. You're not going to drag me through the courts and make my life a living hell. You're not going to do anything that will garner the attention of the press, that will expose our daughter to harm. I don't mean physical harm. I mean the kind of harm that will befall her when she's twelve and goes on to the Internet and sees those stories. Do you think I don't know anything about the man I've fallen in love with?'

His jaw throbbed.

'You're not going to do that. You're not going to threaten me and you're not going to take her from me.' She swept her eyes shut, exhaling as she realised how right she was. 'You're a good person, Leonidas, and you're not capable of behaving like that. Whatever you might feel, you know our daughter belongs with me.'

'And not with me?' he prompted.

'Yes, with you, too,' she said simply. 'And we'll work that out. We'll work out a way to share her properly, to give her everything *she* deserves. For my daughter I would do almost anything—on Capri, I thought I'd even marry you for her. I thought needing her to have a "proper family" and to know her safety to be assured meant this marriage was essential.' She stared up at him, her eyes suspiciously moist, her voice unsteady. 'But I've got to know myself this week. I finally understand who I am and what I want— marrying a man who doesn't, and says he will never, love me would be a monumental mistake; one I have no intention of making.'

Only ten minutes earlier she'd been readying herself to tell him she loved him, and now Hannah was laying the groundwork for her departure.

'You told me this place is impossible to leave without your say-so. I'm asking you to let me go now. Today. This morning. To organise your plane or your helicopter or your yacht, something to take me away.'

His eyes narrowed; he regarded her sceptically for a moment, and when he spoke there was a bitterness in his words. 'And where will you go, Hannah? To Australia? To your horrible aunt and cousin? Or to London where you know barely anyone?'

Her chest pricked with blades of hurt. 'So you think I should stay here because there's nowhere better to be?'

'I think you should stay here because you want to and because it's best for everyone.'

'Not for me. I won't stay and be an instrument of your self-flagellation, another weapon for your sadism. You punished yourself every year by going to Chrysá Vráchia, and now you plan to punish yourself by having a wife you desire but won't ever love, because it would betray Amy. No, thanks. That's not for me.'

He let out a curse and crossed the room, but Hannah was done. She lifted a hand, stalling him.

'I'm sorry I couldn't disconnect my feelings as well as

you did yours. I'm sorry I agreed to this only to change my mind, but I didn't have all the facts.' She reached for the enormous diamond engagement ring that had never really suited her anyway and dislodged it, sliding it over her knuckle and off her hand.

'I'll go back to London,' she said, thinking quickly. 'That makes sense for now. It's close enough that you can see her often.'

He made a noise of frustration. 'I don't want you to go.'

'I know that,' she whispered. 'But can you give me any reason that's good enough to stay?'

He didn't say anything, his eyes running over her face as if he could see inside her soul and find some way to induce her to remain. But there was none—not that he could give her.

'I have a house in London,' he said, his eyes dropping to her lips before he tore them away, looking over her shoulder. 'You should take it.'

'No, thanks.'

'Hannah,' he groaned. 'You're the mother of our child. I need you to be somewhere safe. Somewhere decent. Just… take the damned house for now. We'll sort out the paperwork later.'

'Once she's born,' Hannah compromised quietly. 'But my room is still available. All my stuff is still in it, in fact. I can go back and it'll be like nothing ever happened.' Her smile hurt, stretching across her face, filling her with grief.

'And what of your safety? Do you no longer care for that?'

She felt her stomach twist because he was doing everything he could to get her to stay—but for all the wrong reasons. 'I presume you fully intend to send guards to watch over me?'

He dipped his head in silent concession.

'I will cooperate with you on security, Leonidas.' Her eyes scanned his face. 'I'm not an idiot. If there's even a chance anything will happen to her because of who you are then I want all the help in the world to keep her safe. But that doesn't require marriage. It doesn't mean I have to stay here—with you.' She swallowed, a surreal sense of disbelief that this was happening taking over her.

He swore in Greek, bringing his body to hers, pressing their foreheads together, his eyes shut. 'We can make this work.'

But Hannah knew it was a lie. Not an intentional deceit, so much as a desire to give her what she needed without losing any part of himself. He didn't want to hurt her. He was a good person, and this hadn't been in his plan.

She swallowed past the lump in her throat, a throat that was raw and stinging. 'No, we can't.' She lifted up on her tiptoes then, because she couldn't resist, and pressed a kiss to his cheek. 'But at least we can say we tried.'

CHAPTER THIRTEEN

THERE WERE NO photos of Amy and Brax in any of his homes for one very simple reason. Leonidas needed no photo in order to see them. They were burned into his retinas, his brain, his heart and soul. He saw them readily, and without any effort.

And now, Hannah was there too, and she was imprinted in a way that was impossible to scrub. He fell asleep with her smiling behind his eyelids and woke up with a start, seeing her visceral, deep pain on that last morning.

Her words were a whisper in his ears all day long. *'I'm here, and I love you.'*

Leonidas had become used to the torment of this—and it was a different torment, because, unlike Amy and Brax, Hannah was out there, within reach, a living, breathing person who loved him.

And he wanted her.

He needed her.

But he wasn't messed up enough to know he didn't deserve her. That he couldn't do that to her. Not when she'd fallen in love with him.

She deserved love. Hadn't he known that all along? Hadn't he wished she hadn't fallen pregnant to him purely because he knew she deserved to meet someone who would dedicate their life to loving her? Completely, unreservedly, in every way? She'd find that person, he was sure of it.

And what would happen then? Leonidas wondered. In

fact, in the month since Hannah had left the island, Leonidas had thought about that a lot. When he wasn't drinking Scotch and glowering at the ocean, or snapping at the domestic staff and firing off ill-thought-out emails, he was imagining what Hannah's life post-Leonidas might look like.

Twice she'd agreed to marry the wrong man. Twice she'd let her kind, good heart lead her down the garden path.

Would third time be the charm for her? She was mesmerisingly beautiful, kind, funny, intelligent. She deserved someone who loved her. And their daughter?

Pain gripped his chest, because of course their daughter would be a part of that package. If Hannah met and married someone else, his daughter would have a stepfather. The idea filled him with sawdust, but even that wasn't enough. He couldn't go after her simply because he didn't want anyone else to have her.

He wasn't a spoiled three-year-old.

She'd fallen in love with him even though he didn't deserve that love, even though he could never give it back. She'd fallen in love with him and the kindest, fairest thing Leonidas could do for Hannah was accept her decision to leave.

He had to let her go.

'*Christós*, don't go easy on him, will you?' Thanos asked Leonidas.

Leonidas, sitting at the head of the table in one of the boardrooms of their London offices, threw his brother a quizzical expression.

'Did you see his hands shaking? He turned violet from rage.'

Leonidas shrugged. 'He wants to do business with us? Then he needs to lower his rate.'

Thanos laughed. 'I've never seen you quite like this.'

Leonidas compressed his lips. His personal life was a mess but that didn't mean his business life had to be. He'd become some kind of monster since Hannah had left the island—working eighteen-hour days seemed like the best way to put her out of his mind.

Every morning he'd woken to the security briefings, reporting on her whereabouts. Their only communication had been through his lawyers—him transferring a town house in London to her name, her not wishing to accept. He'd wanted to text her. To call her.

Hell, he'd wanted to see her. He'd wanted to see her so badly he'd felt as if he were running a marathon uphill, every single day that passed in which he didn't give into his impulses and get on a flight and go to London, knock on her door and demand she marry him after all.

He was a tyrannical CEO, so why not make it impossible for her to refuse marriage? Threaten harder, demand more.

But every time he imagined doing exactly that, he saw her as she'd been that last morning, her heartbreak evident in every line on her face, her softly spoken words when she'd told him he was a good person, that he would never hurt her.

And she was right about that—he couldn't hurt her. So he'd let her go, as he'd known he should. And every month that passed had filled him with an increasing ache, a desperation that was tearing him apart.

He needed her, but it was a selfish need, just as it had been all along.

He'd taken what he wanted from her, using Hannah to fill in the gaps of his soul without realising he was only adding to her own pains. He was becoming yet another thing she would need to get over.

He wanted to speak to her, but how could he? He took

his cues from her and she was refusing to so much as acknowledge his gifts.

This week, however, had been by far the hardest. Three months after she'd left the island, a whole season later, he'd come to London. And he'd gone to bed every night looking out on this ancient city, knowing that she was only miles away. Imagining her, and the roundedness of her belly, the sweetness of her face in repose, the sound of her husky breathing.

He had tormented himself with her nearness—and the knowledge he had no right to see her. That he was here in London and not at her side.

'Leonidas.' He looked up as his brother's assistant entered the room. Belinda, somewhere in her fifties with pale hair and a permanently disapproving scowl, had worked for Thanos for almost a decade and it showed. She was tired and almost on the brink of a nervous breakdown—keeping Thanos's life on the rails could not be an easy occupation. At least they compensated her well for such a chore. 'Greg Hassan's on the phone for you.' She nodded sternly towards the receiver on a bench in the corner of the room.

'Thank you.'

Leonidas moved quickly across the room, telling himself not to panic even as the taste of adrenalin filled his mouth.

'What is it?' He had no time for pleasantries.

'Hannah's been rushed to hospital. Her waters broke.'

'What hospital?'

Hassan gave the name. Leonidas slammed the phone down and grabbed his coat without saying a word.

'Leo?' Thanos was right behind him. 'What's up?'

'The baby's coming.'

Thanos's smile was huge but Leonidas shook his head. 'It's too early. There's still a month to go.'

Panic wrapped around him. 'Stay here. I'll let you know.'

'Screw that.' Thanos's voice was firm. 'No way.'

Leonidas didn't want company, but he knew better than to argue with Thanos. Besides, he didn't have the energy and he didn't much care. He just needed to get to Hannah, to know everything was okay.

It was peak hour and the hospital was across London. 'Helicopter,' he muttered, shouldering out of the office with an impatience that was overtaking his soul.

Thanos didn't say a thing, simply nodded and took out his phone, giving orders for the helicopter to be readied. On the roof, they climbed into the sleek black chopper and it fired to life.

'Which hospital?' their pilot asked.

Leonidas repeated the name and the pilot lifted off. Thanos turned to Leonidas, his own features taut. 'Try not to worry, Leo. You'll be there soon.'

It didn't feel like soon enough to Leonidas. Despite the fact the helicopter cut through the sky like butter, he couldn't believe he'd ever let her leave him, leave the island. He couldn't believe she'd gone into labour on her own— that he hadn't been there to help her.

Finally, the chopper touched down on a neighbouring roof to the hospital. The engine wasn't even cut before Leonidas was jumping down, keeping bent low as he ran across the roof.

Thanos caught up to him as the elevator doors opened and neither spoke as the lift careened to the floor. Thanos ran the rest of the way, his heart pounding with every step he took.

'Hannah May,' he said as he arrived, the reception desk mercifully quiet.

'What ward?'

'I don't know.' Leonidas raked a hand through his hair.

'Obstetrics.' Thanos, right behind him, spoke more calmly.

'Let me see.' The nurse moved slowly, pressing her finger to a clipboard, a frown on her face. 'I don't see her.'

'She was brought in earlier. She must be here,' Leonidas demanded.

'Could you check again?' Thanos suggested, putting a hand on Leonidas's chest and pushing him a little away from the counter. His eyes held a warning—a suggestion: *I'll handle this.*

Leonidas paced from one side of the reception to the other, cursing in his head, adrenalin coursing through his veins.

'This way,' Thanos interrupted him, nodding towards the lifts. They went as fast as they could but everything in this old building was slow. When they reached the obstetrics ward and found the corridor they needed to walk down was closed because of mopping, Leonidas almost shouted the hospital down.

'Calm down,' Thanos insisted.

Yeah, right. When they arrived at the desk for the obstetrics ward, Thanos joined the back of a long queue to find out where Hannah was but Leonidas moved through the doors, and he stood stock-still. Because he heard her. He heard her cries and his heart jerked out of his chest.

A scream, pain; he was running down the corridor towards her voice, so close, his hand reaching for the door.

'You can't go in there, sir.' A man was running behind him, an older man, frail. Despite his security guard uniform, Leonidas didn't think he'd have much chance of stopping a terrified six-and-a-half-foot man in the prime of physical fitness.

'Try and stop me.'

'Sir, stop.' A woman now—a nurse. 'This corridor is off limits to visitors.'

'I'm not a damned visitor. My…' *Christós*, what could he call her? Not his wife. Not his fiancée. She was nothing to him now, just as she'd wanted. His chest rolled. 'My daughter is being born in here.' He hiked his thumb towards the door.

Thanos appeared behind the frail security guard.

'And if you wait in the reception, we'll let you know as soon as your baby arrives.'

He swore angrily. 'No. I want to be in there. Hannah needs me.'

For a moment, the nurse's face flashed with sympathy, but then she was all business again. 'Miss May was very clear on this point. There was no one she wanted called, no one she wanted notified. She told me she is alone.'

Leonidas couldn't meet his brother's eyes. Pain and raw disbelief filled him as he digested this, feeling the rejection of that statement, the line she'd drawn in the sand excluding him from this moment—knowing he deserved no better.

'Tell her I'm here. Please.' The words were hoarse, his stomach rolling, his expression full of desperation.

The nurse relented. 'I will. Please go and wait in reception for now.'

'But I—'

'This is not your call,' the nurse insisted with a quiet firmness in her voice. 'If she wants to do this on her own, you have to accept it.'

Leonidas stared at the nurse, then at the doors, then back at the nurse. Hannah's scream tore through the air and Leonidas felt an agonising need to go to her, to hold her, to do *something…anything* to help her.

'Please.'

'It's not my call.' She lifted a hand to his chest. 'I'll tell her you're here. Go and wait for me out there.'

Every bone in his body railed against this; every fibre of his being demanded he stay, that he fight her, that he fight to be with Hannah. But she didn't want him. She was doing exactly what she'd said she would—making her own life.

Despair swallowed him up. He stalked out of the corridor and into the reception room, which was full of happy, waiting family members. Leonidas was the only one who looked as if he could murder someone with his bare hands.

Thanos sat on one of the chairs, his calmness infuriating to Leonidas.

Leonidas was not calm.

Every time he heard her cry out his body was a tangle of pain, of outrage and impotence. How could he let her go through this—without him?

What could he do to help?

Nothing.

But that didn't change the fact that he was living a moment of sheer terror, that he'd spent the last three months in a state of agony and now it had come to this. Her pain filled him and worry—irrational, desperate anger at his own stupidity—drove through him like a blade.

He'd wasted time. He'd gambled. And now he could lose everything.

When a team of two nurses ran through the waiting room and disappeared into the corridor, he followed. When they pushed into Hannah's room, his heart dropped. A doctor followed.

Leonidas couldn't bear it.

He pushed into the room, and almost wished he hadn't when he saw the pain on Hannah's face, the look of sheer terror.

'Sir, I told you, you can't be here.' The nurse who was at Hannah's legs shot him a fierce look but Leonidas ignored her.

He strode to Hannah's side and took her hand in his, his eyes burning into Hannah's.

'I belong here.'

She looked up at him, her expression showing him only pain, only hurt, and he swallowed, fear tearing through him. 'I belong here.'

She didn't say anything, so he stayed; he kept her hand in his and she squeezed it so hard he wondered if circulation might completely stop, half hoping it would so he could feel something like the pain she was enduring.

He stroked her hair at times, and she said nothing to him—nothing to anyone—there were only the indiscernible, guttural sounds of her cries.

She dug her nails into his flesh and gave one last, agonising cry, the nurse lifting a pink and red baby with a shock of dark hair into the air, wiping her quickly with a towel and hitting her on the back until a robust cry emerged into the room.

Tears filled Leonidas's eyes, emotions swirling through him. He looked down at Hannah and she was sobbing, but a smile was on her lips as she held her hands out for their daughter, pulling her to her chest. Leonidas had never seen anything more beautiful, more perfect.

They were his family—they were his.

'You didn't have to come.' Hannah had recovered enough from the delivery to be trying to make sense of what Leonidas was doing at the hospital—and how he'd got there so quickly. Seeing Leonidas again was going to take a lot more recovery time. It had been three months. Twelve weeks. So many nights wondering if she'd done completely the wrong thing, wanting to crumble and beg him to take her back, needing him on every level, loving him enough to take whatever crumbs he would give her.

And in this moment, when her hormones were rioting and she was looking at their beautiful daughter, it took all her wherewithal to remember why she'd left him.

To remember that he didn't love her, didn't want her, that his heart belonged to someone else and always would.

He'd mercifully left the room again after the delivery under threat of the police being called, so Hannah could be cleaned up in privacy and transferred to a different room— one that was smaller and less medical in its design.

She was exhausted, but her heart was bursting—their daughter was asleep in a tiny crib across the room.

'Did you think I wouldn't?'

She shook her head.

'Did you really want to keep me from this?'

She swallowed, looking at him and seeing him almost for the first time. He was so handsome but there was a torment in his face that robbed her of breath.

'I was going to let you know once she was born.'

That her statement had hurt him was obvious, but when he spoke it was quietly, gently, and that somehow hurt even more.

'No doubt.'

He paced across the room and Hannah's eyes followed him hungrily before she realised what she was doing and looked away. A nurse had brought a tea in a few moments earlier, before Leonidas had returned. Hannah reached for it now, cupping the mug in her hands gratefully.

'You were in so much pain,' he said slowly, turning to face her, his eyes roaming over her in the same hungry way she'd been looking at him a moment earlier. 'I thought you were dying.'

'So did I, believe me,' she quipped, but without humour. She sipped her tea then held it in her lap.

Leonidas moved to the crib, staring down at their daughter, and Hannah had to look away—so powerful was the image of the father of her daughter, the man she loved, the pride on his face, the love she saw there…it tore her apart.

Tears filled her eyes and she blinked, sipping her tea again, jerking her head away so she was looking at a shining white wall.

'Three months.' He said the words as though they were being dragged from deep within him. 'You've been gone for three months.'

The tone of his voice had her pulling her face back to him, and she saw pain there, disbelief. Hurt.

'Three months and it has felt like a decade.' He swallowed, his Adam's apple jerking in his throat.

Her own grief was washing over her. 'I had to leave.'

His eyes narrowed. 'Because you love me.'

She swept her eyes shut. 'Yes.' There was no sense denying it. True love didn't disappear on a whim. It was love. Simple, desperate, all-consuming love.

'*Theos*, Hannah.' He moved towards the bed and she stiffened, bracing for his nearness. She'd come on in leaps and bounds, was learning how to live without him, but she wasn't ready to be touched by him. She couldn't.

'You don't have to be here,' she said urgently, arresting his progress across the room. 'You really don't.'

'I want to be,' he said simply, walking once more. He stood at her side, staring down at her, and her heart flipped in her chest, heavy with love, pain, rejection, fear, need.

'No,' she whispered. 'You don't understand. You can't be here. It's too hard. I don't want you here.'

'Hannah,' he sighed, looking at her, perhaps innately understanding she couldn't bear to be touched by him, not now, not after how he'd rejected her love. 'I've spent the last three months telling myself I was doing the right thing. I knew you were safe, I made sure of that, and I told myself I had to give you what you wanted. I had to let you live your life away from me because I couldn't return your love.'

Hannah made a small, strangled noise of panic.

'And then Greg Hassan called and told me you were on your way to the hospital and—*Theos, agape mou*—I have never felt anything like this fear and panic.'

He pressed his hand to his chest, staring down at her. 'I was so terrified that something had happened to you and all I could think was how I'd wasted all this time. *Christós*, Hannah.' He dropped his head forward for a moment, catching his breath.

'I've been so focussed on what I lost, so angry at what happened to Amy and Brax, at the fact it was my fault, because of who I am, that I didn't stop to realise how lucky I am to have had that time with them. If I could do it all again, knowing how it would end, I would still choose this life.'

His eyes showed such strong emotions then, and her heart cracked. 'I had a son.' His voice was wrenched with grief. 'A beautiful, perfect boy.'

Hannah sobbed; how could she not? And her eyes shifted to their sleeping daughter, her heart twisting inside her.

'I lost them, and it nearly killed me. I spent four years afterwards living some kind of angry half life. Until I met you, and something shifted inside me, something elemental and important, and it terrified me because I thought the only way I could atone for what happened to Amy and Brax was to keep myself walled off from anyone for the rest of my life.'

Another sob escaped Hannah.

'I avoided human contact, I was rude and arrogant, an impossible bastard. And then I saw you…'

His eyes held hers and Hannah was back on Chrysá Vráchia, the power of that moment, of their connection, searing her blood.

'Greg Hassan called and told me you'd been rushed to hospital and I thought something had happened to you, and I realised I've been shutting myself off to what I have no doubt would be an incredible life with the woman I love because I'm afraid of what *might* happen.'

Hannah's eyes flared wide, her expression showing disbelief and confusion.

'That lightning bolt got me too, Hannah. It struck me and I have been trying to pretend it didn't, fighting you this whole way.'

She shook her head but now he bent down so their faces were level, and so close she could feel his warm breath fanning her cheek.

'You are so brave—do you know that? To have been hurt like you were by Angus and still put yourself out on a limb, telling me you've fallen in love with me—'

She shook her head urgently, and, despite the emotions rioting inside her, she was clear on this point, because she'd had months to think it over, to see it as it was. 'Loving you freed me up to realise I felt nothing like love for Angus. How I feel for you is so different.'

'I know.' He leaned forward a little. 'You love me, and you love me even though I have pushed you away, even though I have been stubbornly clinging to a kind of anger that is ruining my life. You love me even when I took your love and refused to acknowledge I returned it. You have loved me when I was so far from being the man you deserved.'

Hannah bit down on her lip, her eyes holding his. 'Love

isn't a choice.' She frowned, lifting a hand to his cheek, because the words had come out all wrong. 'And even if it were, I would choose to love you. You deserve happiness, Leonidas. You deserve it.'

'I wanted to give you everything,' he said quietly. 'When you spoke about your aunt and uncle, your cousin, Angus, all the people who had you in their life and didn't appreciate you, I wanted to scream. You should have the world at your feet; I wanted to give it to you. But you don't really want private jets to Paris, do you?'

She shook her head. 'I mean, that's all well and good, but it's not what really matters.'

'No, it's not,' he agreed, dropping his head to hers, pressing his lips lightly to her forehead. 'All that matters is here, in this room, with you and me. Please tell me I haven't permanently ruined things between us.'

She swept her eyes shut, fear shifting inside her because she didn't want to be hurt again; she didn't want to feel pain.

But nor did she want to live a life without Leonidas in it.

'I'm completely in love with you,' he said. 'Madly, utterly, in every way. I was transfixed by you at Chrysá Vráchia but presumed it was just…that. Infatuation. I couldn't stop thinking about you. I don't know when I fell in love with you, but I do know that from the beginning you have been under my skin and a part of my being. I do know that I want to spend every day we have together showing you that you are the meaning to my life.'

She bit down on her lower lip to stop another sob—a happy one—escaping.

'Life is a gift, and I was wasting it. I don't want to do that any more.'

She expelled a shaky breath, inhaling his masculine fragrance, her stomach swooping and dropping, happiness beginning to flow into her body for the first time in a long time.

'That day on the island—our wedding day—'

She turned to face him, waiting silently for him to finish his thought.

'It was hard. Nothing about marrying you quickly, in secret, away from loved ones, felt like what I wanted. Making you my wife, yes. But like that?' He shook his head, and then reached into his pocket, pulling out a black velvet box. Hannah's eyes dropped to it, her smile transforming her face.

'So I would like to ask you again, Hannah, if you would do me the honour of becoming my wife. I love you with every single part of me. My heart and soul are, and always will be, yours.' He took her hand and lifted it to his lips, pressing a kiss to her inner wrist. 'You brought me back to life and made me myself again. But better, because you've taught me so much about compassion and love, respect and patience. You are so much more than I deserve.'

At that, she shook her head silently, because her throat was filled with tears and she wasn't sure she'd be able to get any sensible words out.

'But I will spend the rest of our lives, however long that may be, striving to be good enough for you, *agape mou.*'

Hannah sobbed then, as he handed the ring box to her.

She hadn't loved her engagement ring—it had been so enormous and flashy. But she'd come to love it because it had promised a future with Leonidas. She cracked open the box and smiled, because it wasn't even the same ring.

Instead there was a single diamond, still large but not break-your-finger huge, surrounded by a circlet of emeralds.

'It's beautiful,' she whispered, her eyes filling with tears.

'Two weeks after you left the island, I was in Athens. I saw it in a window and bought it without even realising what I was doing. I have been carrying it around ever since, as though it made you close to me in some way.' His smile was rueful. 'I told myself I could give it to you as an "I'm sorry" gift, if nothing else. But in my heart, I imagined you wearing it on this finger.' He ran his hand over hers. 'And wearing it as a promise to become my wife, to live this life by my side.'

She sobbed then, and held her hand out, so he could slide the ring onto her finger; it fitted perfectly.

'And this is my promise to you,' he said gently, fixing her with a look that seared her soul. 'I will love you and cherish you, be faithful to you, care for you, protect you, adore you and worship you for as long as we both shall live.'

Hannah nodded, still too choked up to respond with words. And really, what words were needed? They'd said all that was necessary and, more importantly, each felt the truth of their declaration, deep inside their beings—and always would.

The only thing left was to marry, and to live happily ever after.

EPILOGUE

'I KNOW YOU said you wanted me to see the world, but this is more than I ever imagined.'

'Do you like them?'

Hannah gave her husband a droll look before turning back to the golden vista beneath her, her green eyes taking in the flat expanse of the Egyptian desert before focussing on the familiar peaks of the ancient Pyramids. The helicopter hovered at a distance, giving a perfect vantage point over them.

'They're stunning,' she said simply. Because they were. It was hard for Hannah to say which of the countries they'd visited in the past eighteen months was her favourite. They all had a special place in her heart, and for different reasons. Going to a special opera performance at the Coliseum had been incredible, a private tour of the Pantheon had taken her breath away, exploring New York with Leonidas by her side, coming to know his Greek island as though she were a local, snorkelling off the shore, swimming in the pool, learning to speak his language and enjoy his food—it had all been remarkable: but all the more so for having Leonidas by her side.

And though she'd planned to wait to tell him her news, with the ancient Pyramids glistening beneath them, a testament to humanity's strength, intelligence, and determination, Hannah felt the words burst out of her.

'I got an email two days ago.'

'Yes?'

She nodded, pride making her eyes sparkle. 'My application was accepted.'

'Your application…?'

She nodded, excitement a thousand arrows darting beneath her skin. 'Law school.'

Leonidas's smile transformed his face and Hannah's heart clutched at the sight. Love was a lightning bolt, yes, but it was also this—a genuine, complete desire to see your loved one succeed in life. Leonidas had been Hannah's champion, he had supported her, overcome her doubts when she'd worried she wouldn't have what it took to apply for her degree, and then when she'd doubted she'd be able to meet the study schedule.

He'd moved all the pieces effortlessly so she could apply, and still be hands-on with their daughter, Isabella.

Her dreams had become his dreams.

'I never doubted for one second that you would be accepted.'

'Because you're Leonidas Stathakis and I'm your wife?' she teased.

'Because you're *you*,' he corrected, leaning forward and kissing her. 'Brilliant, intelligent, motivated, fiercely strong.'

Hannah's heart was flying higher than the Pyramids, way up in the sky.

She was going to achieve her dreams, and even though she liked to think she could have done this on her own, she was so glad it was happening this way—she was so glad she got to share it all with Leonidas.

Hours later, back on the yacht in the Red Sea, with Isabella fast asleep, Hannah reading in the armchair, Leonidas looked at his wife and felt a quick surge of panic, familiar to him now, whenever he contemplated how close he'd come to losing all this.

He had almost shut the door on love and happiness in life because of fear.

He would never make that mistake again.

* * * * *

THE INNOCENT'S EMERGENCY WEDDING

NATALIE ANDERSON

For the gorgeous Alfie.
You're such a loyal four-legged friend—
the exclamation point completing our family
and the best foot-warmer a writer could have.

CHAPTER ONE

'YOU CAN'T MAKE me marry him. You can't make me marry anyone...'

Katie Collins perched nervously on the plush chair in the vast reception room of Zed Enterprises, gripping her bag and reminding herself to breathe often enough to remain conscious. If she'd had more pride—or any other option—she'd have walked out over an hour ago, but the threats relentlessly circling in her head had forced her to remain. He was the one person who had the power to help.

'If you won't marry him you can leave right now, and you know that would kill her—'

Katie blinked the horror away and focused on her surroundings. Alessandro Zetticci's offices showcased a sleek, minimalist style—steel and chrome screamed masculine sophistication and the wealth he'd accumulated in an astoundingly short time. It didn't surprise her. He'd always had the knack of knowing what people wanted.

It had been a decade since she'd seen him and, while certain aspects of that particular visit were branded in her brain, she was acutely aware that he mightn't even remember who she was. She'd have to remind him before begging for his benevolence.

'You'll be homeless. So will the woman who's spent years caring for you, you ungrateful little b—'

Katie again blocked the echo of the viciousness her foster father had spat at her. Seeking distraction, she glanced at the receptionist. Dressed in a sleek navy skirt and smooth white blouse, the tall blonde looked like a chic French movie star, ageing with impossible grace. Katie was also wearing a navy skirt with a white blouse, but where the receptionist's was silk, Katie's was synthetic, and right now it was sticking to her. Outclassed, out of place...she was never quite good enough—

Katie stiffened, snapping out of the self-pity. She didn't need fancy clothes, given she worked in the orchards and the kitchen most of the time.

'You can't refuse after all I've done for you—'

A trickle of sweat slithered down her back, even though the building was beautifully climate-controlled. Her body was literally leaking her nerves. She uncurled her grip on her bag for the twentieth time. Only to immediately clutch the strap again as if it were her lifeline.

She'd not made an appointment, and it was sheer luck that Alessandro was in the office at all today. Too late she realised she had no idea what she'd have done if he hadn't been. She still had no idea what she was going to do if he said no.

'Don't you want to be a real member of the family?'

That attempt at manipulation had stabbed deep. So after all this time Katie was still an outsider? She'd always felt Brian hadn't wanted her, but for him to state it so explicitly, for him to try to force her into doing something insane... She was still an outsider. Still just someone who *owed*...

'Do you want to watch her devastation?'

And that was the problem. She did owe Susan, her foster mother. She more than owed her—she loved her, and she had to protect her.

'Ms Collins?' The elegant receptionist finally interrupted her anxious reverie. 'Alessandro is ready to see you now.'

Katie's heart skidded. She was seized with the urge to bolt in the other direction. Instead she followed the older woman, drawing in a deep breath as she went.

It was a good thing she did, because the second she walked into his office her lungs, like the rest of her, were rendered immobile. She'd looked at recent pictures on the train ride here, so she'd thought she'd be immune. She'd been wrong. Alessandro Zetticci in the flesh was overwhelming.

Katie couldn't smile as the receptionist left—couldn't even see what the room was like, because she couldn't peel her gaze from where he stood behind his desk. Flashes of rogue memory burned. Alessandro in the orchard. His smile. His low laugh. His broad shoulders...

She blinked, desperately focusing on him here and now and *clothed*.

His jet-black hair was straight and long enough to flop in his eyes. His sculpted cheekbones were emphasised by the razor-sharp edge of a perfectly symmetrical, masculine jaw. Lightly stubbled rather than clean-shaven, he looked as if it wasn't long since he'd left his bed. Long black lashes and dark eyebrows framed his arresting eyes. Powder blue, they were brightly backlit by fierce burning intensity.

If she hadn't known better she'd have thought he wore coloured contact lenses, but Katie had seen him sullen and silent over the breakfast table and at Christmas dinners long gone by, and even then, when he'd been moody and resentful, his eyes had glowed with that brilliance.

His mouth had a natural sinful curve, a permanent wicked half-smile—as if he were thinking something slightly inappropriate. It was a mouth made to kiss. Katie remembered that.

The top button of his white shirt was undone, exposing a deeply tanned neck. That tan was an all-over one. Katie remembered that too.

The man was appallingly handsome. The kind of gorgeous rarely seen in the streets, that made ordinary people turn for a second, third, fourth look.

But it wasn't only his smouldering looks that drew people's attention. It was the energy that crackled from him. He had vitality—a kind of fire that drew everyone around him in. It was what had made his empire so massive, so quickly. Because of that smile and that aura of amusement, everyone wanted to lean closer, seduced by the self-assurance that glowed in his eyes.

More than self-assurance he had arrogance—a pure don't-give-a-damn attitude that made him impossibly popular and his investments an unparalleled triumph. He looked ready for something far more enjoyable and intimate than business. He looked like a man with a wicked ability to have a good time. And he followed through on that appearance. He was irresistible—catnip to pretty much every woman in the world. And he was happy to be played with. But never caught.

Katie *definitely* remembered that.

Yet Alessandro Zetticci had faced hardship too. Katie was counting on that fact to make him human. Make him understand. Make him want to *help*.

Now she blinked again, breaking the mortifying immobility his appearance had engendered and stepped deeper into his domain. He didn't greet her—didn't say anything. His swift glance seemed to take her in and dismiss her all in one second.

'I'm Katie Collins,' she began, her embarrassment blooming in the face of his uncharacteristic frigidity. 'I live at White Oaks Hall with Brian Fielding—'

He still didn't smile. 'I don't need you to remind me who you are, Katie.'

'I wasn't sure you'd remember—'

'How could I possibly forget?' Displeasure and disapproval flashed in his eyes.

Faltering at his unfriendly demeanour, Katie licked her dry lips. She'd done nothing to him. Certainly she'd *meant* nothing to him.

Alessandro Zetticci had stalked into Katie's life when he was a sullen fifteen and she a very shy ten. His father, famed Italian chef Aldo Zetticci, had just married Brian's sister Naomi. Brian and Naomi were close, so Aldo and Alessandro had joined the extended Fielding family for holidays at White Oaks—much to Alessandro's obvious resentment.

Only a couple of years later Aldo had died. Alessandro and Naomi had then clashed on the future of his father's food empire. Brian had backed Naomi. Petulant and fiery, Alessandro had fought hard, flaring up at Brian's interference.

'If you go now, you'll never be welcome back here.'

Brian's banishment of Alessandro had terrified her at the time.

'Don't mention him again.'

Brian had whirled on her when she'd fearfully asked where Alessandro had gone. She'd been too young to understand everything, but had known that in no way had it all been Alessandro's fault. In any case, Alessandro's ideas for his father's company couldn't have been that bad, given he'd gone on to build his own business with such success.

He'd always been determined and strong. But from the look in his eyes now he was also unforgiving.

Katie cleared her throat and forced herself to speak anyway. 'I have a proposition for you.'

One jet-black eyebrow arched. 'How intriguing.'

His tone couldn't have sounded *less* intrigued or any more dismissive.

Irritation stiffened her. She was too desperate to cope with casual dismissal. 'I work at White Oaks,' she carried on. 'I've developed some sauces made from our produce. They sell very well.'

She paused, because so far he was bored-looking. Her desperation swiftly blew up to all-out pain.

'Cut to the chase, Katie,' he drawled. 'What do you want from me?'

She was so thrown by the reality of Alessandro in the flesh, so intimidated by that look in his eyes, that she forgot the little speech she'd carefully prepared to try to convince him. It just tumbled out with no further preamble.

'I want you to marry me.'

His eyes widened, the black heart of his pupils all but swallowed the fiery brilliant blue. The rest of him didn't move. He didn't even seem to be breathing.

'Not for real of course,' she hastened to add awkwardly. 'In name only. And not for long.'

'You want me to marry you?' he repeated slowly. 'That was *not* what I expected you to say.'

Katie tensed, unable to read his expression, but then he threw back his unfairly handsome head and laughed. It seemed he'd not heard anything as entertaining in eons. And it was utterly insulting.

Scalding emotion curdled the raw acid in Katie's stomach. All her life she'd strived to meet everyone else's requests and demands as she'd desperately tried to fit in and stay safe. But in this instance she was sick of staying silent and being good. Because almost no one ever asked what *she* wanted.

Fury filled her, fuelled by total humiliation. 'I'm so glad I could give you a joke for the day,' she spat sarcastically. 'Forget I ever said anything.'

'I'm unlikely to ever forget that.'

He strolled around his desk with deceptively casual strides, swiftly moving to where she stood, only three feet into his office.

'What are you doing?' Her voice veered up in an embarrassing squawk as he stepped deep into her personal space.

He didn't reply. Instead he surveyed her dispassionately, rather as if she was a curiosity in a natural history museum. Then he leaned closer still.

'Are you *sniffing* me?' Outraged, she flinched away from him.

'Yes. Have you been drinking?' He reached out and grasped her chin.

Katie stilled, attempting to fix him with a furious gaze.

Unconcerned, he turned her face to one side then the other, intently studying her features. 'On drugs?'

'What? *No*.' She jerked free of his hold. 'Look, I'm perfectly sane.' The truth slipped out, and so did all the hurt and hopelessness. 'I'm just in trouble, and you're the only person I could think of who might be able to help me. Obviously you can't, so I'll leave now.'

She turned sharply as emotions whacked her with a one-two punch. She'd never been as embarrassed or as violently angry. She suddenly spun back, slamming her fury into his face.

'I don't know why I thought *you'd* understand the desire to protect the person you love most—to prevent her losing the thing she loves more than anything,' she yelled at him. 'I don't know why I thought *you'd* ever understand that!'

He stared at her for a long second, his mouth compressed. Sudden emotion flared in his eyes and he stepped forward. 'Katie—'

She shoved past him, rage giving her strength, but just as she reached the door he slammed his hand high above hers to hold it shut, stopping her from storming out. She tugged, but couldn't beat his weight or strength and the door remained sealed. She tugged harder.

'Katie, stop,' he said eventually.

Belatedly she stilled, realising too late what an exhibition she was making of herself. She breathed hard, trying to block the sensations caused by his invasion of her personal space. He was right behind her, leaning so close she could feel his heat. Something insidious shifted inside her. Something deep…something tempting. Something she intuitively knew she needed to ignore.

She closed her eyes in embarrassment.

'You can't just storm in, demand something so outrageous and then flounce off without an explanation. You need to speak,' he added firmly. 'Sit down and start from the beginning.'

She remained locked in place for another mortified moment. He was right. And she'd been so wrong. She should never have come—what had she been thinking?

But he wasn't going to let her leave without a proper explanation. And didn't she owe him that at least? Hell, she was every bit the useless idiot Brian had called her...

Slowly she released the door handle and pivoted awkwardly on the spot. Because Alessandro didn't stand back to give her room to move. He still had his palm pressed on the door, as if he didn't trust her not to try to escape again. He was still so close she almost felt giddy.

Breathe, Katie, breathe.

But she was looking into his eyes and all kinds of confusion clouded her mind. She'd been such a fool to think she could handle him.

He gazed at her, his clear blue eyes compelling and uncharacteristically serious. 'Take a seat and talk to me.'

He suddenly swung aside so she could walk back into the room.

She quickly bypassed him and sank into the nearest chair, her knees strangely wobbly. 'White Oaks is in debt,' she said in a low voice. 'Apparently we're about to lose it. Susan doesn't know.'

'But isn't it Susan's estate?' Alessandro folded his arms and leaned back against the door, still blocking the exit.

'Yes.'

Her foster mother had lived there all her life—had inherited it upon her parents' death. And now, as she faced the disease that was slowly killing her, it was her sanctuary. Katie couldn't sit back and watch Susan lose it.

'But she left the business side of it to Brian when her health began to deteriorate. She focused on the gardens—you know she loves them. All these years...'

She shook her head. She'd had no idea that the estate finances were so dire—that Brian had mismanaged everything so badly and hidden it, to boot. His betrayal hurt.

'He only told me the depth of the trouble we're in yesterday.'

Katie couldn't let Susan lose all that was her love and her life. She'd thought the garden tours she'd organised and the sauce business she'd started would be enough to keep the books she'd seen balanced, but she'd been wrong.

'Brian says he's made a deal. If I marry Carl Westin, Carl will absorb our debt and Susan and Brian can stay at White Oaks.'

'If you marry Carl Westin?' Alessandro pushed away from the door and walked towards her, his gaze narrowing. 'Of Westin Processing?'

'You know him?'

Alessandro looked shocked. 'He's only a little younger than Brian—'

'And a lot older than me, yes.'

'Not to mention unreliable and—'

'Creepy,' she interrupted fiercely. 'I can't marry him.'

Alessandro rubbed his hand across his mouth, hiding the smile that felled a thousand women. 'This is twenty-first-century London, Katie. I don't think Brian can bully you into a marriage you don't want.'

Discomfort clawed at her innards. Alessandro didn't know the subtle ways in which her foster father had undermined her over the years. How did she explain something so complex? Explain that something so important had been shredded by stealth over time? By subtle comments and control?

'There's physical force, but then there's the more emotional kind...' Her throat tightened, shame silencing her. She hated her powerlessness, her lack of real *strength*.

The remnants of his smile faded as he watched her struggle to finish her sentence. 'Your supposed debt to Susan?'

It wasn't 'supposed'. Susan had cared for Katie. She was the first—the only—person to have done that.

Katie had gone to them when she was almost two, when

Susan had finally got Brian to agree to fostering after they'd spent years trying for children of their own. But Brian had never agreed to adoption, and there'd always been the threat that Katie could be sent back into the care system.

In truth, Brian was as controlling of Susan as he was of Katie. It was only that Susan seemed mostly blind to it.

'She's vulnerable.' She glanced at Alessandro. 'She's in a wheelchair now. She can't be left alone for long.'

As Susan's neurological disease progressed, she lived in her own world, safe in the grounds of the estate. A world Katie cared for with her.

'It would kill her to have to leave White Oaks.' Katie had to keep it secure for Susan until the end. 'It's her life.'

She loved her gentle foster mother dearly. Susan had welcomed her, and they'd spent so much time together sheltered on the estate… Though over the last decade their roles had slowly reversed. Katie now read to Susan, kept her company and comfortable. She'd do almost anything for her.

But Katie couldn't talk to Susan about how bad things had become financially, or about Brian's insane plan—she was too fragile to be burdened with that. For a while now Katie had been shielding Susan from several problems Brian had wrought.

'So, if Carl gets you, White Oaks stays safe for Susan.' Alessandro summed it up bluntly. 'But why does Carl want you?'

She flinched, hit by a hot flash of embarrassment. Yeah, she was hardly catch of the day. 'You don't think he finds me attractive?' she mumbled, knowing her face was blushing beetroot.

He had the grace to shoot her a rueful look. 'If he actually *wanted* you he wouldn't woo you with an ultimatum like this.'

'Maybe he can't get anyone else to say yes to him? Maybe he thinks he'll get an obedient wife?' she said bitterly. 'This way he'll be able to control me. He's used to getting what he wants, however he has to do it.'

Alessandro stepped towards her, the whisker of a smile in his eyes. 'And you think I'm different?'

A hot fury built within her. 'I'm sure you're used to getting what you want. Fortunately you don't want me.'

He blinked and that smile fully resurfaced. 'How do you know I don't want you?'

She laughed bitterly. 'You never so much as looked at me.'

'If I recall, the last time we met you were little more than a child. It would have been unacceptable in every way if I'd looked at you then.' He angled his head. 'But I'm looking at you now.'

As if that was going to make any difference!

'Don't bother,' she snapped. 'You have hundreds of gorgeous women you really want. All of them. At once—' She broke off, realising she'd got herself into a quagmire of excruciating embarrassment.

'Hundreds at once?' he echoed with mild incredulity.

'Oh, whatever.' She shook off his amusement. 'You know you don't need to threaten a woman to get your way with her. You don't need to use blackmail—emotional or otherwise.'

'But that's what Brian does to you.' All amusement had dropped from his expression.

She drew in a deep breath and sighed. 'He's used to me doing what he says.'

Because she'd always worked to keep the peace, for Susan. But in asking this of her Brian had gone too far. It wasn't a business deal he'd arranged, it was marriage— intimate and personal. And Brian's brutal response to her refusal had horrified her. So she'd decided to figure out a deal of her own with the one man Brian despised. The only man she'd been able to think of.

'But you're not his daughter,' Alessandro said.

'Thank you for that reminder,' she said stiffly, swallowing back the burn of pain.

It was stupid how much it hurt. There'd always been those little comments from Brian—constantly reminding her that she wasn't family, that she had to be grateful and good, keep her on her best behaviour... The few times she'd tried to fight back, he'd squashed her.

'I'm no blood relative to *any* of them.'

And that was what gave Brian even more power over her.

'You don't think of me as family?' Alessandro asked.

She glanced up at him. 'You weren't there. How could you be?'

Alessandro had only appeared from boarding school during holidays and formal occasions. Her aloof 'step-cousin' couldn't have been less interested in forming a relationship with his new family.

'And thank you for *that* reminder,' he echoed with a soft jeer. An arrogant smile curved his lips for a fleeting second. 'I chose to leave—why can't you?'

'I'm not like you,' she said. 'I can't just walk out. I can't talk to Susan about it—she doesn't know about any of this.' Katie was protecting her on several levels. 'I'd buy out the debt myself, if I could, but I have hardly any money.'

His gaze narrowed. 'You said your sauces sell well?'

She bristled at his belittling tone. 'They do okay. They're even stocked in Sybarite, here in London.'

She'd been so delighted when the gourmet deli had put in a repeat order only a week ago, taking almost all her stock.

'Sybarite? Wonderful.' He said with light mockery. 'Then why aren't you paid accordingly?'

'I put all the profit back into the business... I don't need a lot personally.'

His eyebrows shot up.

'I live in,' she explained irritably. 'I have accommodation and food. I don't need fancy things.'

He skimmed a glance over her outfit and she shrank at the hint of disdain in his eyes.

But then she fought back. 'I knew things weren't good— that's why I started the garden tours as well. I owe it to them to work hard...to help Susan.'

She'd heard that phrase so many times and Brian was right, she *did* owe them. They'd plucked her from a life of poverty and neglect... Who knew what her life would have been like if it hadn't been for their generosity?

'You don't owe them the rest of your life,' Alessandro said bluntly.

'No, but I love Susan,' she said fiercely. 'And she *needs* me now.'

'There's no one else? Not her husband?' he said dryly.

Katie froze at the disparagement in his tone. 'All the times I've tried to stand up to Brian... In the end I've given in...'

'Because of Susan?'

'Yes.'

But Alessandro was right, wasn't he? She didn't have to sacrifice her whole life.

'I guess because of her...he has a hold over me,' she said lamely.

'And I don't?'

'Of course not.'

But she couldn't meet Alessandro's eyes. He had a hold over her in a way that she could never admit to herself, let alone to him.

'So you think that if you marry someone else then you won't have to marry Carl?'

'Yes.'

But when he put it as baldly as that it sounded crazy.

'Why me?' he asked.

'Because you're outrageous enough to actually do it,' she said bluntly.

No one would expect the infamous playboy to settle,

and somehow she thought he might enjoy that unpredict-
ability.

'And, according to the rich list, you have more money
than you know what to do with.'

'Now, *that's* what I originally expected.' His twisting
smile held little mirth. 'You want me to rescue White Oaks
financially? Why not just ask me for the money? Why do
we have to marry?'

'Because it's a language Brian understands. If I'm not
married—without the protection of a *man*,' she spat sarcastically, 'I'll still be controllable. If I'm married, he'll back off.
I don't want just to be out of reach. I want to be repulsive.'

'Repulsive?' Alessandro echoed awfully. 'And there's no
better way to do that than by marrying *me*? Wow.' He leaned
forward. 'You make it sound so eighteenth-century… Will
you be sullied for ever if you're with me?'

'*Married* to you, yes.'

She'd never forgotten the look of anger on Brian's face
when he'd seen an article featuring Alessandro in the news-
papers.

'Brian will hate that I've come to you.'

He drew in a sharp breath.

Katie suddenly realised what she's said and sent him a
contrite look. 'I'm sorry—'

'Don't apologise for being honest.' He watched her for a
moment. 'You'll do anything to look after Susan?'

'Almost anything.' A welter of guilt swamped Katie.

His sympathetic glance was laced with sarcasm. 'You'd
rather sell yourself to a wealthy tyrant of your own choosing?'

'That's right.'

'So, between Carl and me, I'm the lesser of two evils?
The more attractive?'

A frisson of danger lent steel to his light query. She suddenly felt afraid of something, felt fear slicing through her
too sensitive, too thin skin.

'You're temporary,' she said bravely. 'You like temporary. You never hold on to anything for long. Not women or companies. You take what you want and move on.'

'You really think you've done your research on me, don't you?' He looked down at her, grimly thoughtful. 'How can you go back there if you defy Brian so overtly?'

'I think he'll accept it when he realises his financial problems are resolved. And he'll see he can't reach me any more.' She'd finally be free of his hold over her.

'But what will Susan say about you marrying me for my money? Me, the spurned step-nephew, cast out all those years ago? Won't she be disappointed in you?'

A flush of heat singed her skin. 'I wouldn't tell her... I'd have to...'

'Fake it?' he jeered softly. 'Pretend you're in love with me?'

'It wouldn't be for long. Then White Oaks will be safe and Susan can stay there for as long as she has left. Brian can't bully us into anything. He can't send either of us away if I own it. I'll have the power.'

Alessandro regarded her steadily. 'Sounds like a fine plan when you put it like that.' He hunched down in front of her and whispered. 'But what's in it for *me*?'

She stared into his gleaming eyes, wondering how to convince him—playing to his sympathetic side seemed unlikely to succeed. 'I thought you might enjoy it...' she muttered.

'What—being married to you?' That tantalising smile curved his lips, all arrogance.

She blushed furiously. 'Having revenge on *them*.'

He pressed his hand to his heart in mock distress. 'You really don't think much of me, do you?' he said slowly, but that edge was still in his eyes.

'You don't want to take something from them when they took something from you?'

That glint sharpened. 'What do you think they took?'

'Your father's company.' She swallowed, remembering

that fight and the fury with which Alessandro had stormed out of White Oaks.

There was a moment of pure stillness. She couldn't tell what he was thinking behind those fiercely burning eyes. She only knew that he was thinking rapidly—but what he was thinking was clear only to him.

'Hasn't all your research told you I'm more successful than they are now?' he asked sharply, standing up and stepping back from her. 'I don't waste my time thinking about the past. I don't need their business. I don't need your sauces. And I certainly don't need your insane proposal.'

His rejection hit her in a low, dulling blow. Of course he didn't. Of course she couldn't convince him. She was a fool for having thought this could work, but it had been her only plan. She'd been desperate. She still was desperate.

But in the face of his displeasure she fell back into her automatic safety mode. 'Sorry,' she muttered tonelessly. She'd been conditioned for years to apologise when confronted with conflict. 'I'm so sorry.'

Angrily, he muttered something in Italian. Something that sounded viciously impolite. 'What did you *think* was going to happen here today?'

She had no clue. She'd not really thought at all. The mad idea had come to her in the middle of the night. He was the only man she knew with the resources, maybe the motivation, and truthfully he had been her only hope. So she'd sneaked out early in the morning and caught the first train to London.

'What does Carl say about it?' Alessandro almost snarled. 'Does he know the bride he's buying is so unwilling? Can't you bargain a better deal with him?'

'He came to see me last night.' Her skin crawled at the thought of Carl and what he'd said to her. 'I'd hoped he meant for us to be married in name only, but...'

'He wants you to have his babies?' Alessandro's whole demeanour seemed to sharpen.

It wasn't funny, it was foul, and it made her escape all the more imperative. 'He said he'll take what he wants.'

And apparently he did want her...*like that*.

Alessandro swiftly strode further away from her. 'But you don't want him?'

'Of course I don't!' The thought repulsed her.

Alessandro stood on the other side of his desk, leaning on it. There was a moment as he studied her. She saw him take a careful breath.

'What if you were to marry me?' His expression turned speculative. 'You wouldn't want to—?'

'No!' she interrupted vehemently.

'No?' He smiled at the interruption, and that crooked curve to his mouth was sinful. 'What if *I* wanted to?'

It was horrendous how attractive his smile was—and that lightness to his eyes...

'Really? Does your ego need to get any bigger?' She glared at him.

He'd already said no to her. She already knew he wasn't interested. He was just teasing her now—his amusement was audible.

'We both know you have millions of other options,' she said, completely flustered. 'I wouldn't get in your way.'

His eyebrows shot up. 'Wouldn't you?' he asked dryly, before a soft laugh escaped him. 'You as my wife would be willing to just stand by and watch me with other women?'

She flushed, her brain sending her that one image she'd successfully blocked for years—until today. Because she *had* watched him with another woman once.

She'd come across them accidentally. She'd been walking through the orchards, alone as always, when she'd spotted them lying in a grassy patch beneath a heavily flowering apricot tree. He had been shirtless and his jeans had been undone, slipping down his thighs. The muscles of his broad, bronzed back had moved powerfully as he'd bent over the pretty student who'd been arched beneath him.

Her sighing whispers had been too soft for Katie to decipher from that distance. But she'd heard the wickedness in the tone of his low, murmured reply and the breathless, rapid response of the woman he was bestowing carnal pleasure upon. He'd literally been devouring her.

Katie had frozen—not even hiding—fascinated and appalled at the sight of such complete intimacy—at his raw masculinity. She'd been an extremely sheltered young teen, still figuring things out and not really understanding what she was seeing.

To be honest, she still didn't understand it. She'd never met a man who'd made her want to act so wantonly despite the threat of exposure. To be that hedonistic, that caught up in a moment that she wouldn't care who was around to watch...

After only seconds she'd fled, with the sounds of that woman's delight echoing in her ears.

She'd told herself it wasn't her fault. If he was going to pleasure his girlfriend in the orchard—where anyone could have seen them—well, that was his problem. But she'd flushed almost purple that night, when he'd finally graced them with his presence at dinner that evening, almost half an hour late.

'Got held up,' he'd offered—not an apology, just a careless fact.

She'd seen him again in the village a few days later—with a different girl hungrily kissing him in an alleyway. His apparent infidelity to that first girl had shocked her. There'd been another girl only a couple of days later.

It had taken the young and naive Katie a while to realise he wasn't actually in a relationship with any of them. No commitment, no mess—only fun. Alessandro had been incredibly popular and he hadn't been afraid to make the most of it.

And it seemed every woman who'd crossed his path since was as eager to slide her legs apart and let him do whatever he liked between them... He hadn't slowed down any in the decade since that last summer he'd come to the estate.

Katie's quick Internet search on the train this morning had thrown up a billion pictures of him with a billion different women. All beautiful. All as enthusiastic as anything, judging by the look in their eyes. Alessandro Zetticci was an insatiable, arrogant playboy. Which actually made him perfect.

But he wasn't having her. She wasn't interested in any of that.

Only now he'd rounded his desk again. He gripped the armrests of her chair, bending so that his nose was only inches from her own. Dawning brilliance lit his eyes.

'Would you watch, Katie?' he asked.

Did he somehow know about that awful, embarrassing secret of her past?

'You're trying to intimidate me,' she squeaked. 'It's not going to work. I'm not afraid of you.'

He laughed. 'Perhaps you should be. But perhaps I'm not trying to intimidate you. Perhaps I'm testing you.'

'For what?'

He lifted a hand, lightly exploring her jawline with the lightest touch. 'To see if I can seduce you.'

His touch ought to have been easily escapable, but she couldn't seem to move.

Desperately she quelled the flare of heat deep and low in her belly and deliberately rolled her eyes. 'Sorry. I'm immune. That's why we'd be perfect together.'

'I agree,' he answered urbanely, but his eyes danced with devilish laughter. 'Perfect together. In bed.'

'I'm *not* going to sleep with you.'

'So determined...' His lips curled. 'Afraid you might catch something?'

It was a low, teasing drawl, but there was a sharp warning underlying his tone that made her wary. She'd been offensively rude in her outright rejection of any kind of intimacy with him. But as if it was even a consideration! He was the one being rude now.

You did just ask him to marry you.

And she had implied that he was a complete man whore.

'No.' She flushed uncomfortably, because he kept switching from serious to teasing. 'I'm just—'

'Scared you might like it?' he interpolated with a low chuckle.

Yes, this was the Alessandro Zetticci she'd read about—the irrepressible tease who worked hard but played harder.

'You really can't help yourself, can you?' She glared at him in exasperation. 'You think you can seduce every woman you meet!'

'Most don't need to be seduced.' He shrugged, then muttered with outrageous insouciance, 'Most are willing to let me do whatever I want before I even know their name.'

He was so close his words whispered over her lips...so close he seemed to see all her secrets. She closed her eyes—only to regret it instantly. Because now she was even more attuned to his nearness. His heat. His strength. His will. But she knew his words were designed to shock her, to repulse her. Because beneath the seductive slide of his whisper she still heard that steely anger.

She opened her eyes and glared at him. 'I'm not most women. And I'm not challenging you. This isn't about that and never will be.' She drew in a deep breath. 'If we marry I'll have no expectations, put no restrictions on you. And I'd expect the same for you.'

He straightened, and from his towering height shot her a censorious look as if he'd suddenly become the epitome of virtue.

'I may be many things, but a breaker of promises I am not. Even in a civil ceremony I'd promise fidelity, and I'd never break that promise. If you want me to marry you,

you'd better agree to the same.' He was very curt and very clear.

She slammed her hands on the arms of the chair to stop herself slithering down to the floor. Was he going to say yes?

'You'd—?'

'Honour our vows for the duration of our marriage. Of course.'

'But—'

'Does it really come as that much of a shock?' He pinched the bridge of his nose.

'It's just that you—'

'I've never got married before? No. Never had the desire nor reason to.'

Her jaw hung open. 'Are you saying you're going to—?'

'I'm just ascertaining the rules in play before I decide,' he pre-empted her coolly. 'How many lovers do you take in a month?' he asked. He immediately followed up with another question purely designed to shock. 'I enjoy sex and generally have it regularly. I assume you're the same?'

Katie shut her mouth and swallowed. How could he possibly think that she'd have anywhere near the interest he had?

'The past doesn't matter,' she said briskly, fighting down the all-consuming heat this conversation was creating within her. 'There's only the future. Best not to dwell on what's gone before. I'll not be unfaithful, if that's what you'd prefer. I have no problem with celibacy.'

'Well, see…here's the thing,' he drawled with an impossibly wicked glint in his eyes. 'I don't *like* celibacy.'

'We don't need to be married long,' she said crossly. 'I'm sure six months will be long enough to…to…'

'Ensure you're left utterly undesirable?' he finished for her tartly.

'Get our business affairs straightened out.' She threw him another exasperated look.

'Six months of celibacy?' He clutched his chest and gasped theatrically, apparently appalled at the suggestion.

'Please yourself,' she retorted through gritted teeth, goaded to the extreme.

He cocked his head and that devilish smile spread over his too-perfect face. 'Is that what *you* do?'

CHAPTER TWO

ALESSANDRO KNEW HE was being outrageous, but he figured she'd asked for it by waltzing into his office and demanding not just money but his damned hand in marriage, whilst casting him as an insatiable libertine at the same time. She seemed to think he was some satyr, unable to control his voracious sexual needs.

Her 'research' had flicked his pride, and he'd been unable to resist retaliating by playing it up and making Her Total Primness here blush again. And then again.

Frankly, he'd only agreed to see her out of mild boredom. While he'd remembered her name, he hadn't remembered much else—he'd always refused to spend any time dwelling on that painful period of his past. But his commonplace curiosity had grown acute when she'd determinedly waited almost two hours to see him, and he'd turned his mind to what few memories he had of her.

She'd been a shy little thing, always hiding in the orchard and the gardens of that massive estate. Pale and too quiet. But she wasn't that quiet now Brian was trying to make her marry Carl Westin. And not now *he'd* provoked her.

She was much more interesting when provoked. In fact she'd invigorated what had been lining up to be a tedious day facing a trillion clamouring employees, all of whom wanted a piece of him because he'd spent the last couple of weeks crisscrossing the globe as he shed a stake in one company while acquiring two others. Frankly, he'd wanted a bit of a break.

He'd figured Katie was after money and he'd been right. But her marriage proposal alongside that request had come as a complete shock.

Alessandro had crossed paths with Carl Westin a couple

of years ago and the guy was a total jerk. Alessandro might party hard, but he was upfront and honest about it. He didn't cheat. Carl Westin did—in both his business and his personal life. No way was Katie Collins going to marry *him*.

But, as snappy as she might be with Alessandro, she was vulnerable to Brian's bullying.

Brian Fielding, together with his sister Naomi, had forced Alessandro out of his home. They'd taken the company that should have been his. But, most appallingly, they'd all but killed his father.

He picked up his phone, but didn't take his gaze off Katie.

'Cancel my next appointment, please, Dominique,' he instructed his assistant. 'I'm not to be disturbed.'

His interest was rooted in her absurd request, right? Nothing else. Certainly not physical attraction. From what he could see, given the boring ponytail, she had nondescript brown hair. Her eyes were a mix of green and brown and gold—he supposed they were hazel. And hidden beneath those ill-fitting ugly clothes he suspected there were some tidy curves, but not exactly generous ones.

Alessandro had been with too many women to have a particular 'type' but, even so, if he'd passed her on the street he wouldn't have given Katie Collins a second glance…

Yet there was something about her that was drawing the attention of his more basic instincts. The spark that sometimes lit her eyes, the slight pout of her soft mouth, the luminosity of her pale skin when she fired up… Yeah, it was those unexpected little flashes of spirit. He wanted to see more of them. Actually, to his total bemusement, he wanted to see her sparkle.

What he'd told her was true. He'd achieved far greater success than both Naomi and Brian had in their handling of his father's company. But Katie was more insightful than he'd acknowledged. The chance for a little revenge *was* tempting. He could buy White Oaks outright and evict them all—claim Katie's little sauce company and disband it.

If he wanted to, Alessandro could destroy everything that family owned.

That plan ought to be far more appealing than some mad idea of a mock marriage. But Katie had been desperate enough to come to him rather than run away... She really didn't feel she could. She was desperate. He'd seen it in her eyes, in the way she'd pushed past her natural reticence and snapped at him when he'd tested her. In the way she wanted to do everything she could to protect the woman she regarded as a mother...

That was a desire he did understand. That was the only thing that might actually sway him. Because once upon a time he'd wanted to do that—but he'd failed.

Grimly he shut down that line of thinking. The wound was too deep to heal and too sore to dwell on. He focused on Katie, sitting rigidly in that chair, clutching her bag, too terrified for his conscience to handle.

'Do they know you've walked out?' he asked abruptly.

'I left a note for Susan, so she doesn't worry.'

Alessandro had always thought of Susan as the wraith of White Oaks. She was thin, and had been sort of otherworldly as she'd wandered about the vast gardens, directing operations. Brian had seduced the aging heiress, and he'd married her promising Susan everything. And yet it had come with a price. Because Brian, like his sister Naomi, had the gold-digging gene.

Alessandro's father had lost everything because of Naomi. And now it seemed Susan might lose it all because of Brian, just as her health was deteriorating to the point of complete dependence. And with Katie as her designated carer...

He wasn't seriously considering agreeing to her outlandish suggestion, was he?

But Katie's proposition had fired a reckless burn in his blood that he hadn't felt in a long time. It wasn't all about the amusement of blocking Brian…it was the prospect of sparring with Katie a little more.

'Is there no one else who can be the lucky guy?' he asked.

His question about her sexual appetite had resulted in blushing speechlessness, which in turn had tightened his skin. How innocent *was* she? Surely not completely? No woman got to her early twenties without having at least one boyfriend.

'Or am I the only one you thought of?' he prompted when she didn't immediately reply.

'I don't know anyone else to ask,' she said in a small voice. 'And not many men have your kind of money.'

He stared at her for a second and then laughed, enjoying her guileless ability to cut him down to size. 'Well, at least you're honest about why you're here.'

No sex, please—she just wanted his hard cash. And in return he'd get cold, ruthless revenge.

'We have to keep White Oaks for Susan,' she said earnestly. 'She's vulnerable.'

Once again her loyalty struck that infinitely raw spot he thought he'd buried deep.

'If you do what Brian wants and marry Carl you can keep it all,' he pointed out with ruthless precision, even though every cell rebelled at the thought of her going anywhere near that jerk.

'I shouldn't have to sacrifice the rest of my life,' she said fiercely. 'They'd expect the marriage to last. But it's *my* life. It would ruin my chances of having my own family in the future.'

Alessandro grimaced inwardly. Of course she wanted a family of her own. He couldn't think of anything worse. He had no intention of marrying and having a family. Because, much as he'd disliked her judging tone, she was right—he had plenty of options and he liked variety in his life. One woman for the rest of his days just wasn't going to happen.

'I'll work for them. I'll care for her,' she added vehemently. 'But who I marry? That's my choice.'

More memories stirred, adding to the discomfort brewing within him. He remembered those little digs at dinner. Brian always reminding her to appreciate their generosity in fostering her... Asking her wasn't she so lucky to have been chosen by them? Telling her she'd better remember that and always be grateful, because otherwise...

He realised now that Brian's underlying threat that it could all be taken away from her at any moment had been constant. He had no idea what had happened to her birth parents, but he recalled the mutinous looks she'd sometimes cast at Brian. He also remembered the pleading looks her foster mother had sent her—stopping Katie's rebellion. Keeping the peace, keeping Brian happy, had been essential to her survival.

At the time Alessandro had been too consumed by his own bitter agony of loss to think about intervening. Now he remembered it, and a lick of shame at the emotional abuse he'd witnessed burned.

He'd done nothing about it. But he'd only been a teen himself, struggling to cope with what was on his plate already. And she'd seen something of what they'd done to him, hadn't she? She knew that he'd argued with them, knew that he'd left and never looked back.

He released a tight breath, uncomfortable that she knew anything of that time. It wasn't something he ever thought about, let alone discussed. Even so, she intuitively understood that part of him still wanted to make them pay. She understood because she had that need in common—even if she'd never admit it.

Fact was, she'd been lonely and insecure most of her life. Shy, romantic, idealistic. Of course she wanted a family of her own when she was ready and met the right man. Carl Westin wasn't that man. But nor was Alessandro.

'You know what it's like to lose something—someone—

you love,' she said softly. 'Won't you help to stop that from happening to me?'

Yeah, she knew a little too much about him.

'Are you trying to appeal to my generous nature now, Katie?' he asked, as idly as he could.

'I'm sure you *can* be a kind person...'

Meaning he wasn't most of the time? Her challenge sparked the desire to retaliate, and he was almost undone by the urge to haul her to her feet and into his arms. He'd show her *kind*...

The surge of desire was shocking. And wrong. She already had the unwanted attentions of one man—she didn't need them from another. He'd teased her before, but he had no intention of bullying her into anything intimate with him. No more of those jokes.

He curled his fists and shoved the inappropriate response back down deep inside. 'So, either I do this because I'm kind, and I don't want to see you suffer the same loss I did. Or I do it out of petty revenge...' He sent her a perplexed look. 'You can't have it both ways, Katie.'

'I only said that about revenge to persuade you.' She looked adorably shamefaced. 'I played it that way because you're the only person I could think of who might possibly have a reason to say yes to me.'

He sucked in a sharp breath. Yeah, she was alone and isolated. Didn't he know how that felt? And he'd had far more than her. For the first fifteen years of his life he'd had happy, loving parents...she'd never had that.

His concern for her grew when he thought of Carl Westin's reputation, of Susan's frailty, of Brian's greed...

His father hadn't been frail, but he'd been vulnerable in his own way. He'd badly wanted love. And he'd been taken advantage of just as Susan had.

Alessandro wasn't going to let Katie be forced into marrying anyone. She needed some time out to see her way free of this puzzle. And she needed to feel in control. She obviously didn't feel that she could stand up to Brian for long. Maybe Alessandro could be her temporary fix-it guy. Just not exactly in the manner she envisaged.

He straightened up decisively. 'What exactly did you have in mind? Do we announce our engagement immediately?'

Her jaw dropped. 'You're going to do it?'

'For my sins. Yeah, why not? I'll marry you.' He nodded.

She looked like a terrified deer. She sat utterly still, with her head slightly angled, as if she sensed an unseen predator, was keenly aware of the lethal danger she was in. But then she moved. She almost dived into her bag and rapidly pulled out a piece of paper covered in handwritten notes.

'I've thought it all through…'

She was suddenly a bundle of nervous energy, as if she was afraid he'd change his mind at any minute.

Of course he was going to change his mind—but she didn't need to know that yet.

'I imagine you've thought of everything…' he muttered.

'I didn't sleep well last night, and I had all the train journey to finish researching.' She was so engrossed in her explanation she didn't even seem to notice his sarcasm.

'What's the plan?'

'Las Vegas.'

He stared at her. 'In America?'

'Yes.' She smiled brightly, as if he were a bit dim. 'That's the one. If we have our paperwork with us then it can be very quick. There's an all-in-one hotel and chapel venue. It's open all hours.'

Wow. She made it sound unmissable. And so urgent.

'I imagine you do have your paperwork with you?'

'I do.' She nodded. 'There's a flight later this afternoon. Nonstop. We could catch it…' She petered out as she saw the distaste on his face.

'Are you talking about a commercial flight?' he asked.

'Um…yes.' She stared at him.

'You want me to drop everything and leave *now*?'

Was she really that desperate to escape Brian?

'Would that be okay?' She fiddled with the strap on her horrible fake leather bag. 'We can be there and back in just a few days. I'll be gone less than a week. The sooner it's done…'

She paled as she looked at the screen of the tablet on his desk, and then colour rushed into her cheeks so quickly he wondered if she were unwell.

His entire body tensed. 'Are you that afraid of him, Katie?'

She hesitated. 'I'm afraid I won't be able to say no to him for ever.'

'But you *can* say no to me?' He really shouldn't feel as if that were a challenge.

She nodded a little too vigorously. 'You have no reason to ask anything of me. I'm the last person a guy like you would want in his life. I'm no risk to you and you're no risk to me.'

Instinct argued against that instantly. In fact, he wasn't sure he'd heard a *less* true statement. That feeling was crazy…she was no threat to his business, his career, anything. Yet his sixth sense still warned him.

Did he really want to revisit the miseries of his past when he'd come so far? Would the Fielding siblings come after him?

Bring it on.

'Once it's all arranged with you—once we're married— then I'll get straight back and look after Susan.'

He checked at that comment and shot her a measuring glance. For Katie to spend her early twenties nursing her foster mother round the clock wasn't healthy. She needed her own life, her own career. But he wasn't about to go there—not yet. One issue at a time.

'It'll only be for a few months…to ensure Brian doesn't try anything else,' Katie continued in that rushed fashion. 'You'll get a stake in my sauce company, and you'll get the property in the end—we just give Susan lifelong residency rights. You won't lose any money…'

He waved away her breathy, too-earnest promises.

Katie Collins was in trouble. She just couldn't see another way out of it. If he were to get her out of the country and away from Brian the bully for a while she'd have time to clear her head and see sense. He'd think up a better plan when he was more refreshed too.

'I'm not going on a commercial flight.'

He checked his watch and made a few calculations. He could catch up on some work away from the constant interruptions in the office. She'd get the rest she clearly needed. They'd resolve it easily from there.

'But we can still go today, seeing as you're that impatient.'

'We can?'

Her eyes shone, their amber centres flickering like fire. Her lips parted, reddened and soft, and her skin simply glowed. She was luminescent. Sparkling wasn't the word—she was suddenly stunning.

Alessandro's skin tightened. Suddenly he wanted to get closer and *taste*.

'Thank you so much. I really appreciate your help.'

She sent him a huge smile of gratitude. As if he was some kindly uncle. Alessandro leaned closer, feeling that frisson of danger—of something forbidden—sharpen.

'Don't start thinking I'm *kind*, Katie,' he muttered without thinking. 'Because I'm not. I'm ambitious and I'm always out for myself. Everything I do stems from selfish motivations, so rest assured I'll claim complete payment for this.'

Her smile froze. 'Of course,' she breathed nervously. 'Whatever you want…all you have to do is ask.'

CHAPTER THREE

ALESSANDRO STARED, FLOORED by the husky innocence of her reply. He just needed to ask? He ground back the inappropriate, obvious response. Why was he degenerating into some lame jerk who took every chance to turn the conversation towards the sexual? Why was he thinking of sex at all around her? He refused to be no better than the bastard prospective fiancé she was escaping—full of unwanted amorous attention…

But at the same time Alessandro had never met a woman he couldn't seduce. That wasn't to say he'd slept with every woman he'd met, and he was hardly about to seduce Katie. That would be like a lion playing with a lamb. Disastrous for her and unsatisfying for him.

But as he studied her closer he discovered more—her delicate chin, her high cheekbones—and then he returned to her complex coloured eyes that changed with the light, or perhaps with her mood. Elfin-featured, fine-boned…she was stunning when he teased that worry from her eyes and replaced it with excitement.

And she was as aware of him as he was of her. He needed very little of his vast experience to know that.

Temptation tugged.

No.

He whirled away from her fascinating features, dismissing those wayward thoughts, and picked up his phone again instead.

'Dominique, I need a report on Brian and Susan Fielding, owners of White Oaks Hall—business dealings as well as personal. I also need a complete update on Zetticci Foods. Latest financials, forecasts, reviews, analysis, new product offerings from the last couple of years, plus their performance and internal management structure. The same with any company Carl Westin is involved with. I want *everything*. Email it ASAP.'

He needed information and ammunition.

'I also need the jet ready to leave for the States in an hour. Cancel all my meetings for the next...' He mulled for a moment and factored in the travel time. 'Five days.'

As always Dominique simply said yes, and Alessandro hung up.

'I need your passport.' He gestured to Katie, who was sitting with her mouth ajar. 'For the flight manifest, border control conditions and so on.' He waggled his fingers impatiently.

Katie snapped her mouth shut, wordlessly rummaged in her bag and handed the document to him. As he strode out to give it to Dominique he quickly flicked through it. None of the pages was stamped—which didn't mean she'd hadn't travelled, at least within Europe—but it looked almost brand-new. His curiosity sharpened.

Back in his office, she was still clutching the bag like it was some kind of protective shield.

'Did you leave your suitcase out in Reception?' he asked.

'I...uh...no.' She shook her head.

'You don't have any clothes with you?'

Her eyes widened.

He bit back another laugh, refusing to verbalise the next obvious innuendo.

'Not even a toothbrush?' A hit of pleasure warmed his blood at the prospect of getting her out of that plain skirt and into something that fitted her better. 'It doesn't matter. We'll get you something over there.'

He had five days—an eternity in his usual high-speed schedule. This was a chance to lay old ghosts to rest and to enjoy a mild distraction. Hell, in five days he could easily seduce her into surrender—not complete, of course, just enough to soothe the irritation she'd inflicted on him. She might think he was a shameless playboy, but for all her protests she was not immune.

He smiled to himself. The satisfaction of her acknowledging *that* was going to be good.

All of which proved he'd been working too hard lately. It was past time for some play.

It was all happening so much faster than Katie had imagined—though frankly she hadn't imagined any further than getting into his office, let alone actually convincing him to go to Vegas with her.

But *not* for five days. That was far too long to leave Susan. They needed to fly over today and back tomorrow. She'd suggest that to him a little later, though. She didn't want to say anything that might make him change his mind before they were married.

Nervously she accompanied him to the basement, where a car and driver waited. A few moments later they were on the road to City Airport.

Alessandro took calls for the entire journey. In the majority of them he spoke in Italian, meaning that Katie didn't understand a word, but his urbane, confident tones slipped beneath her skin, stirring a secret response she couldn't bear to acknowledge.

She stared fixedly out of the window, trying to minimise his impact on her senses. He was too handsome, too powerful, too full of wicked humour that made her want to smile all the time.

And he'd agreed to go with her to Vegas.

Get a grip.

But the knots tightened in her stomach as they arrived at the airport.

Another assistant was waiting at the entrance to the private jet terminal and he handed Alessandro a folder of paperwork and a large paper bag. As they walked through the building Alessandro showed her the Sybarite deli logo stamped on the side.

'I'm looking forward to tasting your work.' His lips twitched and he leaned closer. 'Lots of things you can do with sauce...sharpen up even the blandest of dishes, correct?'

She sent him a death look.

He laughed. 'You're easy to bait, Katie.'

Breathless, she failed to think of a reply. Why did she keep reading innuendo into everything he said?

Because he means you to.

He was an outrageous tease. While he'd been intimidating when she'd first arrived in his office, it hadn't taken long till he'd flipped the switch to a playful side that was his natural, wicked self. It wasn't actually anything to do with *her*. Except she kept overreacting.

She had to keep her response in check and not take him seriously—that would be no problem at all, right? All her life she'd played it safe—almost always backing down from causing a scene even when she'd wanted to, rarely disobeying Brian, never fighting back because Susan had been so anxious the few times she had. She'd invariably stayed within the rules her authoritarian foster father had set.

But Alessandro barely seemed to bother with rules at all.

'You own this?' she muttered as they swiftly walked through the terminal and onto the tarmac. To her ignorant eyes the immaculate plane looked brand-new.

'I own a stake in a jet leasing company. Better for the environmental footprint if we share the private planes around a bit.'

He laughed at her withering look of disbelief.

Yes, Alessandro Zetticci had interests in as many companies as he had in women. Fiendishly energetic and astute, he had a knack for knowing what people wanted, what they liked, before they were even aware of it.

She knew he'd used that innate sophistication as a youth and set up his first venue. It had rapidly become the ultimate nightspot for high society, celebrities, models, wannabes... Then at the height of its popularity he'd sold it, taken the stellar profits and reinvested them into a new company—again using that innate foresight.

He created and then flicked on companies with the careless ease with which he traded women. From one company to the next, amassing a property portfolio and personal fortune at the same time.

'What?' Alessandro prompted as she paused to look up at the plane again.

'It's bigger than I expected.'

It seemed massive for just the two of them.

That smile hovered on his lips. 'Oh?'

She shot him another death look. 'Do you put sexual innuendo into *all* of your conversations?'

'As much as I can, of course,' he drawled, the wickedness in his smile deepening. 'Being the lascivious playboy that I am.'

'You're only doing it to antagonise me now,' she said.

'Am I?'

'Or you're just practising your flirty banter. Which you don't need to.'

'Don't I?' A flicker of astonishment lit his eyes. 'Why not?'

No man had ever spoken to her this way, and she'd certainly never answered back. But with a man like Alessandro offence was the best defence, wasn't it? Surely she should fight fire with fire?

She glared at him. 'Any woman with eyes would say yes to you. You don't even have to open your mouth.'

He burst out laughing—all warmth and wicked energy. 'But a closed mouth isn't as good, Katie.' He chuckled again and teased her. 'Don't you want to know what my tongue is *really* good at?'

Refusing to reply, she stomped up the stairs. She was still unable to believe he'd agreed to marry her. But that was him, right? Mercurial, maverick, mischievous. This must appeal to that renegade element within him that enjoyed wild, spontaneous adventures. Indeed, she heard him chuckle again close behind her.

'You react so prudishly, how am I supposed to resist?' he murmured.

She turned her head, taking the chance to look down on him for once. 'You could just try being polite instead of trying to embarrass me.'

He sent her a fake wounded look. 'But, Katie, I'm unfailingly polite.'

She knew he didn't mean it. He was still laughing at her. She had the horrible feeling he knew she was too aware of him. Somehow she needed to keep him at a distance.

At the top of the stairs she shyly followed a uniformed crewman through to the main passenger section of the plane. She drew in a deep breath because it was stunning—luxury leather, gleaming chrome, plush carpet and an outrageous sense of space.

The crewman demonstrated how the extra-wide seats reclined and pointed out the stack of reading material stowed in a gorgeous side table with a glossy finish. Then he showed her a partition further down the back of the plane, beyond which was a beautiful linen-clad bed and a polished bathroom facility. It was pure decadent elegance.

'Thank you,' she murmured as the crewman disappeared back the way he'd come.

'We have three pilots and one assistant for a flight of this duration,' Alessandro explained as he put his folders, bag and tablet down. 'If there's anything you need just ask and it will be done.'

Three pilots? Some oxygen might be good right now.

'Where are they?' she asked.

'Crew quarters.' He sat in the seat opposite the one she'd

taken and smiled as she fumbled with the seatbelt. 'Are you okay?'

'I haven't travelled that much,' she confessed with an embarrassed smile.

His eyes narrowed. 'You've flown before, though, right?'

'I went to Paris on a school trip, but we went on the train.'

'You've never flown at *all*?' he queried keenly, but then he smiled, and it was that wicked one. 'Well, it's always good to begin with the best. Start as you mean to go on, *si*?'

This was definitely the best. And Katie couldn't quite contain her smile as she leaned back and looked out of the window as the plane taxied to the end of the runway.

'You're not scared?' Alessandro asked, watching her curiously.

She shook her head, determinedly keeping her attention on the window as they took off. The view of the city was incredible. 'It's amazing…' she breathed.

After a few minutes she glanced back at Alessandro, absurdly disappointed to see him engrossed in reading something on his tablet. She watched quietly as he swiped through page after page. His frown deepened as he took notes with the pen and notepad he'd balanced skilfully on his knee.

He might be a playboy, but he also knew how to work. That was what those 'most eligible bachelor' articles gushed about—not just his legendary woman-slaying status, but his second-to-none work ethic. He had to be driven to have achieved the success he had in only ten years. How had he managed it? Intelligent, determined, decisive…known for his deals…he was always ahead of everyone else.

She just didn't want him to change his mind. So she sat silently, trying to blend into the background the way she did when Brian was in one of his moods. But she felt hot and uncomfortable, ridiculously aware of that bed behind her.

No doubt Alessandro would bring women on flights

with him all the time—hit that mile-high club time after time in complete comfort. The crew certainly hadn't batted any eyelids when they'd seen her with him. Who knew how many women he'd had in there? It was a den of debauchery.

'You don't want to lie down and rest for a while?' He suddenly glanced up and seemed to pick up on the direction of her thoughts. 'You've had a long day of travelling already.'

'No, thanks,' she answered immediately, her skin burning at the thought. 'I'm fine.'

As he held her gaze his expression turned wickedly quizzical. 'What are you thinking about Katie?'

'Nothing,' she lied.

'So "nothing" makes you blush like that?'

Katie pointedly turned away and buried her nose in the nearest magazine.

Alessandro huffed out a tight breath. He was trying to keep his temper in check, but the reports Dominique had emailed over just before their departure were making it impossible. Brian Fielding might be hyper-controlling over his wife and Katie, but he was very much out of control in his own life. He was one of those jerks who thought he could have it all without doing any work—gambling not only with cards and chance machines, but with get-rich-quick schemes and insecure investments. One of which, ironically, was Zetticci Foods.

His father's former company was in worse shape than Alessandro had realised. While Aldo had been a creative genius—an instinctive, outstanding chef, with innate knowledge and a passion for his work—since his death the company's direction had faltered.

As CEO, Naomi had clearly gone for a splatter gun approach, throwing out a ton of new products and hoping one would hit the market. None had. She'd sacked every one of the chefs she'd brought on board over the years and then turned to her brother Brian for a cash injection.

And what Brian had told Katie was correct. They were on the brink of losing White Oaks, Susan's home and inheritance. According to the brief report, the older woman was now wheelchair-bound and being cared for by family at home. Being cared for by *Katie*—because Brian was regularly travelling to conferences, active on local government board meetings...

Alessandro grimaced. Brian was all about the show.

He glanced up from the report, his gaze unerringly landing on Katie again. When she'd mentioned her sauces earlier she'd lit up enough to nudge his curiosity. He'd got an assistant to track down a sample from that deli and bring it to the airport.

'Are you hungry?' he asked.

She sent him a startled look, then swiftly averted her gaze. He watched with mild incredulity as yet another blush washed over her skin.

'Katie,' he mocked in a low voice, '*you're* the one reading innuendo into everything I say.'

He had to admit he found it both amusing and arousing. The fact that she was so aware of him was a kind of balm—because her effect on *him* wasn't just arousing, it was irritating.

'It's the way you look when you say it,' she grumbled, glancing back to shoot him daggers yet again.

Hugely entertained, he cocked his head and muttered coyly, 'Oh, I forgot...it's my looks...'

'You have no idea what it's like for us mere mortals,' she ground out.

She didn't think herself attractive? He arched his eyebrows at her and waited.

'We're invisible,' she explained when she finally got sick of his silence.

The last thing she'd been to him all day was *invisible*. The more she opened her mouth, the more he was fascinated by what she had to say and by the sweetness of the lips doing the speaking. They looked so lush, and here he was wondering if other parts of her were as perfect...

He was so tempted, so curious to taste and explore, that somehow he'd become every inch the satyr she'd pegged him as. Every thought was related to her being naked and sprawled on a bed before him. Which, contrary to popular opinion, was *not* the way he usually worked. He enjoyed women—always—but he could take it or leave it. He'd never felt desire as if it were an addiction before.

'You know you have power over people,' she added.

'Are you treating me like a piece of meat, Katie?' he muttered, acutely aware of the irony in his accusation. 'Are you sure it's only my looks? What about my money? My charm? My extraordinary intelligence?'

'Let's not forget your outsize ego.'

'Yet you're defining me only by my appearance,' he mocked.

She pressed her lips together. He wished she wouldn't bite back her snap.

'Are you treating me like a toy, Alessandro?' She glared at him. 'Am I here for your amusement? To liven up an otherwise boring day?'

She was so on the mark that he nearly winced. Instead he leaned back in his seat, irritated by his uncontrollable inappropriate thinking and her superficial judgement. Why should he care what she thought of him?

'Is that what women are for you?' she added softly.

'Do you want me to marry you or not?' he growled.

She seemed to freeze. Then she pulled on a tight smile. 'Are *you* hungry?' she enquired, very politely.

He suddenly felt sorry, because he'd scared her into compliance—he'd not meant to, but he'd threatened to take away what she wanted. In that moment he was no better than Brian.

'Always,' he grumbled—and he meant no innuendo in that.

Frankly, he often forgot to eat when he was working flat-out, and he'd been working around the clock these last couple of weeks to pull together some deals. So, come to think of it, he did have a mighty hollow deep in his belly.

She looked down at the table between them and then glanced back up at him. 'Do you want to try my sauces?' she asked.

Her voice sounded huskier than usual, and it was his turn to shoot her a look.

'Really?' He began to laugh, because that had been such a cute little tease. 'Not bad!'

To his delight, she suddenly laughed too. And she was gorgeous doing it.

'Sorry…' she murmured once she'd recovered her equilibrium.

No. He didn't want her ever to be sorry for giving as good as she got. She was prickly, quick to repel any possible suggestion of something between them. But there was something, and now she'd put the image in his head of licking some luscious sauce off her naked flesh. The blast of heat in his body was beyond uncomfortable.

Purely for something to do to distract himself, he lifted four small bottles out of the brown paper bag he'd stashed beside him.

'Nice packaging,' he noted. They looked more professional than he'd expected, with their simple green and white labels. 'Which should I try first?'

She shrugged her shoulders.

He fetched a few small plates from the galley and poured a little from each bottle onto them.

'You don't want a cracker or something to put it on?' she asked.

Or something.

He inwardly growled at his one-track lustathon thinking—had he regressed a few millennia to become some hormone-overloaded caveman? He'd last been with a beautiful woman only a few weeks ago, before work had ramped up so much. It wasn't as if he'd had a dry spell...*ever*.

It's because she said she didn't want you.

His pride was pricked. He hated being told he couldn't do something. Authority issues from the bad days of his late teens, he mocked himself. Being denied something made him all the more determined to do—to take or have—whatever it was he'd been banned from. So, yes, naturally he now wanted to *do* Ms Katie Collins. He wanted it more with every passing minute. But he couldn't be that jerk—she had enough of those in her life already.

Focus on the food.

He tried the apricot sauce first. It punched his tastebuds so hard he closed his eyes, inhaling sharply at the intensity. This was better than good.

He blinked and stared at her accusingly. 'You made this?'

'Well, I have help to pick the fruit—' She broke off warily and coloured.

Diverted, he wondered who helped her with the fruit picking.

But then she continued, 'And I use the kitchen in the house.'

She literally made them all herself? 'Whose recipes?'

'My own.' She sat a little straighter. 'I'm quite good at it... Though really it's the herbs. We grow those too.'

'You have your very own special blend of herbs and spices?' he drawled.

'Is that so hard to believe?' she asked with a little reproach.

He cleared his throat. 'You've done some culinary courses?'

That flush in her cheeks resurged. 'I tried to do a couple of courses at the local institute, but I couldn't leave Susan. So I learned from every cooking channel I could find.'

She tilted her chin with prim defensiveness, daring him

to question her. Her eyes glinted, filling with quiet confidence in the face of his surprise.

'What else do you have aside from these?' he asked, trying to steady his appetite.

'Don't you like them?' she asked, looking as if butter wouldn't melt in her mouth.

'You don't need my feedback,' he said roughly. 'You know damn well how delicious they are.'

Her smile blossomed, igniting a glow that seemed fuelled by something deep within her. 'I *know*, right?' She laughed cheekily.

His gut tightened at her unexpected confidence. Coy little trickster... It turned out that she, like her sauce, was passionate, confident and full of sassy flavour. At least in regard to this. The turnaround from the wet lamb who'd wandered into his office on wobbly legs only a couple of hours ago was astounding. In this moment—in this one thing—she shone.

'Like I said, I use the fruit we grow.' She reached forward, turning the bottles so the labels faced her. 'Those apricots are a heritage variety. Same with the plums.'

Alessandro nodded, slightly dazed. He'd never found discussing fruit trees fascinating before, but he couldn't take his eyes from her. He thought again that she was like her sauces—intense, fiery and sweet.

'Susan's father planted those trees,' she added softly. 'I help her care for them, cook their fruit. I love it.'

And that love came out in the flavour of her creations.

Unsettling long-ignored memories stirred. His father had been like that—guided by instinct and emotion. Alessandro had always been more interested in the business side of things. His analytical brain worked better in bigger picture ways. Katie was self-taught and humble, and she had inimitable warmth.

Another searing shaft of hunger strained his resolve. The

desire to touch her almost derailed his reason. As she blossomed before him he ached to conquer and claim...

A horrible thought occurred to him. Had hideous Carl Westin ever seen her like this?

'Maybe this is what he wants,' he muttered, before thinking better of it.

She sent him a mystified look. 'Who?'

He blinked. 'Carl. Your sauces.'

Her jaw dropped as she stared at him in astonishment. 'You think he wants my recipes?'

No. He did not. But the fact that she honestly believed he might showed just how oblivious to her own beauty she was. Alessandro half laughed, even as he was almost overcome by the urge to haul her out of that seat.

He could have her soft, yielding sweetness beneath him in an instant. He'd discover her true taste. But he swallowed the desire back.

He forced his focus back to the sauces. 'Which is your favourite?'

'The cherry vinegar.' She dipped her finger into the small pool he'd poured onto the plate and sucked the sauce off the tip of it.

Any other woman he'd have thought was making a deliberately seductive move, but there was too much of the innocent in Katie's eyes.

To his total torment, she'd left a tiny smear just above her lip. At that sight all his good intentions melted. He couldn't resist that contrary look in her eyes. Like the myriad of colours it was all reflected there—confidence, caution, humour, haughtiness...and desire. It was beyond temptation.

'Alessandro?' She sat very still as he swiftly rose from his seat. 'What are you doing?'

'Tasting the cherry.'

He braced his hands on the armrests of her seat and slowly bent closer. Hesitating, testing, allowing her the space, the time, to pull away, to say something. She didn't.

Pleasure washed over him and he hadn't even touched her. He gently licked that little smear from her mouth. At the tiny hitch in her breathing he brushed his lips that bit lower, to cover hers.

He'd steal only the lightest, quickest of kisses. A tiny tease…just *because*. She expected it anyway, didn't she? He couldn't let her down, what with all her wild assumptions about him.

'Katie?' he asked, searching.

She stayed still and silent, but the expression in her eyes said it all.

There was a moment, the tiniest of pauses, when his lips were barely pressed against hers at all, and then he returned with a gorgeous, luscious pressure that simply melted Katie. His tongue traced over her lips in a teasing slide until she opened and let him in.

This was a kiss.

This was everything all in one soft touch. In mere moments her heart pounded, suddenly too big for her chest, as he stole—and gave—an experience like no other.

He sparked something within her. A trickle that ran faster, fuller, until it became an intense warmth, flooding her system. She strained closer to let herself taste him the way he was tasting her. He deepened the contact, swirling his tongue into her hungry mouth, and shyly, eagerly, instinctively she matched him.

The dizzying sensation intensified. Delight mixed with heat and an ache for more. She shivered, seeking his touch on her skin. She wanted to get closer and she didn't want this to stop. It was too nice. She'd never experienced anything so nice.

Suddenly she was seized with the conviction that nothing was ever going to be the same. *She* was never going to be the same. He'd awakened a need so intense she thought it could never be met. And in that moment of realisation—

of shocking recognition and burgeoning desire, of undeniable deep need—she moaned.

He suddenly lifted himself away and stepped back.

Katie pressed herself into her seat, desperately putting more distance between them as she tried to recover her breath. She gazed up, dying inside when she registered his casual expression. Why wasn't he breathless?

'You can't... You shouldn't...' She trailed off, unable to scramble a sentence together. Why wasn't he shattered?

It was just a kiss. You're taking it too seriously.

That amused look in his eyes grew as she struggled to regain her sensibility.

'That wasn't fair,' she breathed.

'Not fair?' He returned to his seat and folded his arms across his chest.

'You were only supposed to sample my sauces.'

Instead they'd both discovered he could seduce her with a snap of his fingers. Her flush burned.

'Oh, yes, the sauces,' he echoed with soft irony. 'You really created them all by yourself?'

'Why is that so hard to believe?' she snapped balefully. 'You don't think I can be good at anything?'

'I think we've both just figured out what you're good at.'

She gaped, flummoxed into speechlessness, and felt that wretched burn of embarrassment slide over her skin again. He was so skilled, so charming...no wonder all those women fell into his bed.

Now he smiled at her wickedly. 'If you don't want me to kiss you again, then stop fishing for compliments.'

Her jaw fell open. Was she meant to be *grateful* for his kisses? 'I don't need you to kiss me to make me feel better about myself.'

He reached forward to the plates on the table, swirled his finger in the cherry vinegar sauce and licked it off with a lascivious flourish. 'No, you just need me to marry you to help you escape your evil guardian.'

He made it sound ridiculous. As if *she* was being ridiculous. But she could see no other way to keep White Oaks safe for Susan.

'Yes,' she ground out through gritted teeth. 'And that's *all* I want from you.'

CHAPTER FOUR

BACK IN LONDON it would be almost midnight, but here in Las Vegas it was early evening. Not that there was any sense of time in this city. It was always open…always ready to entertain. And the last thing Alessandro wanted right now was to find himself anywhere near a bedroom with Katie Collins.

He never should have kissed her.

Gritting his teeth, Alessandro guided her through customs clearance and then straight into the limo his assistant had organised.

Their hotel was on the main strip, suitably ritzy and fantastically distracting, with ornate decor and vast, gleaming lounge areas. The receptionist handed him a key card while the porters took his luggage. Of course Katie didn't have any.

He turned and looked at her, standing in the centre of the luxurious lobby. The wide-eyed amazement on her pretty face was priceless.

He never, ever should have kissed her.

He tensed as desire rippled through his body. Pushing it down, he glanced away and rubbed his hand over his face. He was tired, *si*? Hence the loss of self-control. But he'd pull himself together. They'd take in the view, have dinner, have a rational and realistic chat about Katie's future…

Except he didn't think he could actually be alone with her yet. Not after the sensual torture of the plane trip. His awareness of her was shocking, and he was unaccustomed to travelling with a woman like this—to being close, but not being able to touch her more than that kiss he'd already stolen.

A massive mistake.

Maybe once Susan was settled and Katie was away from the horror foster father Alessandro could indulge in a liaison with her, but until then it was too complicated.

'Do you want to head up to the suite or shall we take a look around first?' He offered her the choice to check how she was feeling.

She eagerly accepted the safe option. 'Let's look around.'

He grimaced wryly. Yeah, she didn't want to be alone with him. To her he was the big, bad wolf. And she was right to be wary. He did want to eat her. He'd pounce the second she suggested it.

Instead he followed her into the bar, abandoning any idea of a rational discussion until morning. They were both too tired and tense. Having a moment to lighten up would be good for them. But there was no reason why he couldn't keep teasing her—just a little. To deny himself that last little pleasure with her would be a step too far, and Alessandro wasn't accustomed to self-denial.

The bar was three-quarters full already—people were out to enjoy themselves in all the ways they could in this town.

'Look at the colours in that cocktail.' Katie's colourful eyes gleamed as they passed a table full of laughing women. 'It's beautiful.'

She sounded almost wistful as they took their seats in an intimate alcove with a view across the bar.

'You don't want to know what's in it?' Alessandro asked dryly, sinking into a seat that he knew was going to be far too comfortable.

'Something that beautiful is bound to taste good, don't you think?' she smiled.

Her words struck home if he applied them to *her*. 'You can have one,' he growled.

Her gaze widened, then narrowed. 'I asked you to marry me—not turn into my mother.'

The temptation to kiss her almost overwhelmed him and

he grasped for self-control. 'When did you last have an alcoholic drink?'

Her chin lifted higher and a mutinous look sharpened her eyes. But she didn't reply.

Yeah, she'd never drunk alcohol...she'd never travelled. What else had she never done? Because there'd been inexperience in her kiss. Sweet, shy, hot, totally tempting inexperience.

There'd also been a burst of fire.

'One,' he reiterated unapologetically, and nodded to the waiter. Neither of them needed anything to fan the flames.

The waiter returned shortly, bearing a tray with the most outrageous cocktail Alessandro had ever seen. Given that he'd spent a large chunk of his adult life building hospitality venues, he'd pretty much seen every cocktail there was. This one featured bright green and orange layers of pure alcohol and vaguely resembled a vibrant parrot. Too late he realised that if Katie were to have more than two mouthfuls things might veer off course.

'I'm not sure that—'

Too late. She'd already sipped.

'Oh...' She swallowed and sucked in a breath. Surprise widened her eyes. 'It's even more delicious than I imagined.'

Was this a thirst to drown her sorrows? Or cool her down?

Alessandro swiftly reached across and picked up her glass before she had the chance to lift it again. He was saving her from herself, he thought morosely. He swallowed the vile sweet liquid with an appalled grimace.

'Whisky, please,' he wheezed to the waiter, who hadn't had a chance to get more than five feet away. 'Double.'

'You didn't like it?' Katie enquired meekly, but that tiny twinkle in her eyes gave her away.

He laughed, enjoying her flash of attitude. It was so much better than that cowed, fearful look he'd seen on her in his office. Now she had some sparkle.

'You know I didn't.'

He watched as she pushed back the sleeves of her school-girlish white blouse. He glanced around at the glittering interior of the bar and sternly told himself not to stare at the tiny amount of skin the action exposed. Since when was he fascinated by less than a square inch of skin? When his dates usually wore so much less?

Alessandro took a sip as soon as his whisky arrived, and cursed his inner devil who'd thought this was a good idea. Desperate for distraction, he pulled out his phone and realised he'd neglected to switch it on after the flight. He frowned as multiple messages from Dominque pinged. All asking him to call her urgently.

Before he could, the phone buzzed in his hand.

'What is it?' he asked tersely. Dominique wouldn't bother him unless it was important.

'Alessandro, I've been trying to get hold of you.' Dominque sounded concerned. 'Something's come up in our research on White Oaks,' she continued crisply. 'Katie Collins's engagement to Carl Westin was announced in the papers today.'

'Pardon?' He stilled, unsure he'd heard correctly.

He glanced at Katie. She was watching him, her hand tightening around her lurid drink, her eyes widening with fear as microseconds passed.

'Katie's engagement,' Dominique repeated. 'It only went online an hour ago—that's why I missed it earlier.'

'Where?'

Dominique told him the newspaper's name.

'I'll call you back,' he said briskly.

He reached out and took the glass from Katie's hand.

'What's wrong?' Her voice sounded thin and shadows had dimmed that earlier sparkle.

'Have you checked your phone for messages?'

She rummaged in her bag and hauled out her phone. 'Is

it Susan?' Tears sprang to her eyes. 'I shouldn't have left her. Not even for a day.'

She was actually shaking, and as she fumbled with her phone she dropped it.

'It's not Susan,' he said quietly, scooping up the phone from the floor for her. 'Breathe.' His chest tightened at the concern in her expression. 'It appears that your engagement to Carl was announced this afternoon.'

'That's not possible.' Katie froze, her shocked gaze fixed on him. 'I didn't agree. I said no. I'd *never* agree.'

Yeah, Little Miss Bigamist she was not—but Brian had gone ahead and announced it anyway.

'He can't actually make me, can he?' She snatched her phone from him and switched it on. 'I've got lots of missed calls.' She stared at it in horror. 'Brian, mostly.' She paled even more as she held the phone to her ear.

He could hear the berating tone of Brian's message even from across the table. And he could also hear Katie's breathing quicken.

His own anger pounded in his ears. Brian the bully was ramping up the attack, telling her the engagement was now public knowledge so she couldn't bring shame on the family, couldn't embarrass Susan. Susan who'd gone to bed, so distressed that Katie had left...

Alessandro reached out and took the phone from Katie, turning it off before tossing it onto the table between them. He rubbed his forehead, struggling to think clearly. He regretted the long flight and that one whisky, and all the hours in the last fortnight during which he'd worked and not slept. But he had to do something—anything to help ease Katie's anxiety.

The obvious solution stared him in the face. They'd come this far so they might as well complete the picture. Right now it felt like the fastest, easiest option. The decision was easy.

He'd be the villain of the piece. The scoundrel who had seduced some other man's fiancée away from him...

With the added scandalous frisson of the family connection between them, people were going to love the gossip. But Alessandro didn't care about his own reputation. Right now all he cared about was clearing the panic from Katie's face and stopping Brian from browbeating her into something she didn't want.

They'd forced him out all those years ago, but Alessandro had his own resources now, and he had no one else to worry about. Katie had Susan, and without some extra support she'd be trapped.

'Should I call him back?' Katie asked in a horrified whisper.

'No,' he growled, but then softened his tone. Brian's greed was coming to an end. 'Not yet.'

She swayed a little as she stood. He put his hands on her shoulders to steady her and looked into her eyes.

'You came to me for help, Katie. That's what you want, right?' he asked.

'I want to know that Susan—'

'I'll ensure she's okay. Trust me.'

The sooner Katie was tied to him, the more freedom he'd have to act on her behalf.

She stared up at him, the myriad of colours in her eyes reflecting a myriad of conflicting emotions—fear, mostly, but also hope, and a last hint of awareness.

'Are you sure, Katie?' he asked harshly. 'You really want to do this?'

She looked exhausted and terrified and too damn trusting. All he wanted was her smile and those flashing little sparks in her eyes to come back.

She nodded. 'Yes. Please.'

Katie stood still, her face cupped in strong but gentle hands. The lips moving over hers were warm and assured and teasing, sending flickers of temptation along her veins, stirring the yearning that ran so deep.

She moaned, her lips parting, seeking the slide of his tongue. She liked it when he— *Yes*... The trickle of sensation became a torrent within her and she moaned again. *Like that*. She liked it when he kissed her like that. Deep and gentle and powerful.

'Katie...'

'Mmm?'

The whisper confused her. How could he whisper her name like that while he was kissing her so passionately at the exact same time?

'Katie?'

She breathed in deeply, not wanting to move, floating in a cocoon of warmth, relaxed and happy. She slowly blinked, opened her eyes and smiled.

And then immediately froze.

Reality rushed in on her with sickening speed. She wasn't being kissed in some dream world. She was in bed and she wasn't alone.

Alessandro Zetticci was only inches away, lying facing her, his head propped on his hand. There was an odd expression in his eyes.

'You were moaning,' he said, watching her too closely.

She couldn't reply. Was he *naked*? The part of him she could see above the sheet covering them was naked. There was a vast expanse of bronzed, muscular torso on show.

Katie stared. She couldn't breathe. Couldn't move. Couldn't speak.

'Katie?'

'What are you doing in here?'

He blinked and that wicked smile widened. 'Should I leave?' He pushed down the sheet.

'No!' Huge mistake. *Huge*. Oh. *So* huge.

The man just had everything, didn't he? Long, powerful limbs. Long, powerful... Well, *everything*.

She hurriedly tugged the sheet back up to cover him. 'You're not wearing anything.'

He stared at her for a second and then seemed to take in a steadying breath.

'Actually, I'm not *quite* naked,' he corrected her. 'I kept my boxers on—which is kind of me, given I don't like underwear.'

'Of course you don't,' she muttered desperately, wondering how on earth they'd—

'I get a rash from cheap synthetic fabrics,' he offered in explanation, but wicked humour danced in his eyes.

'Are you sure it's from the fabric?' she snapped back before she could think.

He laughed as he rubbed a hand through his sinfully sexy, slightly-too-long-to-be-good hair. 'I knew the kitten had claws...' He drew in a deep breath and stretched out.

'I'm not a kitten. But I *am* devastated to discover you're not perfect.'

'I never said I was perfect—that was your assumption.' He grinned at her. 'I prefer cotton, or silk—or, better yet, nothing at all.' His eyes glinted.

He was a naturist? Wonderful.

They'd been in *bed* together. Of course it was nothing to him to get into bed with a woman—he did it all the time. But *she* didn't. He was the most masculine thing ever to have graced her bed. Okay, he was the *only* thing ever to have graced her bed.

She swallowed as she remembered the madness of the night before.

'Did we...?' She trailed off, still distracted by all the skin he had on show.

His gaze narrowed on her. 'Do you not remember?'

Her brain was too fried by the sight of him in all his near nude glory to remember her own name, let alone much else.

'Did we—?'

'Sleep together? Sure.' His eyebrows lifted. 'Katie,' he

said, as if lecturing an imbecile, 'if we'd done anything *more* you wouldn't need to ask. Your virtue is safe.'

Yeah, she'd figured that. Because while he might be all but naked she was still completely dressed. Her blouse, skirt, bra, panties...everything. But she was still mortified—*so* mortified.

'We got married,' she whispered.

He stilled and his teasing smile froze. 'Yes, we did.'

She closed her eyes. She ought to feel relief. Wasn't that what she'd wanted? Only all she could feel was *heat*.

That dream she'd been having was a memory, and she'd been reliving it. Her brain had picked the highlight to replay. Not those phone messages from Brian, nor that engagement announcement, nor Alessandro's rapid, decisive response. Not even the fact that he'd marched her off and married her in less than an hour. All she could think about was the kiss that had sealed the deal.

'Here.'

She opened her eyes. He'd picked something up from the bedside table and now held it out to her. She gingerly took the photograph, as if she was afraid it might spring to life and bite her.

It showed the two of them next to each other, posing alongside some random staff at the chapel who'd acted as their witnesses.

She read the caption. 'There's a download code for the video...'

'You want to relive the magic?' Alessandro picked up his phone.

Not really—because the flash flood of memories was scalding her with enough humiliation. But it was as if she was stuck on the roller coaster ride from hell.

'We selected the music video option?' she muttered as he scanned the code.

He grinned, apparently as relaxed as ever. 'We're in Vegas—there's every option.'

He scooted a little closer so she could see the screen next to him.

She tried not to blush, but it was impossible.

Set to what she could only describe as a generic boy band ballad—a love song that she didn't recognise but that sounded familiar—a series of appalling images flashed on the screen. She was in her ugly navy skirt and crumpled blouse, while he looked as unbearably handsome as ever, despite that long flight and the horror of the messages they'd got on landing. And he was smiling at her—a smile that made everything inside her light up.

Unable to tear her eyes from the small screen, Katie watched the playback of her exchanging vows and promising to honour him, to *love* him. In the video Alessandro was turning to her with a playful gleam in his eyes. He was framing her face and holding her still...

As if she'd have been able to run when he was looking at her like that. She'd been bolted in place—mesmerised not by his good looks, but by that look in his eyes. That dance of amusement, of warmth and wit underpinned by heat and hunger.

The second he swooped the camera zoomed in. And as a result almost the entire last minute of their wedding video showed them kissing. She watched herself ditch the posy of flowers the hotel had provided. She'd dropped it to the floor so she could slide her arms up his body and kiss him back. She'd forgotten anyone else was even present, let alone that there was a camera filming them.

Katie couldn't tear her gaze from the final frozen frame. She'd got married in a cheap nylon skirt. She'd looked just like all those other girls he'd kissed—as hungry, as willing... Except at the same time she didn't. She wasn't glamorous and beautiful and sex kittenish.

And she'd had stars in her eyes.

But he'd had laughter on his face.

Alessandro had pulled back from the kiss first. She'd

leaned after him—literally swooning into his embrace. He'd held her upright, away from him. And then he'd laughed. He'd thrown his head back and *laughed*.

It was horrendous.

It wasn't the over-the-top decor of the twenty-four-hour wedding chapel, or even her awful outfit and lack of anything pretty. It was the look on her face. She looked flushed and willing and it was so obvious. She looked *infatuated*. And everyone could see it.

Most of all him.

And now he was almost naked in her bed. But that was only because in her overwrought state at the end of last night she'd *asked* him to stay with her.

When they'd got back to the suite she'd turned to him with tears in her eyes and told him she was tired. He'd come to the bedroom with her and sat down beside her. He'd reassured her. He'd *rescued* her. He'd been a perfect gentleman.

And she must have fallen asleep a second later—like an incompetent, dependent child.

She'd never been as mortified in all her life.

Now he put his phone back on the table with telltale quickness and edged away.

Katie's vulnerable heart thudded as she recognised the horrible truth.

He hadn't wanted to do any of it at all.

Alessandro's head was killing him. Tension, not a hangover. He'd stopped drinking to excess years ago—though admittedly he'd contemplated it earlier as a displacement activity, a distraction to deny the desire coursing through his veins. But he hadn't. Because of Dominque's call.

Hell and damnation.

He'd been so tired last night, so thrown by Katie's visible distress, that he'd seen a quickie marriage as their only option. Memories flitted—her softness and the sweet but tart taste of apricots. He'd kissed her off her feet, and right now he was rocked by the urge to repeat the experience.

Except he'd just seen her appalled expression as the reality of their situation sank in. *Si*. It wasn't his dream deal either.

They'd get it annulled—just as soon as he'd sorted out the estate and care for Susan.

His phone suddenly vibrated. It was still on silent mode after the chapel. He picked it up. It was a message of congratulations. A moment later another message landed. And then more. An influx of congratulations and confusion and appalling curiosity filled his screen.

How?

He gritted his teeth and did a quick online search. Somehow their wedding video had just been uploaded and it was almost immediately trending.

He scooped up the print from the wedding chapel and quickly scanned the information on the back of its cardboard cover.

'It seems I neglected to tick the box refusing my consent for the chapel to use our images for promotional purposes.'

His jaw ached from gritting his teeth so hard. How had he not done a better job of this? He'd been so distracted by her distress and his driving need to somehow make things better. Instead he might have made everything worse.

'Pardon?' Katie's pallor had a greenish tinge to it now.

'The chapel has just posted our wedding video online.'

'What?' She paled even more. 'The video of us…of me…' She trailed off, but he saw her glance down at her crumpled outfit.

Yes, it was hardly the most stunning bridal attire the world had ever seen, and the online trolls were ripping her to shreds already. *Beauty and the Boring* was one comment he *wasn't* about to show her.

Instead he lifted the hotel phone and rapidly ordered coffee and carbs.

'How can you possibly want to eat?' she asked the second he hung up.

'It's exactly what we both need.' Better that hunger than the other one currently tempting him.

His customary headache cure wasn't on the cards today—no lazy sex between soft sheets, no finding relief in the surge of orgasm. Not happening. He'd crossed too many lines with Katie already.

He got out of bed and paced across the room to the window. At the touch of a button the curtains opened. He glared out through the window down to the vibrant avenue below and tried to get his brain to work.

'You were going to back out of it, weren't you?' she said quietly.

He turned and watched certainty settle in her expression.

'You weren't going to go through with it until you found out about the engagement announcement.'

She looked so crushed he had to resist a completely foreign urge to go and give her a cuddle.

'I thought you'd come to your senses once you got far enough away from them,' he admitted. 'That you'd realise getting married wasn't necessary.'

'You brought me all this way to give me time to *come to my senses*?'

'It looked like it was going to take a while,' he conceded. 'But then Brian sprang that announcement on us.'

Alessandro hadn't been able to come up with a decent alternative at the time. He'd been compelled into action by the fear in her eyes. They hadn't even arranged a prenuptial agreement, or discussed the amount he was going to pump into the property, or how he'd recover that cost. Or anything.

She drew up her knees, covering herself with the sheet. 'You think I'm pathetic, don't you?'

'I think you're…' He paused and tried to think how best to explain the confusing things he thought and felt about her. 'You're sweet. Perhaps a little…naive.'

She winced. 'But you can't say you're going to do something and then go back on your word.' Her temper flared. 'That's not fair. Especially something as important as this.'

'But I did it.' He gestured to the unfortunate photo on the table. 'Now you've got a husband to protect you.'

She stared at him.

'Well, wife?' He eyed her grimly, barely holding back the anger that surged within him. 'What's next on the list?'

She shook her head slowly. 'We can get it annulled, right? You didn't really want this. We should just…figure out another way. I'm so sorry.'

He was taken aback by her unexpected stand—and the dignity in her apology.

'Maybe that would make an even bigger scandal?' she wondered aloud, looking almost hopeful. 'I've run away to Vegas on a whim…created a crazy twenty-four-hour wedding scandal… Brian will hate it.'

Something contrary swirled in his gut. Truth be told, he no longer cared about what her foster father thought or wanted. He was suddenly angry with her for wanting to walk away already, when he'd moved heaven and earth to do what she'd wanted.

He didn't want to rush into another set of actions that would make things even worse. Because it was impacting on him *now*.

'I might have a certain reputation,' he said coolly. 'But that's a step too far even for me. We're not getting an annulment. We'll stick with your original plan. Six months, minimum. Even that's a little on the short side.'

'But you didn't even want six days…' she argued, appalled. 'Five was enough for you, wasn't it? You didn't even mean to use those—you were just stringing me along, patting me on the head and saying *sure thing, sweetie*—pacifying me like a child.'

She was angry? Well, so was he.

'I don't *pacify* anyone. I just say no. And I'm saying no

to the annulment idea. You made this bed, *dolcezza*, you might as well get comfortable.'

Her eyes widened and her focus skimmed over his body again. Every muscle within him tensed. He shouldn't be thinking about being back in bed with her. Last night she'd been vulnerable and scared...and so soft. He'd not wanted to leave her alone and distressed. He'd fallen asleep still clothed, waking only enough to shuck his shirt and trousers off before curling around her warm body again.

Now Alessandro stalked back to the bed and scooped up his phone. He needed to get on top of this. And to do that they needed to get away from the scene of their madness before any paparazzi turned up. He was no celebrity, but he had money, and celebrities used some of his properties.

'We need the plane,' he said as soon as Dominique answered. 'Departing in two hours.'

'Anything else I can arrange?' Dominique asked.

Alessandro winced at the almost breathless curiosity Dominique was hiding. She'd clearly heard the news too. 'I'll message you with the destination and other details shortly.'

'We're leaving already?' Katie frowned as he ended the call.

He felt a perverse need to provoke her. 'Yes. We're going on our honeymoon.'

'Honeymoon?' Colour flooded not just her face but her neck, and all the skin he could see...

Her wide-eyed gaze dipped to his bare chest again. He could almost feel it, like a caress on his skin, and he suddenly ached for the reality of her touch.

'It'll give us time and space to sort out the next six months,' he snapped, bending to pick up his trousers and turning his back on her.

Going into any takeover, he needed all the 'i's dotted and the 't's crossed. He'd get his team to work out all the options regarding the marriage, then he'd get Susan's care sorted, acquire Brian's debt and stockpile the ammunition to ensure his compliance. He started mentally drafting emails—anything to stop himself from thinking about getting back into bed and taking up the offer in her beautiful eyes.

'But I need to get back to Susan—'

'You asked for my help, Katie. Let me get on with it.'

'But—'

'Trust me to do my thing,' he interrupted again roughly. 'I'll explain later.'

There was only one place to go. 'Okay.'

At the chastened obedience in her voice he swung back to look at her. She was watching him warily, and then she looked down. He hated it that she'd gone quiet on him.

'I need a shower...' She trailed off. Tension surged in the atmosphere.

She also needed clothes.

He struggled to breathe. 'I'll get some stuff sent up while you're in there,' he offered huskily.

She shot him an embarrassed look as she awkwardly got out of bed and smoothed down her crumpled skirt. 'Thanks.'

He couldn't help grabbing her arm as she passed him. The colour in her cheeks deepened as she looked up into his eyes. He needed to get to know her better—slice through this tension enough to get them to a point where they could coexist happily for a while.

But how did they stop the chemical reaction between them igniting?

Inner tension tightened his grip. 'Just so you know, I'm not agreeing to extra-marital affairs. For either of us.'

He felt her tiny shiver, but she held his gaze with that determined one of her own.

'Fine. But just so *you* know, I'm not agreeing to anything intimate. This is a marriage on paper only.'

Really?

He smiled. The electricity flowing through his veins chased away his headache.

Alessandro was all for making the most of his opportunities—and his acquisitions. And he was going to have so much fun teasing her. Because there was no way she could deny their chemistry any more than he could.

'Fine.' He echoed her with soft sarcasm. 'Of course you're welcome to change your mind any time. I won't hold it against you if you do.'

Because he'd held her in his arms already, and he'd kissed her, heard her moans. And, if he so wanted, he'd have her mind changed in minutes.

CHAPTER FIVE

KATIE HAD DISCOVERED an appalling appreciation of Alessandro's obscene wealth. Being whisked through airport security with privacy and speed like some VIP had been jaw-dropping, and there was a lot to be said for the luxury of a private jet. As the plane now levelled out after take-off she sank deeper into the plush leather seat. The speed of it all was good. The sooner they got back to White Oaks the better.

'Go and lie down in comfort.' Alessandro tore his attention away from his tablet to send her a searching look. 'You're barely able to keep your eyes open. We'll be in the air for a few hours yet—plenty of time for you to get a decent rest.'

She couldn't. It was only now that she had a moment to think that she realised she'd forgotten the most important thing.

'I should have phoned Susan,' she muttered. 'She'll be so worried. I never go this long without contact.'

She was shocked at how selfish she'd been. Alessandro had moved so quickly she'd simply been swept along on the tide of his dynamism. But that wasn't good enough.

'There's already been contact,' he replied easily.

'Pardon?' She stared at him.

'My team,' he explained. 'The lawyers have already made contact with Brian while you were in the shower.'

'Your first contact was through *lawyers*?' In a split second her nerves had tensed to total strain.

'It's fine.' He smiled, but his expression seemed more wicked than reassuring. 'They've made Brian an offer he can't refuse. Don't worry. White Oaks is safe.'

Don't worry? Her heart pounded. 'What about Susan?'

'We're engaging nurse companions. She'll have round-the-clock assistance. Something she should have had for months already.'

At that simply spoken truth the sickening heat of shame swept over her. She'd always tried her best for her foster mother, but now her inadequate efforts made her shrink.

'Brian's accepted that?' He'd never liked people in the house. Had always insisted she and Susan could cope on their own.

'He either accepts my terms or we make him bankrupt. But even if he chooses that option White Oaks and Susan will be cared for.'

Katie blinked rapidly. 'Just like that?'

'Brian's not stupid. He'll agree.' Alessandro said with arrogant certainty. 'Especially if he *loves* her.'

His bitter edge made her look at him. Was he so cynical he didn't believe in love? Why? She blinked again. Would he ever love anyone enough to sacrifice everything for them?

Inwardly she rejected the idea. He was so self-sufficient and self-assured he'd never *need* to sacrifice everything. He'd simply figure out a bunch of alternative solutions. He was too capable. And she felt too useless.

She watched as he went back to his work, typing on the tablet's keyboard like a demon. Astute and agile in his dealings, he was a fast mover—snapping up acquisitions with speed before other buyers even spotted the opportunity. Now he was ferociously dealing with the disaster she'd created, and his ruthless, uncompromising streak was exposed as he coolly exerted his authority over Brian.

His kind of confidence was something she doubted she'd ever have. All her life she'd been insecure—always worrying that she'd displease Brian to the point where he'd refuse to house her any more. She'd tried hard to curb her inclination to fight back, working instead to pacify him—staying out of sight, not raising her voice, not being an inconvenience or an embarrassment.

She'd done that for herself, but also because the emotional strain on Susan had been almost as bad. When Brian was in a good mood he was generous and gregarious, showering her foster mother with love and affection... And in those occasional moments Katie had finally felt safe. But those moments had been short, and always broken by periods of glowering moods, snapped commands and veiled threats.

She was to remember her place—where she'd come from—and she should always be *grateful*.

Now she'd irrevocably altered their relationship by brutally defying his crazy 'marry Carl Westin' request. She was finally away from Brian's control.

But Alessandro was doing everything. She'd gone from one powerful man to another...and that truth sat uncomfortably within her.

Making it worse was her infatuation. There was no other word for the way she'd looked at Alessandro at their wedding—in a way that everyone who saw that video would see...

There was only one thing she could do. She needed to step up, take the responsibility onto her own shoulders somehow. For now that meant falling back on her old survival skills—staying out of sight, staying quiet—while she built her strength and came up with her own plan.

So she did as he'd suggested and retreated to the safety of the sleeping quarters, where she couldn't stare at him like some starstruck teen with a crush.

On the bed, she pulled up one of the soft blankets to cover her legs. The comfy jeans and cute Las Vegas tee that he'd magicked up for her from that hotel's gift shop were great, but she was cold.

As she lay down her mind whirled through replays of the previous night—Alessandro's decisiveness and speed. Her own relief. And then those moments when she'd woken this morning, to find him in bed with her, so full of his amusement at her embarrassment...

She listened to the rhythm of his fingers stabbing at the keyboard over the hum of the plane's engine. And in that dusky dream space between waking and sleeping she let herself remember the warm comfort of his embrace and finally relaxed...

'Katie?'

She felt the mattress suddenly depress and swiftly sat up.

'I managed to spend a whole night in your bed without ravishing you.' Sardonic amusement flashed in his eyes as he shifted to sit more comfortably on the side of the bed. 'You don't need to be afraid of me.'

'I'm not afraid of you,' she argued instantly.

'You're afraid of yourself, then.' That gleam in his gaze intensified.

She rolled her eyes, despite her suddenly sprinting heart. 'Are you ever serious?'

'All the time.'

Something within her tingled—caution. For all his playboy flirtation she felt he was telling the truth. That compelled her to deflect the conversation away from the personal. 'How long have we been flying?'

'We've less than an hour to go.'

'Oh, good.' She'd slept through most of the flight.

'You think?'

An edgy expression tightened his features. She shifted an inch further away. He noticed, huffing out a breath before he rubbed at his forehead.

'There really wasn't any other guy you wanted to run away with?' he suddenly asked softly. 'You didn't have some boyfriend back in the village who Brian tried to chase off?'

Her mouth dried at the intrusiveness of the question. Wordlessly, slowly, she shook her head.

'What about those students who picked the fruit at the end of summer? There were always lots of those.' He waited, a frown growing in his gaze. 'You didn't flirt with any of them over the years?'

She knew *he'd* enjoyed those students—but she hadn't. She'd been far too shy, and far too aware of risking the wrath of her foster father or disappointing her too-gentle foster mother. Besides, none of them had ever so much as looked at her.

The one time she'd put on some lipstick a school friend had given her, Brian had seen it.

'You look cheap.'

His belittling comment hadn't just been unkind, he'd laughed as he'd said it. In one breath he'd killed Katie's desire to try and attract someone. So she'd repressed her youthful yearning for attention, refused to acknowledge her own secret needs. Because he'd confirmed what she'd known already—she couldn't get it right. She wasn't enough as she was. She'd probably never be enough.

Alessandro was still watching her closely, more serious than she'd ever seen him. 'You've had no boyfriends at all, Katie?'

She shook her head yet again.

'Not ever?' His voice tightened. 'So you've not—?'

'No.' She forestalled any further highly embarrassing questions angrily. 'No boyfriends. No kissing. No sex. No *nothing.*'

He sat very still, his gaze not leaving hers. 'I don't think I've ever met a woman in her twenties who's still a virgin. It's not that common, Katie.'

He said it as if there was something wrong with her. Of course it had to be *her*—yet again *she* was the one at fault.

'Maybe not in the circles *you* hang out in, but I don't think it's that abnormal,' she said stiffly, barely masking her inner rebellion. 'No doubt I'm the most untouched woman you've ever met. And you've *married* me. The irony is extreme, don't you think?'

She tossed her head—embarrassed, defensive and

wary…but mostly with herself. With that little weakness she had within her when it came to him.

'Does Carl know you've not had a boyfriend?

She paused, horrified at the question. 'I don't know.' She stared down at the blanket covering her. 'You think he wanted to marry me because of that? Like I was some kind of virgin sacrifice?' She rejected the idea completely. 'Marriage is for a long time. Brian could've just offered him the use of my body for a night…'

Suddenly she was bitterly hurt. Anger forced her to look back into Alessandro's too-handsome face.

'You can't think why he'd want me for a wife at all, can you?'

'I can't understand why *anyone* would want a wife at all,' he countered calmly. 'Or a husband, for that matter. It's not you personally.'

'And yet here you are, married to me,' she pointed out.

Alessandro stared back at her. They were locked in a still, silent moment.

'I think Carl wanted someone controllable. A doormat,' she finally said, slicing through the strained atmosphere.

'You're not *that* controllable,' he muttered.

'No. I'm not.' She lifted her chin, embracing the defiance he sparked within her. 'And I'm not going to struggle with six months' celibacy because I've been uninterested in *that* all my life,' she said scornfully.

Desperately she wanted to believe her own words. Desperately she wanted to score a point against him because he made her so uncomfortable.

But he didn't rise to her bait, he only goaded her more—with that smile.

'I don't think you're "uninterested" in that,' he said softly.

'You can't imagine *anyone* being uninterested,' Katie scoffed.

'Lame call, Katie.' He sent her another considering look from beneath those long, dark lashes. 'You might be inexperienced, but you're not that immature.' He paused, his head cocked. 'Who gave you your first kiss?'

She stared down at the blanket between them and refused to answer.

'Katie…?'

The hint of appalled incredulity in his voice let her know he'd figured it out.

'Don't let it go to your head,' she gritted.

'It's not going to my *head*,' he drawled wickedly.

'Really?' She lifted her chin and glared at him. 'Do guys seriously get off on this?'

He laughed, but it didn't sound easy. 'Don't try to distract me. Denial is unworthy of you, *dolcezza*. I've kissed you. You kissed me back.'

'And let's agree not to do it again.'

He shook his head. 'You are afraid—why?' He frowned at her as if she was a conundrum. 'If you've waited this long there *has* to be a reason.'

Oh, he had to be kidding…

But his insistent prying had pushed her past her learned reticence. She'd make him as uncomfortable as he made her.

'Maybe I was waiting to give my virginity to my husband,' she said in dulcet tones, and sent him a demure look. 'That's a reason why a lot of women wait.'

He stared at her, as still as a predator waiting for his moment to pounce, an unreadable expression on his face.

She rolled her eyes again, masking the intensity this conversation was building within her. 'The only reasons I'm a virgin are lack of interest and lack of opportunity.'

That devilish look lit within him. 'Why, how convenient… You have both now…' he murmured.

Surely he didn't mean—?

He leaned closer. '*I'm* interested. *I'm* your opportunity.'

She just stared at him.

'Right here, right now. We both know how well we'd get on together. What do you say, Katie?'

She was almost certain he wasn't serious, but the awful thing was part of her had already melted in complete surrender…and she was angry with both herself *and* him for that.

'I say I'm not interested.'

His smile swerved. 'Are you sure about that?'

Her breathing quickened. 'I also say you're mean.'

'Opportunity is *not* the only reason.' His lips twisted in mockery as he proved her a liar. 'Are you waiting for love, Katie?'

'Well… I'd have to at least *like* the guy,' she retorted furiously, pushed to the extreme.

He winced and pressed his hand to his heart. 'After all I've done for you…?'

'Don't tease.' She borrowed his look from under lowered eyelashes. 'I'm no match for you.'

He stared for a second, then laughed. 'And that little pretence shows just how up to my weight you are, Katie. You're quiet because you've had to be—not because you didn't have something to say. You're not entirely shy.'

He reached out and grabbed her hand, flattening her fingers when she tried to curl them into a fist.

'You're going to have to get used to a little touching, Katie.' He traced circles on her palm with his index finger as he spoke. 'If you want to prevent Susan from being anxious you'll have to present a blissfully happy façade to her. You said it yourself: you'll have to fake it. You'll need to look and act like you're in love with me and you can't talk to her until you're certain you can do that.'

He spoke lightly, but she understood that he meant every word.

'I'm not having the world know this marriage is a sham. You wanted this, you've got it, but you'll have to act the part. I will touch you. I will kiss you. Everyone knows I'd never be cold with my wife.'

She realised that beneath that tease, even as he touched her so softly, he was angry.

'I've seduced you away from your fiancé after all,' he mocked. 'You're going to have to look spellbound.'

Waves of heat rose just from those tiny tickling circles. His skilful fingers cast sensations like confetti—skating caresses that sent shivers of anticipation down her spine.

She swallowed the hard lump in her throat. 'You're sure that isn't for your own ego?'

'You know my ego doesn't need the boost.' He held her hand more tightly and leaned closer. 'You can't blush every time I come within two feet of you. You can't pull away or look shy…'

She didn't want to pull away. Unfortunately she suspected he knew that too.

'We're going to need to practise,' he added softly.

'You're kidding?'

He shook his head and smiled wickedly. 'As serious as ever—that's me.'

With that he tugged her closer and pressed his mouth on hers. It was a teasing, light kiss, one she could have broken from easily. But she didn't. Instead she stilled, uncertain whether to push him away or kiss him back. Then her body overruled her brain and decided for her and she leaned closer.

Instantly he slid his other hand to the nape of her neck, holding her so he could kiss her even more deeply. His lips roved gently, firmly, and his tongue stroked in a light tease. His fingers still clasped hers. His touch felt beyond intimate, bathing her in rose-gold heat. He was warm and strong and giving.

Delightful, dizzying wisps of wonder trickled through her veins. She tasted his smile in his kiss and somehow she smiled too. Who'd have thought kissing could be so easy or feel so right?

Yet the second she thought that a flicker of something else rose. Once again he'd unleashed something long hidden—something so sharp she wasn't quite ready for it. But she couldn't stop. She couldn't pull back. The desire to keep kissing, keep touching, keep connected to him was too strong.

This was a mistake. Alessandro wrestled with his conscience and his want, but his ability to reason was slipping further the longer he had his mouth sealed to hers. The longer he lost himself in her sweetness. And she was so very sweet.

Anyway, since when did he even have a conscience? There was nothing wrong with just kissing. It was simple fun that meant little…only short moments to enjoy.

But she was a virgin. And she was also his wife.

Those facts clawed at his gut. How was he supposed to stop their chemistry from combusting for six whole months? It was an impossible ask.

He forced himself to break the kiss, lifting his head to stare down at her. Her heavy-lidded eyes contained a dazed sparkle and her lips looked soft and lush and reddened. Her ragged breathing gave her away, as did the building heat of her skin beneath his fingertips.

She was no porcelain doll, no unfeeling automaton. She was full-bodied and hot and the sexiest thing he'd seen… And he'd never wanted a woman the way he wanted her now.

With a muffled groan he slammed his mouth back on hers, pulling her fully into his arms, needing to feel her against his chest. She was as soft and lithe as he'd imagined. And he was doing them both a favour, *si*? Their marriage would look real enough and they'd rid themselves of the frustration riding them both. She'd become a little more worldly…

His reasons, justifications, excuses faded as he succumbed to the pleasure of caressing her. He obeyed the driving urge to touch more, taste more. He pushed gently so she fell back onto the bed and he followed, his body tensing as he felt her hands slide to his waist.

He kissed her neck, marvelling at her soft, smooth skin. He ached to touch every inch of her. He swept his hand down to her hip, feeling the supple arch of her body, listening to the rise of her breathing and then another of those little moans, followed by a gasp as she tried to catch it back. Hell, he loved those moans of hers.

He toyed with the hem of her tee, tempted to lift it and seek out the even softer skin of her waist, her breasts. He'd kiss and caress them until the pleasure sent them both insane...

'Stop...' she said in a small breathless voice. 'Alessandro, please stop.'

He froze, cold shock tossing immediate regret over him. He'd lost control when he never did. But he'd thought she was with him.

He braced his fists either side of her and pushed up, refusing to give in to the overriding urge to touch her again. Her eyes were closed, and her full mouth was turned down in an expression of complete misery. Had he misread all those signs he thought he'd felt?

'Katie...?' he questioned hoarsely.

'You don't have to...' She trailed off.

Confused, he watched the emotions flicker across her face as he tried to get his brain to catch up with her conversation. He didn't 'have to' what?

'You've proved your point, okay? I'm...' She drew in a shuddering breath. 'You don't have to do anything more.'

Wait—so this wasn't about her not wanting more...this was about her thinking that *he* didn't want more?

He was utterly thrown. The low burn of shame angered him—because her accusation was partly true. Hadn't he wanted her surrender? Hadn't he plotted to tease her, to prove she wanted him? But that had been for ever ago. Within two seconds of touching her all pretence, all gameplaying, had burned away, revealing the raw reality of the attraction between them.

'This isn't about me *proving* anything, Katie,' he said bluntly.

She still didn't look at him. 'Like I said, I'm no match for you,' she muttered.

'I kissed you because I wanted to. I want *you*. Because, as infuriating as you are, you're also fascinating and I want to touch you. Everywhere. Sorry if you find that offensive.'

Rosy colour swarmed over her skin and she finally opened her captivating eyes. 'You think I'm fascinating?'

'And infuriating,' he repeated bluntly. But he couldn't help smiling at her.

Her glare was impressive, but undermined by the fact that she was still frozen with shy awkwardness on the bed before him.

'I thought you were just… I thought it was just a game.'

'Katie.' He half laughed, half sighed. 'It's *always* a game. That's what sex *is*. I enjoy baiting you, but only because I genuinely want you.'

He leaned closer. Provoking her was more fun than he'd had in ages. But touching her was shockingly sublime. And quite possibly addictive.

Her baleful expression didn't ease. 'Because I'm inexperienced?'

'Are you really this insecure?' he growled. 'I've kissed you every chance I got, in case you hadn't noticed. Long before I knew that you were inexperienced. If anything, that puts me off.' He rolled his eyes. 'We shouldn't… *I* shouldn't.'

'I'm sorry if it's an inconvenience,' she said sarcastically. 'Maybe it's hard for me to believe when no one's ever wanted me before.'

He laughed. But then swiftly sobered as he realised that in that last she had been entirely serious. A powerful harsh heat built inside him—something more than desire.

'That's only because you've been hiding.'

He glanced down at the jeans and tee she wore. They

revealed only a hint of her figure. She had cute curves, and long legs for a short person. She should be more confident—the way she was when she talked about her work.

Tension swelled within him again. 'I'm not sure we can keep this a marriage on paper only, Katie.'

The likelihood of them getting to six months without having sex was virtually nil. The chemistry he felt, she felt too.

She'd been sheltered—imprisoned, actually—but he would show her the world if she'd let him. Both literally and in this most personal of spheres. She was warm and sweet, passionate and strong. And they'd be free to continue with their lives at the conclusion...

He suddenly stood, turning away as he grappled with the discomforting thought of her being free to find someone else after their marriage had ended. The thought of some other man making her moan in that soft, pleading way she had when he'd kissed her. It had been a primal purr, asking for more. But the thought of some other man being the first to show her just what she'd been created to do...

He clenched his jaw. With one damn kiss everything had changed. This was everything he didn't want. He was ill-cast in this role of rescuer. He'd never wanted marriage. He wasn't cut out to make that 'for ever' commitment to one person. But they were locked in it now, and he was going to have to exert better self-control.

Katie constantly blushed because she was an inexperienced romantic. He couldn't be further from either of those things.

And now her silence spoke volumes.

Too late he remembered her offer to pay him back any time, anyhow. Did she think this was the *how*? Revulsion and regret at the power imbalance between them surged. She'd been raised to be too polite—required not just to be obedient, but *subservient*.

Did she feel as if she couldn't say no to him now he'd

married her? The thought of her saying yes only to please him, or because she felt she owed him, was horrific. But she'd responded to him—he knew she had—and he'd stopped the second she'd asked him to. He could and would always do that.

'I want you,' he said roughly, unused to admitting anything he felt deeply. And this was beyond deep. 'But I'll only do what you want me to. And you have to *really* want it Katie.'

She had to want it the way he did.

Almost uncontrollably.

Desperately he glanced at his watch and made himself walk further away. 'We've less than thirty minutes till we land.'

'Will we go straight to see Susan?'

He froze, then turned back to face her. 'We're not landing in England, Katie.'

'What?' Her eyes rounded. 'Where are we going?'

'Italy.'

And the sooner they got there, the sooner he could straighten out his head and regain control over his wayward body.

But he couldn't resist one last tease. 'We're going on our honeymoon, remember?'

CHAPTER SIX

KATIE WAS SWEPT along on the tide of Alessandro's dynamism all over again. She'd never encountered someone who could get so much done in so little time or with such apparent ease. They'd landed, cleared Customs, been ensconced in another gorgeous car and driven to another fabulous hotel.

Completely different from Las Vegas, this was a beachside hotel, next to a harbour filled with billionaires' yachts and stylish people drinking coffee and looking impossibly glamorous even at this early hour of the morning.

Feeling hot and sticky and tired, Katie wanted to skulk into a corner and hide.

Alessandro was pure practicality again, turning to her the second they were alone in another large suite. 'You need more clothes. Do you want help selecting them?'

She did need more clothes, but there had to be a limit to what she could take from him—besides which, she really felt like arguing with him.

'I am not parading a selection of outfits in front of you like some…some *courtesan*,' she said stiffly.

He smiled appreciatively. 'I didn't mean me. I don't have the time to take you shopping,' he derided softly. 'Anyway, I'd rather see you getting out of clothes than into them. I meant would you like a personal shopper? Like a stylist?'

He thought she needed one. Katie sank into another mire of embarrassment, furiously trying to think of some smart retort and failing. Because the fact was she'd had very few sartorial options until now. The local village didn't have any particularly stylish stores, and since Brian's stinging judgement that one time she'd dressed up she'd hidden in baggy jeans and tees.

But she wanted to take charge of herself, didn't she? Perhaps she could surprise Alessandro? Because, judging by that gleam of amusement in his eyes, he thought she'd be annoyed by his offer.

On one level she was, but on another she was quite grateful. Truthfully, she had no idea what to wear, and for once in her life she wanted to look good.

'Actually, yes, please. I think a makeover might be just the thing to lift my confidence.' A spark of defiance lit within her. She wanted to look *better* than good. 'Maybe I can look like people would expect your wife to—should I get short skirts? Low-cut tops? Totter about in heels?'

'Are you judging other women by their clothing choices?' he queried blandly.

She took the hit—she deserved it. Hadn't she just done to nameless, faceless other women what Brian had done to her? She deserved better from herself. And she needed to allow herself to deserve better too.

'Point taken.' She licked her lips awkwardly. 'So...thank you. I appreciate the offer and I'd like the help.'

Something kindled in his eyes, but he seemed to smother his smile. 'I'll arrange it.'

Being Alessandro, he made the call immediately, speaking rapidly in Italian.

'She's on her way,' he informed her after a few minutes. 'Don't worry about the budget. You'll need casual, and perhaps a couple of outfits suitable for evening functions. I'm going to work for a few hours—I'll be here when you get back.'

Katie stared at him, struck again by his ability to make things happen. 'Do you work all the time?'

He shot her an amused look. 'You know the answer to that.'

'Work hard, play hard?' She shook her head. 'Such a cliché, Alessandro.'

'Are you sure you want to keep baiting me, Katie?'

She was saved from that lethal whisper by a knock on the door.

Alessandro swiftly crossed the room. Katie was struck with sudden nerves as a slim brunette walked in. Dressed in black, with beautiful make-up and her hair in a sleek chignon, she strode confidently straight up to Katie with an appraising gaze.

'I am Julia,' the woman declared, as if Katie ought to be impressed. 'This will be good, *si*?' She studied Katie again and nodded, as if pleased. 'You have great structure.'

Nonplussed, Katie couldn't think what to reply.

Alessandro murmured something in Italian to Julia, which left Katie feeling gauche and clueless and as if she was being dismissed. But it was Alessandro who stood to leave.

He paused beside her on his way and whispered in her ear. 'Don't dress to please me, her, your foster parents or anyone else. Dress to please yourself.' He brushed his lips against her cheekbone, the light touch leaving a burn on her skin. 'I dare you.'

Katie's pulse skidded. She had *carte blanche* with a credit card, complete self-expression and she had no idea what to do.

But it turned out that with Julia—stylist to Italian stars—personal shopping didn't mean traipsing around a bunch of shops and getting exhausted. Personal shopping with Julia meant Katie being ensconced in the hotel beauty salon to spend an hour perusing various lookbooks online and discussing the styles that appealed to her.

Julia made notes and sent messages on her phone. Then she led Katie to a team of beauticians to be buffed and polished to gleaming perfection. She enjoyed both salt and sugar scrubs and rubs, a manicure, pedicure, a haircut, a facial and a make-up lesson. Meanwhile Julia sourced a huge variety of garments.

'We'll create the perfect capsule wardrobe for your honeymoon,' Julia announced with her thick Italian accent. 'A combination of casual, dressy, totally sexy. He says to please yourself, and that is good, but you can also make *him* speechless, *si*?'

He'd told Julia that Katie had to please herself? Shaking her head, Katie tried on literally dozens of dresses, skirts, trousers, blouses, tees... And slowly she got into it. It was impossible not to discover the joy of soft, fine fabrics—silk, cashmere, linen. She wasn't used to wearing clothing that was so beautifully tailored.

'This flatters your subtle femininity.' Julia nodded in approval as Katie emerged from the dressing room in a floral dress with a deep neckline.

'Subtle' was right. Katie ruefully studied her reflection. Making the most of her meagre assets still didn't turn her into anything like those models Alessandro was so often photographed with.

Pull yourself together. None of this pity.

She was his wife for a few weeks—she couldn't complain. And she did look better than she'd ever looked. She was *passable*.

'Try this as well.' Julia smiled at her as if she'd found missing treasure.

Katie stared at the tiny metallic bikini Julia held out to her. 'I'm not sure...'

'It will highlight your eyes. He'll be...how do you say?... putty in your hands.'

While that was a tempting thought, the truth was more the other way around.

Julia grabbed her phone. 'I am going to lay the clothes out in a variety of looks, so you have some ideas to scroll through and select.'

'Thank you.' Katie decided that Julia was worth her weight in gold.

'You're leaving this evening, so I'll pack the things you

do not need today and the porters will bring the bags up to your room.'

Katie simply nodded, hiding the embarrassing fact that she had no idea of Alessandro's plans while this paid stylist apparently did.

An hour later she finally returned to their suite. Alessandro had his back to her and was talking in rapid Italian, seemingly endlessly, on the phone. With his shirtsleeves rolled up, and surrounded by pieces of paper, two tablets and a laptop, he looked every inch the busy entrepreneur.

He didn't turn as she walked in, which was fabulous—because she didn't want to endure his appraisal and sardonic compliments on her haircut and new clothes. That would just be awkward.

So she chose not to wait or to interrupt him. She'd check out the pool instead. She was uncomfortably hot all of a sudden.

In the luxurious changing room, she slipped into the bikini and scooped up the shawl Julia had told her to accessorise it with, and slid on the matching bronze sandals.

It wasn't until she was sitting on the edge of the pool, paddling her feet, that she had a qualm of guilt over just how much Julia had encouraged her to buy.

She'd somehow lost her head in that deliciously scented room, with all those beautiful flowers and gleaming mirrors, and Julia had made her feel as if it was perfectly normal to buy six pairs of shoes, seven dresses and a huge assortment of skirts, trousers and tops. Not to mention the beauty case Julia had also insisted she needed—and the curling wand for her hair, the make-up, the moisturiser and the special sunscreen... And then there were the leather luggage bags to put all the clothes in...

Far too late Katie realised she'd bought far too much. She paddled her feet faster. She was going to have to apologise to Alessandro and then beg Julia to take half the stuff back. It could be returned, right?

Pondering how best to extricate herself from this latest mess, she laughed beneath her breath at her own uselessness. So much for letting herself deserve more...accept more.

'Katie?'

She turned at the husky calling of her name, still smiling at her own madness.

'Alessandro...' She bit her lip, unsure how to confess. 'You've finished your work?'

He towered over her, his hands on his hips as he surveyed her. She couldn't see his expression behind the sunglasses he'd put on. But when he didn't say anything more she had the sense he was irritated in some way.

It's not necessarily anything to do with you...it could be work.

'You were busy. I didn't want to bother you.'

He glanced about the pool, his eyebrows drawing together as he looked at the other guests.

'I wanted to cool off,' she added when he still didn't answer.

'Here.' He picked up the beautiful wrap Julia had included and handed it to her. 'Put this on.'

She clutched it close, shocked mortification chilling her. Was the bikini awful? Was he embarrassed by her?

He suddenly hunched down beside her and pulled off his sunglasses so he could glare into her eyes. 'Don't look so terrified.' He reached out and ran his forefinger along her bare shoulder. 'Your skin is too fair to sit so exposed in the sun. Either I rub sunscreen on you or you cover up. It's your choice.'

He was concerned about her *skin* burning? Suddenly she was all but incinerating on the spot from the brilliant fire in his blue eyes.

'I've already put lotion on,' she whispered.

She didn't want his hands on her body again. At least not in public. She wasn't sure she'd cope.

'There are people watching us,' he whispered back, a reluctant smile tugging his mouth into that tempting curve. 'You might want to rethink your scowl.'

There were? She pulled the wrap over her shoulders and made herself smile.

'Good choice,' he drawled. 'We're leaving in twenty minutes. I understand your bags are ready?'

'Why are we leaving? This place is amazing.'

'Amazing is acceptable, but I prefer paradise.'

She relaxed at the return of his arrogance. 'Big promises.' She arched her eyebrows at him. 'Is paradise another plane ride away?'

'Are you finding that relentless round-the-world travel isn't everything?' He chuckled. 'Don't worry, it's just a short hop by helicopter.' He glanced down at the almost sheer wrap she'd covered herself with. 'You can stay in the bikini if you want. I don't mind.'

She wasn't staying in the bikini.

'Did you have fun today?' he asked slyly as he accompanied her back to their suite.

'Actually, I think I spent too much,' she confessed in a breathless guilty rush. 'Far too much. I think I got a bit excited by it all and just said yes to everything.'

He laughed. 'Excellent. That is good practice.'

'I'm sorry…'

'Of course you are sorry, *dolcezza*,' he murmured. 'And here I was, thinking you were making progress.'

She frowned, unsure what he meant. 'I'll pay you back.'

'I'm sure you will think of a way.' He chuckled again, as her blush burned like a fever, and lifted a finger to feel the heat flaming her cheeks for himself. 'Your mind, Katie… I'm beginning to think it's *filthy*.'

'No, it's the way you say everything that makes it all seem so…*naughty*,' she grumbled awkwardly. 'You're a tease.'

'Yes.' He nodded. 'I suppose I am. But it's just words. My

payment is the pleasure I get from seeing you like this.' He gazed into her eyes. 'Confident and smiling,' he explained softly. 'Nothing more. You don't have to please me. You have only to please yourself.'

He expected nothing more from her?

Katie fought off an absurd feeling of disappointment. He might want her, but he didn't have the desperate desire she did. Somehow she needed to rein in her own pulse.

CHAPTER SEVEN

As THE HELICOPTER rose up from the roof of the hotel Katie's death grip on her safety belt slackened, as did her jaw, because the view was so stunning she forgot her first-time flier nerves. Speechless, she stared at the sparkling water, studded with sleek, gleaming boats. It was a vast crystalline playground for the ultra-stylish, famous and fabulous, and it went on for as far as she could see.

For almost twenty minutes they flew high and fast, and she gazed in wonder at the emerald coast and the scattered array of small islands. Then they began descending, right above one. High cliffs rose on one side, while stone walls bracketed a small beach on the other. In the middle a breathtaking building stood amongst verdant perfectly planted gardens. Hewn from traditional stone, accented with tiles and glass, it was a modern architectural masterpiece, designed to enhance and appreciate the majestic vista.

Katie's heart skidded at the beauty of it. And at the isolation.

She caught a glimpse of a couple of smaller structures in the distance before they landed on the helipad. Then Katie's stomach fluttered as she ducked and ran alongside Alessandro, conscious of his firm arm across her shoulders. Only moments later the helicopter lifted up again.

'Please don't tell me you own this island,' she breathed, conscious of the sudden silence.

'What should I say instead?' His smile chased the remnants of a frown from his face and he drew in a deep breath.

But Katie's lungs had tightened. 'You have staff?' she asked, trying to sound casual.

'A couple who usually live onsite act as caretakers.' He

scooped up the bags the co-pilot had left for them. 'They've gone to the mainland for a few days.'

Leaving her utterly alone with him?

Her nerves flipped from that light flutter to a loud jangle.

Ironic speculation turned his eyes an even more brilliant blue. 'Shall I show you around?'

Katie followed him along the path towards the house. The gardens were gorgeous—established trees offered shade and privacy, while flowers filled the air with a sweet, summery scent.

'It's big for just you,' she murmured, trying to distract herself from her too-intense thoughts.

'I sometimes lease it out when I'm not here,' he answered lightly. 'It's an investment as much as anything.'

Yes, people would pay huge amounts to spend time in such a private, perfect escape. It was architecturally impressive and luxurious, offering a rare level of comfort with space enough for a party.

A shard of cold reality pierced the sweet air. She'd bet he'd had some hedonistic, decadent parties here. She could just imagine millions of beautiful women in their bikinis, draped around the pool.

Alessandro didn't take her to the towering main entrance, but led her to a vast, plant-lined terrace, with a beautiful blue swimming pool that ran down the side of the building. He walked half the length of the terrace, then opened the fourth set of double doors and stood back to let her enter.

'This is your bedroom.'

She felt a quicksilver urge to flee, but instead she stepped through. The room was airy, light and luxurious, with soft-looking furnishings and a huge bed. Transfixed, she licked her dry lips, trying to stop the immediate surge of rampantly inappropriate thoughts in her head.

'It's beautiful, thank you.'

Too awkward to move, she watched him set her bags

at the end of the bed. 'I'm down the hall,' he said. 'Near if you need me.'

She shot him a quick look and glanced back to her bags, half wishing she could snatch them up and escape. Yet at the same time the last thing she wanted to do was run from him.

'You didn't want to be alone last night,' Alessandro reminded her softly when she failed to reply.

That had been different. She'd been overtired and overwrought and, frankly, freaked out. She wasn't freaked out now. She was something else altogether.

Slowly, irresistibly, she looked at him. Her gaze was instantly ensnared by his. Her breath stalled. So did time. Unable to look away, unable to move, she was intensely aware of the irregular skip of her heart as heat rose. In these last days she'd somehow been restrung inside—all her senses were working more acutely, making her even more aware of him—of his size, his strength, his scent…his sensuality.

And his sinfully delicious humour.

She'd never met anyone who made her smile the way he did. And all she wanted was to stay near to him. He was a source of fascination and fun and she didn't want to be alone at all any more. She'd had the smallest of tastes on the plane, and now she was starving—*craving* more of that contact.

But she couldn't speak…couldn't ask. Katie had never asked for anything like that in her life. Not intimacy. Nothing personal. And while he'd said he wanted her, he'd wanted lots of women. It didn't make her special in any way.

'Come on. I'll show you the rest.' He abruptly turned and stalked out of the room.

She followed, trying to breathe out and release the tension that tightened every muscle.

The magnificent kitchen provided the perfect distraction. She actually laughed aloud when she realised there were many fantastic appliances to stare at instead of gazing at him.

'Oh, Alessandro, this is gorgeous.'

'You're turned on by my oven?' He leaned back against the marble bench and laughed briefly, only to pause and shoot her a deliberately smouldering glance. 'Good, I'm hungry. Are *you* hungry?'

He's just teasing.

His mouth twitched as she didn't—*couldn't*—reply.

He eventually relented and broke the silence. 'There are vegetables prepared, and fresh fish in the fridge. I'll get on the grill.'

She glanced out of the window and saw a well-planted kitchen garden conveniently near. 'I could find some herbs or something…?'

'Perfect. Run away and hide, *dolcezza*. I'll be waiting here.'

She shot him a look, but left the room. She wasn't going to run and hide—she was going to do what she was good at.

Outside and alone, she sucked in a gulp of fresh summer sea air to clear her head. His effect on her was increasing with every moment and it was mortifying.

Pull it together.

Just because they were married, it didn't mean anything. All that flirtation was just talk—nothing to be taken seriously.

She plucked at plants almost at random, then determinedly walked back into the kitchen, armed with fresh herbs and a wide smile.

'Let me do that.' She moved next to where he stood preparing the fish at the counter.

'You don't have to.'

'Not because I *owe* you—even though I do.' She shook her head at him. 'Because I enjoy it. It relaxes me.'

He put the knife down on the marble counter. 'Well, if you insist…'

She did. It was the perfect way to avoid looking at him and falling deeper beneath his spell. Except he stayed to watch her, and even though she was skilled, it took every ounce of concentration to prepare the food without dicing her fingers in the process.

'I cook every night,' she chatted inanely.

'For Brian?'

'Don't sound so disapproving.' She laughed.

'He takes advantage of you.'

'I'm not a total Cinderella. I love cooking. I do it even when I don't have to...'

When she'd finished plating the food Alessandro stepped forward, putting the plates onto a tray he'd loaded with silverware and glasses. She followed him to the terrace, with its stunning view and sumptuous surroundings. It really was paradise.

'Would you like a drink?'

'Um...'

'I have non-alcoholic.' His eyes twinkled.

'Oh, okay...thank you.' She watched as he poured her a glass, then filled his own from the same bottle. 'Don't let me stop you from—'

'*I'm* stopping me,' he said quietly, but there was steel beneath his soft tone. 'I don't need anything that might take the edge off my resolve.'

Awareness slid like silk over her skin, and for a second she was tempted to throw all caution to the wind and suggest they drink from the other bottle together and then...

But she saved herself from speaking by tucking in to the food she'd prepared. He too seemed to be determined to be distracted by the food.

'You're really good at this, Katie,' he finally said with a satisfied sigh.

She nodded. 'Do you often stay here?' She winced inwardly at her banality. Why couldn't she act like a normal person—not a desperate woman on the edge?

'Ideally for a week or so each month.' A rueful expression flickered across his face and he shrugged. 'Usually not quite a week.'

'Every month?' That was more than she'd expected. 'And you bring people with you?'

Was it party central? Curiosity cut at her, and again she imagined those bikinis by the pool...

His rueful smirk broadened into a real smile and his eyes gleamed, as if he knew what she was really asking. 'No, I prefer peace and quiet when I'm here. I can get a lot of work done.'

'You prefer peace and quiet?' She cocked her head. 'Then you didn't like running that club?'

He'd started his property empire by opening the most popular nightspot in London.

'It was hard work. Late work. But it got me where I needed to be.'

'And where was that?'

'In control. Of my business, my finances, my life.'

Her curiosity deepened. 'You didn't have that control before?'

'It's not always that easy to get, is it?' he said lightly, pointing his fork at her with a teasing look. 'You don't have it. Until today you didn't have any control—'

She stiffened. The edge in his voice raised her defences. 'That—'

'You've been locked away.' He ignored her interruption and spoke faster, the bite of his fury building. 'You should have what you want. Have it *when* you want it. You don't need anyone else's permission or approval. It's your life to live.'

'And that's so easy? Shouldn't I consider other people's feelings at all?' she countered, trying not to get angry in return. 'Or stop to consider that what I want might not actually be all that good for me?'

The thing she wanted right now would *definitely* not be good for her.

He suddenly laughed. 'Ah, you're afraid of getting yourself into trouble...'

He made it sound as if she was a goody-two-shoes, but he didn't understand how important being good had been. She'd have lost everything if she hadn't.

'And you consider other people far too much—at personal cost to yourself,' he added, as if he knew it all.

'Perhaps you don't do it enough?' She couldn't help striking back at him.

'Consider other people's feelings?' He adopted a pious look. 'I'm very careful with other people's feelings.'

'Really?' she muttered sarcastically.

'Are you judging my relationships?'

'Do you even *have* relationships?'

'Sure. Short…sweet. Hot.'

She paused, struck by the honesty underlying that snappy answer.

'Maybe that's not all that good for *you*,' she challenged softly. 'You don't allow yourself to go deeply into relationships so you don't get what's truly good.'

He chuckled, as if she were the most naive creature he'd met. 'I get the good stuff—don't worry about that.'

'There's more to life than good sex, Alessandro.'

'And you would know?' He laughed.

'I might not be experienced in all that—'

'You're so sheltered you've hardly *lived*,' he interrupted with a jeer.

'I've lived a lot, actually,' she argued. 'A great life doesn't always have to mean exotic travel and endless orgasms. Little moments are amazing.'

'How old are you again?' He propped his elbow on the table and pinched the bridge of his nose. 'Are you ready to retire in that orchard?' He shook his head slightly. 'Bury yourself away for all your youth? For heaven's sake, Katie, live a little. You said yourself you don't owe Brian everything—'

'I know that,' she snapped.

'But you're still stuck,' he snapped back. 'Still acting as if you can't break any of his rules.'

She stared at him, silenced. Because he was right.

But she wasn't like Alessandro—not as fiercely independent nor as hedonistic. It wasn't just anyone else's permission or approval that Alessandro refused to need. He refused to *need* anyone in any serious way at all. At least, not for long. It seemed to be his philosophy on life. And good for him.

But she hadn't been entirely useless either, and she resented his implication that she had. 'I *chose* to stay and look after Susan.'

'Of course you did,' he acknowledged. 'But it wasn't like you had any other real option. He'd told you often enough that you owed them.'

Her anger resurged. She hadn't cared for Susan only out of obligation. 'I love her. I *wanted* to…'

She trailed off as his expression altered.

'I know that,' he answered quietly. 'But *Brian* should be the one taking better care of her.'

The bitter note in his voice made a spot in her chest ache. Why was he so bothered by Brian's treatment of his wife?

'Yes, he should,' she acknowledged with a sigh. 'I should have made him.'

'How were you going to do that when—?' Alessandro broke off his too blunt comment and jerked his head in a sharp, negating gesture. 'Naomi didn't take care of my father and I couldn't change that situation either,' he said. 'She and Brian are very alike, unfortunately.'

The curiosity within her deepened into a well. How had Naomi hurt his father? Had things gone wrong before he'd died? Was that why Alessandro had left with so much anger that he'd never returned?

She drew in a breath of courage. 'How—?'

'Do you want to talk to Susan?' he interrupted as he glanced at his watch. 'Now would be a good time.'

She knew he was deliberately diverting her. But she let him. 'Yes, of course. I should have talked to her already.'

'She knows you're okay. Dominique has been in constant contact with her since we married. And she's okay—a nurse companion has started.'

Katie felt guilty all over again. Alessandro had done so much...arranged so much...while she'd just—what? Been unable to think about anything other than him kissing her? She was appalled at her selfishness.

He pulled his phone from his pocket and passed it to her. She quickly tapped in the number.

'Susan?' she said, as soon as her foster mother answered.

'Katie? Is that you?'

'Yes, how are you? Are you okay?'

'Where are you?'

'You're really okay?'

'Is it true?'

Katie half smiled as she realised they were simply firing questions at each other, with neither stopping to answer. She took a breath and slowed down. 'That I've married Alessandro Zetticci? Yes. That's true.'

'I had no idea you'd even seen him since...' Susan drew in an audible breath. 'Why didn't you tell me?'

Katie bit her lip. 'I thought you'd disapprove—'

'Of Alessandro? Is that why you ran away?' Susan sighed. 'I would have talked to Brian. We could have had a lovely ceremony in the gardens...'

Katie slid lower into her seat as relief eased her tension. Susan must be okay if she was able to focus on her precious gardens. She glanced across to Alessandro—clearly he could hear, because her own amusement was mirrored in his eyes.

'I guess we could have...' Katie murmured. 'I'm sorry—'

'Are you happy, Katie?' Susan interrupted.

Katie froze, thrown by her foster mother's serious tone. She'd *thought* she was happy enough at home. She'd been grateful for what she had, and she'd not *let* herself wish for anything more. She'd focused on caring for Susan, on making her sauces, and on the few occasions she'd stopped to think she had hoped that she'd have more eventually. She'd been coping.

But, no, she hadn't been entirely happy. She'd felt constrained by Brian. Following his rules, never feeling good enough, always wary that he would pull the rug from beneath her. As he had when he'd ordered her to marry Carl.

But now she'd had the smallest glimpse of the world beyond White Oaks. Alessandro had done more than enable her—he'd *shown* her. In the few hours she'd been with him she'd done more, seen more, than she had in years. Truthfully, in all her life.

'Katie?' Susan asked her again. 'Are you happy?'

Right this second?

She couldn't look away from the warmth in Alessandro's brilliant blue eyes. Couldn't halt the bubbling sensation in her chest. She could barely answer, but nor could she lie.

'Yes.'

The atmosphere turned electric as the warmth in his eyes was replaced by an indefinable intensity.

Katie swallowed the sudden tightness in her throat and strove to speak. 'I'll be home in a few days. I'll come and see you right away.' Those bubbles fizzed as Alessandro steadily kept watching her. 'Okay?'

'Lovely, darling. I look forward to seeing you both.'

Katie ended the call and handed the phone back to Alessandro, wary of what he might say. More than wary of what he made her feel.

Another flame of guilt licked at her heart. Poor Alessandro. In the last twenty-four hours she'd been demanding and difficult and at times almost rude. But she'd never released her rebellious antagonism towards *anyone* before. It was almost a fire in her blood, pushing her to defy him. To provoke him. She had to settle it somehow.

'Thank you so much for everything,' she said softly.

'I don't want your gratitude,' he snapped. 'That's the last thing I want from you.'

She was transfixed by the blaze in his eyes—not mere warmth, it was blistering. The air thickened, trapping his fierce words between them. One word.

Want.

Her forbidden giveaway reply whispered out. 'What *do* you want from me?'

Heat rose in her cheeks as her mind raced with every intimate possibility her inexperienced self could think of. Her heart skipped, and then skidded to a sprint that left breathing impossible.

But Alessandro slowly shook his head. 'No,' he said harshly, his gaze not lifting from hers. 'You're not transferring your need to people-please to me.'

Katie flinched, because she'd been strung out waiting for his reply. For those few moments she'd been willing to let him do anything he wanted. And that was mortifying. Because he didn't want her. Not really. He had been playing with her on the plane, because she was inexperienced and it was mildly entertaining for him.

'Sex is always a game.'

The worst thing was that he knew what she'd been thinking. He could read her mind as easily as a front-page headline.

He suddenly pushed back from the table and stood in a jerky moment. 'You owe me *nothing*—understand?'

CHAPTER EIGHT

ALESSANDRO STALKED TO the kitchen and tossed their plates into the dishwasher. He'd insisted he didn't want her help because he needed ten minutes alone to get himself together.

Except the kitchen was now tainted with echoes of her scent and sound and the sight of her at that bench.

She'd relaxed in here, swiftly preparing dinner with skill, her smile small and private while she focused intently on her task.

He'd been almost unable to do anything other than stare at her. He'd been staring at her pretty much all afternoon. He was still recovering from the bronze bikini that had brought out the amber lights in her eyes.

Those three guys by the pool had liked it too. She hadn't appeared to notice them, but Alessandro sure as hell had seen them eating her with their eyes. Protective—*possessive*—he'd pointedly wrapped his arm around her, leaving them in no doubt she was taken.

His jealousy, his loss of control over his own body, horrified him. She made him feel as if he'd been starved of sex for centuries. Which he hadn't. Yet he was struggling to control the urge to touch her. His desire burned hotter than an exploding supernova.

Her hair was no longer in that low ponytail, but hung loose and shining after her trip to the salon earlier today. He was glad she hadn't cut much of the length. It gleamed a gorgeous brown, flecked with strands of gold—a myriad of colours to match her eyes.

The dress she'd chosen was bolder than he'd expected—a bright splash of summer colour with a fit that emphasised her narrow waist. He wanted to rip the pretty thing off her like some lust-crazed monster. The longer he was around her, the stronger that wildness within him grew. But it wasn't her new haircut or the clothing that had made the difference. It was her blossoming confidence, that lick of awareness, the anticipation in her eyes.

The memory of her response.

Kissing her had been a massive mistake. He'd discovered too much that was tempting—her sweetness, her heat, her innate passion. And he didn't think he could resist it. He who could walk away from anything—anyone—had had to *run* from her.

She'd infected him—injected a fever into his veins. Now the fever was spreading and all he wanted was *more*. All he could think about was her.

He left the kitchen and walked along the terrace, stopping at the balustrade overlooking the pool. He didn't notice the view, or the scent of the summer flowers, or the warmth of the evening air. He was too busy stopping himself from going to find her.

He was deluding himself that he'd just talk to her—talking to her was oddly easy. But that set another alarm off. He didn't talk to his lovers. He gave pleasure. Took pleasure. And then left.

But he'd had to bite back talking more about Naomi and his father. Of all things that was the one he never discussed with anyone, and yet he'd been so close to telling Katie every silly little thing—even his personal history with this island too…

But he needed to maintain the distance between them because soon enough they'd separate.

He gripped the railing with both hands. He shouldn't have brought her here. It was his private space. But he'd thought he'd be able to prepare her for the charade they were to play for the next few months here—get her over the wobbles. Instead *he* was the one on edge, struggling for self-control, almost consumed by temptation when he knew he shouldn't take advantage of her.

But she's using you.

She wanted his help, his money, his power...for protection. For him to seduce her in return would be too much of a personal price for her to pay, even if she was willing. And if he were any kind of a decent human being he wouldn't even consider it.

But she wants you too.

She hadn't just responded when he'd kissed her—she'd ignited. Sure, there had been some gratitude mixed up in it, but there had been raw, red-hot desire for him there too. He was experienced enough to know that. What was more, the carnal curiosity in her eyes brightened with every interaction they had.

And it was killing him—death by temptation. Maybe they could indulge just a *little*...?

He twisted his lips at that devil inside, tearing him apart, and at his confusion. Why did she captivate him so completely? He'd had plenty of women—all more classically beautiful, more successful, certainly more experienced...

He glared into the blue water. Her virginity wasn't what aroused him... That appallingly inconvenient little fact was the complication that made having her impossible.

Gritting his teeth, he gripped the railing so tight his knuckles turned white.

'Alessandro?'

He turned towards her voice. She warily walked nearer, watching him the way a zoo-keeper might watch a pacing barely caged tiger.

'Mmm?' He tightened his grip to stop himself grabbing her.

'Are you okay?'

'No,' he muttered bluntly, unable to lie because he was tired and too tightly wired to hold back—at least verbally. 'Not okay.'

He'd never struggled with his self-control before.

He'd never wanted one woman with this intensity before.

'Anything I can do?'

Oh, of *course* she'd offer to help, wouldn't she? So willing and eager to please. Which was exactly what he wanted and yet everything he didn't, all at the same time.

Her expression dimmed and a frown slowly formed. 'If you're in a mood I'll leave you to your thoughts.'

Again, everything he wanted and didn't want.

'You confuse me,' he ground out. 'Or rather my feelings for you confuse me.'

She reached out for the railing beside him and held on as tightly as he was. 'You have feelings for me?'

He cleared his throat, grimacing at his uncustomary clumsiness. He did not struggle to think around women. And he never let them wonder what he wanted or definitely *didn't* want from them.

'Perhaps urges would be a better word.'

He heard a soft gasp and her bubbling laugh warmed the air. 'Oh. *Those*.'

'You have them too?' He shot her a sideways look, unable to stop his own small smile.

As her gaze meshed with his her laugh dissolved into a sigh. 'I'm trying to ignore them.' She bit her lip.

'Why?' *And how?*

'To prove to myself that I can.'

He frowned. Why did she need to do that? She'd been so sheltered, and she seemed far too focused on self-control. Alessandro knew that life was short, and Katie seemed to have spent all of hers so far trying to please other people. Why couldn't she just please herself for once?

That temptation spiralled. He knew that her pleasing herself would definitely please him.

'Okay, so how are you going to reward yourself?' He released the railing and moved closer to her. He simply couldn't resist any more. 'Once you've proved your self-control?'

Her eyes widened with every step he took. Her quickened breath was gratifying. Maybe it wasn't as easy as all that for her to ignore those urges.

His body tightened in response and readiness. Damn this restraint. He was sick of trying to be a goddamn hero—it wasn't a natural fit. In the school of life he was a player, not a prefect.

'How am I going to...*what*?' she asked breathlessly.

He smiled at her distraction. 'Going to reward yourself?' He stopped right beside her. 'It seems to me that you're very good at doing what others ask of you. You're very good at keeping yourself in check. Very good at doing what you need to.' Or not doing what she thought she shouldn't. 'So how do you reward *yourself*?'

She didn't—that was obvious.

'The reward is in the action,' she said, her nose wrinkling, as if she were confused by his question. 'By doing— or in this case *not* doing—I feel good.'

Did she really? He didn't think so. He thought she felt as achy and restless as he did. She was watching him too keenly, her whole body was strained. And, heaven help him, he could see the sharp outline of her nipples against the pretty fabric of her dress.

'But it isn't going away, Katie. In fact, it's only getting worse.' Which was intensely unusual for him.

Her luminous eyes widened. 'Are you suggesting that my reward for *not* tangling with you should be for me to tangle with you?'

'You don't actually have to do anything.' He reached out to run his hand the length of her shining hair. It was a beacon he could no longer ignore. 'You can just lie there and take your reward, *dolcezza*.'

He wanted her on a bed—writhing, welcoming, arching in ecstasy. What he'd do to make her scream... She'd be so beautiful.

Sheer shock immobilised her, and then desire glazed her eyes. 'Alessandro...'

It was a caution. But it was also shy need.

And it was surrender.

He wrapped his arm around her waist and pulled her to him. He stared down at her, reading her expression, the softness and the sensual tension in her body. She put her hands on his chest—but not to push away. In fact she arched nearer. Her lips parted on a pout, her breathing hitched. She wanted to touch as much as he did. She was every bit as willing.

'Let me be your reward,' he dared her huskily.

'I'm afraid you're my poison,' she shivered. But her hands slid up his chest, shyly exploring. 'You're such temptation...'

He shook his head, leaning closer, his body aching for her fingers to skim further. 'That's *you*.'

'You can turn any woman on,' she moaned. 'It's so unfair.'

'If you like I can give you some pointers.'

She half laughed and looked down, letting the fall of her hair hide her face.

He cupped her chin and made her look up into his eyes. 'I'm not going to apologise for my past, Katie. But you must know this kind of chemistry doesn't happen every day. It's rare. And seemingly almost impossible to restrain.'

'You're just saying that...' she mumbled.

'No, I'm not. But even so it's still just nothing...' he whispered, brushing closer to her. *It was always nothing.*

'Can something this intense be just nothing?' she asked.

He groaned at what her question gave away. He didn't answer. He couldn't. All he could do now was succumb to the savage need to kiss her. He'd show, not tell.

Intense, yes. Nothing, yes.

His relief at her immediate response lasted mere seconds before restraint became almost impossible. Her lips were luscious and pillowy and so sweet. He tried to ease back so he didn't bruise her, but he heard her little moan of outrage and felt her rise on tiptoes to keep him close. And instead of easing back he slipped his leash—smashing his lips on hers, almost brutal in his possession.

And she met him, matched him. Her hands slid around to his back and held him tighter. Her tongue lashed against his...her breasts pressed close to his chest. He lost his breath, lost his reason. He was unable to resist deepening everything—taking them swiftly to a desperation beyond anything even he'd felt.

Desire combusted. He ought to release her and run— lock himself away until he had himself under control again. But he ached to hear her scream and see her sated—to see the smile of satisfaction on her lips. Determination flared as he felt her trembling need and the tight clasp of her fingers on his shirt. He could control himself enough to see her release. He could make this about her. It was the only acceptable outcome now.

'It's only a moment, Katie.' He was reminding himself as much as reassuring her. 'Only to ease the ache.'

He picked her up and carried her through the open doors before reason could return. He gently placed her in the centre of her big bed, determined not to take everything. He'd not give in to the urge to claim her completely. Not for him that ultimate pleasure. Not with her. She deserved more than he could ever offer her.

But he could give her something. He kissed her, swept away by all the sensations of touching and tasting her— all caramel and honey, silken warm curves. He didn't undress—not himself, nor her. It was the only way to maintain his control. Because in those kisses he'd felt her shivering surrender.

She softened, her legs spreading, offering more than she could possibly realise. He couldn't resist cupping her. Fury swamped him as he felt her damp heat through the thin barrier of her panties.

'How dare you deny yourself when you're this hot?' he

rasped. 'Why do you hold back from something you really want?'

He was oddly furious, because this was about more than this moment with him now. This was about her whole life. She'd denied herself so much.

'You should have what you want,' he told her roughly, bending to tend to her hungry mouth. 'You should always have what you want. What you deserve.'

He wanted to see her undone...all the way to completion. He hated the way she treated herself. As if she believed she didn't deserve more.

She trembled as he strummed her lightly and kissed her hard. She moaned into his mouth, her body rippling beneath his. He lifted his head and stared at her. They'd barely started and she'd ignited. So on the edge. So needy. She'd been restrained too long...as if she were afraid to have her voice heard.

He wanted to hear her voice—her scream. It shot him to the edge too. He wanted time to cease so he could hang in this moment, where he had her where he wanted her— spread before him, hot and wet and willing. He choked on his own groan, holding back as he felt her full-bodied feminine response to his touch.

She was so supple, sweet, eager. Her scent, her warmth, all her responses were beautiful. His body tightened to the point of pain, and the urge to claim and conquer almost overpowered him. He was close to losing his head. But it was imperative to him that she should feel maximum pleasure. This time the desire to please was all his.

Focus only on her. Utterly on her.

Katie gasped, struggling to hold herself together. She shouldn't just lie here...she should touch him back... But what he was doing felt too good, and the reckless desire consuming her was uncontrollable. The ache was so much more than she could handle. She couldn't deny herself, couldn't make herself move—too scared to in case he stopped. She wanted his touch more than she'd ever wanted anything. And he knew it.

He let out a low little laugh—the sexiest sound she'd ever heard—and teased and stoked the flames higher. He kissed her with fierce passion, only to ease back again, roving leisurely down her neck to nibble along the neckline of her dress. Her breasts tightened, wanting some of his attention. But his hands swept down her sides, lifting the silk dress to skim across her thighs.

She sighed, lifting her hips as he sought out her secrets, guiding her along a rapid current of heat and want. Her lips felt hot and a little swollen, and all she wanted was for him to kiss her again—to tease his tongue inside her mouth the way he had before. She ached for the weight of him above her, for him to pin her down and fix her in place with his powerful body.

She couldn't say it, couldn't ask. She could only clutch the sheet beneath her to help hold back her screams.

He lifted his head to look down at her with those smouldering eyes. 'I dare you to do what you want, say what you want—to take what you want, when you want it.' His words were slightly slurred and his strokes up her inner thigh quickened.

'You don't think I've done that already?'

She circled her hips again on pure instinct, wanting him to go higher, wanting more to the point of madness. Wanting it enough to be provoked into answering with all the rebellion she'd normally deny herself.

'Are we not now married because I was ballsy enough to ask you?'

'You were compelled to do that because you wanted to protect Susan.' He stroked her higher, faster, and lowered his head until his mouth was tantalisingly close to hers. 'But you didn't want to marry anyone. Not Carl. Not me either.

You did what you thought you had to, for someone else. When did you last do something for yourself?'

He was teasing, tormenting, pushing her, whispering provocation against her lips.

Silently she stared up at him and pushed her legs a little further apart, granting him unrestricted access. Wordlessly telling him what she wanted.

He slid his hand higher, almost to where she ached most.

'You don't do it often enough,' Alessandro growled. 'What do you want, Katie? *Tell* me.'

'Kiss me,' she whispered in a breathless rush.

In an instant her wish was granted. His kiss was carnal and hot, and at the exact moment his tongue plundered her mouth his fingers teased her secret, most sensitive spot. It took only that stroke and suddenly all the fireworks in the world exploded within her.

She screamed as intense convulsions radiated from where he cupped her core. She twisted in his arms but he didn't release her. His mouth moved to her neck, kissing her while his fingers kept up the delicious torture that tore her into nothing but shreds of sensation.

'So hot. So quick.' A soft exultant laugh followed the last echo of her cries. 'You can't tell me you didn't need that.'

She couldn't answer because she couldn't move. She couldn't see how she was ever going to recover from something that felt so good.

He gently caressed her, keeping her close until the orgasmic quivers began to ease. She felt boneless, weightless, as if she were floating along a warm river of bliss. She opened her eyes and looked straight into his.

The remnants of his smile faded as he gazed down at her until lines of tension bracketed his mouth. When she arched her back just a little his jaw clenched. And as he lost the battle to mask his strain a new energy coiled within her— embers to spark that driving desire.

Not enough.

The sharp knife of need sliced through the last vestige of her relief.

More.

It should have been impossible—only a moment ago she'd experienced an intense orgasm, the most intimate embrace of her life. But he'd roused a hunger she'd never known she had, nor that she was capable of. She needed to know—to share all of herself with him and have him with her...*in* her. What he'd just done wasn't enough, and she had not done enough.

But at the exact moment she realised that he pushed away from her, vaulting off the bed.

'Where are you going?' His vehement speed had shocked the question out of her.

'Out. Before I do something I promised us both that I wouldn't.'

'Alessandro—'

'No.' He shook his head.

Her heart pounded. 'But you...' She trailed off, unable to say it. He hadn't had the release she'd had.

His lips twisted as he read her expression. 'I'll survive.'

'But—'

He stepped forward with a swift movement and pressed his hands into the mattress either side of her head, as if he didn't trust himself to touch her again.

'Don't.'

'But—'

With a growl he bent and caught her mouth in a kiss. She melted, opening to let him in, curling her tongue around his hungrily, the way he'd taught her. But too soon he tore away, with a choked noise in the back of his throat.

He didn't speak until he got to the door. Even then he didn't look back.

'Sweet dreams, Katie.'

CHAPTER NINE

IT WAS IMPOSSIBLE to relax, to forget, to deny, because the bone-deep satisfaction didn't stay—instead bitterness and confusion built.

But worst of all was the desire. It surged more powerful than ever, pacing within her like a creature of the wild, caged in a prison too small. It strengthened with every unstoppable memory—every caress, every kiss that she couldn't forget—until finally it morphed into a fire of frustration that flashed through her system, rendering sleep impossible.

After a few burning restless hours she gave up trying. Needing to cool down, she walked out through the open doorway from her bedroom to the courtyard. The moon cast a silvery path on the darkened water and in the far distance moored boats gleamed in the moonlight. Gentle waves lapped against the beach below.

'You can't sleep?'

His low query didn't startle her. Somehow she'd known he'd be out here too.

And of *course* she couldn't sleep.

Alessandro was sitting at the table where they'd dined, his expression indecipherable in the shadows. But his tone held an edge of mockery. Her frustration flared but she refused to react. She wasn't going to try to provoke him again. She was ignoring that shameless, wilful part of herself.

'It's beautiful,' she murmured, turning back to the water and trying to think of something innocuous to mask her inner turmoil. 'No wonder you come here as often as you can.'

Her tension pulled tighter when he didn't reply. She wrapped her arms around her waist, even though her new

silk nightdress was already too hot. She was conscious of
her breathing, aware of the distance between them, of the
thrum of desire beating relentlessly in her veins.

She finally looked from the water back to him. She could
see the gorgeous gleam of his eyes but couldn't read anything in it. Earlier he'd left her so easily. Which meant he'd
not really wanted her. It hadn't even been a game for him,
so why had he…?

She couldn't hold back the question. 'Alessandro—?'

'Go back to bed, Katie,' he forestalled her huskily.

'No.'

'Katie…'

She hated that tone. 'You don't want my gratitude?' She
tossed her head proudly. 'Then I don't want your pity.'

'Pardon?' A thread of molten steel had entered his voice.

Power flowed through her veins. Control. Pride. Dignity. *This* was what she needed to do. She needed to tell
him what she *didn't* want.

'Don't do me any more favours.'

'Is that what you think that was?' He pushed back from
the table, his chair scraping loudly on the flagstones. 'I
can't—'

'You don't want to,' she snapped.

'Katie—' His muttered oath rubbished her accusation.
'There's no going back.'

Her anger sparked at his hesitation, at his treatment of
her as a naive fool. 'You told me to ask for what I wanted.
I finally did. But then you walked away.'

He stood, planted his feet wide and stared at her like a
determined statue. Too damned heroic.

'I've been regretting it ever since.'

He regretted stopping? Excitement roared through her
at his response.

'Be very sure about your next move, *dolcezza*. Because
if you ask again I'll say yes. And I won't leave. Not until
we're both done.'

Could she be this selfish—take more from him?

'But I can't give you everything you want,' he added harshly. 'I'll never be able to do that.'

'How do you know everything I want?' she replied, her spirits rising. 'I've never said I wanted "everything" from you. I just want *now* with you. Just for me.'

He remained motionless and unyielding.

She stared at the fierce intensity in his eyes. 'I can make up my own mind!' Katie's frustration at his unnecessary protectiveness exploded. 'I don't need *you* to make the decision for me.'

His breath hissed out between clenched teeth. 'No? You're claiming control? Fine.' He took one barely leashed step forward. 'But some elements I *do* get to decide.'

The steel in his voice sent a shock of anticipation into that secret part of her—so thrilling, so stunning, she was rendered speechless.

'My room. My bed. My way.'

He punctuated each word with another step towards her.

She couldn't move, locked in place by the burn of blue. He was so strong, so consuming, and as he stalked closer she felt the overwhelming desire to surrender—to simply melt before him. *This* was what she wanted. His attention. Nothing but now. All physical.

She closed her mind to the complications of the future, not even daring to consider the next five minutes. She couldn't bear the agony of embarrassment.

She chose just him—just now. 'Okay.'

He swallowed and took the last step towards her. In the moonlight she saw the faintest sheen of sweat skimming his skin. He wore only boxers, and they did little to hide the reaction of his body. For a moment she just stared, her heart thudding with a roar of both anticipation and anxiety, before she made herself look away.

Her knees weakened as desire rushed to pool low in her belly. But with his all-seeing eyes he knew she'd peeked.

'Not pity,' he teased softly. 'You're getting something far more powerful than pity, Katie.'

That old playboy arrogance was tinder to the spark of rebellion that smoked only in his presence. To the need to fire back at him.

Her heart quadrupled its pace. She ran her tongue over her parched lips but was barely able to mutter the response that he'd provoked. 'Prove it.'

His lips curved, but that sly smile didn't soften the steeliness in his eyes. 'Next time you dare me, try taking a breath first.'

'It's impossible to breathe around you,' she confessed.

His hand cupped her jaw. 'Katie…'

For a horrible moment she thought he was going to deny her. But then he bent towards her. His kiss tasted of lemon and mint, cool and refreshing. His body brushed against hers, his skin burning through her silk slip. She uncurled her fists, reaching out to touch him, resting her hands on his waist. The kiss deepened. Emboldened, she traced more of his skin, discovering his strength and height and heat.

His muscles tensed beneath her touch and he tore his lips from hers. 'Katie—inside.' He paused and then stepped back.

He didn't reach to pick her up and carry her this time. Instinctively she knew he was testing her, ensuring that this was her choice, her decision. Her legs trembled—but not from fear. It was anticipation…pure yearning.

This once, she promised herself. There was no one else she wanted—that she'd ever wanted. He was a present to herself in this fantasy place for this one perfect night. She couldn't deny herself and she'd have no regrets.

His bedroom was even more vast than hers. The curtains weren't drawn and in the bright moonlight the spacious bed gleamed—a pearled place for private pleasure. She noticed the white coverings were untouched—had he not even tried to sleep tonight?

Her pulse thundered as she sat on the bed. Her senses were so heightened that the luxurious linen felt deliciously soft and cool on her overly sensitive skin. He didn't move to join her. Did she have to ask him again?

But then he released a harsh breath and came to her. As he knelt on the bed beside her he framed her face in his hands and kissed her hard and deep and long. She tumbled into the sensation—all sweet heat and relief—because finally she was here, with him, having what she wanted... needed...from him. With nothing held back.

He lifted his head and took his time. To her infinite torment he touched her slowly, slipping the thin straps of her soft silk nightgown from her shoulders. Then he tugged it lower, exposing her breasts to his gaze. To his touch. To his kiss. Then he pulled the gown lower still, until she was bared completely. He paused and cocked his head, one hand rubbing the back of his neck as he surveyed her with hungry eyes.

'You're beautiful,' he muttered hoarsely, and bent to kiss her belly, then to kiss her lower still.

'You don't have to flatter me...' she moaned, turning her head to press her cheek to the cool sheet, briefly closing her eyes at the intensity of such an intimate touch.

'Don't hide behind your judgemental ideas of me to reject my appreciation,' he growled, lifting his head and waiting until she turned and looked him in the eyes. 'Accept the compliment, Katie.' He placed his hand on her—intimately. 'Accept the caress. Or we cannot continue.'

His gaze, his touch, burned into her—through her—until she had no recourse but to release the pent-up tension in a deep sigh and slide her legs a little further apart.

'Yes,' she whispered.

'Good...' He smiled. 'Because I need to see you. I need to taste you. I need to have you.'

His words shook a fierce response from her, and his hands stoked it even higher. His fingertips swept over her and his mouth followed, bestowing caresses and kisses both firm and gentle, playful and passionate. All the length of her body sensation ignited—blissful pleasure and a desperate, driving need for more.

He chuckled as she arched, to encourage him to stroke harder, to touch her right where she was so tormented. But he didn't. He held back with deliberate devastation.

'Not yet.' His words sounded slightly slurred as he shifted and began again.

He teased her to the brink and back again. Once, twice… until she was writhing, shaking and finally asking all over again—begging, in fact. She couldn't take it any more.

'Please, Alessandro…'

He smiled that wonderful, wicked, infuriating smile that always made her tumble towards him. And then he moved closer, kissing her lower, then lower, while his hand cupped and his finger teased.

She shivered as he discovered her hot, wet secrets. Slowly, gently, he slid a single finger inside her. She moved uncontrollably, then tensed as a moment of lucidity hit—as she realised the total intimacy of his touch.

'Let yourself go,' he breathed against her. 'Your instincts are good.'

She had no choice but to obey the dictates of her trembling, aching body, because then he sealed his mouth to that most sensual private part of her. She arched, driving her hips high against him, and screamed in ecstasy as he relentlessly subjected her to the most intimate, most incredible experience of her life.

The orgasm shot through her, racking every muscle and cell, twisting her inside out in a series of pleasurable pulses, until she finally fell back on the bed in a limp heap. But even as she breathed out that last sigh of supreme delight she realised her body was charged—fully powered and ready for something so much more. Something she instinctively knew only he could give her.

He lifted himself right away from her.

Shocked, she watched him stand. 'Seriously...?'

He shot her a look—tension intertwined with amusement. 'Absolutely.'

She realised he'd retrieved a box from the drawer in the small table beside the bed. Her heart thudded as he finally removed the boxers that had been the only barrier between them and rolled a condom down his length.

Katie ran her tongue along her lip and then swallowed—unable to look away, unable to speak.

'I'll take care of you, Katie,' he said softly.

But that steely determination was still audible.

It made her shiver. 'I know.'

The moment he came back to her on the bed the chemistry between them combusted. He gently nudged her legs apart with his, bracing himself over her and kissing her beyond anticipation all over again. He was so, so close, and she'd never been as excited, as aching, in all her life.

But then he paused to look deep into her eyes. 'Are you—?'

She twisted beneath him in an agony of desire. 'Don't you *dare* ask me again.'

He half laughed, but she could see the strain around his eyes. She put her hand on his jaw, feeling the heat of his skin, the sheen of sweat covering him.

'Katie...' He cupped her face in return, then slid his fingers to lace them through her hair. His eyes locked on hers. 'You're beautiful,' he said. 'More beautiful than is comfortable,' he added in an almost inaudible murmur.

He pressed closer. She drew in a shocked, sharp breath, her eyes fluttering shut as she strained to take him.

His low groan felled her. 'Katie... Breathe.'

She trembled, yielding on a soft sigh as he pushed right inside her. He was so big, his invasion hard and thick, and now he paused, searching her eyes as he slowly took what she offered and gave what she needed.

Silently they stared at each other as he pressed ever so slightly closer, sliding deeper into her tight, slick body. She moaned at the sensation—so full, so overwhelming. And just at the moment when she thought it was too much he kissed her—tenderly, but taking her totally. His tongue caressed her slow and deep, matching the rhythm of his hips, pressing close and then releasing before thrusting closer, then closer again.

She more than melted. She moved—breaking free of his kiss to gasp in delight and arch closer as she suddenly realised just how good this was.

'That's it,' he muttered, bearing down on her again. 'Take me.'

His hand swept lower, his fingers teasing the secret place where they were pressed close. She felt his rigid length deep inside, stroking her. It felt so good. Her mouth parted as her breathing became erratic and moans of excitement escaped. Her gaze was locked on his. She felt his determination, his approval as she tumbled deeper into a vortex of intensity where heat and darkness coalesced.

She cried out again as pleasure swept over her in a great wave. She wound her arms tight around him and literally rode him through it—the cause of her pleasure and her anchor through the storm of sensation.

And then…when she finally returned to calm…she refused to release him. She held his roughened jaw between her palms, looking right into his eyes.

His smile slipped a little. 'Katie…' Half warning, half praise. 'You okay?'

She nodded. She could hardly speak for the intensity of her satisfaction. She simply sighed his name. 'Alessandro…'

He smiled, then kissed her as if he was pouring his soul into her. 'A little more,' he whispered. 'Just a little more. Okay?'

'Yes.'

It was more than okay. She didn't want this to end. She

hadn't had everything yet. She hadn't had him shaking in her arms the way she'd shaken in his.

He smiled as he watched her, apparently able to read her mind. 'Come with me this time.'

It should have been impossible. The orgasm she'd just enjoyed had been so intense. Only his words triggered a lick of electricity that she recognised. She felt the heat and damp of his skin, the tension holding him fiercely still as he locked against her and her own desire surged. She wanted him to let go too.

Primal instinct kicked in and her body took over. She curled her leg around his waist, locking him deeper to her, and slid her arms more tightly around his back.

'Your instincts are good,' he'd assured her. And he was right. Because this felt even better.

The look in his blue eyes became even more brilliant. 'Katie—'

'More, Alessandro. Please.' She'd loved all his tenderness, but she wanted his passion too.

With a groan he pressed his hands beside her, levering himself up so he could drive deeper into her. This wasn't pleasure. This was beyond anything that could be defined that simply.

Her lips parted as she panted with every pounding thrust. She squeezed him with her arms and legs, aching to hold him more tightly, more deeply inside her. She couldn't get close enough. She *still* couldn't get close enough.

'Katie...' he choked. 'Katie...' He lapsed into unintelligible Italian.

This was what she wanted.

This was even better than before.

The ripple took her by surprise, tearing through her, seizing every muscle, making her fingers like claws that dug into him. And he was the same with her—buried to the hilt and then some. Rammed together—clutching, kissing, totally connected—they shared every inch, every sensation.

'I had no idea…' she gasped.

It wasn't a trickle of goodness. It was a river—a shimmering cascade of delight spreading throughout her body and beyond. Seeping into him too, into this bubble they'd created. This cocoon of such intimacy, such connection.

She'd never felt as close to anyone. Never felt as secure. Even if it was only for these few moments, it was the best feeling of her life.

'Thank you.'

'Katie…' The lightest puff of teasing disapproval.

She couldn't summon the energy to open her eyes, but she smiled a little sadly. 'I mean it.'

He held her close and rolled, lifting her to lie on his chest. He cradled her as the last shivers of delight skimmed her skin.

'Thank *you*.' He released a long, satisfied sigh.

She'd not expected words of love—of course she hadn't. But now she felt their absence. It was an alarmingly vast emptiness that ached.

That 'everything' she'd said she didn't want from him…? *No.*

She refused to recognise the extent of that yearning. This would only be a temporary pleasure. That was what it was for him. This gnawing feeling inside was simply lust all over again. Purely physical. She'd be satisfied with his body, his skill, and she'd have her fill of him.

And now, impossibly, when she'd been exhausted only moments ago, she was energised again.

'Katie?'

Of course he'd sensed it.

His hands tightened on her waist and he shifted, sliding her beneath him.

'Show me more,' she said, and kissed him before he could answer, desperately drowning the doubt that was trying to curl its cold tendrils around her heart.

Oh, Katie, what have you done?

CHAPTER TEN

TROUBLE SLITHERED LIKE a clever snake, avoiding detection until it was too late to stop its strike. While last night had been wonderful, it had also been dangerous. More than she'd thought possible.

Katie showered beneath cold water, desperate to settle the confusing thoughts and feelings swirling in her head. It was just sex. Natural. Normal. Nothing profound. Nothing out of the ordinary. Yet her heart pounded. Instinctively she knew her response was more intense than 'normal'. *Her instincts were good*, and they were right on this.

This wasn't some 'people-pleasing' problem like Alessandro had teased her about. She'd been utterly unable to resist the temptation of him last night, and this morning that impulse was even stronger. She'd naively thought it would have eased. Wasn't that what happened when you scratched an itch? It went away. It wasn't supposed to itch more. Lots of people had casual flings or one-night stands and moved on.

Only she'd sunk deeper into the pool of infatuation. Truthfully, she was halfway to falling for him completely. He'd helped her. He'd listened. He'd been kind. But he also challenged her constantly, while invariably making her laugh at the same time, and that just made him magnetic. Add the way he could please her physically and she stood no chance.

She mocked herself for being sentimental—for weaving fairy tales into her fantasies. As a lonely teen she'd dreamt of being swept off her feet and being ravished, of being taken away to some wondrous kingdom where she was safe and secure and *loved* for all time…

But Alessandro wasn't Prince Charming. There was no happy-ever-after in his world. This was only fun—moments that meant nothing. Last night had been merely that for him, and while she knew that he'd truly wanted her, soon enough he wouldn't.

Already that thought terrified her more than it ought. Because she knew too well how being unwanted hurt.

She had to protect herself—she had to be stronger. He'd told her to take what she wanted, but how could she when she knew she was putting herself at risk?

He'd also wanted honesty…and that she could give him. She'd grown some courage in the last couple of days. She could do what she *needed* to do—what was best for *her*.

Alessandro sat out on the terrace and scrolled through his emails, trying to distract himself while waiting for Katie to emerge. He'd slept late, but when he'd woken she'd still been in a deep slumber and he'd not wanted to disturb her, despite the ache in his gut tempting him to touch her.

Grimly he put the tablet on the table, giving up on any semblance of concentration on work. He shouldn't have said yes to her, but he'd been powerless to say no when he'd wanted her more than he'd wanted anyone.

Unfortunately, he still did.

His skin tightened at the merest recollection. Unease tensed his muscles even more. Her lack of experience and her lonely upbringing made her vulnerable. Yet she'd teased him that he didn't go into relationships deeply enough. Why would he need to when he'd never intended to get married? But now he had—and he didn't want to hurt her. Somehow he needed to keep this from getting more complicated.

He gritted his teeth, because the obvious way was by shutting down the physical aspect of their relationship. Except all he wanted was to get back into bed with her.

'Good morning.'

He glanced up at her soft greeting and couldn't help smiling as colour flooded her face as she walked towards where he sat. There wasn't a part of her he hadn't kissed and yet she still blushed. He hungered to peel off her clothes and see that flush over all her skin. Right now.

No.

He lifted the coffee pot and poured her a cup. 'How are you?' He tried to keep it light, but tension tightened his throat.

'Good.' She accepted the coffee, keeping her gaze on the cup and not him. 'Sorry I slept so late.'

'You needed it.'

He coughed out the huskiness in his voice. He hated it that she still apologised and felt she needed to explain her behaviour all the time.

She kept her eyes averted. Wariness prickled down his spine. Already he knew that look. She had something on her mind. That made two of them.

'What's up?' he prompted.

She sipped her drink, bracing herself as if nervous. 'I've been thinking...'

'Sounds dangerous,' he teased when she trailed off. 'You have another crazy plan in your head?'

A small smile crossed her lips and she nodded.

He drew in an exaggerated breath. 'Okay, hit me with it.'

She hesitated, her glance skittering away from him again. 'I just want you to know I had a great time last night...'

He narrowed his gaze, all senses suddenly on full alert.

'But I don't think...'

His brain sharpened as she trailed off again. Was she attempting her first 'one-night-and-walk-away'—her first ever break-up? Her thinking was more dangerous than he'd imagined.

'We shouldn't do that again,' she said quickly.

'Do what again?' He wanted to make her spell it out. Wanted to make her blush awkwardly all over again. Because he was feeling oddly wounded.

'We shouldn't sleep together,' she said more firmly.

'You mean have sex?'

'That too.'

He blinked. *Wow*. Even though it was exactly what *he'd* been thinking less than five minutes ago, now the idea seemed like pure madness. Had he disappointed her in some way? He refused to believe it.

'I made you—'

'Yes,' she blurted, interrupting him. 'I had too good a time.'

Was that even possible? He relaxed a little and rubbed his hand across his mouth to hide his smile. 'So the problem is...?'

'It's simple pleasure to you,' she said, straightening. 'You said it's just a fun pastime. And I can see why... It's amazing.'

He dropped his hand and stared at her warily.

'The thing is...' She paused to cough the frog from her throat and sent him an apologetic smile. 'I think it might not be that simple for me. I liked it...too much. I know it's probably just because...you know... I'm not that experienced and you're really—'

He held up his hand to stop her. 'I can't make out if you're insulting me or paying me a compliment.'

'You're really good at making a woman feel good,' she said earnestly, regardless of his interruption. 'The problem is if you keep making me feel that good I'll probably end up fancying myself in love with you.'

'And of course that is beyond the realms of possibility?' He forced a smile past the hollowness in his chest. 'Once again, I thank you for your honesty.'

'It's just better if we don't sleep together again.' She held the coffee cup close to her chest.

'One night really was enough for you?' Rebellion bubbled in his blood. 'Straight back to self-denial, Katie?'

She'd scuttled into her box, hiding away when she didn't have to. He was tempted to stand up and take the two steps to get close to her again. One kiss and he'd convince her otherwise.

'Self-preservation,' she corrected quietly.

'Are you trying to scare me off?' he asked, attempting a small tease when in fact he felt the furthest from laughing he'd felt in years.

'I'm not like you…' she breathed. 'I don't want to be just another lover for anyone,' she said.

He rubbed his forehead. 'I'm not the complete playboy you seem to think I am.' His gaze narrowed when he saw the disbelieving arch of her eyebrows. 'I played that up because you were being so judgey. How do you think I got my clubs so damn popular? It was all part of the image.'

She shook her head at him, her eyes serious. 'No, Alessandro. I *saw* you.'

He paused. 'Saw me what?'

Her blush deepened. 'You were about eighteen…it wasn't long before you left White Oaks for the last time. I saw you in the orchard. You were…entertaining one of the summer workers. A few days later you were entertaining another. You've *always* had lots of women. It wasn't about building your business then.'

'You saw me "entertaining" one of the student workers? What was I doing?' He racked his brain, trying to remember who or when, but honestly that period in his life had been hideous.

She didn't reply but that flush under her skin deepened in colour. Clearly he'd been doing a little more than kissing a girl.

'Did you like watching me?' he asked roughly.

Her eyes widened in surprise and the colour mottled all down her neck. 'I was only… I didn't know what I was watching.'

Definitely more than just kissing. He gazed at her searchingly, compelling her to tell him more.

'I was curious,' she muttered. 'Okay, maybe I was jealous.' She shook her head, her mortification evident. 'You never even looked at me.'

'Of course I didn't.' He was shocked into speaking

frankly. 'You were a child who hid in the kitchen all the time. I hardly saw you. And, yes, I was having a good time with other distractions. I needed those distractions then.'

'Because of your father and Naomi?'

Her soft question pierced his cool armour.

'I hated her.'

He was so shocked by Katie's confession, by the tired confusion in his head, that the truth washed out of him. His father's new wife had made them leave the home he loved and then...

'She took everything from me. She made him—' He broke off and strove for simplicity. 'He died and I blamed her. I still do.'

His father's heart had already been broken, but Naomi had delivered the fatal blow.

He glared at Katie, angered at what she'd made him reveal, but somehow unable to stop more words tumbling out. 'I was *alone*. It felt good. I'm not going to apologise for that.'

It hurt enough to admit even this. The truth was he'd been miserable. Bereft and grieving. And at the time he hadn't handled what was happening. The welcome of those lovers had been a brief respite from the bruising reality of his world being ripped apart.

'I was...'

'Seeking solace?' Katie finished his sentence softly.

He stilled. Solace? No. Not solace. That sounded too romantic, too refined. It attached too much meaning to what had been...

'No, it was just an escape,' he corrected her, blinding himself to the welts on his heart as he spoke. 'Sex feels good.'

'It's always just physical?' She frowned. 'Orgasms for everyone?'

He stiffened. 'Everyone loves a good orgasm, Katie, even you.'

'So there isn't an emotional connection?'

Her query caused him discomfort... He wasn't a user. He was a giver, right?

'I always ensure my partner has a good time,' he said, avoiding answering the actual question.

But she'd got what she wanted anyway. She'd exposed his shallow soul and he was angry with her. Because maybe it *wasn't* about all those women he'd been with at that time. Maybe he had just been seeking a fix—as temporary as it had been. Maybe he hadn't wanted to confront the hurt he'd been hiding from. He still didn't.

Yet even as he justified and deflected he felt flawed. Flayed. And he didn't like what she'd found in him.

'Yes,' Katie said, her face falling. 'I get that now.'

That was a knowledge she had because of *him*.

The thought of her enjoying escapist sex with some other guy skyrocketed his blood pressure.

'Damn it, Katie.' He frowned and sighed heavily.

'Maybe I *was* naive and judgey before.' She clutched her cup closer to her chest. 'But I'm right about stopping this now. You know I'm right.'

Yeah, as much as he hated the idea, he agreed with her. And he could hardly argue with her when he was the one who'd told her to speak up for what she wanted.

'Okay.' He nodded. 'No problem. I can handle a woman saying no to me.'

'Really?' As she turned he glimpsed something sharp in her eyes. 'That's not a challenge? Isn't it always a game to you?'

'It was when you were lying to yourself about how much you wanted me,' he said roughly, resenting the way she was challenging him now.

'You wanted me only to prove how much I wanted *you*?'

'No.'

At that first meeting in his office she'd hit his pride and he'd wanted to bite back. He'd told himself he'd get her to say yes for sport. But the truth was that real desire had taken hold in seconds. And now there could be nothing but blunt honesty.

'I just wanted you.'

He still did. But he didn't want to admit how different last night had felt. Not to her, and not to himself.

It was only because these were unusual circumstances. He'd never brought a woman to his island—that was what had made last night unique. There wasn't anything actually meaningful or special between them.

She stared at him for a moment. 'I'm sorry.' Worry straightened her soft mouth.

He realised she had actually been afraid of his reaction—of telling him what she wanted, denying him.

He pulled his head together and sent her a genuine smile, wanting her to relax. 'I can handle rejection, Katie. I'm not going to ask you to leave or end our arrangement just because you've had enough. You're allowed autonomy over your own damn body. Always.'

But she'd left an ache in his. And it was not unquenched lust. This was a loss that went deeper than that. In only a couple of soft-spoken sentences she'd stripped him of something he'd never realised he had but that he'd held dear.

His self-delusion.

Katie pulled on her bikini, bypassed the pool, and headed to the small beach she'd seen from the helicopter. She'd avoid Alessandro by exploring the island.

For almost an hour she walked along the waterline, paddling her feet and contemplating his reaction. But then she heard the chug of an engine growing louder. She paused halfway along the beach and watched the sleek little motorboat slowly come closer. Judging by the gleaming boat and its occupants' glamorous attire, she guessed they were friends of Alessandro's. And they'd clearly had this destination in mind.

'Ciao, bella!' the man called, a wide smile on his face as they came close to the shore.

'I'm not Bella,' she replied coolly.

The man wasn't put off—in fact he laughed. 'So it's true, Alessandro!'

She turned swiftly. Her husband was standing at the top of the beach behind her, wearing nothing but swim shorts. Katie swiftly suppressed her gasp of surprise that her spirits soared just at the sight of him. She blinked and tried not to stare like some lust-crazed nympho at all his bare skin. Acrid, smoky regret curled in her.

'What are you doing here, Vassily?' Alessandro asked, walking to join her at the waterfront.

'Satisfying my curiosity. We're all agog at the events.' The man was unabashed by Alessandro's even cooler tone—clearly a good friend, then. 'Since when have you been caught?'

'I keep my most precious things private—you know that, Vassily.' Alessandro ignored the question.

An unspoken communication passed between the two men before Vassily turned a bright smile on her. 'Come out with us for a quick spin,' he invited wickedly.

'Say no, Katie.'

She glanced at Alessandro and saw an unreadable brilliance in his eyes. She knew his friend was trying to goad him in some way, and while she should probably side with him, she was curious to know more. The imp of defiance blossomed within her.

'I only want to interrogate you,' Vassily added with roguish charm.

And she only wanted to escape Alessandro.

Rebellious fire raced in her veins. 'I've never been on a boat like yours.'

'Alessandro!' Vassily was audibly shocked. 'Have you kept her imprisoned on this island?'

'Getting into that rust bucket would be beneath you,' Alessandro informed her dryly.

Katie met Alessandro's gaze and read the displeasure there. For a moment she wondered if he was going to grasp her by the hand and hold her to his side.

She turned back to Vassily and forced a light laugh. 'He wants me to say no, but I'm not going to.'

'Defiant *and* beautiful…' Vassily taunted Alessandro.

Alessandro stared at Katie for another moment, a hint of retribution in his eyes, and then he splashed into the water.

'Are you coming too?' Vassily groaned with disappointment. 'How am I to torture the truth from her?'

'You're not touching her.' Alessandro turned and held out his hand to help her into the boat.

'Possessive?' Vassily commented dryly.

'Of my wife—yes.'

Katie couldn't look at either man as Alessandro helped her into the boat. He was only playing up his 'possessiveness' in front of his friends. She quickly sat and pasted on a smile for the woman who'd been watching the proceedings from behind her glamorous sunglasses.

Alessandro climbed aboard and shot Vassily a lazy look. 'Once around the island. Thirty minutes. That's all.' He leaned forward. 'Katie, this is Nina and Vassily. Both of them are untrustworthy annoyances.'

From his tone she knew he was teasing. Nina just had to be a model. She had gleaming black hair to her hips, smoky eyes, and a white string bikini that showed off every inch of her stunning physique.

'Would you like a drink?' Vassily offered with a laugh. 'There's champagne in the picnic basket.'

'No, thanks, it's a little early for me.'

So this was his world. Katie listened to their glib repartee, noting their insouciance and glamour. These were wealthy people avoiding boredom with their fast boats, fast women and party lifestyle.

She saw the glance Nina shot Alessandro, heard her low, laughing whisper, and stiffened. In a few months' time he'd be free to follow up that invitation if he wanted. She knew he wouldn't now, though. He'd made a promise to her in Vegas and for as long as they were married he'd keep it. But even so jealousy twisted. It was stupid of her when *she'd* said no to him. *She'd* stopped it.

Only three hours in and she regretted that rash decision. *Don't think about it.*

'Do you stay here with Alessandro often?' she asked, thinking she'd distract herself by getting what information she could from Vassily.

'No one gets to go on Alessandro's island—it's sacrosanct.'

'He doesn't lease it out when he's not here?' She frowned lightly.

'Oh, I wish! We'd all lease it year-round.'

Why had he told her he leased it out when he didn't? Why lie? And it didn't make sense. Alessandro was too astute a businessman to leave an asset like this unoccupied and not making him money. Moreover, he was known for his rapid turnaround of businesses. He flicked them on at a profit and moved to the next. Why hadn't he sold this place?

Well, actually, that she could understand—no one in their right mind would ever sell this slice of heaven.

She masked her frown with a smile as they circled around the island and sped past the high cliffs. They'd circled around half the island already.

Another small cove came into view. 'That beach is amazing.'

Vassily glanced at her and turned to Alessandro with surprise. 'You've not taken her swimming here?'

'We've been busy with other things.' Alessandro ran his fingertip across her bare shoulders. 'The sun is hot. We should get you back.'

'You've brought out his protective instincts,' Vassily said in apparent amazement. 'I never knew he had any.'

Katie turned back to the beach.

'A blushing bride, Alessandro?' Vassily positively marvelled. 'I'd never have thought.'

'You don't often think,' Alessandro retorted mildly. 'Take us home.'

'You can always come and stay with me if he gets too grumpy,' Vassily whispered to her as they returned to the main beach and he pulled the boat back into the shallows.

'I never get grumpy, Vassily. Unless someone tries to mess with what's mine.'

It was a barely veiled threat, playing up to his protective, possessive image. After all, for him it was always a game.

'I want to be alone with my wife—does that really surprise you?'

'No. And I don't blame you for keeping her your secret captive, Alessandro.' Vassily smirked. 'I'm only sorry you met her first.'

Katie breathed out in relief as she jumped back into the water and splashed to the relative safety of Alessandro's private beach. 'Bye, Vassily—bye, Nina.' She waved.

'Did you have fun?' Alessandro asked with an ironic inflection as they walked the path to the house.

'Your friends are nice.'

'They're too curious.'

'Because they care?'

He shook his head. Of course he'd deny any depth of emotion in any of his relationships.

'I bet you two make a fabulous duo. Two playboys on the prowl.' She grimaced.

'You're forgetting Nina,' he drawled.

She didn't want to think about Nina—it just made that stupid jealousy flare. 'I'm going to change,' she muttered.

'Wonderful.' With a vicious movement, he peeled off the path by the pool. 'I'm going to cool off.'

CHAPTER ELEVEN

KATIE SPENT THE night tossing and turning alone in her bed. She should have fallen asleep almost instantly, given she'd hardly had any sleep the night before. Instead she spent hours awake—burning up with restless regret.

They'd had a quiet dinner, talking about things that were not intimate, not important. He'd mentioned that the paperwork for White Oaks was well underway, and she'd be able to see it and sign it when they got back to London.

She'd spoken to Susan again, avoiding difficult questions by keeping the conversation about her foster mother's new carers. Susan seemed to enjoy their company. She sounded well cared for and happy—so Katie could relax a little, right?

Surely she'd made the right decision regarding Alessandro and her…? This feverish ache would soon ease. She'd lived without sensuality all her life—she'd get used to that again quickly, wouldn't she?

She rose early and opted to avoid both the pool and the beach, taking refuge in the garden, fossicking for fruit and herbs as she went. The plants were varied and verdant, and so diverse that she hurried back to the house to grab a basket to put her samples in.

Then she followed the crisscrossing paths through the formal gardens, eventually following one out into a forest-like area. She searched for wild herbs for a while, and then came upon another less-defined track. The small *Proprieta Privata* sign provoked her curiosity.

A few minutes along she saw a small cottage. It wasn't the quarters of the couple who lived on the island full-time—that was on the other side, nearer the new mansion. This small structure was clearly much older than any of the others, and it was tiny. As she paused to look at it the front door suddenly opened—and Alessandro walked out, an open book in his hand.

As he saw her a look of genuine shock flashed on his face. He was quick to recover, but his smile didn't quite smother the unguarded sadness in his eyes.

'I'm so sorry,' she said hurriedly, and backed up a step, realising she'd come upon him at a private moment. 'I didn't mean to intrude. I was just…'

'Avoiding me the same way I was avoiding you.'

She smiled ruefully. 'I've interrupted your reading. I'll go.'

'No, I wasn't even seeing the words.'

Embarrassed, she didn't know what to say.

He seemed to gather himself and glanced at the basket she was carrying. 'You've been busy.'

'Oh, yes.' She glanced down and belatedly realised just how much produce she'd picked. 'I hope you don't mind?'

'Why would I mind?' he growled. 'I like it when you speak your mind, Katie. I like it when you do what you want. You don't have to fit in to my schedule—you should feel free to do whatever you want here. I'm not going to send you away. Not because you don't want to sleep with me, or do whatever I want. I'm not like your foster father. You don't have to fall in line. You're safe. Nothing you could do would make me force you to leave. Just be *you*.'

She blinked, then smiled, surprised and touched by his mini-rant. She wished she could slide back into that teasing banter that she enjoyed so much.

'*Nothing* I could do?'

'I'm your husband—not your boss, your gaoler. Not any kind of authority. You don't have to ask my permission to do anything,' he added gruffly. 'Just do whatever you want.'

'Okay,' she agreed quietly.

He knew, didn't he? That all her life she'd had to seek permission, and that too many times she'd been scared to answer back when she'd wanted to. Maybe she ought to be embarrassed that he knew how weak she was…only he didn't seem to think she was, exactly…

He tossed the book down on an old wicker chair that stood near the cottage doorway and walked over to pick through the herbs in the basket. 'How do you know which ones aren't poisonous?'

'I don't know if you've heard of this thing called the internet…?'

He chuckled and lifted one of the leaves to sniff it, that smile lingering in his eyes. 'My father would wander around with bunches of herbs, or some weird vegetable he'd picked from this garden.'

'You know, he was the one who taught me how to forage in the first place.'

Alessandro cocked his head, his eyes widening in surprise. 'My father did?'

'Those couple of summers he had at White Oaks, before he died.'

'You were just a kid.'

'That didn't mean everyone had to ignore me.' She shot him a sharp smile. 'He found me in the gardens when I was hiding from Brian's wrath one day… I think he took pity on me. He showed me some herbs and taught me various combinations.'

'He understood your interest?'

'He ignited it. He was an amazing man. Full of vitality and so generous.'

Alessandro scooped up the old hardback book he'd tossed down and gestured for her to sit. 'I had no idea he talked with you—but of course he would have.'

'He was nice to everyone. Socially gifted—like you.' She watched as he leaned against the old wall beside her.

He stared into space, seemingly lost in thought for a long moment. 'This was my parents' home.'

She was confused. 'The island?'

'This very cottage. We holidayed here when I was little. All our summers. Weekends.'

Really? No wonder the place was so special to him.

She sat very still, not wanting to interrupt him, hoping he'd tell her something more.

'After my mother died...my father didn't want to come back here.' He sighed. 'And then he and Naomi grew closer. She'd been working at the company for a while, establishing the London office. He brought her here, but she didn't like it.'

Katie's eyebrows lifted. How could anyone not like it here?

'There were too many memories of my mother.' He answered her unasked question with a pained smile. 'This is where Mamma convalesced when she was ill. Cancer. The hospital across the water is where she died. Naomi convinced him to sell the island just before they got married.'

Katie couldn't hold back. 'I can't believe Naomi wanted to get rid of this island.'

'She wanted everything *new*. She wanted him to live in England. New house. New life. More money. More success. Nothing of my mother or his heritage and their past. She wanted that wiped out. I think she was jealous of her. And I think Naomi's request broke his heart all over again.'

Alessandro gazed towards the cottage.

'It was the one thing I wanted,' he said. 'It took me years to get it back. The things are gone but the memories are here.'

She realised now that this place meant everything to him—more than his companies. More than anything. This was the one thing he'd chased and held on to.

'My father had plans for the big house, but Mamma always loved the cottage. This was where she liked to sit in the sun and read when she was too tired to do anything else.'

Katie waited, then looked at the stunning view over the waters to the mainland beyond and not into Alessandro's

face as she finally asked a question and crossed her fingers
that he'd answer.

'She was sick for a while?'

'Years,' he said flatly. 'It was hard on my father. He was
managing the restaurants, expanding the food production.
He wanted to make it a success and he nursed her at the
same time. He'd come home late from the restaurants and
do all his testing during the day, in the kitchen here. She'd
sample everything for him.'

Katie smiled softly. 'What about you?'

'I'd try them too.' He half smiled.

That wasn't what she'd meant, and he knew it. But he'd
deflected her away from himself—something she realised
he often did with humour. And now she knew he'd been
here all through his mother's illness.

'You helped care for her?'

There was a long moment of silence.

'When Mamma died, he had a kind of greyness to him…
He had a heart attack a couple of weeks later. A broken heart
from which I don't think he ever truly recovered.'

Katie's heart ached—it must have been terrifying for
Alessandro. After his mother's long illness, to have almost
lost his father so soon?

'And then Naomi…?'

'She came out from the UK to help with the company.
They got together so quickly. I think he was trying to bury
his grief, to feel better. Naomi wanted him to take the head-
quarters to England and focus on building the market there.
He married her, gave up the island, his home, and worked
himself into the ground. He gave her everything until his
heart couldn't give any more. Love literally killed him.'

'And hurt you too.' So deeply.

No wonder he sought solace in sex—even if he denied
it, that was what he'd been doing. He'd been torn from his
home because he had wanted to support his father, probably while still grieving his mother's death. Only then he'd

lost him too. And then Naomi had cut him out from his father's company.

'I'm okay, Katie,' he said.

'Really? You watched your mother suffer for a long time…you looked after her with your father. That's why you know what Susan needs—why you're angry with Brian for not doing a decent job. You lost your mother, you lost this place, you lost him… Alessandro—'

'Are you feeling sorry for me Katie?'

He sent her a semblance of that old wicked smile. But it had changed. It no longer hid the other elements within him. The vulnerability.

'Because don't. You know my life is amazing—'

'I'm glad you have this place back now,' she interrupted him. 'Your parents would—'

'I know,' he said quietly. 'It's the one place I won't part with. Never.'

'No.'

His heart was here. Deeply hidden and huge.

'I guess you feel this way about White Oaks,' he said gruffly.

Not quite. When she thought of her home now it was tinged with sadness. She realised how suffocated she'd felt there.

'I feel that way about *Susan*,' she said. 'White Oaks is beautiful, but it's also been a prison—like you said. Full of rules. And I was always afraid I was going to get sent away.'

She understood why Alessandro had helped her now. Because he understood so much more than she'd realised. He presented this carefree playboy façade, but beneath that was a hurt guy who'd lost everything that mattered to him most.

'What are you going to make with all that stuff?' he asked, pointedly looking back into the basket.

'I'm not sure.'

'Well, you've got to do *something* with it. It can't all go to waste now you've picked it.'

'Okay, I accept the challenge.'

Slowly they walked back along the path to the main house together and she desperately tried not to think about touching him. But she ached to hold him again.

'I thought you said you leased out the island, but Vassily told me you don't.'

Alessandro laughed, and cursed beneath his breath. 'In the early years I did, to help make it pay. I don't have to do that any more. I didn't *quite* lie to you.'

'No, you just didn't want to tell me how important it is to you.'

He paused and looked at her.

She turned to face him. 'Is it so hard admitting how much things might mean, Alessandro?'

The tension swelled between them again and he sent her a long, considering look. Then his gaze dropped to her basket.

'Go and concentrate your dangerous thinking on the contents of that basket, Katie. I think we might both prefer the results of that.'

She actually did as he'd suggested. Working in the kitchen had always been a kind of therapy for her—a displacement activity, a distraction from difficulties.

She lost track of time as she toyed with the assortment she'd gathered, trialling different herbs both in baking and in making something decent for dinner. But she couldn't quite shake her sadness for what he'd lost.

'You don't want a rest?'

She looked up as he walked back in, his face one big frown.

'It's been *hours*,' he added.

'It's been a good distraction,' she said with a rueful smile. 'It always is. Work is for you too, right?'

'Stop thinking you need to figure me out, Katie. I'm not that complicated. Work hard, play hard—every bit the cliché you said.'

'Really?' She gestured to a tray of lemon curd tartlets and tried to make a joke. 'So, you want to sample my wares?'

There was a pregnant pause and she glanced back and caught his eye.

'You know I do,' he muttered ruefully.

She knew he'd bitten back worse banter. She shot a look at him and laughed.

For a moment he joined in, but his laugh soon ended on a rueful sigh. 'The trouble is I know how good they're going to be already. I think that once I start I'm not going to want to stop.'

He rubbed his hand through his hair and looked at her with that old, wicked amusement.

'That *is* a problem,' she agreed with a light laugh.

He bit into one anyway, and closed his eyes briefly before nodding. 'Yeah, I knew it. These are even better than that sauce the other day. You're very talented, *dolcezza*.'

'No—'

'Take the compliment.'

She fell silent, pressing down on her smile.

'You tried to tell me it's all about those heritage fruit trees. It isn't, Katie. You're not reliant on the orchards at White Oaks. You can make amazing creations no matter where the ingredients come from. Have more faith in yourself. Your stuff is good because it's *yours*. Trust your taste. Your judgement. Make other things yours too.' He leaned over the bench, energy suddenly radiating from him. 'You know, I could launch a bid for Zetticci Foods…'

She stared at him in amazement.

'A hostile take-over. They're in a bad way. With you at the helm we could turn it around.'

She gaped for another second, then laughed. 'You're kidding?'

'Maybe it's time for Naomi to retire.' His energy somehow seemed to increase. 'You make a premium product, Katie. You could make a huge success of it.'

'You're crazy.'

'You just made me the most delicious thing I've eaten using little more than a few leaves from the garden. You know taste. Flavour. I believe in you, Katie. You should believe in you too.'

'I couldn't run a whole massive company.'

'I'd put in a management team to support you.'

She couldn't take her gaze off the fire in his. 'You want the company back? The way you have your home here back?'

'Actually, no.' He shook his head. 'It's only one option for you. You could expand White Oaks if you don't want to take on Zetticci. Or you could start something completely new. Whatever you choose, you need to make the most of your gift. You need to do something, *dolcezza*, you're too talented to go to waste. And I can help you.'

He truly meant it and she was truly touched. The fact that he believed in her gave her a lift that no one had ever given her.

But she knew what would happen. As soon as she was established and the company was viable he'd get bored. He'd sell and move on... He was always able to walk away because he never became emotionally involved in anything. He'd locked what heart he had into this place—where his history was.

'All of those options would take months, maybe years, to really become something,' she said. 'You don't want to be tied to me for that long,' she added bravely. 'We shouldn't complicate this even more.'

'I'm good at separating my business life from my personal life, Katie.'

He didn't have a personal life. At least, not a meaningful one.

'Yeah? Well, I can't compartmentalise as well as you can.' She paused. 'I appreciate your support, but I'm not going to be your latest business project. You've done enough for me.'

He watched her for another moment, then seemed to withdraw. 'Okay. Then we should go back to London. Check on Susan...face Brian. I don't think there's any point delaying any longer.'

She maintained her slight smile with all the control she could muster, but she'd frozen inside.

'It will remove us from temptation too.' A lopsided smile didn't quite reach his eyes. 'We'll figure out our living arrangements. I travel a lot. You won't have to see me all that often. I just ask that you stay at my place through the week. Weekends with Susan. Something like that?'

'Of course,' she readily agreed. 'Anything.'

He shot her a look and they both laughed, that newly forming ice thawing a fraction.

She only just bit back the apology she knew he'd hate to hear. Smiling, she looked up into his face. For a moment they faced each other, frozen for a beat of time. She just knew he was thinking about kissing her. For a moment she wanted him to. He would be so easy to have an affair with, but even easier to fall in love with.

But that was the last thing he wanted, and she thought she understood why a little now.

'Old habits are very easy to fall into,' he said softly.

'And very hard to break.' She nodded.

She made herself look away from him. He was too handsome, too tempting. Smart, funny, loyal, kind...but emotionally contained.

He wasn't the wild playboy she'd once thought he was. He was private and hurt. And actually as isolated and as alone as she.

CHAPTER TWELVE

ALESSANDRO DRUMMED HIS fingers on the steering wheel, releasing the tension building within. He was so aware of her emotions he seemed to be absorbing them. She seemed unnervingly attuned to his moods too. As he'd told Vassily the other day, he kept the things most precious to him private, yet somehow he'd ended up spilling half his life story to her back in Italy. And as she'd listened the soft compassion in her clear eyes had made him speak even more.

Now yet more memories stirred as they drove through the village near White Oaks. Memories long-buried that impacted his usual carefree demeanour. Usually nothing meant enough for him to get that upset about it. It made making deals easier when he could be clinical. He'd be clinical about this too—somehow.

'The village seems smaller,' he commented, to slice through the strained atmosphere.

The energy in the car crackled.

'I'm sorry I've made you come back,' she said suddenly in a small voice.

He hated hearing that apology—the anxiety that simmered beneath her beauty. But he knew he wasn't really the source of her upset. She was worried about Susan. And scared to see Brian.

He was compelled to reassure her with the reality. None of this was her fault. He smiled at her. 'I'm the one driving—you haven't dragged me here.'

She didn't smile back. 'They kicked you out when you'd already lost so much. They took Aldo's company.' She dragged in a breath. 'You must hate the place—and I've made you *buy* it.'

'I could have said no,' he pointed out simply. 'Stop worrying about me. All that was a long time ago. Zetticci was Dad's. I know who I am. I know what I've done since.' He reached out and squeezed her hand. 'Don't feel bad for me, Katie. I know you've spent all your life caring for Susan and being careful around Brian. You don't need to do either of those things with me.'

Beneath his hand hers tensed, and he saw her blink a couple of times.

'I think I should still care about how you're feeling,' she said huskily.

A ball of discomfort tightened low in his gut. She was so disarmingly honest sometimes. He turned back to focus on driving instead of staring at her.

He cleared his throat as he turned down the long driveway of the estate. 'The gardens look even more magnificent than I remember.'

'Susan might be in a wheelchair now, but she still supervises the plantings like an army general.' She looked at the trees and exhaled shakily. 'I can't wait to see her.'

But when he pulled up outside the main house Katie didn't undo her seat belt, or make any attempt to move.

'You're worried about seeing him?' he prompted.

She swallowed and nodded.

Alessandro unclipped his belt and leaned across so that he could look into her pretty eyes properly. 'You have no trouble standing up to me,' he murmured lightly. 'I'm a brilliant businessman, but you negotiated with me and won. You have me wrapped around your little finger and saying yes to your every request.'

A small smile slowly curved her lips.

'You've put me in my place with no problem at all,' he reminded her with a little wink. 'Besides, what can he do to you now?'

* * *

Katie squared her shoulders and knocked on the door. Alessandro was right. She could handle Brian—and more importantly she was going to see Susan.

To her surprise, Brian was smiling as he opened the door and welcomed them into the wide foyer. He was also alone.

'Where's Susan?' Katie frowned as she looked around for signs of her foster mother.

Brian ignored her question. 'It's been a long time, Alessandro.'

'Where's Susan, Brian?' Katie asked again.

'She'll be here shortly.'

Brian's smile seemed superglued on, and he still hadn't so much as looked at Katie.

'I thought we should have a minute to fully settle the situation first.'

'The situation is settled,' she said crisply. 'We're only here to see Susan.'

He finally faced her. His swift glance took in her new clothes and that horrible crocodile smile widened more. 'I underestimated you, Katie. Alessandro's backing is even more secure than Carl's would have been. We can restore White Oaks completely. You won't have to spend hours making those silly sauces any more. All that effort for such little return.' He stepped closer. 'You've done well. Everybody wins.'

He was so dismissive, so ignorant, and he didn't even realise how cruel he was being. He had no idea how much her work meant to her.

'Seriously…?' Katie muttered with appalled amazement.

This was why he was smiling and not shouting at her for defying him? Because he thought she'd done a better deal than the craziness he'd arranged? And now he was acting welcoming in order to manipulate her, because it was in *his* best interests?

'Alessandro.' Brian turned back to her silent husband. 'Why don't we—?'

'Where's Susan, Brian?' Katie interrupted impatiently. He shot her a displeased look.

She turned her back on him and walked into the hallway. 'She knew we were coming. I talked to her about it last night…' She trailed off and listened, but the house was eerily silent. She looked back at Brian.

He glared at her, and that old meanness tightened his features. 'I knew we had things to discuss privately, so I told her you'd changed the time you were arriving.'

'You…*what*?'

'She's out with one of her new companions. They're very thoughtful and caring, those nurses. Susan's happier than she's been in years.'

Katie brushed off that deliberate dig, still getting her head around what he'd done. 'You lied to her about when I was coming?'

Her pulse roared in her ears. How typically controlling. He'd know how much Katie wanted to see Susan. This was a petty way of inflicting pain. But Susan had been looking forward to seeing Katie too.

'How could you do that to her?' Katie stared at him.

'She'll see you soon enough,' Brian shrugged.

Hurt exploded. 'The only reason we're here is to see *her*. I want to ensure Susan's happiness and security at White Oaks.'

'And apparently you've achieved that by marrying Alessandro. Well done.'

She gaped at him. 'All that matters to me is her happiness. You know, I have no idea why she stays married to you, but that's her choice. Here's *my* choice—you can live here, but only as long as you care for Susan properly. No more "conferences", Brian. No more gambling. If you put one foot out of line it's all over.'

He stepped closer. 'You can't tell me what to do.'

'The way you've told *me* what to do all my life?' She'd laugh if she didn't feel so bitter. 'You don't *have* to do as I say, but as I now own this property—'

'You manipulative little—'

'What?' she interrupted furiously. She wasn't going to let him berate her again. 'You never let me feel safe here—or like I belonged. You always threatened me to make me do what you wanted. No more, Brian. You can't bully me now.'

'Because you've brought *him* with you?' he sneered.

'Because I don't care any more,' she yelled. 'Because I'm doing what *I* want. What's best for me and what's best for Susan and that's it.' She drew breath and stared at the defiance in his eyes. 'She's not coming back for hours, is she?'

He didn't answer.

'Do anything like this again and you're gone.'

She turned on the spot and walked out of the house, instinctively turning towards the silent shaded safety of her youth—away from Brian, away from the conflict that had always festered...away from Alessandro. She didn't want him to *see*—

'Katie.'

He caught her shoulders as she stumbled. She bowed her head but didn't turn. She didn't want to look at him. She was too hurt.

All her life Brian had made her feel inadequate, as if she were a disappointment—only there on sufferance because Susan had wanted her. He'd controlled her with that sense of obligation—playing on her gratitude and guilt.

'You were amazing,' Alessandro muttered, pulling her back to rest against him.

'No...' She shook her head and resisted his embrace. 'No, I wasn't. I ran away.'

He turned her in his arms and searched her face, muttering something low and indecipherable, then pressed her head against his chest and cradled her. 'I'm sorry he hurt you,' he muttered gruffly into her hair.

She knew he saw her turmoil and sadness. Her hands reached out of their own accord, resting on his waist. His warmth and strength burned through his shirt. All she wanted was to feel better. To feel that someone wanted her. Her birth parents hadn't wanted her. Nor had Brian. And he'd kept her from seeing Susan today. Susan who loved her but whom she was going to lose too soon…

Her heart tore. 'How can he still hurt me?' she whispered.

'Because you care,' Alessandro muttered against her hair. 'It's complicated. He raised you…part of you might always want his approval, might always love him. Even when he's let you down.'

Katie lifted her head and gazed into Alessandro's eyes. How was he so compassionate and insightful and complex… and so right? Was it because he knew something of how she felt?

'Did it feel as if your father had let you down when he married Naomi?'

He froze for a moment, but then nodded. 'I wanted him to be happy, but I couldn't understand how he could be happy with *her*…'

Katie smiled sadly. 'Was *any* woman going to live up to your mother?'

He sent her an equally sad smile and admitted it. 'Probably not. But he could have done better. He could have found someone kind. She wasn't. And he wasn't strong enough to move, to work all those hours… But he wanted to please her—he wanted to be loved.'

Katie's heart curled in. 'I can understand that,' she said softly. 'Most of us want to be loved.'

Alessandro shook his head. 'No. Some of us don't want that at all.' He smiled at her. 'Too much drama.'

She knew he was deliberately making a joke, but she couldn't smile back. 'Too much hurt?'

He paused. 'That too.'

The truth hovered between them—an invisible, impenetrable wall.

He pressed his palm to her cheek. 'Katie—'

She didn't want to talk any more. She didn't want to think any more.

'Don't be nice to me,' she whispered.

He could never give her what she really wanted but she didn't care about that. She just wanted to feel better.

'What should I be, then?' he asked with a remnant of that old teasing glint. 'All mean and horrible like him?' He cocked his head and the glint brightened into something fiercer and his smile faded. 'I don't care if that's what you're used to—you're not getting it from me.'

A fierce bubble of emotion fizzed in her chest. 'What *am* I getting, then?'

'What do you want?'

Pure emotion pulsed. Hurt, angry, aching for something, she gazed at him. 'Solace.'

His chest rose and fell, and she snatched a glimpse of turmoil reflected in his eyes. But then he bent and kissed her gently. Too gently.

'Why have you stopped?' That wasn't what she wanted.

With a rough groan he kissed her again—and the floodgates were opened.

Katie clung to him, pouring her need into his kiss. She lost everything in that one searing kiss—all reason, all hurt, even her footing. She was literally swept off her feet. But somehow he was with her, pressing so close on the warm summer grass. And there was nothing smooth or practised in this. It was simply a kiss—soul-deep, urgently seeking to satisfy a longing so intense neither could stop.

She shook, unwilling and unable to break the seal of their kiss. And he was too. As their mouths clung their hands moved the clothing necessary and suddenly he was there— *all* there—right where she was hot and wet and hungry and needing his fierce, hard strength.

She sobbed into his kiss as he gave her what she needed. Locked together, their connection was deep and intimate, and somehow their physical closeness became an exposition of something else altogether. A welter of emotions tossed within her—and warmth of a different kind radiated over the intense heat of pure passion.

But she couldn't stop to define it because she'd already exploded, her body radiating that desperate, devastating delight.

But even as she struggled to recover, struggled to stand and walk with him back to the car, she knew the difficult truth. It still wasn't enough.

'We'll come back soon. We won't tell him when. You'll see Susan, I promise.'

'I know.'

Alessandro glanced at her quickly, then turned back to the road. He was struggling not to speed, not to get them the hell out of there as fast as possible—away from what had just happened.

Not Brian and his petty meanness. But Katie and him.

He'd done the one thing she'd asked him not to. And while she'd been willing at the time that was only because she'd been emotional. Vulnerable.

His emotions churned—want, pain, denial. He'd wanted to reach out to her. He'd been desperate to see her smile again—to hold her close and comfort her. Yes, to offer solace.

But holding her close had led to other things. The need to connect with her had been primal and he'd done it the one way he knew best. Physically. He'd meant only a kiss, but passion had overtaken him. All he'd wanted was to heal the bruise on her heart, but what he'd done was put her at risk.

'I'm sorry,' he said tightly. 'I shouldn't have—'

'I wanted it too,' she interrupted quietly.

'No, I lost control. I didn't use anything' He'd had unprotected sex for the first time in his life. He'd never lost control like that before. 'You might—'

'I'm on birth control,' she said softly.

He was so stunned he almost slammed on the brakes. That flash of a future, that wisp of an image of Katie cradling their baby, wasn't the shocking possibility it had been a second ago.

'Since when? You were—'

'I'm on it for other reasons,' she mumbled. 'But it means that what just happened won't…'

'Have long-term consequences?' he finished for her.

But it felt like a lie. When he ought to feel instant relief, he felt a sinking inside instead. Surely not disappointment? What was wrong with him?

That hadn't been escape he'd sought to offer her. It hadn't been solace. Hadn't he taken advantage because it had eased his *own* demons to hold her? Because he'd been desperate to touch her? He'd ached for her softness, her surrender.

He'd hated the exclusion and isolation from her in these past days. He'd hated the restrictions she'd put on them. He'd assumed his fascination with her would fade, whether they burned out their desire or not. He'd thought that if it were starved it would die. It hadn't. And even sated again it still hadn't.

Could he really blame this on old habits? The other day he'd recoiled from her suggestion that there was something emotionally needy in his liaisons. But wasn't it exactly that? Yes, he used sex as an escape—for fun, to alleviate boredom or stress…but he also used it to hide from his hurts.

The trouble was that now he'd recognised that those hurts were still there… But, even so, what he'd done with Katie hadn't just been about using sex to assuage their pain. It hadn't been just rampant libido either. Those weak justifications minimised what had happened.

The truth was that too-quick moment under the trees had been the most intimate experience of his life. Never had he wanted to feel as close to someone, to give to someone. And in the aftermath he ached.

Grimly he parked the car in the basement garage of his London apartment and escorted her into the elevator. He'd have to remove himself—temporarily shift into another apartment. He walked through the lounge, tossing the keys on the table as he went. He'd call the building manager and see if there was a unit free.

'Alessandro.'

Reluctantly he glanced at her. She stood in the middle of his lounge. Her face was pale and tear-stained and her pretty dress was crumpled. She'd never looked as beautiful. If he was going to leave, it had to be now.

'I'm taking you to bed, Alessandro,' she said, with that quiet boldness he loved to see in her.

'Are you?' He swallowed and felt his self-control slip. He tried to joke. 'I thought you didn't want to make things any more complicated?'

'I think it's a little late for that.'

'No, it's not.' It couldn't be.

'You like control. Are you afraid that if you give too much away you'll lose control altogether?'

'Katie—'

'I'm not going to hurt you.' She stepped towards him.

As if *that* was the issue! 'You're no longer afraid that I might hurt you?' he growled.

She shrugged carelessly. 'I want that escape. Just for a while.'

'Is that really all it is, *dolcezza*?' It didn't feel like it to him any more—and suddenly he was angry. 'It's always been an escape for me,' he said harshly. 'It wasn't always about the woman I was with—more about the thrill of the chase, the orgasms.'

She flinched—then froze.

'I get off on seeing my partner get hers too. I always like doing that for her. But you...it's different.' Somehow it mattered more. 'I don't just get off from making you climax,' he muttered, almost malevolently. 'It's an imperative. I ache to taste you. To make you shake. To hear you scream. I want nothing more than to render you mindless...so that all you can do is beg for me. Because that's how much I want you. I don't get off from that. I live for it.'

He drew in a sharp breath, half appalled at what he'd just admitted. He watched as Katie's skin was burnished with the most beautiful blush.

But she brushed a lock of hair behind her ear and didn't take her shy but hungry eyes off him. 'So why are you all the way over there?'

Because he couldn't seem to move.

Because he couldn't quite process the depth of this.

She walked over until she was a mere breath away. 'What do you want?' she asked. 'You asked me to say what I wanted. Now I'm asking you.'

His tongue was tied.

Her expression softened. 'It's hard, isn't it?'

He swallowed. 'Harder than you'd believe,' he huffed in a lame quip.

'I'm not going to help you with that unless you speak up.' She smiled and leaned that little bit closer. 'It's only fair, Alessandro.'

She'd turned his own tease on him—except he didn't want it to be a tease any more. The threat of denial—of her leaving him aching—felt like a whip over his heart. He curled his hands into fists. It was too intense.

'Tell me what you want from me.'

He just wanted her. Not to forget, or escape, or soothe all his aches... He just wanted to hold her close. But it seemed he'd lost his words.

'I...'

'What?'

He could hardly think. He felt too hot, too broken. Her flecked eyes flashed with confusion, compassion, heat.

He dropped his gaze and stared at her mouth because he couldn't continue to drown in her eyes.

'You want me to kiss you?' she breathed. 'Where?'

He didn't care. Anywhere. He just needed her touch. *'Accarezzami...'*

She understood. She was there already. Sensations swept over him as her hands caressed him and she kissed him with her soft, sweet mouth. For one last second he stayed still, trying to hold it all back. But then it was too late.

Almost savagely he scooped her into his arms and stormed towards his bedroom to have it all.

CHAPTER THIRTEEN

KATIE DIDN'T JUST say yes. She demanded more. And he didn't let her down. He sent her into a world she'd known existed but had never dreamed she'd step into. A world of freedom and choice.

Each morning Alessandro took her to a different market—they'd scoped them out together online, part of the research he reckoned she needed to do. Laughing, but loving it, she chose ingredients, tools.

On their return to the apartment he'd shut himself in his study to work while she tested her new finds in the kitchen. A few hours later he'd emerge and taste what she'd been working on.

By then their sensual tension was too fraught to ignore. Beneath his ministrations Katie had unleashed a hidden, long-denied side of herself—the demanding side. And she had more than accepted it—she indulged it. Again and again.

Alessandro was intense, passionate and insatiable. And he held nothing back from her now. It was so intense, so physical…it was almost frantic. And it always felt fantastic.

He refused to let her cook dinner. Instead they worked their way around the finest restaurants in the city. More market research, according to Alessandro. Sometimes then they went straight home. Sometimes they went to the gilt champagne bar half a block from his apartment and met up with Vassily and Nina and a few other of his friends. It turned out that Nina owned a leisurewear company. And now Katie had pushed past her own insecurity she realised the glamorous woman was really nice—and helpful.

As the days passed she grew increasingly comfortable in her clothes, in her conversation, and with her lover. She even teased him as they talked. But the more she settled in to his lifestyle the edgier Alessandro seemed to become. More attentive. More protective. Almost *possessive*.

'You guys should still be in Italy on honeymoon,' Nina teased her suddenly as they sat together in the bar one evening.

Katie looked at her in surprise.

'I just intercepted that look Alessandro sent you from across the room and you should definitely still be on that island, away from everybody else.' Nina laughed. 'Uh-oh, he's headed this way and looking at you like you're some tasty morsel he's going to swallow in one mouthful.'

Katie glanced over and her gaze instantly collided with his. Electricity arced—and it wasn't his dangerously handsome good-looks, it was the intensity in his whole demeanour, that aura of something unleashed. Tingling awareness shot to her toes as he strode over and held out his hand.

'Bye, Nina.' Katie shot the woman an embarrassed smile as she laced her fingers through Alessandro's and left with him.

'Is something wrong?' she asked him once they were out on the pavement.

Waves of emotion rippled from him. 'You can't look at me like that and not expect me to react,' he muttered.

'You were looking at *me* like that!' she laughed.

He smiled, but she still sensed tension within him. Ripples of sensuality swept through her as they walked.

'I was jealous,' he said gruffly.

'I was talking to *Nina*!' Katie laughed again.

'Nina enjoys the company of attractive people, male or female. She's fascinated by both…'

Katie laughed again, hugely amused. 'Well, Nina is not fascinated by me. We were talking about running a business. She has a lot of experience. I can learn from her.'

'You can learn from *me*,' he pointed out with roguish arrogance as he held the apartment door for her. 'I too have a lot of experience.'

'As a woman in enterprise?'

He chuckled, but then his sensuality simmered over again. 'I don't like it when other people look at you. When other people interest you. When other people make you laugh,' he said, pure seduction. 'You're *my* wife.'

'So only *you* can advise me? Only *you* can make me laugh?' she teased, placing her palm against his roughened jaw.

'No. But only I can do this.'

He pulled her closer and kissed her.

It was no longer solace, no longer an escape. It was all ecstasy.

Katie closed her eyes and drowned in desire, denying the edge of desperation still sharpening within…

He should have known she'd surprise him. In the last week she'd blossomed. She held her own with the likes of Vassily and Nina and his other friends. She saw through their banter for what it was and threw equally teasing barbs and brilliant smiles. She'd come alive as they explored the city, trialling all kinds of creations in the kitchen…

Yet why should any of that be a surprise? She'd made a success of her sauces. She'd made those recipes. She'd picked the fruit, sold to customers. She was outstandingly capable. Just because she'd barely travelled more than twenty-miles from White Oaks, it didn't mean she was going to be shy and socially inept.

She just hadn't had the chance before. And now she was taking to it like a duck to water.

Yet he still felt oddly protective of her, knowing that she'd do anything for those she barely knew and every-thing for those she loved. Knowing that, though her smile came more readily, that rosy flush still swarmed over her skin at his touch.

She was a sweet woman who burned hotter than any other and he didn't want her to change. But she hadn't. She wasn't. She'd just become more herself. She shone—beautiful, proud, confident. Part of him enjoyed the way she glittered when they were out together, and yet part of him wished he'd kept her hidden, so she was all just his.

But that wouldn't have been fair. She'd been hidden most of her life. Kept on that old estate, starved of true freedom by a foster father determined to control her. And Alessandro couldn't keep her for ever—life didn't work like that.

The next night Katie spoke at length to Nina again. Alessandro watched from a distance, knowing she was aware of his scrutiny. She smouldered at him from across the room. He let her tease him until he had to hustle her out before he lost control altogether.

He saw Vassily's arched eyebrow as he whisked her away. He didn't damn well care.

He kissed her as they were driven back to his penthouse. He didn't make it to the bedroom—pulling her to the floor to satisfy the searing lust that overcame him. Her enthusiasm for life literally had him on his knees.

She laughed, and her emerging playfulness arrested his heart. So he worked until she screamed. And then he carried her to his bed and did it all again, until she sighed and drifted off in sated, exhausted slumber.

But he couldn't sleep. He couldn't shake the sensation of impending loss. It knocked against his ribcage, trying to break in and hit the block inside that was his heart. He wasn't going to let it in.

Hours later, he was still awake. Still bothered by a worry he couldn't define, still feeling uneasy at the intensity with which he needed to be with Katie.

Maybe he needed to restore his usual routine—he couldn't ignore the rest of his life for ever. Katie seemed settled, happy, they were managing the moment just fine... Things could return to normal, right?

* * *

'I need to go into the office. I've avoided it too long.' Alessandro walked into the kitchen early, looking far too fine in his navy suit and tie.

'Sure thing.' Katie masked her disappointment with a smile. 'I promise not to burn the place down while you're gone.'

'Great. Then I'll see you later.'

She couldn't quite look at him as he left, and their goodbye was too awkward. They weren't anything like a normal newly married couple.

She worked in the kitchen for a while as a distraction. It wasn't quite enough, so she phoned Susan as well.

'Lemon filling today,' she said, and smiled as she held the phone under chin and stirred the mixture at the same time. 'I think it's pretty good. I'll bring some to you in a few days.'

'You'll be able to see the Madame Hardy rose that's just bloomed.'

'The white one?' Katie had her head around all the herbs, but the roses not so much. And in this old familiar chat her heart ached. She missed her foster mother. 'I can come and see you today, if you like. The train wouldn't take—'

'No, darling,' her foster mother said softly. 'You should be with your husband.'

Should she?

She knew her foster mother was as old-fashioned as the roses she grew, but Katie couldn't understand how Susan could accept Brian's controlling behaviour. How could she not see his lack of kindness? Katie wasn't as forgiving. She wasn't as accepting of…*less*.

Alessandro's image flickered in her mind. She pushed down the wave of discomfort. What they were doing wasn't *less*, wasn't it?

Distractedly she ended the call to Susan, then walked through the apartment. She wished he hadn't gone to work—she missed him a stupid amount already and he'd only been gone a few hours.

She tiptoed to his study, unable to resist her curiosity. It wasn't as neat as she'd expected. Various folders were scattered over a table in the centre of the room. She recognised the names on some of them—buildings he owned, mostly. But then she spotted one with her name on the front. It was set to the side of the others and not hidden at all. A sticky note on the top had a reminder written on it: *Get Katie to sign*.

Her heart skipped a beat, then sped up. In Italy he'd said the White Oaks paperwork would be ready for her when they returned to England. She opened the cover and blinked at the number of pages inside. It wasn't just the documents about his purchase of White Oaks. There was more—about them.

Three pages detailed all the options for declaring their marriage voidable if they wanted to seek an annulment. She glanced at the date at the bottom. It had been written the morning after their marriage. There was also a draft divorce agreement. She blinked at all the zeroes on the pay-out figure she was to receive on settlement. Cold sweat filmed her forehead. The inevitable end of their marriage was presented here with perfect clarity, in simple black and white.

Why had he wanted to do all this so soon after that hideous wedding? Why was he being so financially generous upon her release?

Because he wanted to be free and he'd needed to know the best way to proceed.

He'd never intended on going through with their marriage of convenience in the beginning. He'd only strung her along to get her far enough away from Brian for her to be able to think clearly. He'd openly admitted that. Only then they'd had that message about the engagement announcement and she'd got scared. And he'd whisked her up the aisle to stop her breaking down.

He'd given in.

He'd even given her the sex she'd wanted. He'd known she'd wanted that right from the start. No doubt an experienced man like Alessandro always knew. Besides, women always wanted sex from him.

She'd been so naive. She was his pity project—his Cinderella. He'd dressed her up, he'd taken her to parties, he'd even helped develop possibilities for her own company, had believed in her skill... He'd been soothing over all her insecurities because beneath that arrogant playboy persona he was actually a nice guy. And of *course* he had to protect his company, his own interests, his *name*. He couldn't let this marriage fall apart too soon. He'd been keeping her happy.

But all the intimacy they'd shared was based on a sham. And it had always been going to end.

She stalked through the apartment, unable to release the frenetic energy that was coiling tightly within her. She needed to take action. She'd thought she'd escaped the restrictions of her old life, but in reality she'd ceded control of everything to Alessandro the second she'd sought him out. While he'd done all she'd asked, and then some, he'd always had his exit plan, and he'd want her to sign on the dotted line eventually.

She needed to reclaim not just her own future but her own *now*.

She ought to feel free. White Oaks was secure, Susan was happy and cared for, and she'd silenced Brian and knew she could now ignore him. She had everything, right?

No. Now she knew what she really wanted. A real relationship. She didn't want to be with a man she'd bargained into marrying her. She wanted to be with someone who actually wanted her—only her—for *her*. That wasn't Alessandro. He didn't love her. She wasn't what he wanted, and she wasn't enough for him. She'd known that from the start, but somehow she'd forgotten for a while—he was so seductive, so good at making *her* feel good.

This reminder of reality hurt.

She dragged in a shivering breath. It hurt a lot.

She'd been the one to initiate that kiss in the orchard. Alessandro probably hadn't wanted to reject her at that moment because she'd already been crying. She'd even asked him for it—for escape, for solace. He hadn't said no because he was too *kind*.

And she'd asked again back at his apartment. In fact, she'd demanded. Again he'd said yes. For a moment she'd felt all that warmth and intimacy and believed in unions and love. But that didn't mean he cared for her in any great way. No more than he cared for any other woman who'd been in his life.

The guy adored sex. He was the first to admit that. It wasn't an expression of *love*, it was physical pleasure— escape and release. Even when he'd said it was different with her, he'd still meant it was only physical. Her instincts after their first time together had been right. She'd known it would mean more to her.

Anger shot through her. Why didn't she ever get it all? Why was she never enough?

She'd not been wanted by her birth family. Not wanted by Brian. Not wanted enough by Susan for her to really fight for her...

And Alessandro would want someone else very soon.

He had no intention of this relationship lasting. He never had.

She'd been starved of attention for so much of her life she'd been willing to accept anything he cared to offer her. That made her more like Susan than she'd realised. But, worse than that, she'd been like Brian too—*using* Alessandro, taking advantage of his innate generosity.

The realisation hurt.

She had to deal with it. She couldn't maintain this facsimile of a marriage. Couldn't stick around waiting for him to get bored and pull out the divorce document. No more lies, no more pretence. There had to be nothing but honesty.

Three hours later she froze halfway down the hall as she heard the door unlock.

'Katie?' Alessandro paused just over the threshold, a wary expression stealing over his face as he studied her. 'What's with the scared rabbit look? Is everything okay?'

Nothing was okay.

'What's happened?' He closed the door behind him, his eyes narrowing on the overnight bag she'd placed by the entrance. 'Are you going somewhere?'

'I need to leave, Alessandro.'

'Leave? Why?' His expression sharpened. 'Is it Susan? You need me to take you to her?'

His concern shattered her. 'It's not that. I can't ever thank you enough for helping me with her. But you were right,' she said softly. 'I didn't need to get married to help her. I don't have to feel like I owe everyone everything. Not even you. I can just say no.'

'So you're saying no to me? To *us*? Just like that?' He cleared his throat and walked towards her. 'You've just decided it's over?'

She held her hands together tightly. 'You asked your lawyer to check the validity of our marriage.'

He checked his pace and then breathed out. 'Is that what this is about? You looked at the paperwork?'

'There was a lot of it. You explored all the options.'

'Of course—that's what due diligence is. I thought you'd want to see it. I've never held anything back from you, *dolcezza*.'

'Haven't you?' She threw him a sceptical glance. 'You thought I'd want to see that amount in the divorce settlement? How much you're prepared to pay to be rid of me?'

'To be rid of you? Or to help you?' He stopped about three feet away from her, but he seemed to be looking right into her soul. 'In the eyes of the world, we're married.'

It was all about that façade… 'But it's not real.'

'Isn't it?' he asked sharply. 'Are we not living as a married couple? Aren't we intimate? Sharing?'

'*What* are we sharing?' she asked. 'I am *taking* what you are *giving*. And I'm saying you don't have to give any more.'

'I don't "have to give"?' He laughed that bitter laugh that sounded so wrong on him. 'I never "have" to do anything, Katie. I've wanted to do everything I've done with you.'

But he didn't want to give her what she really wanted. 'This was a mistake from the start.'

Seeing that report had been the catalyst to finally make her see sense. She'd used him too much for too long and in the process she'd lost her heart.

She whirled away from him, hurt and unable to hide it. 'I should have married Carl.'

Hard hands on her shoulders spun her around. 'Take that back.' He glared at her.

Somehow she was against the wall and she couldn't escape his fury.

'Take that back *now*,' he demanded roughly.

His anger astonished her. Worse was the familiar tug low in her belly. Would she always want him beyond reason? Beyond caring even for herself?

'You would have been miserable with him.' Alessandro's gaze drilled into her, daring her to deny it.

'I'm more miserable now.'

His eyes widened and he actually paled. 'You regret being with me that much?'

No. She didn't regret a second of it. How could she? When it had been the most intense, amazing, infuriating time of her life? But it mattered so much that it hurt to *breathe*. She'd always be on edge. Waiting. Knowing that soon enough he'd be bored and decide to initiate the divorce. And then he'd be gone. How could she put herself through that?

'I never would have slept with him,' she explained with pained honesty. 'Then this wouldn't have happened.'

'It's only because we've been sleeping together that things have become complicated?

Her eyes filled with acidic tears. 'Of course not.'

It was because she'd fallen in love with him. And that was the last thing he'd want.

'You don't want to stay?' His bafflement hurt all the more.

She laughed weakly. She'd give almost anything to stay. But she'd slowly shrivel up and die a slow painful death here. Because her heart would beat alone, ripped out to remain where it wasn't wanted, slowly bleeding out its last.

'For what?' she asked bitterly. 'You to finally get tired of me?'

He looked shocked. 'Katie—'

'Why does all this have to be on *your* timeline?' she exploded as she heard the denial in his voice. 'Why can it only be over when *you've* had enough?'

He brushed the backs of his fingers down her jawline. 'Have you really had enough, Katie?'

'Don't be cruel.' She pushed back against his too-powerful persuasiveness. 'It's over, Alessandro. It has to be. I'm sorry if its inconvenient, or embarrassing for your reputation…but I can't go on like this.'

'Like what? What is so awful about this? You hate going out with me? You hate the way I make you orgasm?' he growled. 'We're living as a married couple. We're out every night, displaying our relationship.'

She recoiled in complete mortification. Was *that* why he'd taken her out? Was it all part of the act? Those moments when he'd looked at her he'd intended his friends to see it? Had that been part of his performance?

Too late she remembered he'd told her right at the start that she'd have to fake it.

'I don't want to live a lie any more. You never wanted to

be my husband. You don't love me. But I've fallen for you, Alessandro,' she muttered sadly.

He stared at her, frozen for a moment, then dropped his hands to his sides. 'You're confused, *dolcezza*. This is just a crush…'

'A crush? What do you think I am? Eternally naive because I never had a boyfriend before you?' She felt sick. 'And what am I to you? Just another notch on your bedpost?'

'Katie—'

'Don't *minimise* what's between us. Tell the truth.'

'We're…having an affair.'

'Right.' She curled her hands so tightly together her nails almost pierced her palms. 'You *never* wanted to marry me— not even pretend. And you shouldn't have. You just felt sorry for me that night when I panicked…' She dragged in another burning breath. 'You want to be free and you can be. I can too.'

'I did what you asked of me. I did *everything.*'

'And I never should have asked you. I didn't know what you'd been through.'

'What's that supposed to mean?' His expression shut down.

'You don't want to love because you don't want to be hurt. And I get it. You lost everyone. Your mother died. You saw your father's heart break in front of your eyes. Then you lost your home and him and everything he'd worked for. Love has brought nothing but loss to you.'

'*This* is not love.'

'Not for you, no. But don't deny my feelings. Don't deny what I'm saying.'

'I *do* deny it. You're just bewitched by my looks—what was it you said? I don't even need to open my mouth?'

His cruel rejection of her affection hurt. Because it was a denial not just of her but of his own real worth. Or did he think she was too stupid to see what was really in front of her?

'It's not that, Alessandro. Nor is it your money or your power. It is *you*. Your discipline, your insane work ethic, but also your compassion, your belief in me. You *have* done everything I've asked—because you're loyal and protective. Yes, it's also your sensuality…you know it is…but most of all it's just *you*. You're impossible, but you always make me laugh, you always lift me up…' She gazed at him and the truth whispered out. 'You've made my life so much more than fun. I love how I feel when I'm around you.'

He didn't move. 'If I'm all that, why won't you stay?'

'Because you deserve better too,' she said huskily. 'You deserve not just to be loved, but to feel this kind of love for someone else.' She blinked away the burn of tears. 'You don't invest in anything. Not really. Not relationships, not even companies. You enjoy the game—the chase, the catch… And when you're done you flick them on. You're never emotionally invested in anything except the memories on your island.'

In his pale face his eyes flashed wildly. 'Have you finished critiquing me?'

Her anger sparked. 'Sorry, are you bored already? That's your usual get-out excuse, right?'

'Katie—'

'This is the last thing you want, isn't it? This terrifies you—someone who truly loves you. But don't worry. I won't die of a broken heart. Don't feel guilty about hurting me.'

He flinched.

'But really *you're* the one who doesn't want to get hurt. Fair enough.'

'No, Katie. You're reading into things that aren't there.' He shook his head dismissively. 'You're just tired. It's been a whirlwind… It won't be this intense for ever. It never is.'

His denial shocked her. It was as if he hadn't heard a word she'd said. Because he didn't feel the way she did. 'So let me leave now, then.'

His jaw tensed. She watched ice harden his eyes.

'You can't give me a real reason to stay,' she said softly.

It seemed he couldn't say anything. He'd frozen.

She waited as a last little spark of hope flickered before fading. 'You never wanted to marry anyone. No marriage. No kids. No love. No drama.'

He still didn't reply—didn't say the words she desperately wanted to hear. Of course he didn't. She wasn't enough. He wouldn't want her for ever. No one ever had. Not even Susan needed her now...

Katie had never felt so alone.

And now he literally stepped back from her.

'What are you going to do?' he asked.

'I need to get out and live—see and do everything I've missed out on for so long.'

'What can you do without me?' He glared at her. '*No one* can give you what I can give you.'

'But you can't give me what I really want. You know you can't.'

He flung his head up, as if he scented danger. 'So you want to meet someone else?'

'Eventually, yes.' She wanted to find someone who'd fall in love with *her*. Just for her.

He looked furious. 'Not while we're still married—'

'Don't worry, it's going to take me a while to get over you.'

She blinked back tears, because the thought of finding someone else appalled her. But he wasn't going to stop her. Because he wasn't going to say what wasn't true.

'I don't want to accept less than I deserve. And I don't want to use you any more.'

His jaw clenched. 'I'm *helping* you.'

'No, I'm *using* you, Alessandro.'

He hated the thought that she had any control over him in this. She drew in another breath.

'I'm not going to be like my family. But I'm not going to be like you either. You're kind, but you're also a coward.

Life hurts. Love hurts. We lose people along the way, we get rejected, and it hurts. But not you—not any more, right? Because you avoid possibilities, chances. Your entire existence is as fake as our marriage. You have so much more to offer someone, but you choose not to. It's such a waste.'

'We had a deal—'

'Just be *honest*!' she cried. 'You don't love me. You don't want to be married. You never did. You need to let me go.'

CHAPTER FOURTEEN

IT TOOK ALESSANDRO a moment to realise that the loud ringing noise in the room was coming from his pocket, not inside his head. He'd ignored it for so long it had gone to voicemail, but less than three seconds later it began ringing again. With far less co-ordination than usual he pulled out his phone and glanced at the screen. He'd never been so glad to get an urgent call.

'Really?' Katie gaped, fury lighting her eyes. 'You're going to answer that *now*?'

'It might be important,' he muttered.

'And this conversation isn't?'

It wasn't a 'conversation' they'd been having. 'I just need a minute.'

Alessandro stalked into his study, slamming the door behind him and answering the phone as he went. He barely heard Dominique's query about a major deal that suddenly seemed utterly unimportant. He couldn't even answer. He couldn't tolerate the torrent of emotions Katie's stormy outrage had unleashed. He couldn't think.

'I'll call you back later.'

He abruptly ended the call to Dominque and took a breath. It didn't help. Why was Katie so determined to destroy what was a perfectly good thing? Why stir up stuff that didn't need to be—?

He turned and strode back to the lounge, pausing on the threshold. It was empty. One icy thought sliced through the chaos. He immediately glanced down the hall. Yes, her hold-all bag had gone. He quickly checked the other rooms in the apartment, even though he knew. Half her clothes still hung in the walk-in wardrobe she'd used. The ice inside him began to burn.

He crossed to the window overlooking the street—two taxis were waiting at the rank over the road. She'd have had no trouble getting a ride. Or she might have headed for the train station around the corner... It didn't really matter. All that mattered was that she'd gone.

He discovered the note in the kitchen. A single sheet of paper on the counter, a single line written on it.

Thanks for everything.

Her words coldly echoed the warning he'd given her that night he'd taken her to his bed for the first time... *'I can't give you everything.'*

He scowled. When had she written this? He'd been out of the room so briefly. She must have snatched her bag and sprinted. She couldn't have stopped to scrawl a message. Had she written this before, because she'd actually intended to leave without saying goodbye? He'd returned home earlier than he'd meant to because he'd been unable to stay away...

And she'd been unable to give him even one more minute.

Rage erupted. How dared she? When he'd done everything she'd asked of him? More, in fact.

He phoned her—naturally she didn't answer. He didn't leave a message. He paced the floor. Then phoned again. And again.

Sheer fury and shock made it impossible to process anything properly.

Apparently she'd made a stand and moved to get on with her own life. She'd fought for the independence and freedom she'd never had. Good for her, right? But *he* wasn't her enemy.

'I can't stay here with you.'

That was so unjust. He wasn't cruel. She'd said he needed to let her go. She'd said it would hurt her to stay. He couldn't believe that—they were getting on well. Really well. It was all just fine...wasn't it?

But then she'd said she loved him.

His innards iced all over again. She did *not*. Every cell rejected that. It was gratitude. Because she'd had so little kindness in her life she was mistaking her response to his actions. He'd helped her and she was overly appreciative because she wasn't used to it.

And it *was* a kind of crush. Her want for him was hormone-driven—she'd discovered she liked sex. It wasn't *love*. She was too inexperienced to know any different. She was naive and sheltered and she was confused.

How had he gone from not wanting to mess with her to messing everything up? *He* wasn't naive or sheltered and yet he was completely confused.

Liar.

He slumped into a chair and stared moodily out of the window.

He knew exactly what had happened. Everything he'd happily avoided all his adult life. Emotional intensity. Vulnerability. Real *risk*.

Maybe she was right to say he'd never invested that most valuable part of himself. Not his heart. And why was that? Because he'd never wanted to care so particularly for one person that if they left he'd be wrecked.

He'd been wrecked before when he'd lost his parents and his home. He'd rebuilt himself. Now he had power and privilege and the capacity to do pretty much what he wanted. He had everything, didn't he? And he'd been perfectly happy until she'd come along. And then he'd been happy with how things had been between them...they'd been *good*.

Why had she ruined it? Why had she pushed? What was so wrong with how things had been?

Unable to rest, he worked round the clock. Unable to socialise, he ignored calls from Vassily and the others. He would've gone to Italy and immersed himself in the island—except it was now permeated with her presence and he couldn't bear the thought of feeling this emptiness there.

He prowled around his apartment like a wounded beast. She was constantly in his thoughts, in his dreams, in his aching heart...

It would get better. Things always did.

But two days later it wasn't improving any.

Not almost a week later either.

Slowly he realised that for all the challenge in his work, for all the wealth he'd accumulated, he had nothing he really wanted to *hold*. The one thing he wanted had walked out on him.

His 'amazing lifestyle' had merely been masking an empty core. Katie had ripped off the façade and exposed that painful truth to the light. He'd refused to give himself fully. Not for him that all-consuming, life-changing, bigger-than-both-of-them love... He'd never wanted that. So he'd never let anyone in. Deliberately cut relationships off at the knees.

But then Katie had catapulted into his life and he hadn't been able to cut her off. He'd been unable to say no to her on almost anything. She'd exposed him, and she'd also soothed him. She'd made him feel so much that was good. But he'd been wary and defensive, and so focused on staying his precious bulletproof self he'd not given her what she really needed. Even when she'd finally braved up enough to ask for it.

'You don't want to be hurt.'

He'd scoffed at her words at the time. But she was right.

'Coward.'

When she'd thrown that at him he'd frozen, his action proving her accusation in that exact moment. She'd not asked for much—only to know his feelings—but he'd remained silent, denying her. He realised now what a betrayal that silence had been. The same betrayal she'd had for years. Her foster-father had never told her she was loved, safe, wanted...

He'd done the worst thing possible to her. And hurting her had been horrific.

He was an idiot, and now he was suffering the kind of pain he realised he'd spent half his life trying to avoid. And he was such a fool because he hadn't even let himself have the flipside of that risk. He hadn't had all the good things—*time* with her. Love. Laughter... All that contentment and possibility.

She wanted *family*. And she should have it. She should have a husband who adored her, who could fill her life with children and all the warmth and laughter she'd missed out on.

He'd thought he'd never want any of that. He'd thought he'd remain free for ever. But it turned out he wasn't 'free'— he was lost. He'd been enjoying affair after affair, as superficial as she'd once suggested. And that judgement of hers had only hit so hard because it was true.

For once he let himself sift through those memories he would never normally recall—the happiness and joy of his parents. Watching them, being loved by them, bathed in security. He'd been so fortunate to have had it at all. Katie hadn't had any of that. Yet she was the most loving, generous, loyal person he'd met. And so courageous.

Only now she'd run away. And she only ran when she felt she had no other choice. When she was too hurt, too scared to fight.

He had to fight for her.

He had to ensure she had everything she wanted and needed.

He had to be the one to give it to her.

Because he wanted—needed—it from her as well.

Actually, he just wanted her. He'd never wanted anything or anyone more. But when she'd told him she loved him he'd frozen. Not only denying himself, but denying *her*.

His pain worsened. Not for his past, but for his future—his *now*. He'd *failed* her.

But that didn't mean he was going to *quit*.

Energy and determination surged through his body.

He'd find her. He'd fight for her. And he'd damn well bring her back and tell her *his* truth—that she was his heart.

CHAPTER FIFTEEN

KATIE THREADED THROUGH the crowd of tourists as she headed towards her hostel. The café where she'd been working for the last few days was busy and she was tired. Hopefully that meant she might actually sleep tonight. Because while the long working days were good, they didn't stop her from thinking about Alessandro all the time, and the small hours alone and awake at night were the worst.

'I've finally found you.'

'Oh!' She lurched to a stop in the middle of the footpath.

'Sorry. I didn't mean to give you a fright.'

Alessandro had materialised out of nowhere. Tall, stubbled, intense and far too intimidating, in black trousers and an open-collared shirt.

Slack-jawed, she stared. A too-powerful thud walloped her heart. 'What are you doing here?'

'How could you just vanish?'

She blinked rapidly at the reproach in his eyes. 'I didn't mean to worry you.'

'Didn't you?' Anger flashed across his face. 'Or did you think so little of me you thought I wouldn't worry at all?'

She swallowed as her anger surged in response. She'd told him what she thought of him and he'd dismissed it as a *crush*.

'Why run away and hide?' he growled. 'You said all those things and didn't give me the chance to—' He broke off and visibly sought for control. 'I thought I could keep this... I don't think I can.' He jerked his head in the direction of the hostel. 'You're staying there?'

She nodded.

'Living the life you've missed out on until now?' His lips compressed.

'Living a life, yes. Working at a job I got for myself, spending money I've earned.'

He gazed at her for a moment, and slowly the faintest suggestion of a smile flickered in his eyes. Then he took a careful breath. 'I'm in the hotel across the road. Will you come there so we can talk?'

'You have something to say now?' she asked smartly.

'As it happens, I do. I'll do it here if I have to, but I think we'd both prefer some privacy.'

Heat flared, skimming over not just her skin but every muscle, every organ. That electricity had always been a strong current within her and she had to resist. 'I don't think that's wise.'

'I thought you'd discovered your courage, Katie?' he dared softly.

She stared back at him, knowing how much he enjoyed challenging her. How much she enjoyed it too. His expression slowly altered, revealing something more—something she truly didn't have the courage to face.

'Give me a chance, *dolcezza*.'

And that she couldn't resist. Even though she was more terrified than at any time in her life. Not even Brian's worst threats had made her feel this vulnerable.

Hardly aware, she crossed the street with him. The silence simmered, thickening the air while time twisted. Her pulse raced but her breathing felt slow, and all of a sudden they were alone.

His hotel suite was too quiet, too small for comfort despite its opulent spaciousness. She crossed the room to the window and looked down at the bustling Edinburgh streets as her panic rose.

What was the point in this? Why rehash that pain of what had been said…and not said?

She wasn't ready to face him. Why did seeing him now hurt even more than when she'd walked out?

'Katie?'

She closed her eyes against the soft contrition she heard in his voice. This wasn't what she wanted.

'Katie, I'm sorry—'

'Don't *pity* me,' Katie whispered sharply, screwing her eyes closed. It was too much.

'Actually, I've been feeling sorry for myself.'

He'd moved closer—she could feel him right behind her. But she didn't turn and face him. She didn't want to listen.

'I've had a chance to think…' he added slowly. 'And I think I like being married.'

Her heart lurched, and then anger scorched it. 'Go find someone you *want* to marry, then,' she wheezed.

'I already have.' He put his hands on her shoulders. 'Katie, *dolcezza*, breathe.'

She couldn't step back—couldn't escape. 'Don't…'

She shook her head, glancing over her shoulder—beyond him—to the door so far across the room.

'Don't run away again.' He applied a little pressure until she pivoted to face him. 'I let you down with my silence the other day and I'm sorry for that. I just… I was just so stunned. Please don't run away. Stay so we can talk.' He drew in a shaking breath. 'I needed time before you left. I need just a little more now.'

Her flare of defiance faded. Her whole body hurt too much—her throat felt so tight she couldn't speak. He looked more serious than she'd ever seen him, the blue of his eyes deep and almost bruised.

'You've been waiting all your life for someone to love you the way you ought to be loved. I am so sorry I've made you wait longer.'

Her eyes suddenly filled. Stinging unwanted tears that she had to hide, even as she ached to lean forward and wrap her arms around him, to forgive him anything, accept anything, and never let him go no matter what. She wanted to *hope*.

But she couldn't let herself. She couldn't even look at him.

'Please, don't…' Swallowing hard, she wrapped her arms around her waist and bent her head to stare hard at the floor.

He cupped her face in hands so gentle it was as if he were afraid she might disappear before his eyes. It was the lightest of caresses that compelled her to look back up at him.

'*Dolcezza*, don't cry.'

'You shouldn't have come here. You shouldn't have…' She looked into his blue eyes and a tear slipped down her cheek. 'It's not fair.'

'Life isn't always fair, is it? Sometimes we win, sometimes we lose. Sometimes we just run away.' He edged nearer, his voice dropping. 'And sometimes we throw the game because we're afraid of winning.' He shook his head ever so slightly. 'I threw the game, Katie. And I wasn't fair to either of us. I couldn't be honest with you before because I couldn't be honest with myself. I couldn't bear to face how much you mattered to me.'

She couldn't keep up—couldn't accept what she thought he was trying to say. She only heard the resistance. 'You don't want to care about me.' And it hurt *so* much.

'I didn't want to care about anyone.'

He didn't deny it, but he didn't let her go. Rather he stepped nearer, until his eyes were only inches from hers and his breath warmed her face.

'I didn't even realise how safe I was playing. I thought I had it all figured out. But you were right. I was just afraid. Underneath it all I was empty—maybe I'd never got past that hurt from years ago. But I thought I could handle you. I thought I was doing you a favour—what a hero, right? The truth was I wanted you and I knew you wanted me. I thought it could be an affair like any other…'

'It *was* an affair.' She made herself say it. 'Our marriage was never real.'

'Actually, it was. It *is*.' He brushed away her tear with the backs of his fingers in the lightest of touches. 'Our feelings are real, Katie.' He gazed at her. 'My feelings are real.'

Her eyes filled all over again and she rapidly blinked. 'Don't—'

'You were too generous in saying I'd sought solace in the past… I think I was being selfish. I avoided getting close to anyone, subconsciously protecting my heart, because…poor me… I'd been hurt. But who hasn't in life? I was just taking what I wanted and giving little in return. I was a jerk.'

His self-recrimination shocked her. '*No*. You were just… *living*. And then you helped me. You did everything I asked of you—' It was just that she'd asked for too much.

'Only the easy things—money, sex… But real caring? The way *you* care for people?' He leaned closer. 'I didn't even realise what that was until you showed me. Not until I was doing it for you without even realising—'

'I don't want you to feel you have to take care of me any more,' she interrupted fiercely. 'I don't want you to rescue me.'

'Who's rescuing who, Katie?' he asked.

A gorgeous rueful smile flitted across his face before he became more serious than ever.

'The day you left you asked me to be honest, and at the time I couldn't be.' He huffed out a harsh breath. 'Now I *have* to be. You were right. I've been a coward. I hurt you in the worst possible way. I hurt you by my silence. Because you have the capacity for the kind of love that terrifies me. The kind that is so huge, so deep, that you'd do almost anything for someone you love. The kind of love my parents had. The kind I've secretly always craved but never wanted to admit. The kind I have for you.'

A rushing noise in her ears muffled his words. She couldn't tell if what she was hearing was… What had he said? The soaring sensation inside threatened to make her faint.

'I love you, Katie. The best kind of all,' he muttered. 'It isn't a game, *dolcezza*. It's real. And it's everything.'

She swayed and he caught her around the waist, pulling her flush against him.

The sigh she released was jagged and painful. 'What did you say?'

'I know it's going to take a while for you to believe me. That's okay. I'm not going anywhere. Because I can't be without you. I can't believe I let you go. These days have been hell.' Emotion shook not just his voice but his body, and he pressed her closer still. 'You're not walking out on me ever again and I'm never walking out on you.'

His kiss burned through the dizziness. He was here and he wanted her and what he'd said was real.

Katie gasped as his passion swept through her and she soared. There was so much emotion in his touch, in his broken apologies. He was so powerful, so possessive as he pulled her closer, his hands raking down her body as if he couldn't quite believe she was there, melting into him.

But suddenly he pulled back.

'What…?' She couldn't quite breathe enough to get the words out.

He too seemed breathless, his chest rising and falling fast as he reached into his pocket.

'On the way up here I thought maybe we could have another wedding ceremony…one we put a little more thought into. We could invite Susan and our friends. I'd like to wear a decent suit. You could wear the dress of your dreams…'

Katie couldn't move.

'I need you to understand that I *choose* you, Katie. I love you and I want you alongside me always. So will you marry me all over again?' He opened the box. 'Will you mean it with me this time?'

He wanted to marry her again? He wanted to show his feelings for her to their world?

'You don't need to…' Katie saw the ring and winced. 'You've given me too much already.'

She didn't want any more of his money. She didn't want

him to think he had to do these big things for her. She
wanted only him.

'Not everything Katie. Not yet. You've given me more.'
He took the ring from the box. 'You're everything to me.
And I want to celebrate it. I want the world to know.'

'Alessandro…' Her heart burst—he wanted to publicly
profess his feelings for her, claim her as his? A rush of
warmth and pride and pleasure overwhelmed her.

'It's…'

He slid the ring down her finger. 'A perfect fit.'

The diamond sparkled so brightly she had to blink again.
Rapidly. 'You didn't have to—'

'I wanted to. Accept the gift, Katie.'

He kept hold of her hand and smiled at her. It wasn't the
wicked, amused smile of always—it had something else in
it as well. Something infinitely more.

'If you need to find confidence in me you can look at this
and remember. And I like seeing you adorned in my gifts. It
gives me a sense of security. I figure it wards off other men.'

She couldn't help a little chuckle, and then she shook her
head to try to stop those tears from falling again. 'What
other men?'

'You have no idea how beautiful you are,' he teased gen-
tly, then tugged at her hand to pull her back into his arms.
He caressed the length of her spine to pull her closer still.
'So let me tell you.'

Her eyes filled, but he tilted her chin so she couldn't
hide her face again.

'Listen, *dolcezza*—listen and believe. You need to know
you're more than gorgeous. Your hair shines, and so does
your skin, and your eyes are truly bewitching…all those
colours in them gleam. But you light up with this kind of
magic.' He angled his head. 'There's no one else with your
vitality, your generosity—'

'Alessandro—'

'It's true. And I know you won't believe me yet, because you've never been told before, you've never really been shown. But I'll tell you, and I'll show you, every day for the rest of our lives. I love you, Katie, and I will never leave you.'

He knew just what she needed to hear. Because he knew her. He understood her. And he'd come for her. It meant everything.

She hugged him back tightly and instantly he cradled her closer.

'I thought relationships weren't worth it.' He closed his eyes. 'But *you're* worth it. Being with you, having you, then losing you…' He groaned. 'Never leave me again, Katie. It was the absolute worst.' He gazed deeply into her eyes. 'Stay with me always. Love me always.'

His vulnerability broke her open. Because he'd been hurt in the past, he'd been lonely and so had she.

'I'm yours,' she admitted on a shaky sigh. 'I'll always be yours.'

'I've missed you so much, *dolcezza*,' he whispered.

He gave her what she needed—his touch, his kiss. She breathed him in and began truly to believe.

He didn't hurry, instead undertaking the most tender rediscovery of her body. He murmured constantly—how much he'd missed her, how much he loved her—in English, in Italian, in his touch. And when he finally claimed his place in her body and soul she sobbed in sheer ecstasy.

It wasn't a mere escape or a moment of pleasure. It was so much more. Their intimacy deepened as the last knot locking her heart away loosened. Joy surged within, like lightning that transcended the physical. He had all of her—but he held her with such care, such reverence. It was tenderness and passion and a promise of pure security.

She finally understood how much he cared. And it was a long, long time before either of them could speak again.

It was Alessandro who lifted his head from where he'd

been resting on her breast and sent her a teasing smile. 'You smell delicious.'

She giggled. 'I spent the afternoon baking cinnamon buns.'

Laughing, he lowered his head and nuzzled her neck, as if he couldn't get enough of her taste. 'Come home and make something for yourself.'

'I'd like that. I think I'd like to start afresh. Not White Oaks, not Zetticci. Something completely new.' She quivered a little inside at the excitement of the prospect. 'Will you help me?'

'Try and stop me.' He nipped her skin with his teeth and tugged her closer to him again, pressing against her intimately. 'We could build lots of things together. A company, a home, a family…'

'You really want all that with me?'

'More than I've ever wanted anything,' he said simply.

She melted, welcoming him completely.

They were more than a match—they were a *team*.

'Ti amo,' she whispered shyly.

He stilled and she saw pure vulnerability flash in his eyes as he blinked rapidly. *'Dolcezza—'*

'Accept the gift, Alessandro,' she challenged softly.

He nodded. 'If I have you I have everything,' he said. 'You *are* everything.'

She finally believed that she meant that much to him. He treasured her just as she treasured him.

He slowly traced a gentle path over her heart with the tips of his fingers. She'd never felt as close to anyone, never as safe, never as content.

She smiled past her own tears and kissed him again. Together they'd soften old scars. Together they'd create new joy.

And together they would always, *always*, love.

* * * * *

COMING SOON!

We really hope you enjoyed reading this book. If you're looking for more romance, be sure to head to the shops when new books are available on

Thursday 17th October

To see which titles are coming soon, please visit **millsandboon.co.uk/nextmonth**

MILLS & BOON

Coming next month

BOUND BY THEIR NINE-MONTH SCANDAL
Dani Collins

"Señor Navarro," she said, offering her hand.

"Angelo," he corrected. His clasp sent electricity through to her nerve endings as he took the liberty of greeting her with, "Pia."

"Thank you for coming," she said, desperately pretending they were strangers when all she could think about was how his weight had pressed her into the cushions while her entire being had seemed to fly.

His eyes dazzled, yet pinned her in place. There was an air of aggression about him. Hostility even, in the way he had appeared like this, when she had literally been on the defensive. He seemed ready for a fight.

She had almost hoped he would leave her hanging after her note. She could have raised their baby with a clear conscience that she had tried to reach out while facing no interference from this unknown quantity.

As for what would happen if he did get in touch? She had tried to be realistic in her expectations, but Poppy had stuck a few delusions in her head. They seemed even more ridiculous as she faced such a daunting conversation with him. How had she even found the courage to say such frank things that night, let alone *do* the things they'd done? Wicked, intimate, carnal things that caused a blush to singe up from her throat into her cheeks.

"I need a moment," she said, voice straining.

She had already declined invitations for drinks, fearful her avoidance of a glass of champagne would make her condition obvious. She only had to say a last goodbye to the committee and, "Thank you again, but I must take this meeting."

Moments later, trembling inwardly, she led Angelo into the small office off the lab where she had worked the last three years when not in the field. She had already packed her things into a small cardboard box that sat on the chair. She was shifting from academic work to motherhood and marriage. That was all that was left of her former life.

Angelo seemed to eat up all the air as he closed the door behind him and looked at the empty bulletin board, the box of tissues and the well-used filing cabinet.

Pia started to move the box, but he said, "I'll stand."

He was taller than her, which made him well over six feet because she had the family's genetic disposition toward above average height. His air of watchfulness was intimidating, too, especially when he trained his laser-blue eyes on her again.

"Your card was very cryptic," he said.

She had spent a long time composing it, wondering why he had sneaked into the ball when he could easily have afforded the plate fee. At the time, she had thought his reason for being on the rooftop was exactly as he had explained it—curiosity. She had many more questions now, but didn't ask them yet. There was every chance she would never see him again after she told him why she had reached out.

Memories of their intimacy that night accosted her daily. It was top of mind now, which put her at a further disadvantage. Her only recourse was to do what she always did when she was uncomfortable—hide behind a curtain of reserve and speak her piece as matter-of-factly as possible.

"I'll come straight to the point." She hitched her hip on the edge of her desk and set her clammy palms together, affecting indifference while fighting to keep a quaver from her voice.

"I'm pregnant. It's yours."

Continue reading
BOUND BY THEIR NINE-MONTH SCANDAL
Dani Collins

Available next month
www.millsandboon.co.uk

MILLS & BOON

THE HEART OF ROMANCE

A ROMANCE FOR EVERY KIND OF READER

MODERN

Prepare to be swept off your feet by sophisticated, sexy and seductive heroes, in some of the world's most glamourous and romantic locations, where power and passion collide.
8 stories per month.

HISTORICAL

Escape with historical heroes from time gone by. Whether your passion is for wicked Regency Rakes, muscled Vikings or rugged Highlanders, awaken the romance of the past.
6 stories per month.

MEDICAL

Set your pulse racing with dedicated, delectable doctors in the high-pressure world of medicine, where emotions run high and passion, comfort and love are the best medicine.
6 stories per month.

True Love

Celebrate true love with tender stories of heartfelt romance, from the rush of falling in love to the joy a new baby can bring, and a focus on the emotional heart of a relationship.
8 stories per month.

Desire

Indulge in secrets and scandal, intense drama and plenty of sizzling hot action with powerful and passionate heroes who have it all: wealth, status, good looks…everything but the right woman.
6 stories per month.

HEROES

Experience all the excitement of a gripping thriller, with an intense romance at its heart. Resourceful, true-to-life women and strong, fearless men face danger and desire - a killer combination!
8 stories per month.

DARE

Sensual love stories featuring smart, sassy heroines you'd want as a best friend, and compelling intense heroes who are worthy of them.
4 stories per month.

To see which titles are coming soon, please visit

millsandboon.co.uk/nextmonth

MILLS & BOON
DARE

Sexy. Passionate. Bold.

Sensual love stories featuring smart, sassy heroines you'd want as a best friend, and compelling intense heroes who are worthy of them.

JOIN US ON SOCIAL MEDIA!

Stay up to date with our latest releases, author news and gossip, special offers and discounts, and all the behind-the-scenes action from Mills & Boon...

 millsandboon

 millsandboonuk

 millsandboon

It might just be true love...